HEART OF SHADOWS

AN EPIC ROMANTASY SAGA

EMPIRE OF BLOOD AND MALICE
BOOK ONE

MEG COWLEY

*To those nurturing embers of great dreams
—stoke them to an inferno.*

to the elven Realm of AURAURIA
TIR-NA-ALATHEA
(THE LIVING FOREST)
THE HIGHLANDS
THE LOWLANDS
Pelenor
Eyre

The Great Sea
Summer Palace
Kingsguard Academy
Tournai
PLAINS
PELENOR
Well of Life
Asnirheim
Himmelheim
Keldheim
VALTIVAR
DRAGONTOOTH MOUNTAINS

READING GUIDE

Dear Reader,
It's important that you have a wonderful reading experience.
In light of that, please take note of the content guidelines of
this book if you have any reading preferences or aversions
pertaining to violence, trauma, or romantic content. Full
content guidance for this series can be found on the author's
website.

It is also advised to enjoy the series in order for all events to
flow coherently.

Warmest wishes,

Meg Cowley

1

HARPER

Sheer desperation bought Harper another day from death. The rabbit's lifeless eyes reflected late autumn's woods. Steely skies and scudding clouds, stretching trunks and bloody leaves—and the darkness of her looming shadow extinguishing all from those glistening orbs. Harper eased the snare from its neck before resetting the trap, then fastened the animal to her belt next to two of its dangling kin. She muttered a small thank you to it as she always did, and stroked its silken ear. Her slim fingers pressed the cord back into the pile of sodden leaves, concealing it from view on the game trail once again.

She stepped back to appraise it. Invisible. Betta had taught her well. The old woman was no longer as independent as she had once been and a shadow of her former self. She relied on Harper to keep her safe, warm, and fed more than she liked to admit. Harper did not begrudge it. Betta had saved her from the streets of Glymouth as a young and hopeless waif, and without the taciturn woman's pragmatic kindness, Harper would have long since starved to death.

Harper's stomach growled in anticipation. She stirred into action. That day, it would not be empty. Her willowy figure might have been praised as elegant and attractive in some circles—but it was no town fashion. Her jutting bones were a testament to the slow starvation of poverty. For a change, she had both surplus meat and hides to sell. The pittance they would fetch were the heights of her prospects.

Harper wiped her wet palms on her breeches. It did little good. The steady drizzle, which had persisted since that morning, had soaked through every layer of clothing she wore. The sun soared far above, wreathed in mist and fog—nothing more than a baleful disc that cruelly mimicked the moon's grace with its cool disdain. Down in the bowels of the forest, there was no light or warmth to comfort her. Harper suppressed a groan at the stiffness of her limbs as she stretched.

It was time to return to the village. Soon, dusk would come, and with it, creatures she was not armed against. Her feet sank through wet loam and layers of fallen leaves with each step. The trees were half bare, the forest floor a kaleidoscope of oranges and browns. It made tracking both a blessing and curse. The mud made every print stand out in sharp relief, yet following the game trails was a difficult wade through boggy thickets. It was lucky she knew the woods like the back of her hand. Where the rabbits lived, where the deer grazed, and where the denizens prowled.

Over the rhythmic squelching of the mud on her leather boots, Harper's heightened senses scanned her surroundings. The overwhelming scent of damp, natural decay clogged her nose, making it impossible to trace the natural haunts of predator and prey and requiring all her other senses to bridge the gap. A flicker of leaves falling spiked her pulse as crashing betrayed a presence beside her own. It sounded big enough to be a bear that was too far down the foothills for comfort. Her heart thudded in her chest, strong and alert, ready to thunder into action at a second's notice to spirit her away should danger approach. But the leaves fell of their own accord—and the noise faded.

Harper skidded down the last embankment as the village came into view. There was the smallest wave of relief at the safety it promised, before dislike rose in her. It always did. The village meant people and she had no fondness for them. She would be glad of the tavern's hot fire that night, but not who would be there too. The street was half empty. Those who weren't huddled inside from the weather were out on the bay fishing for their own suppers, braving the edge of the coming storm. Harper made her way straight to the lone public house, letting herself in.

Tam, the landlord, clattered downstairs at her entrance— and raised a brow as he appraised her. His gaze caught the bounty strapped to her waist. "Very nice," he said with an appreciative nod. "They'll do for tonight's stew." Cook would whip up a batch of hot, filling, meaty stew. Harper usually managed to slip a bowl for herself from the fresh pot before all the patrons, though Tam always charged her for it if he caught her.

"Three coppers apiece, and I keep the hides," she said as a starting negotiation. She'd get more for those from the tanner.

Tam sucked the inside of his cheek for a second. "Two coppers each, but I want a hide—a tanned one. Need to patch up."

"Three each and you'll keep a hide." She would not give him an inch. Not when the difference meant her starving. He could afford it, the miser. She kept her face blank from the resentment seething inside her.

"Hmph." Tam jerked his thumb toward the kitchen, a silent invitation for her to take them by way of the cook, and ambled upstairs. It was as close to an accord as she would get.

Harper skinned the rabbits and left them on the counter, then retreated to the hearth, almost grasping the flames in her desperation for warmth. Her cloak was heavy and sodden as she peeled it off and hung it by the fire. Soon, steam rose from it. She turned this way and that until she had mostly dried, her attention on the flickering flames. The first of that night's patrons ambled in. One of the fishermen from the bay, wanting his own warmth and a place to dry off. Harper stirred with a sigh. Time to work.

Harper wiped the globule of spittle from her cheek with her sleeve as she twisted away from the man, his cold and clammy hand wrapped around her wrist. She suppressed a shudder of distaste and schooled her expression into bland boredom as she backed away, her hands full of empty tankards.

"What do yeh say, lass?" Old Robson roared with laughter as he raised a paddle-sized palm to try and slap her on the bottom, but he was far too drunk and she far too nimble. All the same, she thrust the tankards before her as a barrier and tried not to gag on the stench of his hot breath fanning across her face bearing stale beer, tobacco, and something she couldn't identify—and did not want to.

Her eyes slid over his toothless grin, his grizzled, unkempt stubble, and the stains on his tattered tunic. *I wouldn't take you to bed in a thousand years*, she thought. *Not even if you were the last man in Caledan.* She vowed she would never need coin *that* badly.

"Are yeh accosting my girl?" shouted Tam from across the bar, leaning over it to peer into the dim corner. "Yeh wouldn't leave me without a hand now, would yeh?"

"I'll leave you wi'out those two hands," said Old Robson, leering at Harper, who hastily turned away. "I bet they make short work of my—"

"All righ'. That's enough," Tam called as raucous laughter erupted from the inebriated patrons.

Harper's cheeks burned as she rushed behind the counter, longing to curse the lot of them.

"All right?" asked Tam. His eyes roamed over her, but not in the same predatory manner as Old Robson's. He was a slightly better man than that. He liked to make sure his staff were not accosted, though not out of kindness. It was bad for business to have it on the premises. What his staff got up to elsewhere was their own business. Harper appreciated the illusion of safety all the same.

"Fine," she muttered, slipping past him to dunk the empty tankards into the pail of water in the kitchen out of sight of the patrons.

She dropped to her knees to scrub them, using a sticky hand to push a wisp of loose hair out of her face—and immediately regretting it. Now she had a smear of goodness knows what on her cheek. Her eyes stung from the long day, the smoke curling in the air no help, but she resisted rubbing them with the back of her hand. In the dark corner of the kitchen, she allowed herself to pause for a long moment. Her eyes slipped shut in exhaustion. She inhaled deeply through her mouth if only to avoid the fullness of, for just one breath, the rank stench of spilled ale, sweat, and worse that hung heavy on the dank air.

Harper dunked her hands into the bucket and scrubbed furiously at the skin the old man had touched, but the ghostly feeling of his fingers still clamped there, despite her best efforts. With her eyes closed, she could pretend she washed with clean water. By that time of night, it was usually more beer than water, but Harper wasn't about to dodge through the crowd again to go fetch a fresh pail from the well. She could not block out the din from the next room. The silence of home was always golden after each shift. *Not long now*. Her head thumped dully.

At a clatter behind her, she rushed to appear busy, nearly slopping half the pail onto the floor with her sudden movement. Tam shoved open the door, thudding it into the wall. "You could appease them, you know. Earn a bit of extra coin."

She whipped around to look up at him, mortified. "You mean…?"

"Well, aye." Tam shrugged. "There's no shame in it. Take 'em home. I don't care what yeh do outside my place to earn your way." And now, he *did* look at her in the way that made her skin crawl.

Hidden by the water, she clenched her hands deep in the bucket. Harper bared her teeth at him and turned away, scrubbing at the tankards furiously, as though she could take out her anger on them. "How dare you. I'm not whoring myself out to them."

"What?" She heard the creak as he leaned against the slanting door frame. "It's not like you have anything to lose. What are yeh now? Five and twenty?" Her jaw dropped. Was that how bad she looked for twenty-three winters? He tutted, oblivious to her indignation. "Well, y'aren't gonna find a husband as you are anyway, so you might as well do better for yourself than that shack of yours. There ain't no shame in it. 'Specially with winter comin' and your old gal to care for. Pride don't keep a bed warm or a belly full."

Harper knew that. She felt it so deeply her bones ached, but that was a line she wouldn't cross. Her body was the last thing she had of value that was *hers*. She wouldn't give that up unless there was no other way—and she'd always found a way. Every winter seemed to be tighter and leaner than the last, but she'd always survived.

She looked into the pail of dirty water. This was freedom —wasn't it? Making her own way in the world? The feeling in her stomach soured, and her throat tightened. This fell so short of the dreams nestled so carefully against the slivers of her wanting heart.

At her silence, Tam straightened and shrugged. "It's your choice. You're pretty enough to catch a decent fellow's eye. Not like *him*." Tam jerked his head in the direction of the bar. The thought of those hands roaming her, and worse, assailed her. Harper shuddered so visibly that Tam chuckled. "Aye. He's not much of a reward. Besides, his coin is gone by way of my coffers."

"You're welcome to it," she spat.

He laughed. "It's a shame you don't come with a dowry. With spirit like yours, I'd have kept you for myself." He grinned, pausing, as though he expected a thank you for the compliment.

Indignation rose, burning hot through her belly, but she swallowed the bitter words forming on her tongue, for they would not serve her to utter. Was that all she was to be seen as in this world of men? Chattel to be owned? An object of their pleasure and the subject of their will?

His smile fading at her scowl, Tam muttered under his breath and sauntered out to the bar to call last orders. It was only when he had gone that Harper allowed the stiffness in her shoulders to ease.

This was not it. This was not to be the sum of her life. Harper could not take one more winter of this miserable drudgery, scraping an existence so hard and pointless it barely merited the effort, to line the pockets of the men that ruled that land. She wanted more—she wanted freedom for herself on her own terms—and she would make it so. Harper vowed it to the suds floating before her, the dirt on her knees, and the rain battering the roof above.

2

HARPER

Soon after Tam had tossed the last of the patrons onto the street, the worst of them still lying in puddles of mud and their own vomit, Harper made her way out. She paused by the door to accept her wage for the week, eyeing the full bag of coin Tam kept as he counted out a meagre handful of coppers for her.

After Tam's deductions for taxes to the Lord of County Denholme—almost half of her coin—and a bit more for the suppers he docked from her pay, there was barely enough to scrape by. Certainly none to save, though she always tightened her belt an extra notch to put something away when she could bear it. Her hand closed around the coppers, a bitter taste upon her tongue. They were so small against her palm it still felt empty. Where were her grand dreams in the face of such a harsh reality?

"See thee tomorrow," Tam said. He stepped aside so she could cross the threshold.

Harper did not reply, resolve hardening within her. There would be few tomorrows left here. She was done with this godforsaken place one way or another. Harper threw the hood up on her cloak and tucked it tightly around her before she brushed past him. The wind bit into her skin as it brought the chilled sea air inland. There was nothing but black as she looked out at the bay. Only darkness lay out there, the stars obscured by steely grey storm clouds, the ocean an inky void.

She often wondered what misfortune had landed her in this bleak and unforgiving corner of Caledan alone, and what had happened to her parents, but there was no time to do so that night, for fingers of icy wind pulled her cloak aside, stealing what little warmth she had in her moment of stillness. Without delay, she ducked into an alley for shelter, and to take the less trodden way home. Outside the village, the woods swallowed her up, the night blacker under the canopy. Harper did not dally. Wolves and worse prowled at night.

One encounter with a wolf had been enough for her. A day three years hence, and in a clearing, a young, lone she-wolf had crossed her path. They had stared each other down, and in that moment Harper had thought the wolf as proud, wild, and wary as her. Neither had broken the other's gaze for a long moment—and then with a flash, the wolf had gone, blending back into the shadow of the trees with such silence that Harper wondered if it had been a dream. Why else had the wolf not attacked? Only the paw prints pressed into the mud at the stream's crossing up ahead had proved it to be real.

Harper let out a ragged breath when she saw the small candlelight glimmer amongst the dark trees through her sole window, if it could be called that. It was a shard of salvaged glass from the town, far from transparent, that she had built into the woodwork of what Tam had called her "shack", though she had fonder feelings toward it. It had been the only home she had known for as long as she could remember.

Thud. The rising howl of the gale and the dark shadows of the night vanished as she shut and barred the door behind her, glad for the relative peace. Her ears still rang with the noise of the tavern and the storm, banishing the telltale creak of wood as the abode flexed around her and the whistle as that persistent storm found a way inside through the cracks. She would return to the tavern tomorrow, and the day after that, and seemingly all the days after that until she could finally leave—but for now, her time was her own.

Harper dragged off her cloak and hung it on the crooked iron nail that served as a hanging peg near the fire, then knelt to coax life into the embers. The floor, hard-packed earth, oozed cold through the paltry layer of rushes and a sheepskin rug. The rug was old, tattered, and nicked with holes from poor skinning—the only reason she had been able to afford to trade for it in the first place—but it did the job of sheltering her from rising damp, and the matted wool was a rough comfort on her knees as she knelt to tend the hearth.

Harper moved with practised silence, not disturbing the prone form huddled on one of the two pallets. Betta's wheezy breathing had started getting worse, she noted. The drawing in of winter would see Betta suffer this year. Harper stoked the fire again, prodding it into life, and eased another log on. At the very least now, she could keep Betta warm and fed, as the old woman had done for her in winters past.

Guilt flickered around her edges. Freedom meant leaving Betta behind too. The old woman had already refused on many occasions to move, even simply closer to the towns where she might have found an easier way of life. Harper owed Betta for everything over the years, and Harper's conscience wrestled with the tally that felt so one-sided against her favour. She could not abandon Betta to a life of greater hardship in her absence. There had to be a way to both free herself and ensure Betta's comfort and care.

The fire flickered to life, soon growing before her. It flooded the small space with heat and Harper consumed the warmth greedily, basking in the light. It was so much purer than the murk of the tavern. The fresh scent of the pine boughs always cleansed that stench from her nose. Still chilled to the bone, she put an extra ration of wood on it to keep them toasty that night. It was a small pleasure that meant a disproportionately huge amount—she would never forget the pervasive cold of having no roof over her head.

Over a beaker of hot brewed roots and leaves made from whatever she could throw together, Harper examined her hoard, kept in a wooden trinket box under the head of the pallet where she slept. Two silver marks and fifteen copper pennies piled within. She added one of her coppers from that week. She could not afford to add another. Even that would send them close enough to starvation. More than likely, she would end up taking the copper back out to buy enough food, as she always did in winter. The prices went up when there was little available.

Harper never stopped dreaming of leaving, of building a better life, but it was too hard to think about when that might be. It seemed as endlessly and impossibly far away as ever between one year to the next of eking out an existence and with nowhere else to go and no means to leave in any case. No family. No friends. No ties calling her anywhere. She tugged her other treasure from the hiding place. The leather cover was tatty and worn, but she caressed it as though it was the most precious trove. The spine cracked as she opened it, the amber light of the fire barely illuminating the handwritten sheaves. Harper strained her eyes to read them anyway.

This was why she saved. Out there, beyond the woods, the sea, and the black sky, lay better lands, better places. Powerful warriors, honoured ladies, terrifying dragons, clever magic. Mountains, forests, seas, verdant lands… Adventure. Prospects. Hope. Her corner of Caledan was a grey and lifeless place. Out there, she dreamed of real places like those. Places where it was possible to warm right through to her bones, enjoy a full stomach, and a safe night's sleep. Places where she wouldn't feel as though it was her destiny to live and die in obscurity, working herself to the bone to survive, pay taxes, and then end up in an unmarked grave at the communal cemetary.

As the fire died down and the night darkened, Harper lost herself in the tales. No matter that she had read them so many times before. No matter that she ought to have slept instead. This was a chance to leave her life behind for a few hopeful moments. To step into shoes where she would be powerful enough to decide her own fate and carve her own place in the world. Someday, drunk patrons would not paw her as she served them. Harper clung to that.

3

DIMITRI

imitri buttoned his collar one-handed. His other forefinger and thumb stroked Princess Rosella's slim chin for a fleeting second before his lingering fingertips slipped away. She huffed in annoyance, fluttering her long lashes and pouting as she propped herself on her elbows atop the plump, silken cushions.

"Are you *sure* you have to leave, Dimitri?" she asked, cocking her head to one side so he could see the slender, pale, perfect fall of her neck below her pointed ears that, not too long ago, he had kissed his way down. He gazed at it, his lips twitching in a light smirk.

She lay on her belly, nude and flushed on the rumpled sheets and entirely unashamed, making no attempt to cover herself. Rosella was the supposedly innocent daughter of the king, his youngest and adopted child—some said his illegitimate daughter by another she-elf. But Dimitri was no longer fooled. Rosella knew *exactly* what she was doing. He had been a willing, though naïve volunteer for her affections before she had trapped him into her service. Now, he was a master of meaningless intimacy to keep her pleased. One way he ensured a space at her father, the King's side—and his own survival in a royal court brimming with betrayal and ruin.

"Your father requires my attendance at the council, Princess, and I am already late due to your *last* request for me to remain just a little longer."

"But it was worth it, wasn't it?" The minute tightening of the skin around her eyes was a warning sign he had learned to read early on.

He could not disagree. "Of course."

Rosella sighed and rolled onto her back, exposing two perfect breasts as temptation. Her golden hair pooled around her, glowing in the candlelight. How she loved when he ran his fingers through it. He clasped his hands firmly behind his back and lowered in a bow.

"My lady."

"Fine." She huffed, rolling away to snag a silken dressing gown. He caught the flash of genuine annoyance.

"I'll return soon, as always."

"Yes, yes. When business allows," she snapped.

Pressing his lips together, he suppressed a retort and strode forward to catch her wrists as she stood. Dimitri drew her close, sliding his hands down her sides and placing the ghost of a kiss upon her lips, then one on her neck. She melted into his touch. He retreated before she could ensnare him again.

Her last glimpse of him was his usual wolfish grin and a wink before he vanished from her chambers, his cockiness undiminished as he swaggered past her attendants, each one more disdainful than the last. Dimitri straightened his clothes as he strode toward the great hall. It would not do to turn up at a council meeting late and ruffled. After all, he could only push his usual reputation so far. It was a careful line, dancing between all the masks he wore to keep himself and his people safe.

Storm clouds chased him across a courtyard inside Pelenor's royal palace—autumn came early, nipping at the heels of a hot summer. The shivers across his skin had little to do with the weather, though. He resisted the urge to rub his arms as he approached the doors, glad for the long sleeves that hid the goosebumps. Great dragons hewn of oak guarded the way, their ruby eyes gleaming.

Dimitri schooled his expression into blandness as the guards heaved open the ornate doors. In he strode, his steps quiet on the polished marble floor that stretched across the huge, vaulted space. Before him, council members sat or stood on the chequered marble floor like game pieces upon a playing board. Standing before them all and the centre of attention was the King of Pelenor himself.

A few heads twisted toward Dimitri, then swiftly turned away when they realised who it was. He did not grace any of them with his attention, not even his own father, though he noted in the periphery of his vision the customary disgust in his father's curled lip and the curt shake of his head before he turned his gaze back to the king. That was nothing new. Dimitri had long given up on his father's gratitude. His family's current fortunes were entirely Dimitri's doing, however accidental, but no appreciation ever came. No one ever thanked a bastard son.

"—no concern of ours," the king said, not stopping speaking at his entrance. Dimitri breathed out with silent relief, soothing the frisson of fear that rose in him to always remind him of the boundaries in this hateful place. His lateness had most certainly been noted by the elven king, whose ears were as sharp as his own, but Toroth had deigned to ignore him. Dimitri preferred it to be so.

"Your Majesty, if I may," a councillor interjected.

Toroth ceased speaking and fixed him with a stern gaze. He did not like being interrupted.

The councillor cleared his throat and shuffled his feet, uncomfortable. "These are our own borders that are under threat, so would it not be prudent to—"

"No, Thaeus, it would *not* be prudent. The goblins do not threaten our borders." The king's glare burned the room in a brazen dare for anyone to contradict him. No one did, though a few cloaks rustled—as loud as dissent became in that court before Toroth crushed such notions. Shadows pooled around them, light and shade starkly contrasting the king's face as he stared them all down.

"Their strife is with the dwarves, as ever it has been. It is Valtivar's borders that are threatened, not Pelenor's. If the goblin dissent grows, so must the response of the dwarves. I will not lose our men to their petty battles. If the dwarves cannot control their own homelands, if they cannot control the scourge of these pests, then frankly, they are unworthy allies. I will most certainly not commit the Winged Kingsguard to assist, as you earlier suggested. It is beneath their notice."

But a rain of dragonfire and magic would be mighty helpful. Dimitri did not voice the thought. The king was a law unto himself.

"My sources inform me that the goblin uprising is mostly confined to the eastern reaches of Valtivar," continued Toroth.

Dimitri held back a scoff. *He* was the king's source. That was how the illegitimate son of a minor elven lord had built himself a standing of power and fortune in the elven court—

by utilising his skills in trading truths, lies, and secrets. Rosella was the unwitting origin of half of it, for ladies talked amongst themselves in circles the menfolk were not permitted to enter. Through her, he had a window to it all as she blathered to him during their trysts. He wondered if she knew he used her as much she used him, furnishing his own nest with everything she gave him. Surely, she had to know he felt no genuine affection or attraction towards her, much as he expertly repressed the repulsion her touch brought him. Certainly, there was no affection on her part—she used him to dig at her father and to do her own dirty work in the court when needed.

Over the years, Dimitri had found secrets were a currency beyond blood or money that held their own value —not that the king liked to admit the wealth of his knowledge came from such a source of low standing. It was a path Dimitri relied upon for his own survival in a court of lies and backstabbing, where his fall from favour or worse lay just around the corner at the feet of fate's fickle twists. Living under the king's rule always felt like one step away from ruin. But, Dimitri was used to the unadulterated edge of anxiety that was his constant companion. It kept him alive.

"Remote holdings and abandoned outposts in Valtivar have been targeted. It seems the goblins seek to build their own kingdom and cast down the dwarves."

Dimitri's lips thinned. Now Toroth parroted him almost word for word. "The dwarven lords hold enough power in their armies to defeat any such uprising." Exactly as he had told Toroth on first delivering the news.

The king turned toward Dimitri at last. His lip curled. "You have no business here. Out."

Dimitri opened his mouth in indignation, but remained silent. He could not find a retort that would not land him in irons. The king advanced a step. Councillors shrunk from him. All heads turned to Dimitri. He closed his mouth into a firm, thin line. A paper thin defence, but his air of disdain was all he had to draw upon. Now it seemed he was worthy of their attention—their full, undivided attention—as they mirrored the king's disgust. He reflected it back to them.

Let's play this fickle game again, shall we? Dimitri stood taller, his face impassive, violet eyes meeting the king's own. "Your Majesty?" He allowed not one flicker of fear to edge his voice. It was ever the same—Toroth came to him when he wanted something, and was the first to turn the other cheek when Dimitrius no longer suited his company.

"Do not presume that because you defile my daughter you are permitted to attend such meetings." The king flicked a ring-laden finger at him in dismissal and turned away to address the rest of the council once more.

Dimitri swallowed his retorts. The king ought to have been glad Dimitri brought him news of goblin uprisings that threatened to cripple trade across the borders, and bedded the king's daughter so he didn't have to put up with her petulant tempers. Seeing guards converge upon him, Dimitri gave a low bow to the king—who ignored it entirely—shoved his hands into his pockets, and strolled out nonchalantly before they could lay a hand upon him. He would not suffer the reputational harm of that indignity. His blood boiled, wrath seething hot and angry underneath his skin with every footstep.

His father's gaze followed him out, but Damir made no move to support Dimitri. Dimitri resented his father more than the rest of them combined, for no matter what, Dimitri's efforts would never be enough. Dimitri had long ago given up trying to seek his approval. His father's successes were entirely accidental, and certainly not wished for—but Damir had wasted no time trading on Dimitri's usefulness to the crown. It had only further cemented Dimitri's opinion of his father—and his worth.

Dimitri had long wished for his father's demise. In Dimitri's eyes, Damir deserved nothing less for punishing Dimitri for his existence all these years when it was Damir's own indiscretion that had begotten him. At least Dimitrius took precautions to never be so careless, especially in Rosella's servitude. His nightly preventative tonic came second in importance only to guarding his life. Dimitri had no children of his own, and he would keep it that way. The illegitimate child of an illegitimate child would have no hope for a good life in a court where purity of blood was prized. He might have been dastardly, but Dimitri would not force his own damned circumstances on another. Not of his own choice.

The king and his daughter were another matter. Rosella was a consenting female of age. Toroth had done nothing but grumble about her for years, and he made no secret of it. In particular, her delight in spending his fortune, no matter that she was the sweetest and least conniving of all his children— which was saying something. She was only a jewel in so far as extending his dominion with her marriage, but Toroth had never deemed a suitor and their assets worthy of taking that prize—and Dimitrius was most certainly not the one to change his mind of that. Dimitri returned to her chambers, bitter as it always tasted and unclean as it made him feel. He was not sure whether it was out of loathing for himself, or the king.

That night, Dimitri watched her from the shadows, far from the rumpled silken sheets they had left in her chambers.

Rosella, wearing a gown of starlight and diamonds, twirled on the arm of an elven princeling. He tried to suppress a pang of jealousy, unsuccessfully. He was not envious of her shared attention—far from it, it was a relief-filled respite—but oh, to be free of the maligned attention that dogged his every step. He was barely welcome in the first place. He stood far outside the globe of light, brilliance, and laughter that graced the finest ballroom in the city of Tournai, instead favouring the cold darkness of the gardens that were wet after the storm's passing.

A figure melted out of the shadows beside him.

"Yes, Rook?" Dimitri's informants all went by coded names. It was safer that way.

Light glinted as coins changed hands. Rook tucked the money away before speaking. "Dissent in the north. Those whom we spoke of. Avoiding duties at the ports by landing their most choice goods elsewhere. The ships turn up to the docks half empty."

"The king thanks you," Dimitri said, as he always did. Rook vanished into the night without another word.

Dimitri chewed on the knowledge. Did the king deserve it? Not at all. Was it worth hiding? Even less so. He sighed and turned his eyes to the heavens for a fleeting second. No answers would come from the cold stars above him, hidden by their blanket of dark clouds. He was duty-bound to report it, whether he liked it or not. At least in some form. Dimitri picked through which information to feed onward. He always kept some choice morsels for himself, or for ears other than the king's.

He'd give those traitors a chance to save themselves—and owe him—before he turned them in, he decided with a small smile. Some of those who had looked down their noses at him earlier that day would tomorrow be begging him to keep their secrets, lest they incur the wrath of the king and see their heads roll or their bodies burn in dragonfire for treason. This small hold of power was the only form of insurance he had found to soothe the edge off the raw fear that lurked at the fringes of his mind, ever present, in the court. The more he held of others' secrets, the less his own could bite him. The bastard son of an elven lord had to make his own fortune one way or another.

4

AEDON

The gigantic trees of the living forest rustled and contorted, but there was no wind to move them. It was as if the very trees themselves were angry. Aedon knew it to be true. The forest was *furious*.

He dashed across the rope bridge walkways that soared above the forest floor, clinging on for dear life. The living trees, the *dhiran*, buckled their limbs around him, sending the walkways swinging like ribbons in the wind. Aedon was lucky he had always been a nimble elf. Even so, he struggled to keep his footing. He ducked and wove as branches tore at him with razor sharp leaves. Every splintered arm of wood stabbed at him like a jagged blade, leaving his skin peppered with nicks and grazes.

Still, it was better than descending to the forest floor. If he did, the writhing roots would rip themselves free from the earth and strangle him before they wrenched him limb from limb. Tir-na-Alathea was a special place, but a cursed one. No one left if the forest did not wish it. Luckily, Aedon had a better plan—he hoped. He chanced a glance over his

23

shoulder and redoubled his efforts. The two elves pursuing him had murder in their eyes. He could not blame them, he supposed. The elves of Tir-na-Alathea were not the forgiving type, even though he *had* asked nicely. It wasn't his fault they had refused the trade. They'd left him no choice but to take it. This was all on them—but their howls of rage told him they felt otherwise.

One hand returned to his breast, checking and rechecking that the lump was still there. That *it* nestled safely within the protection of his leather jerkin. He could not afford for that to tumble to the forest floor and be forever lost. He strained for breath, every muscle screaming in pain as he pushed himself harder. He was a fast elf, but this was their home. Escape was far from guaranteed. El'hari and Ta'hiir would pursue him to the death on their Queen's orders, if that was what it took.

As though the forest itself had eyes, faces stared from within the trees, with agony carved in the flowing whorls of their rippling bark. That gave him renewed cause to flee. If he were caught, that or worse would be his fate, for those were not the trees, but the eternal prisoners of the living forest. Those who had wronged it never saw the light of day again, thanks to the magic of the wood. It was a magic so strong, Aedon had to blink back the headache that threatened to engulf him. Every pulse of anger from the forest had the very fabric of the magic of this place trying to crush him until even the air seemed to squeeze him from all sides.

There was a break in the swirling leaves ahead. Beyond it, a chink of sky and a flash of tumbling water—the falls. His escape. His eyes flicked skyward as a shadow engulfed him. Giant, eagle-like wings soared over the canopy. They were utterly silent like a hunter at night. Relief overwhelmed Aedon. He had never been so relieved to see an Aerian, particularly *this* legendary winged warrior, in his life. Aedon swallowed, hoping his plan would work, but there was no time for doubt. The edge of the trees approached. It was now or never.

The forest continued for many miles at the bottom of the cliff. The rumble of the water was indistinguishable from the roar of blood pounding through his ears. At the trees' edge, the walkway ended in a balcony open to the skies. Without slowing, Aedon vaulted the slim rail and hurled himself into the abyss. His heart rose into his mouth as he fell with a soundless scream, the wind tearing at him just like the trees had done seconds before. He forced his watering eyes open. The trees below raced up to meet him. The cliff face was close—too close. Just one snag of his body on the stone and he would meet an even more grisly fate, smashing into the cliff and then tumbling to his death. His heart jerked in a frenzy of panic.

Suddenly, he was tackled from the sky. The impact knocked all the breath from his body. Stars burst in his eyes as Aedon gasped for air. Two bare, muscled arms, riddled with scars, locked around his chest in a protective cage. Aedon clutched onto the familiar, worn leather bracers, but neither relief nor safety was his yet. They still plummeted. His savior slowed their descent, his giant wings outstretched as they glided over the forest, then he pumped them powerfully, sending them up—to Aedon's relief.

"Well met, elf."

"Brand," Aedon managed to croak out. His ribs felt shattered. With each wingbeat, they rose into the sky. Aedon did not struggle in Brand's grasp. The Aerian's grip was a vice around him, crushing Aedon to his solid, leather chestplate. It dug painfully into his back, yet Aedon relished the metal studs and hard, ridged edges cutting into his flesh. They were safety. He breathed in a shaky breath to steady himself, inhaling the scent of leather and sweat. Never had he been so grateful for that stench.

"I was scared for a moment you weren't going to catch me," Aedon spluttered with his first draw of breath. He tried to sound nonchalant, but he was unable to keep the tremor from his voice. The pounding of his heart continued to deafen him. He looked up. Brand's expression was impassive, his attention on the horizon.

"I nearly didn't," Brand growled in his gravel voice. "The peace and quiet I'd have without you was tempting, but Erika would kill me if I dropped what you carry. I thought I'd better not."

Aedon ceased moving. The forest was far below them now. His head swam, nausea threatening to overwhelm him as his stomach roiled. Elves were not meant to fly. Not without a dragon. He turned his head as far as he could as Brand banked higher. Now he could see them. The elves of Tir-na-Alathea. They crowded the balcony he had jumped from. From such a distance, they were too small for him to see their features in detail, but their raised fists were unmistakable.

It'll be about three hundred years before I can set foot there again, Aedon thought with a moment of ruefulness. It was a shame. The Tir-na-Alathea elves were some of the most talented spellmakers in all of the elven kingdoms. Their wares and services were definitely closed to him now.

"You do have it, right?" Brand asked. He squeezed a little. A warning not to joke.

Aedon's hand wormed around Brand's iron grip, slipping under the neckline of his top. The tips of his fingers brushed against the cold, hard, crystal vial digging into his chest. It was there. Safely stoppered. A grin of triumph broke over his face. "Oh, I got it all right! Right from under their noses! They said it could not be done. Stealing from the elves of Tir-na-Alathea, escaping the living forest, all without paying the price," he crowed. "The legendary Thief of Pelenor strikes again!"

Brand's arms loosened. "There's that annoying noise I was so keen to get rid of," he threatened.

Aedon silenced at once, and his belly somersaulted until Brand's arms tightened around him again, but he could not stop the grin that split his face until it ached. *This* was the best part. Forget the thrill of the chase. What Aedon loved most was the smug enjoyment of a successful mission.

5

HARPER

Harper wove through the crowded streets of Glymouth, wending her way through the town's lower levels. Past the docks where the stink never left the air and the gutters ran red with the guts of butchered fish. Past the market traders hawking their wares, though hardly anybody boasted fresh produce, for it had been an even barer harvest than usual from the barren lands of Denholme County. Past the inns, lodges, and hostels that housed travellers like her. Harper would return home that day. She could not afford even the most meagre of them.

It was busy, unusually so, and abuzz, but Harper did not know what would be so interesting in such a remote place. They could hardly still be talking of the birth of the new prince, far away in the capital city. That had been last month's gossip.

The tanner had hides already drying in his cobblestone courtyard when she came upon it, gratefully ducking into the empty square away from the crushing throng and the sweat and musk clinging to it. For a moment, she paused to watch him before he perceived her. He bent to his work, wielding the blade skillfully to scour and scrape the hide before him without nicking a hole in it.

Those muscled shoulders towered over the rack. His arms bulged—forearms visible under rolled up sleeves—as he scraped down a bearskin, sweat beaded on his brow. Something still coiled low and deep in her core for Alric. Handsome and honourable, he was a rare breed, but she had not personally enjoyed the angles and planes of his body for years now. Still. It was some small pleasure to look and remember how it had felt to run her hands down his body as she had worshipped him in the woods. She wrenched her glance away before he caught her staring.

Harper swallowed her dismay as she looked at the fine stags and even finer wolf hides surrounding him in the yard. Her paltry rabbit skins would fetch hardly anything. It would barely be worth the effort of coming and missing a shift at the inn. She pushed the thought from her mind and gathered up her hides, straightening her back.

"Hey, lass," the tanner said, grinning when he saw her, that one-sided smile something she knew he saved just for her. She smiled coyly in response and followed him inside.

Oh yes—Alric was still as handsome as ever, though he would never be hers. Their adolescent romance had been a whirlwind and half a dream, but nothing more, though he had always been kind to her since, and she him. Alric had been promised to the harbour master's daughter, whether he liked it or not, and Harper had not dallied with him in the five years since they had wed, nor had he sought her warmth out. In the cold, dark, lonely hours of the night she sometimes resented that honour of his that she had first been so drawn to.

His sharp-eyed wife lurked in the shadow of the stairwell,

and Harper wiped the heat from her attention upon Alric. The woman knew exactly who had come a-calling. Knew their history. Had lorded it over Harper when she'd married Alric. But Harper knew they'd had no babes—five years, and not one. None would come now, Harper reckoned, if they had not already, but she took no pleasure in that. Alric would need someone to carry on his work when he grew old. Harper carefully avoided her gaze all the same.

Alric paused his work and straightened with a grimace from being hunched for so long, bracing an arm against his lower back and stretching out with a groan. "What have you brought me this time?" As he spoke, he wiped the sharp blade on the rough leather swinging from his belt to clear it of the flesh he'd expertly scraped from his latest hide.

"A bunch of coneys, Alric," she admitted. "But I'd like to make a deal if I can." She held up the rabbits by their ears for his examination.

"Sure, sure," he said, but she saw how the anticipation faded from his eyes. "I can take 'em, but I can't give you much, lass. Rabbit hide i'nt worth much this season, what with the bounty of wolves I've been a-having from the hunters." Harper waited until he finished, then offered the hides to him.

"I understand," she said, strangling her pride as much as her desperation. *Whatever you can give me will help.* She swallowed the words. She would not lower herself to beg. "Mind, these are from the west woods. Rarer than what anyone else'll be bringing your way of rabbits. From my best warrens. The hide on these is supple and soft. Highest quality. Ladies in the town'll need these for their slippers or whatever ridiculous fashions they're wanting this winter."

There was that smile again. He shot her a small look that made her toes curl and ran his finger over the soft fur, examining the inside of the skin. Harper remembered the feel of those calluses grazing her inner thighs. His hands were soft and gentle for a man so large.

"You did a good job skinning these. You're getting better."

"I learned from the finest."

He batted away her compliment with a giant hand. "You're too kind. But I'm glad all the same. A better hide means a better price when I sell it, and I can give you a copper more for them. You do bring me the finest. There's good trapping down your neck of the woods, Miss Harper."

He counted out the coins. Satisfaction coiled in her belly. Wife be damned, he never haggled and always gave her the highest price, right on the edge of what they were worth, leaving little room for his own gains. That he still cared meant more to her than she could express. "I'll see you soon, Miss Harper."

Harper clamped down on the warmth that bloomed at the promise of those words. She absolutely wouldn't be seeing him soon. Not for *that*. And if her growing determination to leave bore fruit, she'd not be seeing too much more of him ever again. She wasn't quite sure how that made her feel —that was lumped in on the edge of the complex bundle of feelings that the thought of leaving Betta elicited.

Harper paused on the threshold so her eyes could adjust from the darkness inside his workshop to the weak sunlight piercing through the grey clouds. It made the city appear ever more bleak. The grey stone under the grey sky by the grey sea. She tucked her cloak around her before diving into the maelstrom, keeping her eyes and ears open—to soon find it was a celebration for the marriage of the lord's daughter to one of his most decorated men.

Pausing amongst the throng of people cheering the procession past, Harper watched too. A striking warrior parading his glowing maiden. His armour gleamed, his horse's coat shone, and his face bore the plumpness of wealth. And her? Harper could not help but feel a sting of jealousy as she beheld his bride. Soft hair radiated in a golden wave down her back, in perfect contrast with the royal blue cloak she wore, hemmed with white ermine. Silks rippled across her grey mare and jewellery glistened at her throat, her ears, her fingers. Her eyes were bright and clear, her perfect teeth—not a one of them missing—flashing from between blush-stained lips as she took in the adoration of the crowd.

I bet she doesn't have to sell rabbit hides and serve arseholes beer to put food in her belly.

Harper's pang of jealousy turned to disdain as she saw the doting adoration the lord's daughter emanated toward her new husband, fluttering her lashes at him. As much as Harper denied even the rare offers of a dalliance those days, Harper could not pretend it was because she was holding out for hope of marriage. Who would want her? A penniless orphan with no dowry or assets had nothing to bring to a union. Yet neither would Harper be content to play wife and broodmare. And what did she need a husband for? She had survived for years on her own. What value could a man bring that she could not, save for warming her bed every night? Harper was no fool. She knew what would be her sole duty as a wife. She wrinkled her nose in disgust at the thought.

She looked at the warrior. He radiated self-assurance. That was who she envied. Not the simpering slip of a young woman riding at his side, beautiful as she was with her doe eyes and willowy frame draped in luxurious fabrics. As much as the cheering crowd waved to their lady, it was to him the ladies lining the way threw flowers and favours, to him the menfolk looked with respect in their stern gazes. That was the kind of status she wanted—the power to make her own way in the world.

After a warm meal to fill her belly, she turned away from town with a heavy heart. Away from dreams of the warrior and grandeur. Back to her dreary, cold shack and the adventures she lived by re-reading the tattered pages of her much-loved storybook.

6

DIMITRI

imitri rubbed a hand across the back of his neck, closing his eyes for a moment to enjoy the relief of it. It had been a hard morning with the king, relaying just enough information to earn his rewards, but not so much that he lost all leverage over those he had incriminated.

The king had been eager to dismiss him, and Rosella had deserted him entirely that week, too. He was grateful for the respite on both fronts. There were far more important things to do. Rosella had already bored him to a living death with talks of gowns, each more fancy and ridiculous than the last. The king had stretched his patience to within an inch of its tolerance with discussions of grand parades through the city —which, of course, Dimitri was expected to use his accomplices to infiltrate for any sign of trouble. It was a time of celebration, but the king was wise to be cautious. With the city overcrowded and in high spirits for the celebrations, there were bound to be a few dissenters in the midst who would use the charged atmosphere to fuel their warmongering.

Dimitri halted, realising he had wandered into the royal gallery. His gaze flicked to the nearest painting on the wall, and he let out a bark of laughter at the irony. Of all the works he could have stopped before, perhaps it being that one was apt. *The outcast views the outcast*, he thought dourly as he stepped closer. Dimitri had never thought to look at this particular painting before, but then again, he had never cared to visit the royal galleries to look at paintings of rulers long dead and elaborately grand scenes that told of glories far exaggerated by the victors.

Floor to ceiling it stretched, so big, it seemed he could step through the canvas into the scene before him, though he would not have wanted to. Saradon stood there, tall and powerful, in the moment before he was cast down by the small glimmer of hope at his feet. Dimitri regarded him with morbid curiosity, wondering how exact a likeness it was. Saradon stood taller than average, towering over Dimitri, who was tall enough himself. Saradon wielded a dark blade, the match of his armour, shadows and fire seeming to cling to him. The half-elf's brows were furrowed with wrath, and his violet eyes pierced Dimitri where he stood. Dimitri shivered. It was incredibly lifelike, whether accurate or not.

"Five hundred years since you were defeated," Dimitri mused to the painting. He would receive no answer, but how he recalled the legends was curious all the same. "Five hundred years, but no body did they find, no way to mark your death. Were you cast down, I wonder?" He dismissed the notion immediately. "Of course you were. If you had not been, if you had endured, you would have won. The legends say how close you were. Besides which, you would have avenged what they did to your dear mother. And then we would all live in a very different Pelenor." He scowled. Would that really have been such a bad thing to be free of the stifling class system that ruled the land, filled with prejudice, judgement, and inequality?

Outside, however, the country celebrated. Banners and bunting adorned Pelenor's capital city, Tournai. It seemed plays and minstrels sprung up on every street corner to sing and act the tale of Saradon—his uprising and his crushing defeat half a millenia before. Music and joy filled the city, celebrating the endurance of the normal order. Money filled it too. The king was most pleased about that. The taxes this celebration would raise had Toroth rubbing his hands together in glee every time he looked out of the windows at the busy city below.

"You just wanted to break the wheel, didn't you?" Dimitri asked the painting.

Saradon's eyes stared at him, unblinking—and unforthcoming with answers.

"Who could blame you?" Dimitri sighed. "It's a damn broken wheel as it is."

The legends spoke of Saradon. He who had tried to wipe out the monarchy, an evil that grew unchecked. And yet, on the other side of the coin, the tales spoke of a male wronged by society, cast out for his differences, and punished for his quest to right the wrongs of a sinful nation.

"Who could blame you indeed," Dimitri muttered. *Perhaps you wanted a better life for those oppressed like you. Like me.* There were some thoughts he did not dare speak out loud, for there were ears everywhere in the palace. Most belonged to him now, but one could never be too careful. No one would know of the struggles he had faced to climb from the depths of that black pit of circumstance he had been born into to his present status. No one was allowed to see behind the armour he wore.

Saradon had half blood and no magic. Dimitri, brimming with magic but illegitimate and half-blood, bore a similarly stinging wound. Both of them had been cast out for faults not of their own making—and Dimitrius would one day seek revenge for the cruelties of his so-called family. This was one of the few remaining portraits of Saradon that Dimitri knew of. So many had been destroyed. This one was permitted for the final victory the history books reflected.

He gazed down the gallery at the sole other and strolled toward it. Saradon sat in a darkened nook just off the main gallery, appearing just like any other member of the royal family. There was nothing to mark him out. Even his gaze was muted. Dimitri frowned at the picture. It was such a bland and uninspiring portrayal. His eyes flicked to the first one. *In that one, they painted your true fire.* Then back again. Dimitri shook his head. Saradon looked stern and melancholy all in one. Strong and full of hidden depths—or perhaps Dimitri imagined that, desperate to draw something from the art that was not truly there. And yet, he had to wonder. Did Saradon know when they had painted him there what atrocities he would commit? What vile acts would be enacted in his name?

It was so difficult to reconcile the placid male posing here to the one who had wreaked havoc upon Pelenor. Dimitri's lips pursed as he viewed the first painting once more. The symbolism of the stark contrast of light and dark was not lost on him. The small pinprick of light and hope at Saradon's feet. The overwhelming darkness that was him filling the rest of the frame, as if it would spill out. Dimitri found it so trite. So rarely was the beholder's eye untainted.

So very rarely was history told by the losers. He wondered if Saradon would have painted himself thusly.

"What are you doing here?" Damir's sharp voice rang in the empty halls.

Dimitri turned, swallowing his distaste into bland indifference. His usual mask.

"I could ask you the same, *Father*."

His father rankled at that, but answered anyway. "I was looking for you." His eyes narrowed. "What *are* you doing here?"

Dimitri shrugged and turned away, for he knew it infuriated his father. "It does not concern you."

Damir puffed with indignance, and Dimitri allowed a small smirk of satisfaction to show. True to form, his father's thunderous scowl deepened.

"I came to admire the art, of course." Dimitri flourished a hand at the walls with a mocking smile.

"Such a criminal misfit you selected to view." His father's eyes flicked to Saradon towering over them both.

"Perhaps he was simply misunderstood." Dimitri cocked his head to one side, meeting Saradon's gaze once more.

"He was a dangerous, evil thinker who nearly toppled the peace of many nations." Damir's tone rang with warning to cease speaking of such matters. Ears lurked everywhere. Much as Dimitri loved to bait his father, there was a careful line to toe regarding his own safety.

"Curious for one with no magic, don't you think?"

"He had others to act for him. And powerful magics. Why do you think the king, and all those since Saradon, have kept the Dragonhearts and such artefacts under lock and key for centuries?" His father lowered his voice, eyes darting to either side, as if he did indeed fear being overheard. "No one must be allowed to grow that powerful again."

"If so many chose to follow him, perhaps his message was not so hateful after all," Dimitri dared to say, not matching his father's whisper.

"You speak treasons," his father warned him.

"Curiosity is not treasonous." Dimitri's indignance echoed around the chamber.

"Saradon curse your smart tongue, boy!"

I haven't been a boy for a long time, no thanks to you. "I'd have thought you would appreciate the fact your *bastard*—" Dimitri took vicious pleasure in Damir's flinch. His father hated the word, the mere reminder of the indiscretion he had tried so very hard to conceal but could never escape. "—has done so very well for himself, despite your attempts to hamper that. Be thankful I am so clever. If I were not, you would not have gained half the privileges you are honoured with."

Damir had no answer for that, speechless with indignance.

"Well, you clearly haven't come for the pleasure of my excellent company, so what do you want?" Dimitri turned away from Damir, ignoring the pointed glare he received in answer, and pretended to admire an ornate antique. His father could not bear to be ignored. Dimitri delighted in tormenting that whenever he could. It was one of the few small victories he could claim in life.

"No indeed. You need to tread more carefully. I won't have you angering the king." Damir folded his arms across his chest. He was as cold as usual, but Dimitri was well-schooled in being on the receiving end of such indifference. After all, he had learned from a master, not that he would ever admit it.

"As if you have a say in anything I do, dear father." Dimitri flicked an imaginary piece of dust off his immaculate, slate cuffs and strolled down the gallery, stepping from light into shadow and back again as he passed each tall window.

"I'm your father and I won't have you shame our house any more than you already do." His father strode after him, dogging his footsteps.

Dimitri scoffed. "Frankly, the shame is all yours. Aren't I nothing more than that to you? I didn't choose to be born, and yet you have your current fortune to thank me for. I've worked hard and succeeded, despite every limitation you enforced upon me." He stopped and glared at his father. "You're welcome," he added pointedly.

Damir pursed his lips. No thanks came—as ever. Old dragons didn't change their scales. Dimitri's lip curled as he turned away again.

"Do you hear me?" his father insisted. "I shan't have you drag our name through the mud. I don't want the king's wrath upon me for your misdemeanours."

"Oh, don't worry!" Dimitri whirled on his father, his words as scathing as he could possibly make them. "I shan't endanger your delicate little head, nor that of your latest harlot."

"She is my wife!"

"Your *latest* wife."

"You will show her more respect. I command it! She is the lady of your house, not one of the common slatterns you associate with."

Dimitri spluttered with laughter, unable to contain it. "You deign to lecture me? *I* have never fathered a bastard. Please tell me the irony is not lost upon you." His amusement faded to darkness. "And before you so much as say another word, may I warn you that by association, it would very much appear that you call Her Royal Highness a slattern. I am sure you are very much mistaken and do not need to inform the king you hold such views on his most precious daughter."

Damir paled and shrank away.

Dimitri scoffed in disgust. *Pathetic coward.* "I didn't think so. Are we done?"

Damir looked very much as if he wanted to be, but he shook his head. Dimitri raised an eyebrow in silent invitation for him to continue, pursing his lips. Damir gestured for him to follow and set off to the far end of the gallery, which was shrouded in darkness from the shuttered windows that excluded the day's light.

"The goblin massing," Damir muttered. To anyone else, they appeared to be a father and son merely appraising priceless works of art. "I want more news from the borders, more news of the troubles."

Dimitri heard the reluctance in Damir's voice. It killed his father to have to ask him for anything. "The king forbade we take any further part."

Damir scoffed. "I know that will not stop you or your sources. Forewarned is forearmed. The dwarves are not likely to ask for help—not from Toroth—and if the uprising is more severe than we are led to believe, which I fear it is, we may yet have to act. I hope I worry for naught, yet..." Damir trailed off.

Dimitri nodded. He understood his father's motivations. The family lands of Eyre lay close to the border. Too close for comfort to the troubles—and too far away from Tournai to receive the king's aid. Should no one stand in the way, they would be the first lands to fall.

"I'll not promise anything." And with that, Dimitri strode into the shadows, abandoning his father to the solitude of the gallery without waiting for a response.

7

AEDON

edon stretched his toes toward the licks of fire that chased away the dark and threw dancing light on the cave walls. The warmth banished the creeping cold from his feet, for which he was grateful. His sodden boots lay with all the others to one side, gently steaming as the water evaporated. Erika and Ragnar sat around the fire lost in reverie, and for once, Aedon did not break it. Bone-deep weariness settled in him. It had been a long while since they had enjoyed true, safe rest, and he longed for it. They looked up as Brand strode back in, his wings tucked in tightly against the small passageway of the cave.

"All clear," he said, his gaze raking across them all. The night surrounded him in stark shadows, and only his eyes glinted until he entered the small sphere of light beside them.

"Safe?" Ragnar questioned with a nervous glance toward the entrance.

Brand chuckled darkly as he squatted near the fire. "I wouldn't go *that* far. The elves of Tir-na-Alathea are a murderous bunch when they want to be, and we're too close for comfort. This is the most defensible position we have, but we cannot stay for more than one night. I've scouted the area. There are no traces of us—or them. We should still sleep with one eye open and some extra protection." He glared pointedly at Aedon, who inclined his head.

"The wards are already up. Don't worry."

"I still don't trust the trees." Brand scowled toward the entrance, as if the trees were creeping in.

Aedon clapped him on the shoulder. "Don't worry yourself, Brand. The trees here are harmless. They're not the same as the Tir-na-Alathea *dhiran*."

Brand did not seem convinced by the deepening of his frown, but Aedon let him be. He knew the Aerian warrior never let his guard down.

"Are you sure there's no reason to worry?" Ragnar looked toward the inky void of the cave mouth again.

"If Brand says not, I'll trust to that," Erika said.

Brand inclined his head to her, then turned to Ragnar. "You're safe here, Master Dwarf."

Even so, the night closed about them, leeching in from the cave entrance and Aedon was glad for the light and warmth of the fire, though he would not admit it. He leaned back onto an elbow and smirked. "What a tale for the ages, eh? The legendary Thief of Pelenor takes on the elves of Tir-na-Alathea and wins. I can hear the adoration already."

Erika snorted at Brand. "You should have dropped him."

"My apologies," Brand said, shrugging. "He carried our prize. I could not, though I considered it."

"You would be lost without me," Aedon crooned.

"We'd be in a lot less bloody trouble," Ragnar said, jabbing his wooden spoon at Aedon.

Aedon only grinned wider and swiped a taste of the broth from it, making Ragnar rap his knuckles. "Yum."

"If you knew what hunted us, you wouldn't be so cocky," warned Brand.

"I *do* know what hunts us," said Aedon. "Why worry about what we cannot control? They shan't catch us. We're masters of evasion."

"They'll see your fat head from a mile off," the Aerian warrior grumbled, moving closer to the fire between Aedon and Erika.

The only sound besides the crackle of the fire and the rasp of Erika's blade on her whetstone was the sizzle of the roasting meat dripping fat into the flames. The nomad woman's gift to them that day was a young wild boar, caught before Aedon and Brand had returned from their mission. It had been a long trek since for all of them, up into the foothills and as far away from the waking forest as they could travel.

They had fled long into the dark without stopping. Erika had guarded their rear, whilst Aedon magically swept away any trace of their passing. Brand had carried their prize, ready to take to the skies at a moment's notice to save it, should it come to that. Yet, somehow, they had evaded capture. Aedon held their prize before him, the top and bottom of the vial between his finger and thumb, admiring the way the faceted crystal caught the orange light of the fire and shattered it across the cave in hues of honey and amber.

"Is that it?" Erika asked. She frowned and leaned forward, as if it might seem more impressive if she got closer.

"What do you mean, 'is that *it*'?" Aedon spluttered, glaring at her indignantly. "It cost a lot—nearly my head, thank you very much—to get this much!" His numb buttocks protesting, he shifted on the hard ground. Even though the furs beneath them were warm, they grew worn from age and the earth's cold seeped through.

The stoppered vial was a beautiful specimen, the likes of which few in Pelenor would see. The perfectly clear, tear-shaped crystal vessel was small—smaller than Aedon had hoped. However, in the heat of the moment, and having come so far, there had been little reason to *not* take it. The clear liquid within glimmered with every hue of the rainbow and a light of its own, if Aedon squinted at it. However, there was not enough to take even one mouthful.

"We were hoping for more, I think," Ragnar said. His quiet, measured voice made Aedon wince much more than Erika's sharpness. Somehow, his disappointment was worse. Aedon threw a troubled glance at the dwarf, who stared at the vial as he turned the meat on the spit, basting it in its own juices. He sighed. "I would have taken more had it been available. This was it. The sum total of all that distillation."

They all stared at it, and he knew they wondered the same. Did it hold salvation, and would it be enough? The liquid seemed so insubstantial. Aedon swallowed and pushed thoughts of failure aside. That was not an option. They all knew it. "It'll be enough," he said, more strongly than he felt.

No one questioned him.

"We still might not return in time," said Ragnar, his fingers fiddling with one of the embellishments upon his braided beard. "They were quite unwell."

"The sickness was slow, though," Brand argued.

"Aye, but we have already been gone too long. Who knows how their condition has developed."

"We should take some horses on the way. Brand, you can fly, but the three of us will be far faster on horseback."

"We cannot! We should buy some," Ragnar said. He still turned the spit, but it was force of habit. He paid no atten-tion to the roasting meat. He was too busy glaring at Aedon.

Brand barely suppressed a snort of laughter. "With what coin?"

Ragnar's shoulders sank a little, but there was still a plea in his gaze as he searched Aedon's.

Aedon smiled gently. "I'm sorry, my friend. We shall have to take. There's no other way."

Ragnar looked away. A jerk of his head was the only acknowledgment Aedon received.

"I'm *sorry*. I wish it could be otherwise, but you know we never take for the sake of greed. We take what we must to help those in dire need. Of all our quests, surely this is worth it—we can save lives. We can return the horses when we're done, if you're so bothered."

"Don't," said Ragnar. "I know why we do what we do, but it does not make it any easier for my conscience to bear, no matter how great the need. Whoever we take from will be sorely poorer for it."

Aedon's lips thinned. "I feel the same. What is right is not always easy."

"Theft is wrong."

Brand clapped Ragnar on the shoulder. "It is, yet we will steal again as we have stolen before because it is even worse to let innocents die, isn't it." There was no question in his voice.

Ragnar met the Aerian's piercing golden eyes. To his credit, he did not flinch, though it felt like looking into the hunting glare of an eagle. "Yes," he said dully, looking away.

"None of us enjoys this life, of living in the shadows and having to steal to do what we feel is right." Brand's voice was gentle. "Yet I would rather have this kind of unseen honour than every privilege that was afforded to me before." His gaze flicked to Erika, who nodded, face grim. He looked at Aedon. "There's no other way?"

Aedon squirmed. "I won't say we don't have a choice, Ragnar, because you never agree, but you know Brand's right."

Ragnar pursed his lips. "I know. I just wonder when we'll ever *not* have to make such choices."

"Perhaps tomorrow, perhaps never." Aedon shrugged. "I'll make them gladly every time. What we do *matters*. We may commit crimes—but only with the greater good in mind. It makes a difference. *We* make a difference. The world needs us to keep doing what we do."

8

DIMITRI

imitri leaned against the golden stone column. He soaked in the atmosphere, admiring the enchanted domed ceiling of stars and moonlight. It was the most relaxed he had felt in an age. Even the ever-present tightness in his shoulders had faded. He had not been in this part of the palace for over a year since the last summer ball of the previous season. It was one of the few parts of the palace he liked. Warm and inviting, a world away from the cold, grey stone, foreboding gloom, and politics in the rest of the place. Most of his business took place in the older, original parts of the building. The ones constructed for war, not pleasure.

He sipped at his nectar-like drink in the delicate glass flute, raising it in toast to those who greeted him with a dip of their head or a smile. On this one night, all came together. Political agendas, familial ties, personal vendettas… All were forgotten for a night of merriment. He had no doubt that in the morning, along with sore heads, they would have hate for him once more, but tonight, it was nice to feel almost like one of them for a change. To not have to keep the cold and distant mask.

Still, his smile was clipped as he toasted them, and no one stopped to speak with him. They might not have shown their hate or fear towards him that night, but there was a clear divide. He was not one of them, and never would be. He was here as his father's guest, not in his own right. That irked him—and delighted his father, who was convinced he granted Dimitri a great and gracious boon.

Dimitri watched his father stalk past with his wife on his arm. Dimitri looked through the crowd, but his half-brothers were mercifully lost in the throng. His step-mother glowed with a beauty Damir did not deserve, but she was as cold as the rest of them. Calculating. She had not wed Damir for love, but money and position. Dimitri knew a lot more than she thought.

He had been there—or at least his ears had—as her family had arranged the union. It—or rather, she—was one of many strings the family had to its bow, always trying to improve its standing and wheedle its way into royal favour. She was now a lower lady in waiting to the queen, an honour that would have been far beyond her reach otherwise. The queen's favour had its own rewards and her family quick to capitalise upon them. Dimitri had not been overly concerned. Every house was like that. Self-serving, out for their own gain. All friends on the surface, but conniving and conspiring to take the others down.

Now, with warm faelights bathing them all in golden light, they laughed and danced as if they were naught but good friends. On the edge of the swirling bodies of those mingling and dancing, it was the perfect place to observe who spoke to whom, who slipped away with whom, and even who was present or absent. Dimitri was never off duty, much as he softened the hardness of his mask. The king would grill him for the details on the morrow, as he always did.

Dimitri shoved away from the column with casual grace, meandering through the laughter and gleaming smiles for another drink. He would have just one more. It would not do to have a buzzing head and lose his mind. Elven wine was extremely strong. The scent of Rosella's perfume reached his nose before she crossed his path. Once upon a time, it had enchanted him—now it nauseated, sending that swoop of sickness into his belly, every breath a poison. Suddenly she was upon him, giggling, and dragged him into the whirl of dancers. He let himself be pulled, before sweeping her into his arms and falling into step with those beside them with a smile upon his lips that betrayed nothing of his true feelings.

A wispy gown of palest blue like the glowing moon adorned her, swirling around her sculpted figure as her feet danced upon air. Next to Dimitri's black tunic adorned with silver threads, Rosella was the light to his darkness, glowing in comparison and effortlessly eclipsing all those around them. She was indeed the most beautiful of all there. At least outwardly. Her dress floated with her. She was wind and water, her feet seeming to never touch the floor. He followed their neighbours' steps with ease with her long-fingered hand in one of his and her slim waist cradled in his other palm.

For all the limitations of his younger days, Dimitri had been well-schooled in the courtly arts and did not shame her. Even so, he felt the king's disapproval radiating from the dais. He was half sure Rosella had preyed upon him just to cause the king's ire. Dimitri fixed his mask into bland cheer, not letting the king drag his attention as he twirled the princess past her father, pretending that all his attention was on her. All her attention was on the rhythm of the music. Inebriated, she was pure joy, movement, and laughter in his arms.

When they passed Dimitri's father, he allowed his gaze to slide to Damir's and his lips to curl with the hint of smug disdain. As they twirled once more out of sight, Dimitri suppressed a genuine smile at his father's scowl. Damn them all, he decided. Dimitri held his head higher. Tonight, he was off duty. He held his back straighter and tugged Rosella closer. Tonight, he was no one, dancing with a princess, and, king be damned, he would enjoy it. The bastard and the princess. For that one moment, he would be above all their scorn.

As the music crescendoed and died, Dimitri bowed and Rosella curtseyed, holding themselves for a moment. Around them, applause scattered through the dancers, and the musicians struck up another tune. Dimitri handed Rosella off to another willing male, and with his usual wink and a mischievous grin that she mirrored, disappeared to catch his breath and find another drink. The musicians had chosen a favourite, and the floor flooded with bodies.

His heart sank as he saw the king's subtle summons. Toroth could not be ignored. Dimitri inclined his head slightly to indicate he had seen. The king affixed him for a long moment with a stare that promised murder, before vanishing. The dangerous thrill of terror spiked in Dimitri before he forced it down. Dimitri changed course, meandering to one of the exits and a quieter, deserted part of the castle.

The chill blasted him as soon as he left the ballroom and the heat of all those bodies fell away, as if they hated the shadows he now stepped into. It was freezing beyond the protective spells, the nights cool even in the late summer with the proximity of the mountain and the altitude of the place. The breeze seeped through him, cooling his clothes and his skin—but doing nothing to dampen the stoking fire of fear inside him that Toroth wrought amongst his court. The court that existed on a knife edge between the king's tempers. Dimitri was not immune to it. He was a navigator of that tempestuous sea, but not its master.

And so, he found himself as he always did when presented with unexpected summons, racing through a mental list of any perceived infractions. What had he done? When? Why? How? What spin could be put on it to soothe the king's ire, to keep himself safe? Every time, it felt the same crushing weight of life or death—that somehow, Dimitri had damned himself and today was to be the day the king had decided his worth was at an end, and that he would have to fight his way free. Dimitri did not turn as the king silently appeared beside him. He steeled himself, awaiting for the blow to fall.

9

DIMITRI

Toroth did not mention his daughter, though Dimitri knew it was always first on his tongue. His heart fluttered in relief—and then sank further. Dimitri knew, if he did not receive Toroth's wrath at once, he was safe. But for a lack of customary disdain? The king desired a favour. The more tolerable the king, the higher the favour.

"I have something to ask of you, Dimitrius," Toroth said, almost affably.

"Your Majesty?" Dimitri inclined his head. A chilling tingle crept down his spine.

"I require your help with a delicate matter—with your customary discretion, of course."

"Anything, Your Majesty. I live to serve." It was not a question or a request. Dimitri hated every word he uttered, but there was little choice. Even the breeze paused, as if it, too, held its breath.

"I have a list of names that I know to be committing various misdemeanours."

Dimitri stilled. He was the source of most of the king's intelligence, which meant one of two things. One, if Toroth had names he did not know of, then Dimitri had failed in his duties. The thought did not bear acknowledging, for the punishment would be severe, but even so, his heart thundered into life, pulse racing. Or two, they were innocents to be punished for the king's own agenda.

"Your Majesty?" It was a struggle for him to keep the words monotone, empty, not filled with dread of one kind or another.

The king told him a list of names. Dimitri knew them all—but he could not identify any threads that connected them. The seesawing nausea within him swirled. He had missed something. He would be next upon the pyre. It was the only conclusion he could arrive at.

"What is their crime, Your Majesty?" He knew a few had committed minor infractions—at worst, embezzlement. He clutched at smoke to imagine what they might have done that had angered Toroth. What connected them all in this moment? He wanted to vomit, and clamped his mouth shut, forcing breaths through his nose. He could not afford to lose himself. Not there. Not then. Danger approached in the shadows.

"That is none of your concern." Toroth could—or would—not tell him.

Dimitri was not sure which was worse, but relief flooded him. *It's not me.* That thought was followed by horror. What was King Toroth planning?

"They will all be arrested on the morrow, at dawn's break."

Dread curdled in Dimitri's belly. That would be easy. All were present in Tournai to celebrate the five-hundredth anniversary of Saradon's defeat. It sounded as though Toroth had his plot well in hand, whatever it was. Dimitri both did and did not want to know what it was. "What do you require of me, sire?"

"You shall plant convincing evidence in all their homes to suggest they are supporters of Saradon and seek to revive his mission."

Cold flooded Dimitri as the missing piece of the puzzle clicked into place. It seemed even the breeze stalled at his realisation, for the frigid flicker of air had ceased. "You will frame them of this for what end?"

Toroth glared at Dimitri for questioning him, but he answered. "Two birds, one stone. Criminals are punished, and national pride is restored. That is all you need to know." *But you will do the dirty work for me*, was the unspoken implication that laced Toroth's words.

Dimitri bowed smoothly, betraying nothing of his hammering heart or the dread coursing through him. He could read between the lines. This was nothing more than greed. Toroth wanted their assets. The king knew he could not bleed the country dry through more taxes and risk a revolt. In framing them, Toroth would bolster his own coffers and stoke patriotic pride. Who would question him? At the first mention of Saradon, the accused would be abandoned by all they knew and loved. Distanced, defamed, disowned. On such a critical anniversary of the fall of Saradon and the salvation of Pelenor, Toroth would be the saviour of Pelenor, keeping the kingdom safe from evil, and himself utterly beyond reproach. Toroth was no fool.

"Well?" Toroth snapped at his silence.

Dimitri wondered how long the king had planned this. He felt sick to his stomach, but the nausea had nothing to do with the drinking or the dancing. He shifted his weight, choosing his words with care. "They will be killed?"

"For such treason, yes."

"What have they done to deserve it?"

Toroth scowled at him. "Your place is not to ask such questions. It is your duty to do my bidding. Can I count on you, or will you be alongside the traitors?" It would mean nothing to the king to have him rounded up as well.

Dimitri held back the swallow that would betray him. "Of course, Your Majesty. I am yours to command." He executed a smooth bow and stayed, bent low, his back as straight as a rod.

"Good. You have the night." The king did not acknowledge him further. Toroth strode away, back to the ballroom.

For a moment, the corridor became an even darker black. Once his shadow left the doorway, a column of light and warmth spilled out. But Dimitri did not wish to rejoin it. Nothing would halt the frigid claws stealing the warm aura from him. He sagged against the wall, allowing himself a moment of weakness, before pulling himself upright once more. It took all his willpower not to vomit. He softly called a name, and a figure melted out of the darkness beside him. "You heard all that?"

"Yes, sir," his associate replied.

Dimitri paused, his heart heavy. It was already done, and there was nothing he could do to stop it. If he did his job well, perhaps this would be a swift death—and that was all the mercy he could give Toroth's victims. "Make it so, by the king's orders."

There was no answer, just a rustle of movement as his informant disappeared into the night. Dimitri closed his eyes and turned his face to the cold sky as his heart quickened once more and the familiar feeling of panic tightened his chest and rushed through his veins. He took deep, deliberate breaths, but the ice in his blood raced through him until his hands shook with it. He folded his arms across his chest, but it was a frail and useless gesture. They could not protect him from what he would have to do in the name of Toroth.

Breathe.

He forced himself to continue, trying to block it all out and send away each care with the breeze, like a seed floating on the wind, but it did not work. For a wild moment, he wondered what it would be like for the accusations to be true. For Saradon's mission to be alive, perhaps even for Saradon to return. Such an impossible thought. Or was it? Perhaps the king did fear that. Dimitri could not know what Toroth's mind held, but it seemed to be only selfishness and greed. Hate spiked in him. The riven circle sprang to mind—the Mark of Saradon. The broken wheel. This wheel needed to be broken, just as Saradon had sought, and Dimitri wished he were not so powerless. The king was a law unto himself, and the kingdom bled for it.

Dimitri could not linger any longer. His absence would soon be noted. He returned to the festivities, each step taking all the effort he had, but he was no longer a part of the merriment. He felt cut off, as though doused in a cold blast that even the magic of this place could not penetrate. The bland indifference he schooled his expression into was only possible with his years of practice, but rage burned underneath it. It was a cold inferno that crescendoed with the music humming through them all, until all he could hear was the sound of his blood drumming in his ears.

The king was in the midst of the throng, laughing and making merry—with one of those who was to die, Dimitri noted—as though there were nothing wrong or untoward. Dimitri looked at the king's companion, knowing he had less than a day to enjoy his liberty. Perhaps only several at best to live. He had no doubt Toroth would make a spectacle of them all. It was an unsettling feeling to possess such foresight.

Dimitri watched the man jest with the king. As pleasured as that individual felt tonight, he would be in a world more pain as he met his end in one of the most unpleasant ways imaginable. He would be made a scapegoat for an imaginary crime. His land and all his assets would be seized. He would die for nothing except greed. His name and his line after him would be forever shamed—for a crime of which he had never been guilty.

Nausea rose in Dimitri. Informing on legitimate crimes was one thing, but this went a step too far. Already, his soul felt blackened with the knowledge of what was to come and his part in it. The order had been given. Guilt already stained Dimitri, and yet he had done it and would do it again, as he did everything that was asked of him, no matter the cost to his own soul, to survive in this cursed place.

Why do I do it? he asked the enchanted stars above, but they held no answers. Neither did he. Did he? Was there truly no choice? Panic flooded him once more. It rose with the rage and nausea, a maelstrom engulfing him until his senses were overwhelmed and he could not see the ballroom before him. Everything collapsed inward, trapping him, confining him. He could not breathe. Could not break this. Could not escape.

Dimitri fled, stumbling in his haste into the cool gardens under the real stars and moonlight, to a dark corner that matched his soul, where no one could see him fall apart. In the darkness, alone, he gave in to the panic, unleashing his desperate hold on it in relief. The cold air stabbed into his lungs with each sawing breath, the pain a welcome relief. He was alive. And whilst he drew breath, there was hope.

But, the moment of peace did not last. Before he could

take another breath, before the sweet scent of her honey-suckle was barely in his nostrils, hands slid around his waist. Blinded by rage and panic, he spun around and slammed the body up against the wall, but then the familiar perfume teased him. His vision cleared, and Dimitri realised it was Rosella. His rage slackened and his face paled. He loosened his grip, horrified, and tried to back away, but she held him all the tighter. Even in the darkness, he saw how her eyes glittered with the absence of wit. How much had she drunk?

Too much, as always.

She pulled him closer, the drink-fuelled lust clear to see. He raged against that, too, as anger clouded his vision once more. How shallow, gluttonous, and selfish they all were. Beyond the brink, he gave in to the beast within him, crushing his lips against hers. Anything to block it all out, burn through it.

His tongue slipped into her mouth, urgent and seeking, and she responded in kind, the taste of something intoxicating and sweet bleeding across his tongue. She tugged him clumsily towards the rose bushes, staggering to a more private corner. Her hands slipped to his breeches, tugging the laces and grazing across him until he throbbed, filled with the need for relief. Without thinking, he found his hands halfway up her thighs, her skirts gathered up, and pushed her back against the carved hedges, clenching his fingers around her soft buttocks.

She squealed and squirmed in his grasp, and he scented it before he saw it. Blood. Had he cut her somehow? Been too rough? The maelstrom within him stilled as his own blood drained away until he was cold to his core. Then he espied it. Blood upon her arm. A thorn had nicked her skin.

Not him. Relief washed away the darkness for a moment before the next wave rolled in. She was already over the moment. Drunk and giggling, she tugged him closer, but his rage and panic had faded, replaced with something sour and sickening that curdled in his gut. Dimitri dropped the silken fabric and staggered backwards. Crumpled, it covered her, but she was a crushed rose now, the scrunched fabric scarred by his hands.

Gods only know what her father will think.

Then again, she was so inebriated, she might not even remember what had happened. With the barest thought, he healed the cut upon her milky skin with a smudge of magic, and before she could entangle him again, he slipped into the shadows and fled.

10

DIMITRI

way from the overwhelmedness of the ball—and
Rosella—it was far easier to clear his head. Dimitri
fled blindly, the taste of Rosella still upon his lips,
no matter how much he rubbed at them until he finally
stopped, far away from the noise and light. He was surprised
to find himself in the royal gallery. A stroke of something
unearthly ran down his spine. What had brought him there,
of all places? He walked across the smooth floor with his
eyes closed, slowing his breathing, filling his lungs with
clean, cool air. Here, it was not polluted with drink, food,
sweat… and the scent of greed. There was only darkness and
silence.

Why do I do it?

Rosella's face swam before his mind's eye. He envied
them, but the more he acted like the rest of them, the more
he hated himself for it. It was like his own personal brand of
torture. He pushed thoughts of her away. No doubt he would
go to her later—he always had to—but he relished this
moment of reprieve.

He stopped and opened his eyes. Dimitri stood once more before the portrait of Saradon. Not the meek, sitting study, but the one of fire and might as Saradon stood tall, wreathed in flame and darkness. He seemed even more foreboding in the dark gallery, and the stillness of the air, the utter silence, muffled even Dimitri's racing heart—but not his mind. That was as sharp as a razor, unclouded by the drink that corrupted the rest of them.

This was an opportunity.

The king conspired to commit the ultimate crimes in his greed. Dimitri could not imagine a more horrific way to punish those who had done nothing wrong aside from the usual pettiness of the court. They were all as bad as the king, but Toroth was the worst of them all. The sum of their sins.

Now Dimitri's panic and rage ebbed, he saw potential. It would not be easily done, yet perhaps it was more possible than ever. The kingdom of Pelenor had bled for years, but the king had not staunched the wounds. Money. Men. Never-ending tithes and taxes to fund his lavish lifestyle and meaningless conquests.

Dimitri would not be the only one who desired Toroth to fall. Indeed, as his spymaster, Dimitri knew exactly who sought that end, if only for their own greed. Now it was time to use that knowledge, he thought for the first time. A sudden wave of clarity rushed through him, cleansing his mind. How could he achieve it? He stared into Saradon's frozen gaze, as if the painting could tell him. Saradon had done it. The half-elf with no magic had nearly crippled the kingdom.

How? Dimitri asked, but no answer came.

Perhaps it would be as simple as exploiting those who sought Toroth's downfall. Bribery, extortion, threats—but Dimitri rankled at that. Such things were beyond his nature, though he did it daily for the king's bidding. Perhaps it would not be so terrible, for the greater good, but his gut told him that sowing badness would not lead to noble ends. Perhaps he could band them together, united on a common front, though they should hate him, regardless of his part in their greatest desires. Dimitri could not bring himself to that end, either. To do all that and still be hated.

No, perhaps Saradon had the best idea of all—to break the wheel. Dimitri could see Saradon's Mark, the riven circle, burning bright upon his chestplate, as though it were living flame itself. That was beyond Dimitri. He was so close, but he did not have the assets, men, and alliances needed. He would be hard-pressed to find the former, and it would be nigh on impossible to secure the latter.

Moonlight bloomed across the shining floor, illuminating him where he stood amongst the inky shadows and casting its glow onto the foot of the canvas before him. Dimitri froze. Within the portrait itself, in the crystal raised before Saradon, the smallest glittering called him closer. It was such a lifelike painting, Dimitri thought, but the way it twinkled… Paint did not have such properties. He silently stepped forward. Tucked inside the faceted surface of the illustrated crystal, he saw runes, faintly glowing blue and silver. Lunar runes. He had seen few before. These were old and fading. It was a wonder he had noticed them at all. If the moon had not shone at that precise angle, at that precise moment, he would have seen nothing.

Could he read them? Dimitri bent closer. The alphabet sprang into focus, and he murmured the runes aloud. They were scripted in the elven tongue of Auraria—unusual enough in itself—and too subtle to be graffiti. These had been painstakingly included. If they were to only be visible by the light of the moon, they must have held some weight.

And yet, he doubted they had been put there with Toroth's knowledge or permission... or the same of any monarch beforehand.

"'The Heart of a Dragon shall resurrect him. The Heart of a Dragon will cast him down.' That makes no sense." Dimitri frowned at the cryptic message. As he stepped back and glanced at the painting in its entirety, he noted where the runes were written. On an illustration of a Dragonheart. Who would go through so much effort in order to leave a nonsense message? There must have been more to it than he could see, he surmised. What was he missing?

"The Heart of a Dragon shall resurrect him. The Heart of a Dragon will cast him down," he repeated, murmuring it to himself as he raked a hand through his hair. Was it literal? He was not familiar with the intimate details of Saradon's legends, only that the Dragonhearts had been used to make his power far greater than it ever would have been other-wise. Dimitri did not know much about the Dragonhearts, either, other than they had fabled powers of some kind—perhaps more than he had realised. If that were the case, it was no wonder the king hoarded them under ward and key.

He fleetingly wished he could get his hands on one, but it would be an impossible task. No one, save Toroth himself, accessed the king's hoard. He dismissed the idea as soon as he thought it, though a small part of his mind continued to mull over the prospect, reluctant to give up so easily, for Dimitri had often found there was a way to achieve anything. It just required ingenuity, determination, and more than a little measure of luck sometimes. Yet, perhaps this was a match for him. Dimitri did not like to chance failure, or Toroth's cruel ruthlessness.

Clouds scudded across the moon once more. The runes faded before Dimitri's eyes, but they were etched into his memory, and his heart burned with a fire of hope that he had never allowed to grow so much before. Now it was stoked, he could not bear to let it die.

The spymaster, the forgotten son, the outcast... He did not know how he would make it come to pass, but he vowed he would. This was the moment he had waited for all his life. He could see the stars aligning now, almost in place, dancing together. Dimitri looked into Saradon's violent gaze. *I am going to finish your work. I am going to take down the king. I am going to break the wheel.*

AEDON

"They're here," Brand growled. He crouched and drew his huge blade with a quiet hiss. Erika, Aedon, and Ragnar spread out to form an arc, each drawing their weapons. A frisson of fear mingled with excitement rushed through Aedon, and he bounced upon the balls of his feet as he rode it, allowing himself to soak it into his veins and take its power for his own. The sharp edge of those wild feelings would see him through this. Never did he feel more alive than when he sliced into them.

The canyon was the perfect place for an ambush. The only pass through the peaks to their destination. The elves of Tir-na-Alathea knew it as well as they. Aedon felt them skulking nearby, but their magic flowed strangely, warped by the cliffs that hemmed them in. He could not pinpoint it—or them. Unease stirred, disrupting that current of lightning sharp focus within. "Be careful. They have wards up. I cannot tell where they are—or when they will strike."

Granite cliffs soared on either side of them, reaching up into the mountain mists. The eerie silence held, only broken by the ragged tear of their breaths and each step crunching upon the rocky track. Aedon's gaze darted around, flitting from one point to another. His companions sought for any trace of their pursuers too.

He reached inside his breast and offered the small, cloth-wrapped prize to Brand. "You keep it. If all else fails, take to the skies."

The hulking Aerian grasped it and tucked it inside his clothing for safekeeping. "We ought to keep moving. No point sitting here like lambs waiting for slaughter."

They moved swiftly and quietly, loping through the canyon. The scattering of pebbles dislodged with each step seemed painfully loud. But when it came, the attack was silent.

"Unh!" Brand staggered forward with the punch of the impact through his wing. The aerian spun, roared, and charged the familiar male elf swinging down the cliff toward them. Ta'hiir. He had a bow in one hand and a quiver of arrows strapped to his hips—the match to the one piercing Brand's feathered wing. Behind Brand, Aedon slid to a halt. Aedon saw the bloodlust already running in Brand's eyes, for his friend acknowledged no pain from the shot. Without stopping, Brand snapped the shaft of the arrow and tugged it free. He did not so much as glance at the blood pulsing from the wound and blighting his golden brown feathers. In one fluid movement, he swept his blade at the elf just as his assailant landed on the ground before them.

Ta'hiir dodged the blow. His sister, El'hari, following closely behind him, parried it. Her slim blade skittered across Brand's thick steel, sending it slightly off course— enough to strike the stone beside her with an almighty crash. Then she was off. Aedon's attention followed her as he wrenched his dagger free, already calculating how best to disable her. The end of the canyon was so close. If they could just make the break of the pass…

Brandishing her twin blades, Erika gave chase, though she was no match for the elf's speed. Ragnar drew back his axe as Ta'hiir rounded on Brand once more. Just as Ta'hiir's magic began to cripple Brand, forcing the giant almost to his knees, Ragnar threw the axe. Ta'hiir leapt out of the way, cursing. The blade bounced harmlessly into the dust—but it had done its job of distracting him and freeing Brand from the magical assault. Ragnar ran for his blade, pulling his remaining axe from his belt loop.

Aedon followed Erika. Two each against two. Better odds, at least. He did not slow as Brand fell to his knees. The Aerian crashed to the ground, leaving Ragnar, the slow and combat-shy dwarf, facing the fresh-faced and brutal Ta'hiir. The faster Aedon took out El'hari, the faster he could help. Aedon sent his magic shooting after El'hari, pulling her inexorably toward him.

The distraction was enough. Erika pounced upon the she-elf. She gathered El'hari's mahogany hair in her fist and yanked it with relish. El'hari screeched and fell, but at the last second, pitched her weight and sent Erika tumbling instead. Erika crashed to the ground, rolled, and leapt to her feet, but El'hari danced around her, nicking her with cuts and grazes that Erika was not fast enough to dodge. Aedon joined the fray with a howl, barging El'hari aside with a shoulder. She faced him with a snarl, her teeth bared.

"Don't give me the *aleilah*, thief. I want to take it from your hot, fresh corpse!" She launched herself at him.

Breathing heavily, Erika threw herself back into the fight, but with a thrust of El'hari's clawed hand and a burst of magic, she sailed through the air, landed with a thud, and was still. Aedon swore. His blade parried El'hari's, barely able to keep up with her speed. He knew he was no match for her in hand-to-hand combat. As they danced through the canyon in a deadly give-and-take, Aedon caught a glimpse of Brand's hulking form still on the ground, and Ragnar weakening as he tried to keep Ta'hiir at bay.

No! Why wasn't the Aerian up and fighting? Aedon could not pause to give in to the crushing worry that punched him. Poison. The arrow had to be poisoned. The forest elves were too strong. If he did not act, they would all be dead, their promise broken, and the *alailah* lost to the Tir-na-Alathea elves once more.

"Is this the best you have for me?" El'hari laughed. Her taunts stung, but he could withstand them. It was the smug glee in her amber eyes that he despised. "Weren't you one of Pelenor's finest? Not so fine without your dra—"

"*Do not utter her name!*" Aedon thundered, giving in to the magic that was his greatest secret. The inferno consumed him with a roar that drowned out all other sound as the floodgates within him opened. Raw power coursed through him as the magic burnt its way out, blasting the elf before him. Through a golden haze, he saw her alight and fleeing before he turned his attention to her brother. Ta'hiir wheeled on him. His eyes widened with fear, and he fled after his sister before the fire consumed him too. Utterly spent, Aedon collapsed to his knees, his breathing ragged. Ragnar staggered over and helped him to his feet.

"Quickly, Aedon. That was a pretty show, but we cannot be sure they will not come back. You must heal Brand. That arrow is tainted."

Aedon dragged himself to his feet as Ragnar rushed to Erika's side, pulling her onto her back and resting her head upon his legs. Erika stirred under Ragnar's ministrations as he treated her concussion, though he could not fix the sting to her pride. Aedon bent over Brand. He trembled from head to foot with the exertion of drawing upon the old magics without the strength of his former dragon companion to bolster his control. He pushed the ache from his heart at the familiar feel of her magic coursing through him. There was a reason he did not call upon it save for in the gravest need.

It was just as he surmised. Malevolent poison from the arrow oozed inexorably through his companion. The very feel of it left a stinging tang upon Aedon's tongue. With slow, deliberate magic, he drew the poison out of Brand's wound, painstakingly pulling it through each blood vessel until the Aerian's blood ran clean. Finally, Brand's shallow breathing strengthened and colour returned to his dark face. Aedon sealed the wound. A bare patch of skin amongst the feathers on Brand's wing remained—the only indication he had been injured.

Brand groaned. Slowly, he pushed himself into a seated position. His wings slumped to the side of him, like a giant cape, as though he did not have the strength to lift and fold them away. "You cannot keep doing that," Brand mumbled at Aedon as he tried to recover his bearings.

"I know. It really takes it out of me. If only I had more strength to draw on," Aedon said. He smiled half-heartedly, unable to shake the unease that came from seeing his strong brother in arms so roundly beaten. "At least it got us out of that bind, though."

"No more," Brand growled at him.

"Bu—"

"No. More," the Aerian snarled through clenched teeth.

Aedon gritted his teeth as well. "A thank you would be nice. I know what is at stake. If I cannot use the least of my old skills, what good am I?"

Brand grumbled, but subsided. His attention snapped up,

behind Aedon, as Erika approached slowly, limping and grimacing. "Are you all right?" Brand asked in a low voice, the only outward sign of his worry for her. Aedon wasn't fooled. After so long travelling together, he knew what passed between them; the intimacies they would never give voice to.

Holding her head high, Erika met his gaze for a brief moment before sweeping her attention around the canyon again. Her reply was curt and practical. She found no comfort in weakness. "Aye. Enough bickering. We need to get away from this pass and to somewhere more defensible, lest they return."

"They won't." Aedon coughed. His throat was so sore, it felt like he had swallowed a blade.

"You'd better hope not," Brand muttered.

Their collective nerves were well frayed by the time they made camp that evening beneath a painfully indefensible outcrop. Ta'hiir and El'hari were out there in the dark. Everyone knew it, though they did not speak of it. The wood elves would have even greater cause to pursue them now. Aedon did not know what he had hurt more—their bodies or their pride. He clenched the glass vial all the tighter. If she wanted it back so badly, El'hari would indeed have to pry it from his dead hands—and he swore that he would not give her the damned pleasure.

12

DIMITRI

The cold chilled Dimitri to his marrow as freezing wind drove down from the mountains into the wide square. The king sat upon the dais at the head of the square with Queen Idaelia to one side. Off the dais stood the royal family, their faces devoid of any emotion, as the line of soldiers guarding them held back the crowd. Not a body more could fit in the square. They hung out of windows, sat atop walls, carts—anything just for a view. The news had spread like wildfire.

Dimitri stood to one side with the rest of the court. His bones ached, but he would not move. Would not draw the slightest attention to himself. He had a perfect view of the most terrible sight. In the middle of the square, a line of pyres stood. Upon freshly chopped wood were the accused, lashed to the stakes at their centre. They were unrecognisable. Bedraggled and beaten, their finery had been stripped away. Ragged hair flew in the wind, unrestrained and tangled as it whipped around them. They stood, shuddering with cold—and fear—with only thin, cheap cloth to conceal their modesty. It did not protect them from the driving wind in the slightest.

Some sagged in their bindings, already unconscious from their torture. Others shouted, pleaded, begged their case to the king, to the crowd, to anyone who would listen. Toroth silenced them with a wave of his hand. Their mouths did not cease moving, but all the sound of their voices snapped off in an instant. At their silence, the noise of the crowd increased, cursing them all in Saradon's name. Projectiles sailed through the air—rotten vegetables, offal, excrement—to pelt the unfortunates. The king could not have chosen his accusations more perfectly. Even now, the people still feared Saradon and the threat he had posed to their way of life. It was an effective propaganda.

Dimitri stood as immobile as the rest of the court, his face carved with coldness, but inside, he raged. It only fuelled his decision. They did not see that the way of life they sought to protect was one of oppression, fed to them so well from the crown that they believed in their liberties and rights. And yet, Toroth could end them with a word at any moment. Snap their necks. Crush their minds. Steal the life from their veins. It would be easy for one of his power to do on a whim. But this… This was cruelty. It was a spectacle, a performance. An example was to be made of those innocents who stood there—one to keep everyone else in line.

A shadow fell over them, blotting out all light in the square. Dimitri did not look up. He knew what came. A cry rose from the crowd, followed immediately by a hush. The Pelenori were proud of their dragons, but right to fear them. They were the largest beasts in the country and bound by intangible magics that the mortal populace would never understand—or truly trust, when every fibre of their being screamed with the terror of being prey in the presence of such predators.

The black dragon descended from the steel-grey skies and landed with a thud that shook them all. Only the stone of the capital could withstand it without crumbling and cracking under such force. And those claws... Dimitri swallowed at their proximity, but did not allow himself to otherwise flinch away, despite the beast being far too close for comfort.

The tail that encircled the queen's throne close by was an impenetrable, glistening, black wall of scales and spikes, whilst its head curled around to the king. It stood several times the height of Toroth, who was dwarfed by its bulk as he laid a hand upon its cheek. Eyes of liquid gold with dark voids for pupils stalked every movement in the square. Dimitri instinctively shivered as its attention skimmed across him.

A deep rumble came from its chest, its jaw slightly ajar. As if any of them needed reminding it had teeth as long as their legs, and worse inside its belly. As much as dread filled Dimitri at the presence of the behemoth and what he knew was to come, he felt a momentary pang of envy at the thought of what it would be like to have such a fearsome predator at his disposal. Dimitri no longer dwelt on what could have been had he been permitted to attend selection, or had a chance to become a member of the legendary Winged Kingsguard. Even so, he could not help but wonder what it felt like to control such strength. This dragon, and all the dragons of the Winged Kingsguard, were the reason no uprising in Pelenor had been successful in over three thousand years.

Smoke curled from the dragon's nostrils as Toroth stirred, then stood.

Dimitri could not—would not—listen as the king proclaimed the guilt of those standing before them, embellishing his fabricated tales of their treasons and their secret plots in Saradon's name, decreeing that they would die for their sins against him and Pelenor. He stared into the bitter clouds, longing for the wind to rise and toss the king's words into the skies.

The accused openly sobbed. Few stood without fear on their face, for they knew Toroth's mind would not change, and faced their doom. Those golden eyes were death on swift wings. There could be few more painful ways, but at least it would be quick, Dimitri hoped. The dragon's head snaked forward, its tongue flicking out from between its teeth to scent the air. It hissed before rearing tall. In its ashen chest, a glow built, a sun burning inside its chest that was blinding in the darkness of the gathering storm. Up the dragon's throat it burned, until the beast held pure molten fire in its jaws.

At the king's signal, it unleashed its worst.

Dimitri threw his hands before his face, recoiling with the rest of the crowd. The wave of heat rolled over them all, scalding his palms, his neck, the tips of his ears. It stole the breath from his mouth as it burned his lips. Blinding light flared, forcing his eyes shut, as the fire instantly took hold and the wooden pyres ignited in a blaze.

Mere moments, and it was over. Giant jaws clamped shut, cutting off the stream of flames. Its belly darkened. Such was the fury of the fire, the intensity of the heat, that after only seconds, most of the wood had been incinerated. Dimitri looked away from the sad piles of remains as the stench of burnt wood and charred flesh passed them, and a belch of ash and smoke enveloped the crowd. A part of him ached for them.

There was a long silence before murmurs arose—quiet,

fearful ones, as though the crowd did not dare rouse the king's anger further. The storm spoke for them, having no such qualms. The heavens opened to assault them, sleet and rain hissing as it vapourised upon the pyres.

Toroth stared at the destruction before him, stern faced. Then, he rose and departed without a word, followed by his retinue. At his unspoken command, the dragon launched itself into the skies, battering the square with a cruel blast of air that turned the sleet into weapons that sliced into the upturned faces. Dimitri shielded his head under his cloak—and when he looked up, the dragon had vanished into the seething skies. His heart hammering and the nausea of anxiety swimming around the pit of his stomach, Dimitri could not bear to be there a moment longer. He folded himself into shadow and silence and spirited himself away upon the wind, leaving shouts of alarm in his wake. Now. He had to act now. There could be no more of this.

13

DIMITRI

In darkest hours before the coming of dawn, Dimitri poured over manuscripts in the Athenaeum—the royal library—bending close to examine the tiny script in the small, wavering glow of faelight he had conjured. He could have afforded a bigger light, but he was in the restricted section. Whilst his rank gave him privilege to use it, Dimitri preferred to remain below the attention of the archive keepers, slipping through their realm like a shadow.

The fire driving him burnt like the dragon's flame as the idea took hold. Could he use Saradon to rally a rebellion to his name? Saradon might have been long dead, but he was still a talisman of fear and change. It had been plain to see in the square—fear was a dangerous beast. Yet, it was also a tool. Yes, it could stifle and suppress… but it could also *ignite* a frenzy.

"The Heart of a Dragon shall resurrect him. The Heart of a Dragon will cast him down," Dimitri muttered to himself, searching through the passages for any mention of such a prophecy, but none could he find. There were other, equally tantalising references of Saradon, but with no clarity to them. Dimitri sighed. He reviewed what he had—a scattering of phrases and sentences written on a small square of parchment in neat, cursive script in the coded language only he understood.

"'As it was before, so it will be again, and this time, thrice as hard and thrice as deadly. A fated one holds the key. The fated one is a pinprick of light against an onslaught of darkness.'" The portrait of Saradon standing tall before the tiny light that defeated him sprang to mind. "Is this referring to what has already happened?" Of course, the empty night held no answers, only frustration. "This is impossible!" Dimitri tossed aside the book in annoyance. It slammed to the floor, and Dimitri cursed silently as the slap echoed through the shelves.

He suppressed a sneeze as dust from the ancient articles tickled his nose. For good measure, he warded himself so no sound of his presence would be heard, admonishing himself for failing to do so the moment he had entered, having forgotten in his anticipation. He spread a warmth spell, too, for no fires burnt in the place—too much a risk to the precious things gathered within—and the stone halls were draughty with the sneaking night air.

By the time he finished scanning through the stack of literature before him, Dimitri was still and chilled. He scanned the notes he had so far. They were nothing by themselves, but pieced together, he began to construct something. "Still too many pieces missing." He sighed. And yet... He cocked his head, squinting at the map of Pelenor and the surrounding lands that sat beside him. It suggested that Saradon had been defeated and subsequently disappeared—

but not killed. No body had ever been found. Could it have been nothing more than propoganda spread to calm the people, he wondered, whilst the truth was hidden or never truly known?

"Where would he have gone?" Dimitri asked himself. There were so many places Saradon could have hidden, both inside and outside Pelenor. Saradon did not seem the type to lie low and hold a grudge to the death, Dimitri mused. Not after what he had endured—and done. Throughout everything he saw ran a tantalising hint that Saradon had escaped in some way. What had happened?

Dimitri sent out his magic to search for more information on a particular mountain range that perhaps could hold the key to Saradon's escape, then stilled. The magic dissipated, but he now had his answer. Dimitri could seek him. He would need more power and a relic that held magical resonance to Saradon, but it was possible. If he still existed in any form, Dimitri could find him.

If I am to take on his cause, by his name shall it be done, and Toroth will fear the both of us. He did not understand the scraps of prophecy and the mentions of Dragonhearts—yet. Dimitri hurried to return to his quarters and summon one of his associates, who soon appeared, well used to their master's odd hours. Dimitri hesitated a moment. Even this was perhaps too much to trust to another, but Rook was the best at shadowy business such as this, and Dimitri could not risk being discovered. The lunar runes had given him a harebrained idea, but an idea nonetheless.

"Find out where the Dragonhearts are kept presently." He needed to know for certain for this to have any hope of working.

"Yes, Master."

"And… "

"Master?"

"Never mind. As quickly as you can." He would seek out a relic himself. He already knew precisely where he would find one. Excitement thrummed through him as once more, he folded into smoke and wind.

14

DIMITRI

Dark. Earthy. Still. The silence was both peaceful and watchful. As he stood over the tomb of Saradon's mother, Dimitri waited. Not for anyone else, but for his conscience to decide one way or another. It was one thing to speak of breaking the wheel and bringing a new power and peace to a land. Quite another to break into a grave. Desecration. Such a thing would leave a mark on a soul, a stain that would be hard to banish—even for him. The dead had earned the right to be left in peace. The way Karietta had died, she definitely earned her long rest. Her likeness atop the tomb even stared at him with reproach. He looked away.

The cold stroked its way down his spine, threatening to reduce him to shivers. Then Dimitri recalled the burning of the false traitors, and his resolve hardened. No other relics of Saradon existed. Everything had been destroyed, save this. A last gift to his mother, the only woman who had ever shown him true kindness and love, the only one he had ever cared for. It had only survived because no one had dared to do what he was about to—but Karietta was long dead, and the dead had no cares in the world of the living.

Before he could allow the seeds of doubt to grow, Dimitri split the tomb with a wave of his hand, the stone cracking before him as the slab atop the tomb moved. Dimitri trembled with the effort as he slid it aside with the strength of his magic. Open just a sliver, wide enough to retrieve something. He sent his magic to find what he hoped was still there— because although the dead did not care what he took from their corpses, he was not so naïve to think that they had left no curses on this place whilst alive. He sensed the crumble of fine fabrics as his magic passed, and shuddered at the smoothness of bone—and then he felt it with his power. The cold nothingness of metal. When it floated out, he grasped it, tucking it swiftly into a pocket and departing without a backward glance. He would not look at it just yet. The tomb snapped shut behind him.

With every footstep, his heart pounded at what he had done—the shock, the rush, the fear. And the excitement and adrenaline too, as far-fetched as his quest seemed, as infinitesimally small as his chances were. With a relic, he would find Saradon's resting place. With a Dragonheart, he would discover the truth of the lunar runes one way or another. With the truth, he would find a way to cast down Toroth.

Rook brought him news with the dawn. The Dragonhearts were located precisely where he hoped they would not be— in the most secure of the royal vaults alongside the king's most priceless treasures, from gold spoils to unhatched dragon eggs. He sent Rook away. He had answers—but now more questions too. Dimitri's status would gain him access to some of the vaults, but not without the questions he needed to avoid.

Dimitri went about his usual business thinking of little else aside from how to obtain access to the Dragonhearts, only distracted by the unusual flurry of activity at court that day. There was no talk other than what had happened the day before, though most only dared speak in whispers, and away from the ears of the king.

Not far enough from Dimitri, however. His informants brought their whispers of fear and fury long into the following night. They knew exactly what the king had done and why. In building his power and wealth, Toroth had crippled strategic alliances and severed the trust between himself and the court. Dimitri allowed himself a little smile of satisfaction. He would use that to his advantage. He had already ordered Rook to infiltrate the destroyed households and turn their allegiance to his cause.

He would personally see to the rest, as difficult as it would be. He was already the subject of their suspicions. After all, who else would feed the king such information? It was an unneeded hitch, but not impossible to overcome. Especially when he told them all how Toroth had ordered him to plant false evidence. Of course, no one would dare to openly spread such treason—truth or not—but it would spread like wildfire nonetheless. How the king targeted his most loyal friends and subjects...

This would be too enjoyable to watch. But first, Dimitri needed to find out if there were any grounds to the prophecy.

That evening, Dimitri sealed himself in his chambers to prepare for the most daring part of his plan. With meticulous calm, he smoothed the cushions and placed himself upon the centre of the chaise, sitting cross-legged and straight-backed, with the cold metal of the relic in the palm of his hand. A silent talisman of confidence, reminding him why he did this. What was at stake.

Dimitri closed his eyes. He shut out the comfortable, warm room and the fire flickering before him. The fire he now felt a deep-seated unease around after the previous day. Every crackle was a reminder of those deaths. He still scented smoke—he couldn't cleanse it from his nose. The taste of bitter ash had soured everything upon his tongue that day.

He inhaled a deep, slow breath and relaxed his hands upon his knees, before retreating deeper into his mind where the kernel of his power resided. Dimitri sent it into the dark, down through the city, seeking that bright core of energy and magic that would be the Dragonhearts in their vaults. The feather light presence of his shadowy magic too slight to be detected as he slipped past the wards, which were slumbering, exactly as Rook had said they would be. Nimbly, he danced past them all—the guards, the keeper doing his daily tally. He waited, unconsciously holding his breath as his spirit passed another round of guards. There was little time left before the wards closed. Dimitri opened his mind and sought out a Dragonheart.

It was pure, blinding light. Unbridled power. Nothing sentient. No slumbering dragon spirit, but an untapped well of energy that seemed limitless—and intoxicating. He latched onto it, melding his magic with its, familiarising himself with and revelling in the feel of it. He had transported other things through space and time before, but nothing as powerful as this. The footprint this left upon the magical plane was beyond anything he had sensed before. It knocked the very breath from his chest.

No wonder the king hoarded such a power, and Saradon had seemed invincible with it. The thought slipped out before he regained composure. This was much better than having a dragon, Dimitri realised. A dragon, a living thing of flesh and blood, susceptible to death and its own willfulness, was a liability. But the Dragonhearts—they were magic in its purest form, a well of power bound to the wielder. It was a heady thought that sent him soaring into euphoria with the boundless possibilities.

Focus, he admonished himself. Dimitri pulled the well of power closer, flexing the boundaries of his magic until he felt the strain of it holding every muscle in his body taut. Slowly, it shifted. He pulled harder. Sweat rolled down his forehead, stinging into his eyes, and his hands balled into fists, trembling, his fingers clenched so tightly his nails cut into his palms.

Eventually, and with agonising slowness, it moved to him. It accelerated as the ripple of magic raced through the world. But with its movement, a snap cracked through the fabric of the world. He felt the wards around his magic change from inert to active, recognising the theft. Seeking. Protecting. Dimitri bit down a curse and commanded the Dragonheart to him with the last ounces of his concentration, pulling his magic from the jaws of the protective wards. The Dragonheart wobbled in his power, tumbling through the unseen plane with his magic.

Saradon needs this. I need this.

The wards closed around Dimitri, chasing at the heels of his essence as he recalled every tendril of power into his body. Something felt wrong, but there was no time to question what. He was in a race to save his life. If those wards caught his spirit, it would be over. They snapped shut at the fringes of his magic, fizzling it with their stupendous power —magic he knew would kill him in an instant if he were to be snared by it—and then he was free, soaring back into himself.

He opened his eyes with a gasp and fell forward as the magic crashed back into him, catching himself before he toppled off the chaise. Karietta's ring clattered onto the floor. Deep breaths tore through him as he staggered to his feet, overcome by dizziness and exhaustion, as if he had tried to lift a mountain with his bare hands. The tang of the wards' magic seared his nostrils. He retched and bent double, holding onto the wall for support, because the room span. Every limb ached. The rush faded within him, giving way to pain.

By his feet was the relic. He picked up the ring, glancing around—and sending his magic out tentatively to sense throughout the place. The Dragonheart ought to have landed in his palm, but his strength had snapped just an instant too soon. Dimitri looked around, but he could neither see nor sense anything. The Dragonheart was nowhere to be found. Panic flooded through him. He had definitely moved the Dragonheart—but to where?

15

HARPER

Tam sighed. "There i'nt no one else comin' in tonight." He scowled at the darkening skies outside that were barely visible through the single pane of warped, clouded glass adorning the door. It made a change from him scowling at the empty tavern. Or Harper. Somehow, the dark of night became an even inkier black as the storm clouds piled high. Rain lashed at the shutters, as though a barrage of blunt arrows assaulted them. "Go on. Get gone. No sense you bein' out later than y'ought to in a storm like this."

Harper grinned and dashed into the back to fetch her cloak. A tingle of excitement rose in her. It might only be the smallest sliver of her life that she rescued from the drudgery she despised, but it was *her* sliver, rain or not. Her mind was already at home, sinking into bed. She hoped there was still some of last night's warming broth left. Sometimes, one had to take the small victories in life. Before Tam could change his mind, Harper dashed past him, pulling her hood up and her cloak tightly around her before surging outside. As she

87

barrelled through the door, her head tucked down, it was not rain that stung her shoulders.

She stopped in wonder at the end of the alley. The ground was white with hail. Above her, the clouds were a castle. Plumes of lightning flashed unseen in their depths, illuminating roiling walls of obsidian. The rumble of thunder was a thousand horses charging as the atmosphere held its breath. Then the wind surged again, beating itself about her until it snatched the very breath from her lungs. It was beautifully terrifying. Harper lingered, looking up at the grandeur, even as the lightning within her own veins urged her to move, to run from the danger of it. The hail started again. She broke into a sprint toward the trees as the icy shards pelted her. When she reached their cover, the barrage ceased. She heard the shake and shudder as the branches above her bore the impact.

In the gaps between the trees, white piled. Then she realised it was snowing. The hail had ceased, and though lightning flashed and thunder rumbled above her, flakes now fell, twirling on the dying breeze between the trees. The forest lit up with it as it blanketed the ground swiftly, a great white carpet broken by black circles around each tree. Harper's breath fogged before her and the air's cold bite nipped at her face. She pulled her cloak tighter and hurried onward. It had been many winters since the first snows had been so early, and she had not yet repaired her cloak to see her through the cold to come. Already, the chill seeped through it, aided by the fraying holes here and there.

Great, soggy flakes settled on her. Harper looked up, flinching as one landed on her eyelashes. She stuck out her tongue to catch another, enjoying the cold, fresh wetness that lasted a second before it melted. Harper trudged on in silence, each step crunching through the fresh crust. Snow was her least favourite kind of weather—life became harder, survival more strained, when the snows arrived to stay for the season, but that first snowfall? That always brought a childlike wonder, no matter how old she grew. The allure of the white blanket's clean beauty quickly faded when one had firewood to chop and dry and food to find in the harsh months, but she would enjoy it for a fleeting moment first.

A crack of thunder split the air, and a jolt raced down Harper's spine. Her heartbeat increased. She had never been afraid of the dark, but there was something about that noise that had been utterly wild. A child of fear sent to haunt nightmares. Tales of the Wild Hunt and immortal fae stealing mortals from the woods prickled in the depths of her mind. She quickened her steps. Her gaze roamed under the dark trees, and she could not help but grasp the handle of the ever-present small knife tucked into her belt.

It's just thunder. Perhaps a lightning strike. That was not an encouraging thought, either. She continued trudging as quietly as she could, her gaze scanning around her and barely daring to breathe so she could hear. Nothing moved. Crackling through the falling snow, she saw a glow. The rumbles of thunder receded with the fading lightning, but there was warm light ahead. Before her loomed the giant oak tree where, on a summer's day, she would sit under its boughs as they trickled dappled sunlight and warmth upon her. Once, she had even brought Alric there, and the lazy passion of that afternoon remained one of her most favourite memories. Now it was a dark, sentient menace, foreboding as it skulked in the shadows watching her approach.

She had to reach home, but the glow under the tree lured her closer. *A traveller?* An unlikely thought. She crept closer. Something moved within the shadows. A rush flooded her, sending every fingertip tingling—but it was just falling snow, dislodged from a branch. Her frenzied heart did not slow. That steady glow remained amongst the roots, throwing light up the whorled trunk. Harper pulled for her knife and held it before her, prepared to stab should someone—or something—jump out at her. The small blade seemed insubstantial against the wraiths of a stormy night.

She had never seen firelight quite like it. She drew closer, unable to stop herself. This fire was not just ribbons of amber and gold. It crackled with iridescence, like a shattered rainbow. Even as she watched, it diminished, but something glinted within the flames, nestled in the embers and surrounded by an arc of damp earth where heat had melted away the snow. She could not help but be drawn closer, moving cautiously with silent footsteps.

Harper gulped and chanced a look around. Nothing else stalked her across the snow. It seemed as though the entire land held its breath with her. The snow continued to fall, as silent as the grave, settling on her head and shoulders as the thunder and lightning faded farther away.

Isolation pressed upon her. It was too dark, even with the white carpet throwing a pale glow through the trunks. A loud crack rang out deep in the forest. She trembled from head to toe, torn between fleeing and staying.

Run, run, run, her blood sang.

Stay, look, just a little glance, her curiosity answered.

A flash of lightning, bigger, closer. The fire sputtered out. She drifted closer, curiosity warring with instinct, and dithered, torn. It was so small, the night was so cold, and she could not see it properly to assess if it was a threat. Harper inched closer, her trembling hand holding her small knife before her. The oak loomed over her now. A stone as big as her clenched fist sat in a ring of melted snow. Multi-faceted, it captured the light from the dying embers beneath it and sent shards of colour out in every direction. It looked almost like quartz—rough, ridged, and angular, with crystalline protrusions on the outside. It was opaque and translucent at the same time.

Curiosity won as she stepped forward, disbelief fuelling her. The arm holding the knife slowly fell to her side. Harper blinked. She was clearly imagining things. The cold had gotten to her, and she had lost her mind. Yet no matter how hard she blinked, the strange stone, the thing that looked like a Dragonheart of legend according to her book, did not disappear. Never had she thought they truly existed. Never had she seen one. And yet, this seemed to hold true to the mythical stones she had heard of in tales from wandering bards and storytellers. Surely they did not—*could* not—exist. Especially not in a godsforsaken place like this.

The fire was gone and darkness reached toward her as the last embers faded. It felt oppressive, even with the tumbling white snow so close. The branches were reaching hands above her, their dark fingers stretched wide as though they would fall upon her and take her. She could not take her eyes off the stone, even though her body cried for her to run. Worse things prowled beyond the safety of the village at night that her little hunting knife was no match for. This could have attracted attention that she did not want.

It was so beautiful. Somehow, it reflected light where there was none.

"What do I do with you?" she said aloud. She was hesitant to touch it. Dragonhearts were supposedly gifted with legendary powers bestowed by their former bodies, but were they dangerous? Would it be hot from the flames? There was no radiant heat that she could feel when she hovered her hand close to its alluring surface.

She could not leave it. Lord Denholme would want such a treasure. A thought struck her. She could sell it to buy her freedom. Little would stand in her way on such rich proceeds. Her chest tightened for an entirely different reason at that thought. This was all her wildest dreams come true. She could go far on the proceeds for such a treasure. Start over somewhere new, somewhere far nicer than the drab, cold, dank County Denholme. Perhaps even Pandora, Caledan's capital city. It was an irresistible thought, one she had long harboured but never truly acknowledged. It was too painful to be so far from her dreams of freedom and fortune. Dreams where she would always be well fed and well kept, instead of a copper away from starving.

Harper reached for the stone, her will settled by the prospect of a better life. Her senses tingled in the dark night. It was utterly still, as if the blanket of snow muted all sound. She scanned the horizon one last time. Nothing moved in the darkness around her. The tree seemed both protector and enemy, friend and predator. She grabbed the stone, her fingers scraping on the jagged, rough surface. In the next instant, the entire world disappeared.

16

HARPER

Light and energy coursed through Harper until it seemed like she was light and energy herself. Her body felt charged with limitless power, every nerve alight with sensation. Colours whirled around her, flashing far too quickly to distinguish and overwhelming her senses. A pair of wild, dark, violet eyes flashed, locking with her gaze for the briefest instant—and sending a thrill down her spine—before they widened and then vanished into the maelstrom.

The Dragonheart burned her, the only physical sensation that permeated the vortex of energy, and when everything disappeared into blackness, its touch was all that remained. Sound deafened her. Millions of voices whispering, chattering, shouting, clamouring to be heard, their words layering over each other so she could hear not one of them distinctly. It was so loud that her ears hurt and her head split, forcing her eyes shut. She spun weightlessly. There was no up or down, no direction. Utter nothingness. Her stomach roiled.

Then, bright light and heat engulfed her and she fell

forward, crashing into something solid that knocked the breath from her. Temporarily blinded and deafened after the storm, Harper lay stunned as her senses quivered and her winded lungs burned. It was warm. The light was pure. Her fingers twitched. Harper was spreadeagled, and as her senses returned, bare dirt pressed into her hand. Grass tickled her cheek. She scented earth. It tickled her nose and she sneezed, groaning as pain wracked her body in the aftermath. Her hand flexed. The Dragonheart's touch was gone.

She inched open her eyes, blinking to clear her vision. The world was sideways. Not a moment before, she had been in her woods with snow falling around her. Now the sun warmed her back and a gentle breeze caressed her exposed arms and face where her cloak had fallen away, teasing a loose tendril of hair across her ear. It had just been *snowing* at night as winter fought for dominance of autumn. This was a summer's day. She swallowed, her throat parched. The ringing in her ears diminished, and the rush of trickling water, rustling leaves, and birdsong crescendoed around her. This did not sound like home at all. There, it was the depths of the evening. The water was frozen, the trees had no leaves, and the birds did not sing of life.

Harper looked farther afield, squinting in the sun that seemed to shine directly into her eyes. Trees. Hills. Daylight. Her breath caught. Where was she? *I'm dreaming*, her rational mind replied. She had fallen asleep, sick of the dark and the cold. But as she turned her head ever so slightly, the gravelly soil dug into her cheek and a blade of grass tickled her nose. She would wake up any second now. Any second at all. Her chest tightened. Harper rolled onto her side and pinched her arm. It hurt. First Dragonhearts, then waking up in the middle of a countryside she did not recognise. A curl of unease slithered through her belly. Harper propped herself up on an arm. She rubbed her hand across her eyes and her pounding forehead with a groan.

The Dragonheart lay beside her in a circle of charred greenery and blackened earth. When she dared to touch the stone, Harper quickly snatched her hand away, but this time, the bottom of the world did not drop away from her. She reached out with shaking fingers to rest her hand atop the stone again. Smooth facets, sharp edges, and rough planes grazed her skin.

"Where am I?" she whispered. The breeze caught her words and tossed them away. Her chest tightened and her breath stuttered as panic clutched her. Of course, the summer skies gave no reply. Harper suppressed the urge to whimper and stood on shaky legs. She picked up the Dragonheart and clutched it so tightly that its rough edges dug into her palm. And still, that edge of pain did nothing to carve through this dream.

A wave of dizziness overtook her, her stomach growling in protest. When had she last eaten? She could barely remember. Some rushed morsel at the inn, leftovers from a patron's plate to avoid an empty stomach. Not enough to sustain her shaking, exhausted frame. She had nothing. Berries grew in the trees around her—tauntingly out of reach—but she did not know these trees. That treasure could have been sustenance or poison, and she would not know which until it was too late.

She examined herself. Stains covered her from head to toe. Her cloak hem was completely sodden from the snow, right through to her leggings. The cold, clammy fabric clung to her skin, stealing what little warmth the sun afforded her. As she looked around, it was clear it was still late summer or early autumn, though it seemed far milder in comparison. Many of the trees were green and lush, some just beginning to yellow. It was painfully bright and colourful compared to even the finest days in her dreary corner of Caledan.

There was nothing for it. It was the middle of nowhere. No matter how hard she strained her ears, she heard no trace of civilisation. She turned in a circle. Judging from the slope of the ground, she stood atop a hill, though she could not see much of the horizon for all the trees crowding around. No visible paths led in any direction. Harper scanned the trees. No breaks that might signal a road. Through the trees, mountains soared into the heights of the sky. Harper frowned. There weren't any mountains like that where she lived. She swallowed again, forcing down the nerves that threatened to boil over. "Just out for a walk, Harper." *With your Dragonheart.*

However, she cursed at a sudden realisation. She felt in her cloak pocket, fingers stretching right into the corners in the desperate hope one of them hid a secret treasure—as silly as that was to hope for. Lint, a single copper, and the leather bracelet with a single metal charm that she always kept with her was all she had. All her coin was at home. In her box of trinkets and treasures with her precious book, and Betta. How far away was she?

Her heart sank. She spun around wildly, but still, no familiar points of reference jumped out at her. Harper swallowed, tucked the Dragonheart into the crook of her arm, and drew out her bracelet. The worn leather was smooth, the bead of metal cold. She ran a fingertip lightly over the emblem stamped into it, a circle split by a waving line, wondering as she always did what it meant to the person who had it before her. She had possessed it as long as she remembered. Knowing nothing of her past, it was as close to an heirloom as she had. She normally kept it tucked inside her garments so it did not get stolen by one of the many pickpockets and tricksters who frequented the inn or the town. On a whim, she tied it around her bony wrist and took comfort from having something familiar with her in the strange place.

There was nothing else for it. Harper chose a direction at random and walked. The breeze blew the sweet air at her, and she wondered just how far she was from civilisation. There could not be any towns close by. She had not smelt air this clean in years, not unless she went to the depths of the mountain foothills far from the village. There was no pollution on it, a welcome change from the woodsmoke and stench of fish that clogged the air at home.

As the sound of running water crescendoed, Harper stepped under the shadow of the trees, marveling at their size. Looking much like what she recognised as silver birches, they soared into the heights, standing twice as tall as those at home. Out here, she reckoned they had much better soil. Ahead, shattered light sparkled through the trees. A stream. She ran to it, sank to her knees, and cupped her hands so she could scoop up water. She drew in long draughts of it, dipping her hands in several times. Far sweeter than the tainted water of the river in her village.

"All rivers lead to the sea…" she muttered, and followed the trickle of water downhill. Before long, the streamside became a track well worn by animals passing. The faintest trace of woodsmoke lingered on the breeze, tugging her downhill. She quickened her step. Fire could only mean one thing. *People.* And people meant help.

Thatched roofs tucked amongst the gradually thinning trees as the decline of the ground levelled out into the valley. Harper's breath was ragged after the steep and strenuous descent. The ache crept right up her neck and stiffened her shoulders. Harper narrowed her eyes as she looked at the village. Mud and wattle walls, held together by strong, wooden beams, upheld the thick, thatched roofs. There were no streets here, only hard-packed earth paths barely wide enough for a cart to pass. Donkeys and draught horses pulled carts piled high with straw, wood, food, and other wares.

Her mouth fell open. Atop a cart stood a man who was clearly no human. He looked like an elf straight from her beloved tales—pointed ears, slim build, fine features. Slouching in a doorway was a short, stout fellow, as grumpy as she had ever seen, wearing plated leather armour and with a wiry beard taking over half his chest. Seeing a shadow too large for a bird's passing, she looked up. A giant woman with the wings of a great bird of prey alighted behind one of the buildings. Harper's eyes glazed over as she watched the bustle before her, and a whimper escaped her lips. She stopped in the middle of the dirt track.

At an unintelligible shout behind her, in a tongue she had never heard before, she whirled around. With a squeal, she dived out of the way to save herself from being mowed down by a passing horse and cart. As she regained her balance, the village faltered around her. She looked around, seeing everyone turned toward her. Eyes widened. Mouths muttered behind hands. A whisper sounded around her. Brows furrowed. A thickset man strode towards her, shouting in a strange tongue and pointing at the Dragon-heart, which had tumbled from her grip to land upon the packed earth for all to see.

"I don't understand. Do you speak the Common Tongue?" Harper stammered. Foreboding curled up her spine, the unwelcome thought like a claw down her back—she was no longer in Caledan. That meant… She shut down the tendril of uncertain worry.

"Common Tongue?" he growled, his voice thickly accented.

"Yes." She latched onto the suggestion gratefully.

Another man stepped forward, his brows furrowed, a suspicious scowl upon his face as he pointed toward the stone. "Where did you get that Heart of Dragons?" His accent was almost too thick to understand, but his anger was clear.

She snatched the stone from the dirt and clutched it to her chest. "I found it." She did not mention the fact that that seemed to have been in a different country, though now she began to think it was an entirely different world.

"Lies! By the order of the king, all Dragonhearts are held at the capital!" the man retorted.

The crowd advanced on Harper. She took a step back. A woman cried out from the back of the crowd, her shout savage and her tone clear, though Harper did not understand her words. The babble of exclamations and accusations crescendoed.

"Thief!" she heard amongst the foreign tongues. "Criminal!"

People spat on the ground toward Harper as they continued to cry out in the tongue she could not understand.

"I didn't steal anything!" she protested, stepping back as heat flooded through her. Her cloak felt as though it smothered her as the crowd constricted around her. "It appeared in the midst of the storm!"

"What storm?" the man barked. "A lie!"

"No, not here. I—"

"The thief speaks Common Tongue. A foreigner!"

A soldier appeared ahead, drawn by the clamour. He wore leather armour and chainmail, his polished helmet gleaming in the sun. Yet the emblem upon his breast was not the fish and spear of Lord Denholme. Harper fled.

17

HARPER

Harper raced back into the woods, so quickly that her descent careened on the edge of control. Her legs juddered and her knees crunched with the force of each stride, sending bolts of pain spearing through her. The roar of the mob behind her spurred her on —the fear of being caught far outweighing her fear of tripping on the uneven ground. She leapt over exposed roots, and low branches whipped past her face. She cared not when they tangled in her hair, ripping out strands as she dashed past, because fear screamed louder than the pain in her veins.

Her muscles burned as she pushed them harder, leaping from one step to the next. She dropped onto a road that was barely more than a track, following the same direction. Taking to it gratefully, she sped up, knowing her head start would soon be gone. She chanced a look behind her. Some were far too close for comfort. With her head tucked into her chest, she continued, dodging off the other side of the road and through the trees to camouflage herself as best she could, until the terrain forced her back onto the road as it looped down the hill. Her pursuers were even closer than before, but hampered by having to scramble down a precipitous embankment she had somehow avoided. She bit back a curse and rounded a corner.

Smack.

"Oof!" Harper crashed to the ground, her body smarting from the force of the impact and her breath knocked from her. A heavy weight pinned her sprawled form down. "Get off me!" she shrieked—and the weight vanished. She blinked and sat up, gasping.

"Watch where you're going, foreigner!" A hand yanked her to her feet by the front of her shirt.

Harper gaped. She was face to face with one of the most attractive men she had ever laid eyes on. When he peered past her at the advancing mob, she caught a glimpse of pointed ears. *An elf.* His tanned skin radiated life and vibrancy, and coy green eyes were unfathomable pools under a tousled shock of wavy brown hair as his lips quirked in a lopsided smirk. It rendered him boyishly attractive, even though he looked a decade older than her. He was lithe and muscled, the tone that came with athletic endurance, and his perfectly fitted clothes enhanced his sculpted form. He wore a light shirt with green embellishing the collar and cuffs, ivy leaves chasing themselves around the edges.

His chest strained under his leather jerkin with the force of his breathing. Harper could not help but linger over the faded gold embossing upon it, the scratches and gashes that marred the once beautiful design. Her eyes crept down to his legs. Muscled thighs were bound in pants that looked far too tight to run in, and his light leather boots were perfect for a silent hunt through the forest.

"Did you hear what I said?" he snapped.

She blinked. "Sorry. What?"

"Don't you know not to bother someone when he's being chased?" He bounced on the balls of his feet anxiously. "Hey. Is that a Dragonheart?" he added incredulously.

She gathered the now dusty object into her arms again. "I don't have time for this!" Harper pushed past him, but he grabbed her arm.

"Not that way. Tons of angry folks I'm guessing you don't want to run into." His gaze slipped over her shoulder and he frowned. "Oh my. You too? How interesting. That hill really isn't stopping them. Seems we can escape together and ask questions later. How's that sound?"

Harper turned. The whites of their eyes were visible, so close were they. "Good!" she squeaked. Together, they leapt off the road and crashed through the forest, tumbling down the hill in their haste to escape. Harper only had a second to wonder what this handsome stranger was being chased for before she had to give all her attention to the uneven ground ahead.

Harper could not tell whether the crashing belonged to her barreling through the bush or their followers trampling behind. The stranger did not let go of her hand as he dragged her along, somehow avoiding the worst of the rolls and hillocks in the earth that would have otherwise sent her sprawling. His hand crushed hers, but she had no breath to complain. Fuelled by rampant fear and the last dregs of her strength, she clung on. What would happen if they caught her? She had no doubt it wouldn't be good.

"Did you steal that Dragonheart?" he fired at her.

She spared him a glance. "No!" It was all her burning lungs had the breath to reply. She scowled at his raised eyebrow. Curiosity got the better of her—as usual. "Why does everyone think that?" she gasped out.

"Well, it's usually the case. No offense, but you're clearly not from the Kingsguard. You're not a dragon-rider or one of the king's people. Besides that, you're speaking *Common Tongue* with the most strange accent. If you're speaking so, that means you're not native to Pelenor! Which leads me to believe the Dragonheart *isn't* yours. Where in Altarea are you from?" He looked pleased with himself when Harper gaped. "So, did you steal it?" he asked again when she did not answer. He looked excited by the prospect, as though bursting with more questions.

"No!" she gasped, exasperated and breathless. "Look, now isn't the time!"

"Well, come on then. The sooner we lose them, the sooner I hear this tale. I *love* a thrilling escape." He shot a smouldering grin at her that made her stomach swoop with something else entirely, and pulled her faster. Trees and shrubs raced by, and the mossy carpet underfoot put an extra spring in their step as they approached a break in the trees. Rays of sun flashed through the canopy above them, half-blinding her with every step.

"Almost there!" he called cheerfully. "Never let it be said that I didn't help a damsel in distress—and her Dragonheart."

Harper scowled. This man... elf... *whatever*... grated on her, or perhaps it was the frustrations of a long, hard day. No matter. She had just about had it with whatever was happening. Her mysterious companion tugged her in another direction, altering their course slightly. The gaps between the trees widened. Harper saw a flash of blue ahead and forested mountains behind it. *A lake!* The elf did not slow as he approached the edge of the trees. Harper tugged him back, but he pulled her forward inexorably. She couldn't see the edge of the lake, which meant...

The trees ended abruptly, and the cliff edge loomed. Before she could protest, he sped up, tugging her with him, and leapt off the cliff with her in tow. Harper screamed as the ground fell away beneath her. There was barely a moment to take a gulp of air before they plunged into the blue depths. The frigid water forced the air from Harper's lungs and she flailed, panicking, as her mouth instinctively opened to draw breath where there was only water. Her cloak bloomed around her, tangling and folding in upon her. She clutched the stone tighter, and weight dragged her down.

Panic had her screaming into the water—a seething mass of bubbles erupting from her mouth. His hand tightened around hers and he yanked her towards the light. When they broke the surface, she gulped in great shuddering breaths, letting out a sob of belated shock. Panic flooded her, leaving her unable to take a full breath as she kicked her legs and thrashed her arms, trying to stay afloat.

"No time for that. Swim, quickly."

"I can't swim!" she shrieked, choking as she went under for a second and water sloshed into her half-open mouth.

He dragged her up a second later and she hurled out the mouthful of water, choking for a breath and clutching at him as desperation spiked within her. With a muttered curse, he pulled her alongside him and broke into a fast, one-armed stroke that sliced through the frigid water. Above them, the cliff face soared, limestone pockmarked by weather and crushed by the roots of the trees that clung precariously to the top. Panic overcame Harper once more as those cliffs seemed to lean in and crush her. She struggled for a moment in the elf's grasp as the cloak wrapped around her legs before she kicked it loose. The cold crept into her, gnawing at her bones. She couldn't expand her chest to breathe from the fear and the cold suffocating her.

Shouts sounded above them. The mob gathered at the

edge of the cliff, but no one followed them into the water. The elf angled for a small, rocky cove at the base of the cliff —the perfect escape where no one could follow unless they too jumped into the lake, except it was also a trap. How could they escape? She shot a glance at the elf as he swam toward it, his brows drawn down in grim determination. Who was this enigmatic stranger?

"Welcome to your getaway," he announced as he staggered to his feet, the water chest deep on him. Harper, over a head shorter, clutched at him, shrieking as her boots hit the bottom, and immediately swept away in a cascade of loose stones that she could not see at her feet. He hauled her out until they were waist deep. Was the air above or the water below colder? Her teeth chattered, and her entire body shook. She could hardly tell which felt worse. Only fear kept her on her feet, for her legs threatened to buckle.

She looked around, wondering at his words, for they made no sense. The cove was tiny and a dead end. No caves or tunnels. No way up the cliff. The only way out lay across the huge stretch of water. She didn't have a better plan—and now she had no choice but to trust the handsome maniac before her. Harper quickly resigned herself to the fact nothing made sense anymore, and that she had no space to care beyond anything but her own survival.

They scrambled from the shallows, water streaming from them. Compared to the cold water, the air felt warm. Harper's teeth chattered all the same, chilled to her very bones. On all fours, she clambered through the shallows, the sharp rocks cutting her hands and her cloak catching on every sharp edge and yanking her backwards.

"Here," the elf called to her.

She sloshed over to him. Behind a rock, she saw a tiny coracle big enough for one.

"Get in." She looked at him, dumbfounded. *"Get in!"* he repeated. "The cliff won't hold them back forever. There are Kingsguard alongside those peasants. Believe me, they don't want to be denied of their prize catch. Me."

Harper fleetingly wondered what was worse than allegedly stealing a Dragonheart, but she obeyed, giving him an incredulous look as she clambered into the coracle. This tiny, frail thing would bear a person's weight—or two? It looked like nothing more than a few scraps of leather bound around a twig-like frame. As she settled into it, her legs crossed, she held the Dragonheart close. Through the sodden cloak, it pulsed with warmth, as if burning with an inner fire. She clung to that as shivers wracked her.

The elf tugged the small vessel out onto the lake. In the centre of the bobbing coracle, Harper wrapped her arms around herself and squealed as it tipped—threatening to capsize—when the elf got in. Miraculously, it did not. He squeezed awkwardly around her, and she ended up wedged between his legs at the front of the vessel, the Dragonheart clutched tightly in her hands. By some unseen magic, for he had no paddles, the coracle bobbed away from the shore, over each lapping wave, accelerating until it zoomed across the surface of the water, somehow not tipping them out as it crested each wave. With one hand, Harper clung to the rim of the coracle, leaning back into the elf's warm chest as he leaned into her for balance, and willing away the rising churn of nausea swilling around her belly.

"That ought to do it. They're scuppered for now," he said with a grim smile. "They're at least half a day's walk away from where we'll land on the far shore. Well… unless they have a dragon. In that case, we're damned, but I'd wager not. I'm pretty sure if they did, I'd already be dead."

"R-Right," Harper stammered through her still chattering

teeth. She was entirely unsure how to process that. Dragons had not been seen in Caledan for hundreds of years, but it very much appeared she was no longer in Caledan.

Wind whipped against her, sending wet tendrils of hair slapping into her face, evaporating what little warmth she had. Spray drenched them with every juddering impact across the lake. The water was sweet, just as sweet as the stream she had drunk from, but even though she was thirsty, it was too cold to enjoy a mouthful and a shower at the same time. She twisted to look behind them. The crowd at the top of the cliff had faded into the distance, their faces indistinguishable blobs, though snatches of their voices followed Harper and the elf across the lake. The elf grinned, as though utterly satisfied with events.

"Sorry for the tight squeeze. Didn't plan on having any company," he said. His gaze dragged across her, his brow slightly furrowed, as he took her in. Her stomach tightened at the scrutiny—at being at his mercy on this vessel in the middle of a lake in a strange land. "Don't worry. Just a little while more and we'll get you dried off before we figure out what on earth to do with you."

"We?"

He chuckled. "One doesn't plan heists of this nature by himself, you know."

What had she gotten herself into? Harper let out a shuddering breath. The coracle slowed as it approached the shallows on the other side of the lake. Water lapped against the pebbled shore, which receded into coniferous forests stretching up towering foothills as far as the eye could see. Harper held the Dragonheart tighter. She was exhausted, wet, freezing, starving, thirsty, and in shock. There was no fire left in her. When the vessel bumped into the shore, she held back an angry sob. The elf helped her clamber out of the tipping coracle, and she strode through the freezing shallows onto dry land, where she fell onto her knees, her hands throbbing as they crushed against sharp rocks. He rushed to her side. "Are you all right?"

"No! No, I'm not! What in Caledan's name is happening? I've no idea where I am or how I got here. I'm starving, tired, cold, and wet, and I've no idea why all those people were hell-bent on chasing me. I'm not going another damn step until *someone* explains *something*!"

18

HARPER

"Aedon? Who's this?" a deep, gravelly voice asked, a heavy twang twisting the Common Tongue away from the slant Harper was used to in Caledan. Harper looked up. And up. Large, booted feet. Muscled legs twice as thick as her companion's—whose name she surmised now was 'Aedon'. A chest so broad that the armour upon it would have fallen right off a human. Bare, scarred arms with leather bracers. He towered over her so much, her neck hurt from how far back she had to bend it to take him in. A weather-worn, craggy face stared impassively down at her. And... *Wings?* Wings rested on his back, just like the woman she had seen in the village. Except his were far bigger and tawny in colour. She gaped. There was no fear left in her to be scared by this monstrous male.

"Er... I have no idea," Aedon replied. His voice was almost sheepish. He turned to Harper. "Who are you?"

The man-bird groaned. "Not a dead weight. Please tell me you have not picked up another useless mouth to feed. We

109

already have the dwarf. You were supposed to get *horses*. Four legs! Not two!"

"Hey, you'd starve if it wasn't for his cooking. You're just grumpy you can't beat him at *chatura*. She won't be a weight at all," Aedon said, waving at the bird-man dismissively. "Will you?"

Harper froze. She had no idea how she ought to reply.

"See. We're fine. Our band of merry men and women grows one larger, at least for now. Brand, she seems to have had a terrible day of it. I'll wager she has a story that will entertain us as we sup tonight. Surely she can stay for a night?"

Brand huffed and turned, stalking away. "Fine," he muttered. "Keep the stray. She's all yours."

"Don't mind him," said Aedon, winking at Harper and offering a hand to her. She took it mutely and stood. "He's as soft as a dwarf's backside when you get to know him."

The elf drew himself up. "My name is Aedon. *The* Aedon." He smiled at her, as if expecting her to know who he was. She stared at him blankly. His face fell slightly. "Er, right. Not from around these parts, I see. I guess there is a limit to how far my reputation precedes me, and that's wherever you're from, which would be where, Miss…"

"Harper," she replied quietly. "I'm from County Denholme. In Caledan. This isn't Caledan, is it?" It was barely a question. She knew, deep in her gut. Her fingers curled into her palms, nails cutting little half moons into the skin. But no amount of sharp pain made any of this vanish.

"Right you are, Miss Harper. When did you arrive?"

"Today." She hedged her bet—honesty with no detail to incriminate her.

He narrowed his eyes at her. "Today? Here? Hmm… Your lips are turning a little blue, and we could do with finishing off our rather spectacular escape. How about we get some-where safer and you dried off, then we'll talk. Trust me. You're safe for now."

Safe. Did she feel safe? Every nerve in her body screamed of fighting or fleeing, even through the growing haze of exhaustion which threatened to collapse her after the longest day of her life. Aedon strode away, and turned back to her, waiting expectantly when she did not follow. It took every ounce of effort not to sway on her feet—or fall. Harper swallowed, her throat dry and thick. More walking. She was certain her body could not take it, yet she had no choice but to go forward. Backwards seemed absolutely out of the question. "All right."

Aedon nodded. "That settles it then. Tonight, you can sing for your supper." He smirked. "Not literally, if you're a terrible singer. Singing is not mandatory. Then we'll give you a bed for the night. Of sorts. More of a metaphorical bed, to be honest. On the ground. Ahem." He gave her an encouraging grin. "Smile, Miss Harper. There's no need for that wan face. After a hot meal and a good night's sleep, you'll feel far more chirpy tomorrow. Come on. I'll introduce you to the rest of them."

Harper was too tired to even wonder about who that might be as she trudged after him, utterly dispirited. Clearly, her day wasn't getting back on track anytime soon.

Up ahead, "the rest of them" awaited. She could tell they were eager to be off from the way they shuffled their feet, their packs on their backs, looking down the path. Averting her eyes from Brand's burning glare, Harper glanced at the two others. A stern-faced woman, who looked reassuringly human, and a cloaked and hooded stranger, who bent over a pack and did not look up as she arrived. Harper could tell little about him aside from a medium build and short stature.

"Harper, meet the rabble. Erika, Ragnar, this is Harper. Brand you've already met. We'll do better introductions later, but I'm afraid we need to hurry now."

Erika gave him a reproving glare. "We've been waiting for *you* all day, Aedon. It's you being tardy keeping us now—and Brand here tells us you didn't even get what we came for." She shoved a cloak at him, and then her hostile glare swept across Harper. Harper suppressed the urge to recoil.

"Say no more!" With a gleaming smile, Aedon breezed past her, relieved her of the cloak, and marched off down the track. Brand, Erika, and Ragnar followed without a backwards glance. Harper, with a heaving sigh, stumbled after them at the rear.

They walked until they were high into the foothills and the ache in Harper's legs became a relentless burn. Her head hung so low, she stumbled into Brand, so exhausted that she did not realise they had stopped before her.

"Sorry," she mumbled as he turned and stared at her. He turned away.

"We'll make camp here," Aedon said. "Erika, can you do your thing?"

She nodded and strode away.

"She's going to make sure we can't be tracked," Aedon explained to Harper with a wink. "We don't want to receive any unwanted guests now, do we?"

In quick order, Brand laid a fire that Aedon lit without a single word, while the cloaked stranger rolled out what paltry bedding they had. Harper realised the sky darkened, heralding nightfall, and the air had subtly grown colder. Her cloak was still wet. Now that they had stopped moving, her shivers returned, though she had dried off somewhat during the walk. Aedon ushered her closer to the fire, confiscating her sodden cloak and placing his own around her shoulders. She slumped onto a large rock, grateful to be off her feet, and looked around. This forest, at least, looked familiar. The pines could have belonged to her own forests. *Perhaps I'm not as far away as I think.* She clutched hopelessly at the thought.

"So, who's the precious flower?" asked Erika as she returned, casting a critical eye over Harper. "She's not from round here, is she?"

Harper tried not to stare. Standing this close, she noticed that under Erika's rough-hewn fringe lurked a huge scar on her forehead, one that still looked angry and red, though she could not tell how it had been caused. Erika glared at her. Harper looked away quickly.

"Caledan. You arrived today, you said?" Aedon replied. He leaned closer to Harper, frowning.

Unease curled within her. "Yes."

"That's impossible," Aedon murmured. "Logistically impossible to arrive *here* today from Caledan." The others shared troubled glances that set Harper on edge.

"How do I get back?" she asked, desperation tightening her throat. "This is some kind of mistake."

"Well, she can't stay with us," Brand cut her off.

"And where else is she going to go?" Aedon fired back. "She cannot return to Caledan, if that's where she's supposed to be. We're thousands of miles away."

"What?" Harper asked, stilling. That couldn't be true.

"Nothing. All in good time," Aedon said quickly. She could tell his smile was forced. "Get the soup cooking, Ragnar. I'm starving. It's been a hard day's work, you know! Whilst you lot lazed around, I was out grafting away for us all."

Brand snorted with derision.

The hooded figure shed his cloak, and Harper stifled a gasp. The man was not at all what she had expected. Shorter than all of them, he was muscled, with a shock of wiry, dark hair and a beard to match, all of which had been neatly braided, bunched, and tied together with cords and beads of metals and glass. He was older in appearance than the rest of them, with deep-set wrinkles lining his face. Harper looked away as he caught her staring, just as she examined the tattooed skin of his face and hands. *Is he a... dwarf?* Harper wondered, not daring to ask.

She noticed how very differently they all dressed, as though they came from differing cultures. Aedon's refined—though worn—attire clashed with Brand's practical and hardwearing war gear. Erika's mismatched clothes had an air of the nomadic about them—garments patched with fabrics of many textures and colours, fur on her breast, shoulders, and boots. Ragnar seemed a mixture of all three. Rich fabrics, tired though they were, under robust patterned leathers with hints of fur embellishments.

Ragnar unstrapped the small pot from his pack and set to skinning a small mammal, then peeled some strange looking root vegetables. Soon, a soup bubbled away on the fire, and Harper could not help but blush when her stomach rumbled. Whatever time of day her body thought it was, perhaps it no longer cared now food was on offer. The pot was too small to feed them all with Harper there, but Aedon insisted on sharing. Though she tried to refuse, he would hear none of it, wearing her down with a winning smile and friendly glint in his eyes. She mumbled her thanks and accepted the small serving, along with a hunk of hard bread to dunk into it.

He served himself last, then sat next to her, his crossed legs bumping hers as they all huddled around the fire. She tried not to think about it. He was easily one of the most handsome men she had ever seen—his easy charm so different to Alric's rough kindness, his lithe muscle so contrasting to the tanner's ox-like strength—and his kindness left her slightly flustered and tongue-tied in his presence.

They ate in silence, each ravenously tearing into their portions until the food disappeared in short order. The small serving was the most satisfying thing she had eaten in weeks, hearty and whole compared to the thin, watery stew she had last eaten at the inn. Her stomach felt full and warm, banishing some of the chill that had settled deep in her core that day.

Brand sat back with a satisfied sigh. "Excellent as always, Ragnar."

Ragnar dipped his head in thanks, still eating, his attention on his food. The rest of them turned theirs to Harper, who squirmed under their scrutiny.

"So." Brand said.

Aedon shot him a glare. "Be kind," he muttered. He turned back to Harper. "So…" His voice was lighter. He tilted his head. "You're not from Pelenor. Tell us how you journeyed here."

"I'm not exactly sure," Harper admitted. Internally, she warred for a moment. What should she say? How much could she trust these strangers? But, with weary resignation, she knew that she needed their help. There was no one else to turn to. She recounted finding the Dragonheart and what had happened when she touched it.

"You have a Dragonheart?" Erika's hard gaze bored into Harper, who flinched under it. Everyone's attention on her, she tentatively brought it out of her cloak. The group collectively sucked in a breath before they all leaned closer.

"It is a Heart of Dragons, really and truly?" Ragnar looked to Aedon, who nodded slowly. The dwarf raised a hand to his chest and shook his head. Harper thought he seemed filled with emotion, but she did not understand why.

"I've never heard of such a thing happening," Brand said. His gaze flicked between Aedon and the Dragonheart. "Is it dangerous?"

"I haven't, either. Dragonhearts, being gateways to other lands?" Aedon huffed and shrugged. "Dangerous, though? No, I don't think so. But there are clearly greater magics at play here than what I understand. What happened next, Harper?"

"Well, then I found myself here—well, not *here*, but over by that village. When they saw me, they accused me of stealing the Dragonheart. I ran, and that's when I bumped into you."

"Quite literally," Aedon said with a rueful grin, rubbing his chest. "So you really didn't take the Dragonheart?"

"I didn't."

"It's beautiful." Aedon leaned closer. There was a yearning in him, one that ellicited a coil of something uncomfortable in her gut. "May I?" This close, she saw his green eyes held flecks of blue and gold in them. Somehow, she reached out to him even though she had just a moment before thought it not wise to give her rare treasure over. She blinked, startling as his fingers brushed hers. And then, it was in his hands and she felt dazed. What had just happened? That unease coiled anew in her stomach.

Aedon gently cupped the stone, examining it as though it were the most precious thing he had ever seen. Perhaps it was even more valuable than she had first thought. She cleared her throat. With a smile, he handed it back to her, his hands lingering for just a second as she took it. She tamped down on the uncomfortable feeling. Nothing was amiss. He'd given it back. Why did she still feel uneasy?

"Now, I have a question. Where am I?" she asked.

"You're currently in the Kingdom of Pelenor, to the southeast of the living forest of Tir-na-Alathea," Brand said, as though that explained everything.

"Pelenor?" Somehow, it sounded worse for others to voice that she was definitely in a different land. She had never even heard of the place. She knew of Caledan. To the south was Roher. To the east, the steel-grey waves of the ocean. To the north, the biting cold of the ever-winter lands. She knew even less about what lay to the west. She clamped down on a fluttering in her chest, and folded her trembling hands together.

"Yes," Aedon said. "I suppose we don't need to teach you Pelenor geography right now. You probably need some more sensible clothes, though. Yours look a little, ah... *worn*." He wrinkled his nose. "What in Pelenor is that stain on your shirt? Some kind of blood?"

Harper looked down and her cheeks warmed. "Oh. No, it's stew. I don't have much coin. It's at... home." The word felt strange upon her tongue. Harper offered her copper, shameful as it was. She wondered if it were a hidden blessing that all her wordly goods and money had remained behind. Betta would need them in her absence.

Aedon bit it, then tossed it back at her. "Oh, that won't do you any good here. What about your bracelet? That metal looks valuable."

Harper snatched her arm back. "No. Sentimental value. It's not worth anything to anyone else. It's all I have from my childhood." She ran her finger over the single charm, as she had done thousands of times before, and tucked it out of sight up her sleeve.

"Well, if you're sure."

"Look, there's been a terrible mistake of some kind. If you could just tell me how to get home, or send me back, I'll be on my way."

Aedon shared a troubled look with Brand, who shrugged. "You're going to have to tell her sooner or later. Might as well be now."

"I'm afraid there's no way back, Harper," Aedon said quietly.

She furrowed her brows. "What?"

"I mean, it's *technically* possible. You could travel for months, eventually reaching where you call home. Maybe. If you survived the sea crossings. And the wilds."

Harper's chest tightened. That could not be. "There must be some way I can get back!" she said desperately, fighting the nauseating swoop at the bottom of her stomach. Home might not have been much, but it was hers, and the only anchor she had in the world. More important than anything, Betta depended on her.

19

DIMITRI

Dimitri cast his senses out, toward the Dragonheart wherever it might be, seeking for that now familiar feeling of its magic. Nothing. He threw the net wider, out of his quarters and into the city. Into the palace. Into the vaults. Into the sprawling suburbs.

Nothing. Not one trace of that vast magnitude of power.

His heart skipped a beat. Where had it gone? He could not conceivably have made it vanish, yet it was no longer where it had been. He had to find it before anyone else— because he knew they would soon be looking.

It was not long before the king's men arrived, and despite him expecting them, it still sent a bolt of fear through him. They pounded on the door so hard it shook on its hinges. Of course, he would be amongst the first Toroth called upon. Keeper of the king's secrets and entrusted with his darkest business. The very picture of consternation, he accompanied them toward the great hall. He had changed into his night-wear and ruffled his normally neat hair before Toroth's men had arrived to convincingly appear surprised at the intrusion on his evening.

"You sent for me, my king?" Dimitri swept into a low bow, waiting until he spied the jerk of Toroth's hand to rise. He tugged his dressing gown around him for emphasis.

The great hall was cool, though not as cool as he pretended. The fires had already died to embers, and all traces of that evening's meal had been cleared by the servants. Only the hounds lingered by the fire, as close as they dared, and Dimitri did not fancy bedding down with them.

His attention snapped back to the king, whose eyes were wide with rage as he stalked from side to side on his dais. "One of the... Something has been stolen from my vaults!" he growled.

Dimitri could barely see Toroth's face in the darkness of the hall, save for the rage-filled spark in his eyes reflected from the embers.

"I am most sorry to hear that, Your Majesty. Have you apprehended the thief and recovered the object?" Dimitri asked smoothly, with a touch of dismay.

"No!" spat Toroth, now trembling with rage. Rage Dimitri hoped not to bear the brunt of. That current of fear curdled through him and he fought to keep his face blank.

"That is grievous indeed, Your Majesty. How may I be of service?"

"I have every member of the Kingsguard searching, and I shall send every member of the Winged Kingsguard on the hunt."

A large enough treasure to warrant a full dragon-rider compliment to be sent out? Dimitri was slightly taken aback by it. Did the king really place *that* much value on one Dragonheart? Dimitri almost raised an eyebrow at that, but knew to do so would be too dangerous. Even if he did not know what had gone missing, that would have been a clue in itself.

"I will find it." The king gritted his teeth as he paced back and forth like a caged beast. "You will assist." Toroth turned the full measure of his baleful glare on Dimitri.

"Of course, sire," Dimitri answered, sweeping into a low bow. His pulse settled. He was safe. The king had no idea of his involvement. There had been the slightest touch of dread Toroth knew all along—and had lured Dimitri to his demise with false hope of his ignorance. Fear like that was never far away in this court. "What is it I seek?"

Toroth scowled at him.

Reluctant to tell me what you hide in your vaults? Very well. "I must know what I seek if I am to have any chance of finding it for you, my king," Dimitri said in a painfully affable tone, his head bowed in deference for his intrusion into the king's privacy. He knew how to play Toroth like an instrument.

Toroth muttered a curse under his breath. "Fine. They stole the Heart of a Dragon from me. My warden will give you details." The king's tone was short once more, and Dimitri sensed what little patience he had was running out.

"I shall do everything in my power to locate it. Do you have any leads I may follow?"

Toroth glared at him, but Dimitri stood his ground. "No," he finally admitted. "Ask the general of the Winged Kingsguard to be brought up to speed with any new developments. Report solely to me. Discretion, secrecy, and speed. Get. It. Back." With one last glare, he flicked his hand, dismissing Dimitri.

Dimitri bowed and quickly retreated, lest he be subject to the king's ire. His panic had decreased at the confirmation

Toroth knew nothing of his involvement, but now it spiked back to life again. The whole of the kingdom sought that Dragonheart. He would have to reach it first.

20

HARPER

Aedon sighed and ruffled his hair. "Well, I mean, there might be one way back, but it's really very unlikely."

"Tell me," Harper pleaded. Panic fluttered at her edges, threatening to devour her and only kept at bay by years of resourcefulness at surviving any situation thrown at her. But this? This was beyond finding her next meal or a safe bed for the night… this was world-shattering. She was thousands of miles away from everything she knew—and Betta. Guilt stabbed and twisted inside her. Betta would be worried sick that she had not returned home that night. Would the old woman go out to search for her in the storm? Would harm come to her on Harper's account? She could not bear it.

Aedon shrugged, unaware of her inner turmoil. "If the Dragonheart truly brought you here, perhaps it can send you home. Unfortunately, no one here knows how. Perhaps there are elves elsewhere, or even the king's mages, who would know of such magics. But you'd be hard-pressed to find someone who will help you when, no offense, you have nothing to offer in return."

It was clear from Aedon's dismissive tone that he thought the notion hopeless. Harper's heart sank a little at that.

"Mind, I think he'd want his Dragonheart back first, and there's every chance you wouldn't even get to petition the king. You'd be presumed to have stolen it and left to rot in some dark hole for such a treasonous act. Dragonhearts are incredibly precious, and the king lays claim to them all."

Harper recoiled, her arm protectively encasing the Dragonheart. "It's mine! I found it."

"Well, perhaps the king will look leniently on you if he believes that, but as I said, it's a long shot. In any case, there's nothing we can do about it tonight." He leaned back against the tree he sat under.

"I'm stuck here for now?" Harper said, swallowing.

"Yes."

She nodded, silent for a moment as she tried to take in that fact. She had not realised that, having gotten to this strange place so easily, there would be no way to go back. She huffed, a mirthless chuckle. *Way to get what you wished for, Harper,* she berated herself. She hadn't meant this— had she?

"Pelenor isn't all that bad!" Aedon said, nudging her and grinning. She forced out a small smile, but it did not reach her eyes. "I mean, it's better than Valtivar." He chuckled, but no one joined in. He threw up his hands. "Oh, come on, you grumps. Lighten up."

"What's Valtivar?" Harper asked.

"Another country bordering Pelenor. Far to the south of here, across the mountains." He nodded at the dwarf. "Ragnar hails from there."

"What about you?" Harper asked Aedon. "Where are you from?"

"I'm from Pelenor, though I have the blood of the elf realm, Auraria, running through my line." A smile lit his face. For a moment, he looked utterly carefree, staring into the distance as if he could see a different place around him.

"Is that far away?"

"Oh yes."

"Why are you here then?"

Aedon's smile faded as he shot a glance at the rest of the crew, who fidgeted. "I'm an outcast. We all are, in a fashion. Cast out by our families, countries, and people."

Harper's heart sank. "You mean, you're criminals?"

Aedon drew himself up, full of affront. "Not at all!" His shoulders slumped slightly. "Well, I suppose a little."

"You can't be a *little* bit of a criminal. You either are or you aren't."

"We're not in our own eyes, and that's what matters to us," growled Brand. "But if you want to get technical, yes, we're outlaws."

Harper looked between them. They didn't seem very criminal, though they didn't seem too friendly, either.

"Oh, go on, elf. You might as well tell her who *you* are." Erika scowled. "Sate her curiosity—and your ego. But she has no right to know my story, save from my own lips."

"Nor mine," Brand said.

Ragnar remained silent, watching from the shadows at the edge of the fire.

"Oh, if I must!" With a dramatic flounce, Aedon leapt to his feet and swirled into an exaggerated bow. "Aedon, legendary Thief of Pelenor, at your service, miss. Pleasure to meet you."

Harper's jaw dropped. "You're... You're a *thief?*" she spat.

"Again, not in my own eyes, but technically, yes. My reputation far precedes me. I'm rather proud of it actually."

"What sort of things do you steal?" Harper's eyes narrowed as she took in the ragtag crew once more. They didn't look wealthy. She presumed a good thief would at least wear fine clothes, or have a hoard of treasure. Some evidence of the proceeds of their crime. *Maybe they're terrible at it*, the thought surfaced.

"Things that need to be liberated from their present owners." Aedon lifted his chin, and Harper was surprised by how resilient his sense of righteousness was. It oozed from him. But now that she knew he was a crook, it tainted how handsome she had found him. "We take from those who have not earned it and give to those in need."

Something warmer stirred in her at that. She stamped upon it. "That's very gallant of you, but theft is wrong, no matter how you try to justify it."

"You're quite mistaken." Aedon's eyes flashed, and she shrank back at their intensity. "Would you consider it unreasonable to return funds to overtaxed peasants who cannot feed their starving children? Would you consider it unreasonable to liberate commandeered goods, stolen for avarice, and return them to their owners? Would you consider it unreasonable to liberate a cure to a sickness that would otherwise be withheld, costing innocents' lives?"

Harper swallowed, thrown off guard by his passion. "I—I suppose not."

Aedon sat on his rock with a huff. "Well, there you have it. Of course, the king and his guard don't agree. That's why I'm one of the most wanted criminals in the land. Though these three aren't far behind." He nodded at his companions.

"Were you stealing something today?" Harper asked. "You were being chased."

"Yes."

Harper leaned forward.

Aedon sighed. "I can't divulge. I did not get what I came for, if that will relieve your distress." He shared a loaded look with the rest of the group and his tone soured. "But, suffice it to say, it keeps in line with our *criminal* ethos to protect those who cannot protect themselves within the line of the law dictated from those fair few upon their golden pedestals."

Harper coloured. Perhaps she had been wrong to call them criminals, but then again, they were thieves and quite freely admitting it. His arguments made sense, and yet, the law was the law for a reason. Surely no man—or elf—ought to be above it.

"Now." Aedon's tone held an edge of unfriendliness she had not expected, but understood, "we gave you food from our meagre stores, you've had warmth from our fire—and my cloak, I might add—and you are welcome to shelter with us for the night. Frankly, you ought to be grateful we're taking you in. However, if you'd rather not spend the night with a bunch of hardened, moralless criminals, you're free to leave." He gestured at the path.

"May I stay?" she asked in a small voice. "Please. I have nowhere else to go." Goodness knew what roamed the unfamiliar lands. Harper was not afraid of the dark or the forests, but she was not a fool. She was a stranger in these lands and with no means to protect herself. There was safety in numbers, at least. She could have sworn she saw the hint of a smile on Aedon's face at her words.

"She can't fight, she can't survive in the wild, and she has no magic." Erika's assessment was brutal. Harper flinched.

"I can survive. I've hunted and provided for myself for years," Harper retorted with a spark of defiance. The harsh woman continued to glare, but Harper straightened her spine, glaring back.

"What good is a—" Brand began.

Aedon cut him off with a hiss. "She does have a Dragonheart, though. That makes her special. Give her a chance, Erika. I doubt you'd survive in her lands."

Erika huffed. "I could survive anywhere."

"We don't need a wet blanket," said Brand. "She's a liability. We'll get ourselves caught with her slowing us down. We cannot afford the delay—not now—as well you know."

"I'm happy for the girl to stay." Ragnar's voice was quiet, albeit filled with an authority Harper had not expected. The others stopped their bickering to look at him. He met each of their gazes in turn, and there was something accusatory in his that made each person drop their eyes. "I know what it is to be an outcast. You *all* do. You all know how important it is to be accepted, flaws and all. The girl's fallen on hard times, as we have all done. We have a home in each other. Why not one more, at least for a while?"

Brand glanced at his feet, Erika looked uncomfortable, but Aedon beamed. "That settles it then. Three votes to two. Yes, Harper's vote counts. You're stuck with us now."

Harper gave Aedon a hesitant smile. For all their strange depths, he seemed keen to have her. Perhaps, despite his flaws—and illegal habits—he was a generous soul and that deserved its own merit. She had nothing to offer them in recompense. "Thank you. I'll do whatever I can to earn my keep."

Erika huffed, but Aedon ignored her. "That's the spirit!" He threw her a one-sided smile, and his twinkling gaze sent something twisting deep in her core as he reached out a hand to her. She took it hesitantly and he shook it. After he let go, she could still feel the warm imprint of his fingers upon her palm.

"Now that's settled, how about a game of *chatura*?" Ragnar said. He pulled forth a box that contained a folded, hexagonal wooden board and several dozen tiny, intricately carved pieces in three different colours of wood.

Brand rolled his eyes.

"What? You're afraid of being beaten again?" asked Ragnar, grinning.

"Never," Brand growled, his attention snapping to Ragnar. "A farthing says I can wipe the ground with you."

"Easiest money I've made all week," Ragnar chuckled. He lay the board flat and started to stack two sets of figures upon it in a seemingly random order. "Erika? Aedon?"

Erika shook her head, continuing to tend her blade.

Aedon sighed and held up his hands. "I have no coin left, Ragnar. You cleared me out last week."

"And don't forget the 'I owe you', master elf."

Aedon winced. "And that."

"Harper?" Ragnar asked.

She looked at the board. "I don't know how to play." It looked like no game she knew. In the inn, most games centred around coins and alcohol, played with whatever chips the gamblers possessed and whichever vague rules—which were usually as fluid as their drinks—they decided.

"Go on," said Aedon. "Count me in. I'll show you how it's played." He gave Harper a winning smile, which she responded to before she remembered he was a criminal. She looked away, sour-faced.

"That's a poor do for the girl. She'll never learn to play from you. You couldn't win if I was blindfolded!"

"We'll see about that." Aedon stuck out his tongue. "But no money in or out on my part, Master Dwarf."

"Spoilsport."

Ragnar promptly cleared the board of all of them, taking Brand's farthing—a copper coin stamped very differently to Harper's—to the tune of the huge man's cursing. Harper did not have a clue what had happened. Some strange game of strategy, much more complicated than she could follow, with the amount of turns per player changing, different rules for when and how each figurine could move, and a seemingly arbitrary rule system.

When they had finished, Harper's face ached from smiling. Somehow, lost in the game, she had forgotten the shattering of her world for a few precious moments.

"*Chatura* master again!" Ragnar crowed.

"Lucky win," retorted Brand with a scowl. He rose to his feet and stomped off.

Aedon winked at Harper. "You'll pick it up in no time. Ragnar, perhaps we have a future *chatura* mistress on our hands."

Ragnar laughed. "Maybe if she learns from me. Definitely not if she learns from you."

That night, Aedon let Harper keep his cloak and a pelt as bedding, and brushed off her thanks. She wrapped herself in the homely material, noting the faint smell of herbs and woodsmoke. As she lay down away from the others, who piled onto their bed of pelts, she could not sleep, despite her exhaustion.

It was difficult enough to explore the idea of travelling to a different country, but not being able to return home? What would Betta do without her? Then there was the small matter of the Dragonheart. And running with a band of outlaws, including the most wanted criminal in the kingdom. One who had her in a strange and annoying kind of flutter. Harper suppressed a groan.

Silence descended as her campmates drifted into slumber. Before long, Harper's eyes slipped shut, despite the chaos of her mind. She fell asleep snuggled in the warmth of the cloak, the fire before her burning itself to glowing embers.

21

AEDON

Harper was a jewel in the darkness. Firelight threw an amber glow across her and against the stark obsidian of the trees behind. Her worried face was slack and peaceful in slumber, as though she were relieved from the many cares she carried, and her dark hair draped across her face and shoulders like a shroud. Harper was pretty when she did not have her back up, though she did not compare to the elven ladies at court. *Mind*, Aedon thought, *she also has plentiful more attitude*. Which he rather preferred.

The breeze grasped him, a cold edge on the air that told of summer's demise. He looked at Harper's small form just outside the warm glow of the fire and sighed. With a small mutter under his breath, he blew in her direction, sending warm air tumbling around her. At a second thought, he gathered up one of his furs and, placed it gingerly over her shoulders. She shifted slightly but did not wake.

Aedon stayed kneeling beside her for a long moment. Slowly, his hand rose. He hooked her silken curtain of hair in his finger and gently tucked it behind her slightly pointed ear. She appeared entirely innocent in sleep as he took in her features. The jutting curve of her gaunt cheek. The shadows under her eyes. The curve of her lips as the faintest flutter of breath escaped. He examined every inch of her, but there was hardly anything to be seen. She had tucked herself within the confines of his cloak in a futile attempt to break the wind that relentlessly slipped between the trees and through the canopy to bite at them. Only her hand had slipped free, resting under her head, though it made a poor pillow on the hard ground.

Brand sat up and silently motioned to the rest of the group. They rose like wraiths and stalked away in silence, leaving Harper slumbering by the fire, alone and unaware. Aedon sighed and started to rise, but froze as the charm upon her wrist glinted in the firelight. He cocked his head, bending closer for a better look. Worn leather. A roughly shaped silver disc stamped with… Aedon gaped.

A circle split by a line. *The riven circle. The broken wheel. Saradon's Mark.* His stomach dropped, and an icy chill that had nothing to do with the night air speared through him. He scanned her again. Nothing untoward did he find, but she carried Saradon's Mark upon her, and she had clearly shown how precious it was to her. Did she know what it was? he wondered. Did she hide darkness within her? Had he missed something? If so, she hid it well. He sensed nothing ill from her—and he was a master at reading others. Did that reassure or trouble him? Aedon could not be sure.

Troubled, he rose and backed away. His eyes lingered upon her, then her charm bracelet, then Erika. He joined the rest of the group, who stood across the fire at the edge of the clearing. He was still reeling that she had just casually pulled out a Dragonheart. He had not seen one for decades. Something deep within him cracked open and an old hurt ached in his chest. One that he could still not bear to face. Then there was the matter of the mark on her bracelet. It sent the pit of his stomach churning. That changed *everything*.

"She doesn't appear to be lying, however impossible it seems that she has travelled from Caledan in a heartbeat," Ragnar said, frowning. Aedon could hardly see him in the gloom. They carried no lights with them, just in case she awoke.

Aedon cleared his throat quietly. "No indeed. Magic works in mysterious ways. Yet what is a half-elf doing in the midst of Caledan, the kingdom where no elves live, where no magic runs through the veins of the earth?" The wind whistled around them, scattering their words into the trees.

"You're sure she's a half-elf?" Erika asked, her attention fixed upon their unexpected guest.

"I am," replied Aedon. "One elf to another. I can sense the magic slumbering in her blood. She can be nothing else." Of that, he was curious. Did she know? There was such a dearth of magic across the veil in Caledan. Widely travelled as his group was, he thought elves did not exist beyond it. How had she come to be there? And how—and why—had she returned? She was an enigma, and he wanted to unwrap every layer of her answers.

"I do not trust her." Erika's voice was as cold as the night.

"You do not trust anyone." Brand's statement was both criticism and praise. She glowered at him, and he smiled at her with predatory glee.

"I think she is as lost as us all," Ragnar uttered, gazing at her.

"Yes, well," Aedon trailed off, glancing across the fire to her.

"What is it?" Brand asked.

"Speak plainly, elf. It's late, and I'm tired," said Erika.

"She bears Saradon's Mark on the charm on her bracelet," he said quietly. "The thing she would not part with." That she had claimed was nothing more than an old trinket of lost origins born from her homeland.

Erika's hiss drowned the others' murmured surprise. "Then we kill her, take the Dragonheart, and have done with it!"

"No!" Aedon threw out an arm to stop her. He swallowed as her wrath hit him, hatred brimming in every line of her face. Erika had more cause than anyone to care about what he had just found. Saradon had haunted her entire life. And even as Aedon watched the huntress take in their new companion with fresh awareness and a cold, calculating gaze, he saw how it unsettled her, for she subconsciously pressed a hand to her rough-hewn fringe, flattening it against her marred forehead.

"She bears his Mark—she is dangerous, no matter how useless and frail she appears. I will not risk us for a stranger." Venom filled Erika's voice.

"She hides no malice," Aedon protested.

"How can you be sure?"

He flinched at her scathing tone. "I can't be. Just trust me."

"Why do you care for her? Has she corrupted you?" Erika grabbed the front of his shirt and wrenched him to her, glaring up at him as though she could see such magics with her mortal eyes.

"I don't care," he protested, extricating himself, "but can you not see? I believe she is who she says she is, and that something terrible—inexplicable even—has happened to her. That Mark could mean nothing to her in her homeland. You presume too much."

"I presume *nothing*," Erika spat. "Forget that. If she bears his Mark, she is nothing but trouble and we ought to stay clear. We should take the Dragonheart and leave her if you will not kill her."

Aedon glanced at her, eyebrow raised. "That's harsh, even for you."

Erika shrugged and met his stare unabashed. "So? You've always wanted one. Now's your chance. We'll use it for the greater good—she clearly has no idea what she carries. We have no need of her and the dark scum she associates with, so we leave her. Win-win."

Ragnar shifted his weight. Aedon could see the dwarf's discomfort. "That might be too extreme, Erika. I could have called you the same—dark scum—for the stain of your past."

"How dare you!" She whirled on him, blade drawn in a moment. "I'll do it if you are too timid." Erika made as if to stride toward the sleeping girl, but Aedon stepped into her path and stared her down, his fists clenched and his jaw set. Gods above, the nomad was too quick to find her temper, and her judgement was oft swift and harsh. Brand angled so that he blocked her too.

"It's not a case of nerve. It's a case of decency. It seems this girl has nothing, just like us—just like the people we help. Why should we take from her without giving something back?" And, Aedon was curious about her, though he would not admit it. She must have been someone of note for her to come to Pelenor in such circumstances. He did not believe in coincidence.

"What do you suggest, elf? We ask her nicely?" Erika mocked, but he held his ground, drawing himself up to his full height to tower over her. It did not intimidate her in the slightest, but that was not his intention. She subsided when she realised he was resolute.

"We *could* ask her," said Aedon, "but seeing as we cannot

be quite sure of her motivations, perhaps we ought to let her stay with us for a while. Find out more about her and this Dragonheart. Discover where she truly comes from, because it cannot originally be Caledan, whether she knows it or not."

"There's no need to be so hasty indeed," said Ragnar, standing beside Aedon.

Erika glared at him until the dwarf dropped his gaze, then turned her attention to Brand.

"I agree with the elf," said Brand. "Can you vouch for her —that you sense no malice within her?"

"I can." Aedon replied firmly. "We are more than capable of protecting ourselves from her if the need arises—but I do not think it will. I think it is a twist of fate that brought her to us. Let us see where this path leads. Draw out her tale. Play it to our advantage however we can. One way or another, she will travel with us, and so the Dragonheart will, too, and any threat she poses."

"We can keep an eye on her," Brand said, throwing a troubled glance between Erika and Harper. "If she means to harm us, we shall not be caught unawares."

Erika scowled. "Well, we're done here then." She stalked back to the fire, threw herself down on the furs there, and said no more. Brand shrugged and ambled after her, settling on the furs beside her, but her back remained firmly turned to him. Ragnar followed, placing some more boughs gently on the fire so it kept them warm through the night.

Aedon whispered his thanks and arranged his furs in a soft pile. From his position, he saw the gleam in Erika's eyes, her attention fixed on Harper across the fire. The nomad would keep a close eye on their guest that night in light of what they had just discovered. He felt safe, knowing that. Nothing got past Erika—and he could not blame her. Before he closed his eyes, he cast one more troubled glance to Harper, wishing for answers that the darkness could not give them.

Who are you, Harper? What is your story? Why did you come to us?

22
HARPER

arper's first night in Pelenor was miserable. Between her teeth chattering, the screech of unfamiliar wildlife far too close for comfort, and Brand's thunderous snores waking her seemingly every minute, Harper awoke the next morning feeling almost as tired as when she had lain down, and ten times as achy from the tree roots and rocks that had stabbed into her back all night. She groaned and sat up, rolling her neck and shoulders to try and ease the pain, as Aedon bounded into camp with a grin on his face and something dangling between his fingers.

Harper raised an eyebrow. Her stomach grumbled. "Morning."

"Good morning, Harper. Ready for breakfast, I hope." He held up the young boar. "Do you want to skin it?"

Harper's eyes widened, and she stuttered a noncommittal response.

"You don't do that back home?"

"Well, yes, if you've got a skinning knife, but I'm a terrible cook," she admitted, chewing on her lip.

Aedon batted a hand through the air. "Pfft. Any skill can be learned. You obviously haven't had a good teacher. Apprentice yourself to Ragnar. He's a master of the campfire."

Harper stood and smoothed the creases in her tunic, but swiftly gave up and ambled over to Ragnar. He rebuilt the fire, blowing on the smoldering embers and dressing them with fresh old man's beard—the same lichen she used in Caledan to start fires—and kindling sticks to breathe new life into it.

As she watched, scooting closer, Ragnar quietly pulled over a flat-topped rock and set to work. He skinned the small animal, extracted the innards, and cut the joints of meat precisely and cleanly with a small knife, just as Harper would have. It was nothing she did not already know, had not already done a hundred times, though rarely on an animal as fine and meaty as that. The knife had the extensive wear of a much-loved tool. Its worn handle was similarly patched up like her own, and the tiny blade precise in his rough, knobbly fingers. Once Ragnar had finished, she helped him skewer the steaks upon sticks, then sank them into the earth to hover over the fire.

Ragnar nodded in approval. "Good. Come with me. Time to find some tea and berries."

He led her up the hill, browsing beneath the trees, though there was little growing under the dense canopy, until they chanced upon a clearing. "Aha! This will do."

The morning sunlight trickled down in beams laden with dust motes, giving the clearing an ethereal feel. Dew hung upon every leaf and blade of grass, and small mammals rattled the bushes as they went back and forth, not frightened by their presence.

Birds watched them with bright, glossy eyes from the branches of the trees, some carving through the air over their heads. Harper could not help but smile. There was something in the air here. So much more life and colour than there seemed to be in her small village in the rainy mountains.

Ragnar pointed to a plant that looked very similar to a raspberry bush, though the fruits were a bright, vibrant orange. "Pick those fruits—careful not to bruise them, please—and I'll collect the leaves." He gathered up a fold of his cloak, and Harper turned up her shirt to hold the fruit. She bent to pick the fruits one by one, surprised to find them large, juicy, and tender.

"Try one," Ragnar said. She looked up to see him grinning at her as she examined one closely, a wrinkle of suspicion across her nose.

She glared at the fruit, then bit into the tiniest corner of it. Flavour exploded over her tongue, a sweet, nectar-like juice the likes of which she had never tasted in County Denholme's sour and shrivelled produce. "Oh!" She gobbled the rest of the fruit in a hurry, emitting a groan of pleasure. "*Mmm.* That's incredible."

They continued picking the fruits and leaves. Harper watched how carefully he snicked off each leaf, avoiding the thorny vines, his fingers slow and deliberate. Her cloak grew heavier as it collected more and more of the morning dew, but the quickly rising sun was warm, easing the stiffness and chill of her limbs.

"Where are you from, Ragnar?" she plucked up the courage to ask, seeing as he had been kindest to her so far.

He didn't glance up as he continued working. "Keldheim.

It's a city in the mountains of Valtivar, the dwarven kingdom far to the south of here."

He is *a dwarf!* Excitement fluttered. She had heard of them in the tales from travelling bards. Now she had met one in the flesh. She tried to observe Ragnar without openly staring, taking in every detail of his wiry beard that was plaited and adorned with beads and ornaments, the likes of which she had not seen before. Harper's mind already exploded with ideas born of the snatches of stories she recalled. "What's a dwarven city like?"

Ragnar stopped to consider. "I suppose much like any other city, but ours are deceptively large—part underground and part overground. Keldheim was founded upon one of the oldest springs in the country. It wells up from deep under the earth, with the sweetest, most pure water you have ever tasted. The city is full of water. Fountains and aqueducts everywhere. Every house has running water, something you don't see in many of the overground cities in Pelenor. It's an architectural and engineering masterpiece. Keldheim delves deep beneath the earth, and its highest heights are at the summit of the mountain, Keldberg, which is given its name by the spring."

Harper paused picking berries, drawn by the rapture on his face. He spoke of it with love and awe, as though he longed to be there. It sounded far more grand than she had envisioned. "Why did you leave?"

His face clouded over and he dropped back to his task, his motions more brusque.

"I'm sorry. I didn't mean to pry."

"It's not a problem."

"It sounds like a beautiful place. Do you miss it?" she asked tentatively.

"It is, and I do." His shoulders hunched, closed to her as he turned away.

Harper went back to her task, kicking herself for offending her new teacher when he had been so instrumental in securing her a meal for the night and somewhere to belong.

"I am not welcome there any longer," Ragnar eventually said in a low voice. "I do not belong amongst the people. We are too different, and that is not tolerated."

Harper nodded past the lump in her throat. He sounded so desolate. "I'm sorry," she murmured. Something in his words resonated with her—she had not really felt like she belonged, either.

He grunted. "It's been a long time since I set foot there. I'm as much at peace with it as I can be."

Harper wondered how old he was, but she did not ask. *I've caused enough offense today.*

He surprised her when he spoke again. "How about you? You said your bracelet was precious to you—that it was from your childhood. Did your parents give it to you?"

She paused her picking to run her fingers over the worn leather thong and the cold metal bead. "I don't know," she admitted. "I don't remember ever having a family. My youngest memories are with other orphans on the streets—I don't have too many of those. But this is something I've had for as long as I can recall. I assume it came from my family, but I have no idea who they were. I always wondered." She looked up to find him assessing her keenly, and unease filtered through her.

But Ragnar's expression softened, and so too did the stiffness in her shoulders. She supposed she had asked personal questions of him—it was only fair of him to pry in return.

"Hmm. It sounds like a hard life. I'm sorry. Come on now. That should be enough berries."

She followed him back through the forest to the camp, where the smell of roasting boar made Harper's mouth water. Fat crackled and spat as it dripped into the flames. At Ragnar's instruction, Harper ground up most of the berries and smeared them onto the meat to make a sweet glaze, whilst he boiled some water in the pot, adding the leaves and remaining berries to it and setting it aside to steep.

Whilst they worked, she could not help but pause to watch. Brand and Erika danced around them, engaged in some sparring. Erika wielded her slim twin blades like lightning, whilst Brand's gigantic two-handed sword cut the air—and never landed. Harper watched his muscles flex and bulge and the twist of Erika's hard, wiry body with awe. She winced as Brand brought down his giant blade, which looked unstoppable and as if it would shatter every bone in Erika's body—but he could not catch her. She was a blur as she slid away, like water parting before him. There one moment, gone the next. After a while, they tossed the blades aside and engaged in hand-to-hand combat. Despite the size difference, Erika held her own against the giant winged man, and from the way he grunted and growled, Brand did not seem to be going easy on her.

"All right, all right. Call it a draw, you two," Aedon drawled as he strolled into camp. He ran a hand through his tousled hair as he dropped his sword and scabbard by the fire before tumbling into a heap next to Harper.

"Where have you been?" Brand turned to address him with a grumble, his chest heaving. Erika wiped her shining brow on her sleeve and sat to clean her weapons.

"Scouting the area. Why do you always make it sound like

I'm lazing about?" Aedon complained, a hurt edge to his voice, but Harper saw the mischievous twinkle in his eyes that told her he was used to this jesting.

"Because you normally are," Brand growled.

"Hey, I resent that. Whilst you two were playing war games, I was keeping you all safe. Can you two keep the racket down, by the way? I could hear you a mile off. Lucky there's no one about."

"We need to move on." Authority filled Erika's quiet voice. Brand and Ragnar nodded.

"Of course," Aedon said. "It's unwise to linger."

"Then we'll be off after breakfast." Erika stared at Ragnar.

The dwarf waved his spoon, pausing from stirring the tea. "It'll be done momentarily."

Silence fell as they tucked into the hearty breakfast. The tender meat melted on Harper's tongue. It was a strange feeling to eat fresh meat—not dried, salted strips of whatever she could get her hands on, or tough lean rabbit—with a sweet, rich taste she had not expected. She savoured it, not caring that juice dripped down her chin.

The tea had a tangy, surprisingly bitter yet refreshing taste, and she sipped at the pot as they passed it around. She enjoyed the sweetness of the glaze and the sourness of the tea as they mingled upon her tongue. As she took her turn sipping at the tea, she looked into the flickering tongues of the fire, her eyes glazed over in thought. *There's really no way home.* Harper wasn't sure how she felt about that.

It seemed like she found herself on some kind of exciting adventure. On the run with a Dragonheart and a rag-tag band of outlaws, who were each more curious than the last. She could tell they had secrets. From the shared glances, so laden with secrets, to the way they cut each other off mid-sentence and glared at her, as if she might unravel their mysteries.

Compared to this, it was hard to yearn for serving loud, ungrateful customers until the small hours of the night in a dark, oppressive, smelly inn. She glanced around. It was a beauty worlds apart from the woods she knew. Here, even the colours of late summer were so much brighter, the full beauty of the landscape undiminished. Not the faded, dull, grey woods she knew, where darkness and shadow ruled. It made a quiet piece of her heart sing. The tiny sliver that dreamed of more, the fragile thing that never truly dared to believe it would amount to anything. And yet now, she found herself on precisely the kind of wild path she had always dreamed of. When she locked away the fluttering panic that never seemed to leave her now—worries of Betta, and for herself amidst a storm of uncertainty—there was a thrill there. One she wanted more of like a thirst to slake.

Her mouth twitched into a small smile. Perhaps it had been the game of *chatura* the previous night that had persuaded her they were not so bad after all, or perhaps she was a fool. She had not quite decided. The more she thought, the more she realised how thrilling it was. It wasn't as if she had left anything behind. Just her books, her small amount of coin, and an assortment of worthless treasures—pretty stones, carved sticks, nothing of note. *And Betta*, she thought with no small twinge of guilt, but she pushed it aside. Betta was a grown woman, who had survived long before she had come along. Betta would be pragmatic, Harper hoped, when the woman realised Harper was gone. She could take the coin and use it to feed herself if needed, Harper hoped. She would get by like she always had—and so would Harper.

"You all right, Harper?" asked Aedon, tugging the pot from her grasp to have some tea. "You look lost in thought."

"I'm good." Harper grinned, the first true smile she had in a good, long while. Aedon looked at her quizzically, but she only turned her smile back to the fire, savouring her full stomach and the buzz deep in her belly at the promise of the unknown adventure at her feet.

23

DIMITRI

Dimitri glided through the fabric of the world, easily keeping pace with the dragon-riders flying above him. They had offered him, albeit reluctantly, passage with them, but Dimitri had refused. He was not partial to heights, and his own means of travelling worked just as well. Sinking his being into the river of magical energy that flowed alongside the living world, he had slipped from one point to another as he wished upon shadow and wind.

It was a skill few were aware he had and even fewer could master. Not even the king knew of it. It was an elven art lost long ago that he had only discovered through extensive research and more than a little arcane instruction. The dragon-riders of the Winged Kingsguard had openly mocked him, but Dimitri shrugged it off. Let them, he thought. Let them wonder and be afraid when he arrived before them with not a hair on his head disturbed.

As they circled into a descent, he marked their destination—a craggy outcrop on a ridge of hills to the south of

148

Tournai. He picked his own stopping point, the summit of the tallest rocky escarpment, and settled himself on a rock, the picture of relaxed and unspent calm. He wore no cloak, only his usual immaculate, tailored, dark suit, but a small charm warded off the biting wind that nipped at his cheeks. They did not need to see him shiver.

When the three-dozen dragon-riders landed to find him idly leaning on one hand and staring out over the valley before him, their surprise was evident. Yet, they did not ask him how it was possible. No, they would not show him they were curious. They would not admit they did not understand something he could do that lay outside their abilities.

"You found it all right, I see," their leader called to him as he dismounted, an edge of annoyance in his tone.

"Of course, General," Dimitri said. He met his gaze and gave him a sly smile, but offered him no more explanation. It would aid him to unnerve them and their egos.

"Well, don't get in our way. What are you even here for, Spymaster?" General Raedon was far older and wiser than Dimitri, and far outranked him. His long, dark golden hair was braided neatly under his helm, and royal blue surcoat and shining silver armour covered a muscled, heroic figure. Raedon was everything Dimitri was not. Everything he had once sought to be.

Dimitri shoved off the rock and strolled toward him, his hands in his pockets. "I'm here at the orders of the king, not yours. I shall go where I please, do what I please, and *see* what I please, Raedon Lindhir Riel of House Felrian." His use of Raedon's formal title—above his own in rank—was a warning, not a mark of respect.

Raedon knew it, and his jaw clenched. Dimitri could see the infuriation at such insubordination—and overrule by the king. Dimitri smiled casually with a flicker of smugness, just enough to annoy Raedon even further. "The king will be most pleased to hear you offer me every assistance."

Raedon was forced to defer. "The Winged Kingsguard are at your service, Dimitrius Vaeri Mortris of House Ellarian." Every word was forced through clenched teeth.

Dimitri knew Raedon would sooner see him shredded by dragon talons than help, but luckily, they were all still bound by the king's orders—for now. Raedon did not bow, and Dimitri did not expect him to. He could have forced the issue, but there was more than one way to get what he desired.

"Excellent. You will tell me your exact movements that have been planned in advance, and unplanned movements as soon after the fact as is possible. I will conduct my own searches. You need not be concerned with me treading on your claws." He threw a look of disdain at the closest dragon, who rumbled in warning at him.

Raedon nodded, his jaw clenched. Dimitri sauntered off without another word, as if he were out for a walk in the fragrant palace gardens on a summer's eve, not standing on an increasingly blustery peak without a cloak on.

"Lyros. Caren." Raedon summoned his deputies with a snap in his tone, to Dimitri's great satisfaction. "Gather everyone."

Dimitri followed them all day, slipping through the folds of the world as they flew far above him, feeling with every ounce of his perception for that telltale signature of magic, to no avail. By the moon's next rise, Dimitri was in as foul a mood as Raedon as they camped at the foot of the crags, sheltered by the tall pines that grew there and shallow caves under the cliffs.

Unable to bear their less than welcoming company, he slipped away to the top of the crags just as the sun slipped below the horizon, shattering the sky into flames as day burned to night. His worries blazed just as brightly, and he was glad for the barren solitude that afforded him no need to hide the depths of his concerns. The gusty wind chased the shadows from his soul, but the skies held no answers. The question hammered him with every beat of his heart, that ever-present undercurrent of panic thrumming with it. *How far away have I sent the Dragonheart?*

24

HARPER

arper strode alongside Aedon, who looked at her appraisingly as she examined the new outfit she wore, courtesy of him. It was a mismatch of garments, but Harper didn't care. The loose-sleeved shirt billowed on her arms, and she had tucked the long hem into the well-worn leather breeches. The leather boots, at first too large, had molded to her feet, thanks to a few whispers of magic from Aedon. She could still feel his hands upon her calves, stroking the boots into a perfect fit as he knelt before her. That had done strange things to her insides that she did not want to acknowledge. It had been too long since she had enjoyed the touch of another and nothing more, she had ruled, before resolutely clamping down upon the feeling.

Aedon would also not reveal to her where or how he had procured the clothes. Harper had a sinking feeling they were the product of thievery, but she was so comfortable and warm, she did not dare complain. A gentle breeze lifted the scent of lavender water off the tunic and cloak. This one had no holes or patches, and it was far sweeter than the stale sweat and ale that had ingrained in her former cloak.

She pulled the cloak closer, her fingers seeking out the soft wool and fingering the dull metal clasp. It seemed rudimentary compared to Aedon's, but a thing of beauty and craft to Harper. More than that, the cloak was warm. It made her old one seem like a thin, tatty rag in comparison.

"We'll have to get you a weapon, of course," mused Aedon.

Harper snorted. Her hunting knife was one thing. A sword or some such item seemed ludicrous. "A weapon?" She was so lost in the thought, she did not see the root at her feet. She stumbled—and immediately, his hand was upon her wrist, his arm around her waist. She braced against him as he righted her, almost chest to chest.

"Steady there, Harper. Are you quite well?"

For a second, she could not breathe with his verdant eyes fixed upon her. As the heat of his touch seared through her sleeve. As the firmness of his hand at her waist melded them together. She pulled away, heart hammering. "Thank you."

He chuckled. "Not at all. Your first lesson in swordsmanship will be—"

"Stab them with the sharp end," Harper blurted. Anything to rid herself of this feeling.

He shrugged. "Well, I wasn't going to say that, but I suppose that is as good a first rule as any." He grinned. This close, his charming personality was overwhelming and she could not help but be attracted to him. Pushing down the swoop in her stomach, she mentally chastised herself. *He's a criminal, you fool, charming or not.* She stared at Brand's back as they followed him and Erika. Ragnar, at his own trundling pace, followed a distance down the path.

Harper's eyes traveled over Brand's broad, muscled

shoulders, then the length of his sweeping, eagle-like wings —anything to distract herself. They were huge, and she had an inkling of curiousness to see what they looked like fully spread. Imposing, she was sure.

"Don't worry about those two." Aedon leaned closer to whisper. She jumped as his hand brushed hers. "They're not the best with strangers. They have good cause to be wary, but when you get to know them, well, they're as protective and loyal as anyone I've ever met. You just have to bear with them. It'll take a while to earn their trust."

"What is he?" Harper whispered back.

Aedon eyed Brand. "He's an Aerian." At her blank expression, he elaborated. "A winged warrior of the skies."

She shook her head slightly, even further nonplussed.

Brand turned at the noise, eyes narrowed, and Erika tutted at Aedon. "Are you going to chat all day? We have a crucial mission. Head down. Feet forward."

Aedon bowed his head in mock contriteness, but he slid Harper a wink, which seemed to be his cue for mischief.

She bit her lip. "Where are we going?"

Brand and Erika whipped around, both fixing him in a glare as Aedon opened his mouth. He frowned. "What? There's no sense keeping her in the dark. What secret do we have to hide?"

"It's just none of her business," Erika snarled, and Harper's steps faltered at her open hostility.

"She's with us now. Perhaps she can help," Aedon said stubbornly. All trace of his mischief vanished, and the look he gave Harper was full of determination. "In fact, I *know* she can." He lifted his chin and glared at Erika, as if daring her to disagree.

Harper looked between the two of them. She had no idea how she was supposed to help, but she wasn't about to step between the two of them. Not when he fought her corner. To Harper's surprise, even though Erika's mouth was set in a thin line and her disapproval was clear, she relented. "Fine. Only the particulars. No more."

Brand continued walking without a word. Erika huffed and stalked after him.

"What was that about?" Ragnar asked as he caught up.

"They're being difficult, as per usual," called Aedon after their retreating backs. Brand raised his hand in an obscene gesture. "Rude!" Brand made the gesture again. Aedon tutted, but his customary carefree twinkle had returned.

"So, where *are* you going?" Harper asked.

Aedon sighed. "We travel south at present. We're returning to a small village where a sickness spreads. We carry the cure."

Harper frowned. She had not expected that. "Wait… Did you *steal* the cure?"

"Of course," he replied, as if it was obvious. "Not even all the assets in the village could have bartered for it, and people are suffering. Those who held the cure were unwilling to part with it for anything less than a king's ransom. The villagers asked for our help. Naturally, we agreed."

"Who had the cure?"

Aedon grimaced. "The elves of the living forest, Tir-na-Alathea. Stuck-up bunch. Can't stand them. Far too full of their own self-importance, if you ask me. They don't have an ounce of compassion and wouldn't have agreed to trade for anything I could give them, so I took it. But it's for the greater good. The sickness is like nothing we have ever seen before, and it's contagious. Without a defence, it will spread. Many lives are at stake if it does."

"What is the sickness?" Harper asked. A frisson of anxiety fluttered through her. *Careful now, Harper. You're in a land where magic seems to be normal. You have no idea what you're dealing with.*

Aedon shook his head, frowning. "It's a tricky one. It saps strength—both physical and magical."

"Is it so bad that it saps magic?"

"It's different here in Pelenor. Magic is everywhere. It's in the fabric of the very air. Our land and people depend on it. It's like your Caledan without rivers or air. There's hardly any magic in Caledan. You have so few with magical blood there. Frankly, I don't know how you all make do without it."

"I'm mortal and make do without it. I can't believe it's as bad as being without air."

Aedon gave her a strange look. "You're *not* mortal, and yes, it is. You wait and see when we get there."

Harper's eyes narrowed. "I beg your pardon?"

"Who are your parents?" he asked.

The question caught her off guard. "What? I don't know."

"I'll wager not, because they were from Pelenor. Or at least, I reckon one of them was."

Harper stopped dead. "I'm sorry?"

Aedon halted and looked at her, sighing. "I suppose if you don't know, you ought to. It's only fair. Like plenty of folks here in Pelenor, you're only part-mortal."

"And part what?" Harper was pretty sure she'd stopped breathing.

"Elf."

"What?" she whispered. "That's impossible."

"It's true," he said simply. His customary cheeky glimmer was gone, the dimple absent from his cheek, and he looked at her with such open sincerity, she almost believed him. *Almost.*

"It can't be. I'm from Caledan. I'm mortal, like everyone else there." She swallowed.

"You really don't know?"

Erika butted in. "Or she is a liar."

"Surely you feel it flowing through you," Aedon urged, silencing Erika with a glare. "Don't you feel more alive? I can feel it from here. Your blood sings of magic. You even have a little point on your ears!"

"Well, I caught up on some sleep and got some food in my stomach. Of course I'm going to feel better." She resisted the urge to feel her ears. He jested, surely. She had never noticed it before.

"Yes," he said, a touch of impatience in his tone. "But don't you feel far better than that ought to make you? Like you have a spring in your step? Like your muscles don't ache as badly as they did before? Like your head is clearer than it's ever been, despite the fact you ought to be asleep on your feet given the day you had yesterday?"

"Well, I suppose so, but that doesn't mean I have magic. I mean, half-elf? Really?" she scoffed. Her hands rose and she fingered the tips of her ears, then pulled her hair away so he could see. "For starters, explain these. Human ears. Nothing like yours."

"You wait," he said stubbornly. "You've lived for what, twenty or so years in Caledan? Where there's a dearth of magic, what with it being beyond the veil." Harper had no idea what he spoke of. "You've been starved of it. No wonder you couldn't perform any magic, accidental or not. Now you're here. Wait for it to fill that void again. You watch your ears. In a month, they won't be the same."

Harper raised an eyebrow. "You mean my ears are suddenly going to go all pointy?" Her voice oozed disbelief.

"*Suddenly* is the wrong word, but yes. Gradually, you'll develop more of a tip. If your elven blood is strong, from a parent, it'll be quite pronounced and your magic nice and powerful. If it comes from a little further down the line, a great-grandparent or beyond, perhaps your ears won't change at all, but you'll sure be able to feel that magic."

Harper continued trudging along behind Brand's unrelentingly straight back, her own shoulders slightly bowed. She did not know quite what to make of Aedon's fantastical claim, but she could detect no hint of a lie in his words.

"I can teach you, if you'd like," Aedon offered when she did not reply. "To find and use your magic, I mean. With time and help, you'll be able to coax it out of hiding—and then strengthen it."

Harper looked at him quickly, but there was no sign of merriment in his expression. She narrowed her eyes, but her stern expression was a front for the wild storm within her. She spun out of control, and the ground beneath Harper's feet was her only anchor stopping her cascade into open panic. All of her reality seemed to have unravelled and it had no intention of stopping. How deeply did this run inside her?

He held up his hands in defeat. "Fine, don't believe me. Humour me, though."

She could not respond.

"Please?" The sincerity in his eyes was her undoing.

Harper blew out a shaking breath. This was madness. All of it. She would humour him. "Fine. What do you get out of it, though?"

Aedon grinned. "Another elf-blood to keep company with, which will be a nice change from those two misery guts —" He ignored Brand's rude gesture, "—along with the satisfaction of another member of our merry little band being able to spellcast. It's really rather handy."

"Aerians, humans, and dwarves can't spellcast?"

"No. It's proven rather divisive in Pelenor, as you might see. Elves and magic rule. The humans fall to the wayside, and the half-breeds are somewhere in between. Magic means status, power, and wealth. It's just easier to get along here with it."

Harper frowned. "That doesn't seem fair."

"I suppose it's not, but it is what it is, and no amount of disliking will change it."

Harper pondered his words as they strode down a rolling hill and the woods gave way to meadows and plains that stretched as far as the eye could see. A river glinted in the distance, and smoke rose from a settlement on the horizon.

"How far is it?" she asked.

"Oh, a few days' trek yet. Magic can't fly us there, sadly, and Ragnar is a bit too fat for Brand to carry."

"I heard that, you cheeky little bugger," Ragnar called from behind them.

"You were meant to!" Aedon trilled.

Harper stifled a laugh, and her cheeks warmed as he winked at her. They had a strange group here. A friendly, though quiet dwarf, a mischievous elf, and two brooding warriors, all with their own secrets. His offer was over-whelmingly tempting. There were magical beings in all the old tales. If the legends were to be believed, even the elusive Eldarkind, the high elves of Caledan, possessed the skill to perform great magics, though they had disappeared from the land with the dragons. "You're really going to teach me magic?"

"Yes. Real magic."

"The Dragonheart also holds magic?"

"Yes, plenty."

She frowned. It seemed logical. If the stone had brought her here, surely it could take her back. "Is the village you seek on the way to the royal city?"

"I suppose, in a fashion. It's not direct, but it's not too much of a detour. Why?"

"I want to see the king and ask him to send me home with the Dragonheart's magic. If it's his, he can keep it. I just need the magic to leave."

Aedon looked at her, an inscrutable, closed expression upon his face. "It's an impossible task. If you wish to go, you can go, but I think your destiny has summoned you here for a reason, Harper. It's not every day a Dragonheart crosses into a different land to call someone home."

"This isn't my home."

Aedon was silent for a long moment. "Not yet," he murmured, then strode ahead to join Brand and Erika, leaving Harper to wonder at his words—and where she belonged.

HARPER

When they halted to make camp for the night, Harper had had enough of Erika's pointed glances and her quips at Harper's incompetence and naïveté. A hot, heavy feeling clogged her chest and retorts bubbled on her tongue, but that was so twisted with emotion she could not get a word of it out. "I'll catch supper," she said with gritted teeth, having borrowed Aedon's bow and three of his arrows. They did not answer, and she ignored the smile he flashed her as she turned and stalked into the trees, feeling the burn of their attention on the back of her neck.

She strode fast and hard, burning away the burden of the negative emotions churning with her. Soon, her feet had carried her beyond the noise of the camp, and she stopped, breathing hard, to steady herself. Now, she would need to creep, else she would alert the whole forest to her presence and it would all be for nought. She pushed away the thought of returning empty handed. She could not bear that. There was a point to prove today. She had to bring something back to prove her worth and earn her place at the fire that night. She would not be the useless mouth Erika had deemed her. She was a huntress—and a capable one at that.

Harper's gaze roved back and forth as she swept the area until she found a game trail meandering through the trees. She stopped to examine the tracks. Deer. A fox-like creature. Perhaps the hint of a bear. She would have to be careful. She looked around. Nothing moved. Camp was silent in the distance, but if she had to scream, she was certain they could hear her. The woods were deserted too. She had left camp hot-headed—but hunting was no place for emotion and she needed to acclimatise to her unfamiliar tool.

With practised hands, she strung the bow and drew it a few times, testing its strength. The limb bent silently in her hands. *This bow is well made,* she noted appreciatively. It was stronger than her own. She turned slowly, scanning the woods and spotting a rotten log. A soft and easy target. In quick succession, she shot the three arrows at it, straight into the target. *Thump. Thump. Thump.*

Harper retrieved them, wiping the damp, rotting matter from the shafts and tips with the hem of her cloak. After retreating farther away, she shot again, adjusting to make her mark. Twice more she repeated it, until she was sure she could hit what she needed. For the last time, she rustled through the undergrowth and bent low to pull the arrows from the stump. It was time to commence the real hunt.

A twig cracked behind her.

"What is a girl like you doing in the woods so far from… anything?" a deep voice drawled.

Harper whirled around. Her heart thundered into life and adrenaline flooded her system—she nearly fell in her haste to right her balance. Without thought, the bow was in her hands and drawn, an arrow nocked and pointed at the stranger. Their gazes locked, and she could not look away. Violet eyes set under dark brows challenged her. For an instant, they seemed familiar, and then the feeling passed as her blood carried the threat of this male singing through her veins.

Thump. Thump. Thump.

It was no longer the sound of the arrows, but her own heart pounding as the swirling rush inside her spiked with fear. If she had considered Aedon handsome, this was the most perfect male she had ever laid eyes on. Aedon was boyish charm and a tumble on a summer's night… but this male was the promise of sin and darkness. He cocked his head as they appraised each other, and Harper felt as though she stared down the jaws of a wolf.

His build was taller and slimmer, more athletic than Aedon, and his glowing skin paler in stark contrast against his dark, cropped hair. He wore the finest garments she had ever seen. Silks, silver threads, jewelled buttons. They made Lord Denholme's wardrobe look like rags, and made this delicious and intimidating stranger all the more imposing.

Pointed ears, she noted, and that lightning charging through her intensified. He was an elf—which meant he had magic, and she was damn near defenceless. He was utterly out of place in the midst of the woods, with not a speck of dirt or dust upon him. Yet he nonchalantly leaned against a tree, betraying no fear of her or the weapon currently pointed at him.

"Stay back! I'll shoot." Her voice wobbled, and she cursed herself silently.

He smiled, but it was a dark, predatory smile that set her nerves on edge.

"Who are you?" Her voice rang through the deserted trees.

His smile widened even further, as if he could hear the edge of fear in her voice. He pushed off the tree and took a step toward her.

It only took a moment.

Her fingers slipped from the string reflexively. Her arrow flew true. Harper screamed, somehow knowing he was dangerous, hoping they would hear, because she already knew she stood no chance against him if he meant to harm her. In a split second, his hand waved and the arrow vanished.

"That was *rude*, little huntress," he hissed at her. As he advanced, flames flickered in his open palms.

Harper nocked another arrow. Her blood sang with terror, and the shaft wobbled against the string. She would go down fighting—but she knew it was hopeless.

26

DIMITRI

It teased him. Dimitri had lost count of the days. Sunset blended into sunrise, one after another after another, before he finally found some trace of what he sought. A tantalisingly tiny tendril of the Dragonheart's power snaked toward him at his summoning. His whole body lit up with the sensation of it. Simmering worry, his constant companion, was eclipsed by blinding excitement and then relief. Dimitri fought to keep his face utterly blank as he stood at the fringes of the gathered Winged Kingsguard. He rolled a twig between his fingers, casting a glance of bored disdain at Raedon, who lectured them all on strategy for that day's hunt. Yet, inside, his blood held a tingling current of energy, his body longing to spring into action.

Patience was the key. The very last thing he wanted was for the riders to find it. He had to reach it first, then get away from this accursed dank forrest and the Winged Kingsguard, and back to civilisation—with his prize. Dimitri suppressed the urge to abandon the tree that was his shelter. Even there, the morning drizzle was inescapable.

He raised his hand in mock salute as Raedon cast a look of dislike toward him. Raedon scowled and turned away. The rest followed, mounting their grumbling dragons. No one liked the cold here. They were not that far north of Tournai, and yet, with no home comforts, it was a harsh environment far from the luxury the dragons and their riders were accustomed to.

Dimitri did not much like it either, but this was no time to lament the loss of his comforts. He did not show any discomfort, instead slouching on the rock as though it were the most sumptuous pile of cushions in his chambers. In reality, he struggled not to shiver as the pine boughs dripped their cold morning dew down the back of his neck.

When his unwilling companions left, wheeling off into the sky in formation—which he had to admit was impressive, despite his dislike of them—he slowly stood and ambled away, as if on a relaxed morning jaunt. Leisurely. Casual. Random. It was only when they were all out of sight that he raced into the void, slipping into nothingness upon the breeze to chase that faint scent of magic. Closer and closer he yanked it, hungrily seeking. The trace grew stronger until it was everywhere, the powerful item emitting an aura that knocked the breath from him. It forced him to slow. No longer could he track it at speed.

He stepped into the world again and found himself at the edge of a small clearing, staring at a girl. She had not noticed him, too busy bending down in the wet undergrowth, grunting. He squinted, trying to see what she was doing. *Pulling arrows.* And she was no girl, he realised, but a young woman in her early twenties, he estimated. As she stood and wiped off the glinting heads of her arrows, he saw how tall her folded frame was. And within her? Something in him stirred as he felt the faint tendrils of slumbering magic.

They were far from any settlements. What was she doing there? His curiosity piqued. Was it a coincidence? He was not sure he believed in them. A meeting with a strange young woman in the midst of a storm of magical energy roaring around them, and neither linked? Not a chance. The Dragonheart tugged at him. It was as if, out of the vaults, the Dragonheart's essence had spread out over a much wider footprint. One he hoped the dragon-riders would not chance upon. He had to know more.

"What is a girl like you doing in the woods so far from... anything?" he drawled, leaning against the knobbed bark of a tree.

She spun, freezing at the sight of him. Almost faster than he could see, an arrow pointed straight at his throat. The seconds seemed like an age as he dragged his gaze up and down her body, taking in every detail until he met her steel grey eyes. Oh, how he wanted to know the secrets behind them. Could she sense the power around them? She was a nobody, dressed in common clothes, as far as he could see, and that well of magic inside her was pitiful and inert. Disdain filled him. No, he was quite sure she had no idea that somewhere close by, a treasure nestled. More than that, she was no threat to it—or him.

She knew how to handle a bow, that was certain, but she was so painfully thin, he knew she had no real strength to her. Even without magic, he could crush her with ease. Her gaunt cheeks attested to starvation, and the hungry glint in her eyes had flickered with fear the moment she beheld him. That pleased him. She ought to quail before him. He could feel her heart trembling as though his palm pressed against her chest.

"Stay back! I'll shoot."

He smiled a dark, predatory smile at the edge of shrill

fear in her voice, and he could see that unnerved her further. Her shoulders tensed, and her fingers tightened on the bow and string.

"Who are you?" Her voice echoed off the trunks around them. Whoever she was, she was alone. And the Dragonheart was close. He felt it, pulsing through him. Could she feel it? He sensed a taint of magic upon her blood, but she did not sing of power. One way or another, he would find out if she knew something. He had to make sure she could not compromise him. He did not leave loose ends.

Dimitri's smile widened. He pushed off the tree and took a step toward her. Her fingers slipped from the string, and her arrow flew toward him just as her shrill scream split the air. By reflex alone, Dimitri warded himself. The arrow vanished into nothingness. Annoyance spiked. She was either dangerous or stupid—and he did not care for either.

"That was *rude*, little huntress," he hissed, and as he advanced, flames flickered in his open palms.

The young woman nocked and drew another arrow. Her dark hair was tucked behind her ear to afford herself a clear view. Dimitri felt the faintest current of magic stir within her —fear did that in the untrained. Oh yes, she definitely had magic in her blood, and she had no idea how to use it. That served him just fine. Panic and defiance fought within her eyes. Her blood sang of fear. The arrow's shaft wobbled against the string, and her body held as much tension as the bow.

Despite everything, despite the pressing need and the diminishing time driving him, he found himself stayed by curiosity. It was so rare that anything piqued his interest in the monotonous games of courtly intrigue and betrayal he played. This young woman was an enigma. Dimitri did not like the unknown. It was alluring—but dangerous.

Dimitri paused, just far enough away that she stilled, clearly holding back her shot, though she did not lower the bow. "I am Dimitrius Vaeri Mortris of House Ellarian." *Nothing.* Not a flicker of recognition at his name or that of his House. *Who is this peasant?* She must be from far away if she had not heard of him. "Who are you?" He glared at her, fixing her in his stare like prey. He could tell how reluctant she was to fight him, though she had clearly recognised he was some kind of threat.

She remained silent.

"Come now," he said with honeyed venom in his tone. "I told you my name. It is only courteous to return the gesture."

Crashing erupted through the bushes behind him. "Harper!" a male shouted, but Dimitri distinctly heard several figures approaching.

The fire in his palm flickered and died, then erupted again, three times as big, when he saw who approached. "*You!*" Dimitri snarled.

The elf stopped before him in incredulity, staring between him and the girl. He bounded toward her and faced him. She relaxed, the bow slipping from its aim at Dimitri's chest. A protector.

"I never thought I would see your face again," the elf spat at him.

Dimitri's lip curled. "The pleasure is not mine, I assure you. I see the company you keep has fallen." He scoured them all, a ragtag band of misfits. *A dwarf, an Aerian, and two ragged women?* "Aedon Lindhir Riel of House Felrian... or do you just go by Aedon the *Thief* nowadays?"

"None of your damn business, *Spymaster.*" The title was an insult, but it rolled off Dimitri's back. He had suffered worse.

His hands returned to his pockets, the picture of relaxation. He would show nothing to them. "Who is your friend?" He glanced at the woman Aedon had called Harper. What did an elf like Aedon want with her? His other companions had clear worth—armed to the hilt and exuding weaponry competence. But, plucky or not, this woman was a wraith who did not fit.

"Nobody." Aedon shifted to close her off from him, hiding her behind his broad shoulders.

Dimitri cocked his head. A toy of his, perhaps? He shrugged. It would not do to show his interest in any of them. "As you wish. I'll leave you to your miserable existence then. I have more pressing places to be. A pleasure to meet you, Harper." He smiled mockingly at her. She returned it with a scowl.

Dimitri vanished into smoke and wind, only allowing his composure to slip when he was far from them. He materialised against a tree and pressed his hands against the rough bark, leaning his forehead on the trunk. His heart hammered. What had he stumbled upon? The disowned son of House Felrian. A ragtag band of outlaws. A strange girl who fit nowhere. And somewhere tantalisingly close lay the Dragonheart.

How were they all connected? He was only certain of one thing now. This was definitely not a coincidence. Such a thing did not exist where the Thief of Pelenor was concerned. As Dimitri flitted away, he cast a spell of concealment across the entire valley. No one would be able to detect the Dragonheart until he had gotten to the bottom of the matter himself.

That night, after Raedon and his riders returned, Dimitri stared him down. "It's none of your business where I have been or what I have done," Dimitri reminded the leader. "*You* report to *me*, not the other way around."

Raedon scowled. When he did, Dimitri let his smirk show. The resemblance was uncanny. It had been so many years since he had seen Aedon, but he was still the mirror image of his elder brother, Raedon.

"What?" snapped Raedon as he tore off his helm and unclasped his cape.

"Oh, nothing," Dimitri replied airily and sauntered away. Now, at least, he had a reason to stay in the damp, miserable valley.

27

AEDON

Any goodwill Harper had earned from them vanished in the instant they had seen Dimitrius. Even Aedon was now suspicious of her. It was too much to believe none of it was connected. The Heart of Dragons, the Mark of Saradon, and *him*. Annoyance and dislike spiked in Aedon at the thought of Dimitrius.

Yet, Harper was clearly shaken by the experience, and all thoughts of hunting abandoned, for she had returned to their camp and sunk to her knees underneath a tree, rubbing her arms as though she could rid herself of what had just happened. Her glazed expression told him that it was no planned meeting—but Aedon did not believe of any goodwill where the dark spymaster of Pelenor's cruel king was involved. He did not simply appear in the middle of nowhere without reason. And it made unease simmer underneath Aedon's skin. Aedon tugged his collar away from his neck, the fabric suddenly constricting, as he stood with Brand and Erika who argued furiously under their breaths, whilst Ragnar knelt beside Harper with his hand upon her back. He

172

bent low towards her—to check she was unharmed, it seemed.

Aedon did not know what to make of any of this. Only that they were not safe. He glanced up—the sun had gone and twilight deepened the shadows yawning between the trees. It was against Aedon's instinct to remain in their present location for that night, but it was the most defensible position they had against Dimitrius or the Tir-na-Alathean elves who were still out there somewhere. No matter the consequences, he would not have them wandering blind through the dark woods, to be picked off one by one.

Why? The question rang without answer to cease it. Dimitrius owed them less than nothing. Indeed, it would serve his own gain and pleasure to turn them all in. How had he found them—and why had he spared them? Did he know Harper? Worse still—was she somehow in league with Dimitrius? It made no sense, no matter how many times Aedon asked himself. He watched Harper like a hawk, determined to divine her. He would catch her tell, if she had one. He would find out, one way or another, if she knew of Saradon, the mark she bore on her charm, the court of Pelenor—or *that* son of the House of Ellarian. Against every fibre of Aedon's better judgment, which called him to take the Dragonheart, leave their new companion, and flee far into the night, they made camp as the sun set.

2 8

HARPER

arper gathered kindling from around the dell, troubled by her companions' unexplained coldness toward her, and the encounter with the male who had named himself Dimitrius—and thrown her into yet more turmoil.

Dimitrius Vaeri Mortris of House Ellarian.

His name was a song on her tongue, and those violet eyes burned through her. She shook off the shiver they brought and quickly glanced around. It felt like he still watched her, but he had vanished, and Aedon had thrown up every ward he knew around their camp, his easy smile lost in an uncharacteristically thunderous mood that she instinctively shied away from. Nestled in the crook of a gushing stream and surrounded by trees, they were safe from whatever hunted them, Aedon assured her.

But perhaps not from *him*. What did Dimitrius want with her? To have appeared precisely there and then… Harper had begun to believe less and less in coincidences. He found her somehow—and she could not help but wonder if it was connected to the Dragonheart. She was not entirely convinced he would not do it again, and much as she hated herself for it, a small sliver of her *wanted* to see him.

She had never met anyone who had elicited such a storm of emotion within her, one that disturbed the depths of her so deeply that her thoughts were mud churning in writhing waters, turning sense into madness. For, as much as those violet eyes of his promised punishment and fear, there was a spark within them that drew her closer in fascination, like a moth damned to a flame.

The woods closed in around her, so Harper crashed through the brush more noisily than she ought to on her return to camp, on edge from the shadows that chased her. The growing darkness was a threat looming over her shoulder—one that sent a nip to her step and an uncomfortable crawl down the base of her spine. Was he out there even now, watching her?

She joined Ragnar at the fire, whilst Erika butchered the couple of rabbits they had found that day—luckily, it transpired, for Harper's hunt had yielded nothing but questions and danger. Soon, the dark meat bubbled away in a pot with some root vegetables that were unfamiliar to her—purple carrots and potato-like tubers the size of her head with the bizarre appearance of ginger.

As they sat to eat, Harper bit into the rich, lean meat appreciatively, savouring the herb-laden gravy and listening to Aedon's latest tale of grandeur and adventure, for he had already wolfed his meal, as seemed to be his habit. Harper lowered her gaze back to her bowl when she noticed the rest of the group's attention on her.

Even Aedon stared intently as he spoke, now to her. "You told us a story, so it's my turn tonight. Let me tell you a tale from Pelenor of nightmares and monsters..." Aedon's voice dropped into a lower cadence as he hunched closer to the fire. "Let me tell you the tale of Saradon."

The fire threw flickering shadows across his face, morphing the handsome visage into a caricature of light and shadow that delved under his hood. His eyes were faint glimmers in the darkness. Harper instinctively leaned closer. The fire was warm on her front, but cold shadows trailed across her back. They left lingering shivers rippling across Harper's skin as the hair on the back of her neck rose with anticipation. She could not help but be drawn in by his promise of a dark tale.

"Saradon was one of the king's many cousins, a half-elf born to the coupling of an elven mother and a human father, a princeling of the Realm of Pelenor, who would make it even more strong and prosperous in the coming years. Saradon was born amidst much glory and celebration, but alas, something was wrong. Saradon was not as he ought to have been."

Aedon paused and met each of their gazes in turn. The others, who seemed to recognise the tale, sat back, their interest fading. Brand cleaned his weapon, Erika returned to patching up her cloak, and Ragnar picked morsels of meat from his teeth, staring into the flames. Harper leaned forward, breathless with anticipation.

"Saradon was half-elf by blood, yet he possessed no magic." Again, Harper wondered why this was so critical for Pelenor, unable to shake the fact that magic could not really be *that* important if entire nations of mortals in Caledan and beyond survived without it.

"No magic," Aedon repeated, shaking his head. "Of course, it was the greatest shame of the kingdom when word spread that the blood of the royal line was tainted thusly. What could have caused it? Was the babe cursed? Was the very blood of the line, perhaps the king himself, cursed? Rumours grew, spreading like wildfire and changing just as rapidly, until all the Kingdom of Pelenor, and even farther afield, had heard of the cursed child filled with anti-magic.

"Of course, Saradon was just a boy. He was not evil. He was smart and gifted, for all his mortal limitations. He heard the tales, though his mother tried to protect him from them. She loved her boy more than all the world and did not want him to be hurt. Healers were sent for. The finest mages in all the kingdom were called. The greatest elven minds were summoned. Yet no cure could they find, for he suffered no affliction. Random chance, they called it. Ill fortune. He was both a miracle and a mistake.

"His mother loved him all the same, desperate to protect her child from the hurt and sorrow she knew would find him as time marched on. His father was not so kind, giving all his attention to Saradon's siblings, who were as half-elves ought to be—brimming with power. Saradon was hidden away, the shame of his family and the royal bloodline. Saradon knew himself to be different, marked, and not in a way that was blessed. His heart saddened, then hardened, and a darkness was born within him. It was all of the court's fault, from that day to this."

The fire crackled and spat vigorously, making Harper jump backwards. Brand smirked, but Aedon's atmospheric guise did not fall into the shadows of his cloak. Across the fire, Ragnar's impassive face illuminated as he puffed on his pipe, the glowing embers within casting a ruddy hue across him with each breath that flared them into life. The darkness swelled oppressively around them as the last light over the horizon dimmed to nothing.

"As Saradon grew, he saw what an imbalance of power there was in Pelenor. As a half-elven princeling, nephew to the king, he should have been given every right and privilege of his rank, yet he was cut out from both for his lack of magic. He grew bitter—and who could blame him? Slowly, he retreated further into the shadows. Despite his rank, he would never hold power. Despite his blood, he would never inherit. Such was the curse of a mortal life. Saradon grew so angry, so disillusioned, that he sought to make a change. Perhaps his intentions began nobly, or perhaps they were always selfish. Perhaps there were lessons to be learned. That those of mortal blood could be useful in their own way. Perhaps mortality without magic was not a curse after all. Yet all his life, Saradon had been told it was, so what else was he to think? He despised them all for it," Aedon continued darkly.

Harper could not tell to whom the anger in his voice was directed—at Saradon or those who had wronged him.

"In his anger and hate, he decided he would cast them all down, save for his mother, whose love had never erred. He would destroy his father, his uncle the king, and all those who thought he was a blight upon the kingdom. He would take down the elves, magic itself, and rule in his own right, to prove that those without magic could also wield power.

"Perhaps Saradon's cause was noble at first, lifting up those with no voice of their own. At the time, mortals had little say in the running of the kingdom. However, his methods were entirely selfish. Some say the Dragonhearts are what helped him. He stole them and bound them to his will with the darkest of magics, for he was supposed to have none. With the same evil magics, he sapped the king of his strength, then the court, the city, and eventually all those who opposed him, even sending the dragons of the Winged Kingsguard into a slumber from which they could not awaken, all the while absorbing their power. Neither before nor since has Pelenor seen such a dark curse. None could stand in his way. The mighty Kingsguard was rendered useless in a heartbeat. Then he struck."

Harper was frozen, barely breathing—waiting for the hammer to fall. Aedon's eyes fixed upon her, ensnaring her in his gaze as the fire died. She jumped at the crash and shower of sparks as Ragnar tossed another log onto the flames, and her heart raced into a frenzied pitter-patter. A flicker of a smile crossed Aedon's face at her involuntary movement. He was a born storyteller, and she could tell he fed from the energy of his audience by the way he leaned closer, his eyes only for her, making sure she gave him all of her attention.

"Saradon had spent many a year sympathising with those who shared his views in Pelenor. To be mortal, to have no magic, to be anything other than an elf was not a cursed thing. To be forced to live as a second-class citizen was a crime in and of itself, one that wronged them all. In his eyes, and those who followed him, it was something that needed to be righted—and punished. His armies, consisting of humans and other creatures, flooded the kingdom. The king's army, without its magic, was at a severe disadvantage. It seemed all would be lost... until Saradon's plan backfired. The dragons awoke from their cursed slumber and returned to the fight. It was enough to tip the scales."

"What then?" Harper's voice was barely louder than a breath.

"The king's armies swept through Pelenor, annihilating Saradon's forces without mercy. Those who had followed Saradon, as well as their families, were killed or imprisoned. Saradon's entire family was executed, even his dear mother —perhaps *especially* his dear mother—for fear they would support him. That was the last straw for him. It is said his mother's death drove him to the brink of insanity and beyond. That it broke some part of him, the only decent part of him that remained.

"Saradon escaped and fled into exile. No trace of him was found, seen, or heard from again. He was rumoured to have been killed, but no body or proof has ever been offered. His defeat brought peace to Pelenor, but there was a fracture there that is still, even now, not yet healed. There should have been lessons learned—and there were some, but not enough. Those without magic were given greater protection in the kingdom, but it did not go far enough to securing equality. There was too much suspicion and bitterness, fear and anger, hurt and sorrow for all to be forgiven."

Aedon's voice was tinged with sadness. "Wrongs were written between those of magical blood and non-magical blood where none had existed before. Those prejudices still run amongst us. As peaceful as Pelenor may seem now, it is perhaps more divided than ever. Over all hovers one deep-rooted fear to this day. That he, or his likeness, will return." He fell into silence as the darkness closed in and the crackling of the fire seemed unnaturally loud.

"Will he?" Harper whispered, not daring to speak louder.

Aedon shrugged. "No man, elf, or anyone else knows."

"When did this happen?"

"Five hundred years ago or so."

"*Five hundred?*" Harper gasped. "Surely he'll be dead by now."

"Nay. A half-elf with magic will live for many hundreds of years. Even without magic, he will have had a much longer lifespan than most. And he was clever. There are certain dark measures one can take to extend their life, dangerous though they are. With the power of the Dragonhearts, he surely guarded himself well."

"Do you think he will return?"

Aedon did not answer for a moment. "Long before Saradon was even born, there was a prophecy made that the elves connected to him, whether or not it be true, that says he will rise once again, and be many more times as deadly and devastating. Dark tidings indeed, if it is to be true."

"Enough." Erika's voice was unnaturally harsh, even for her. "Do not fill the girl's head with silly stories and nonsense. Saradon is *dead*, gone, and he will not return. It is a story, nothing more."

Harper looked between them, confused. Aedon stared at Erika without replying. The woman clenched her jaw. "What?"

"I know this tale affects you personally. I apologise. I did not intend to cause offense."

"I know, storyteller." All the same, Erika jumped to her feet and stalked from the fire, disappearing into the pitch black of the night.

"Don't leave the wards." Brand's voice rang after her.

Harper continued to glance between Aedon and the spot where Erika disappeared. *What in Caledan am I missing here? Erika was involved with Saradon? Surely she's not old enough.*

Brand shared a glance with Aedon. "It is her story to tell," he said in a surprisingly gentle voice.

"I know," Aedon said heavily, looking back at Harper. "One day, Harper, I hope you will understand why Erika is the way she is, but trust to us, she has endured the greatest of hardships. The fact she is alive at all is a miracle, and that along with the fact she still continues to smile and hope is more besides."

Harper did not understand. His words only made Erika seem even more mysterious and cryptic. *Smile? Hope?* Harper did not think she had ever seen the grimfaced woman's lips crack in anything other than a scowl.

"So the people of Pelenor fear that he, or his followers, will rise again? Those with magic fear those without it?"

Aedon nodded. "Yes, and vice versa. It is why people will fear you, Harper." His dark eyes regarded her solemnly.

"Me? That's…" *Rubbish. Impossible.*

"Yes, you. You carry his mark on your bracelet. And the power of a Dragonheart, a stone that should not exist, at least in your possession. What does that make you? Perhaps a dark sorceress? That scares people."

Harper felt a tingle of unease. "But I haven't done anything wrong."

"*I* know that." He gestured around them. "*We* know that. But fear is hard to overcome. Fear of the past, fear of strangers, fear of danger. You will not be allowed to stroll up to the king and present your case. There will be much explaining to do first, and you must make sure your voice is heard. Otherwise, it will not end well."

"I'm good at persuading people," Harper said, more confidently than she felt. After all, she had managed to remain safe all those years of working at the inn. Old Robson hadn't been the first patron to cross a line. And before that, before Betta had taken her in, the streets had been a terrible place for a young girl. She had endured. Made herself small. Convinced others to ignore her, to disregard her, to leave her be. And when it served, she had made them pity her, to give her charity or a chance. Whatever it took to survive in a world that did not care for starving, penniless orphans.

"Hmm," Aedon replied noncommittally.

She caught his implied undertone, and resentment surged.

29

AEDON

That night as Harper washed the pots out of hearing in the stream, Aedon's companions huddled around him in the dark woods. Doubt raged in him, but his instinct had never led him astray—and it told him that Harper was no threat to them. "If she lies, I cannot detect it," Aedon said, rubbing a hand through his tousled hair and huffing. "She is either truly innocent, or a darkness beyond anything I have ever encountered."

"I think she is the former," Ragnar said.

"The latter," Erika said in the next moment. They glared at each other.

"Why must you believe the worst of people?" asked Ragnar.

"When it is all you have known, why think otherwise? Why are you so naïve?" she snapped back.

"I would hope that we are not lumped in with that," Aedon said to Erika, raising an eyebrow.

She scowled, but subsided in silent, reluctant acquiescence. "Well, I'm not about to believe her word. What can be

183

done about it? It's not safe for her to stay with us. I vote we leave her."

Brand stirred. "If she is dangerous, keeping her with us—in our line of sight at all times—would be the smarter move. Keep your friends close and your enemies closer."

"Or perhaps she is no enemy and you are all mistaken. This could be one giant misunderstanding," Ragnar said.

Erika scoffed, but Aedon silenced her with a glare. "I'll get to the bottom of it."

"How?" Erika pressed.

"By any means necessary." He was not above weaponry, but charm was his greatest weapon, and he would use it to unlock her if it protected his sworn family.

30

DIMITRI

imitri returned to Tournai with the Winged Kingsguard, though not by choice. It was a necessary annoyance. The farther away from the Dragonheart he was, the farther away the riders—and the king—were too. As much as he longed to find it, biding his time was the only sensible choice, no matter how impossibly frustrating. When he returned to the area, he would be able to explore alone. Away from their prying eyes. Hidden from the king's attention.

His attention sharpened as Toroth strode into the study. Dimitri had been inside the study before, but only rarely, and only for his most secretive tasks. It had not changed. It was as cold and unwelcoming as the man who owned it.

Raedon's scowl at being made to wait vanished the moment the king entered. Dimitri suppressed a smile. For all Raedon's arrogance, even he did not dare peeve the king. Dimitri was also fed up of waiting. It had been the longest of days and it was late when they returned, but he did not show an ounce of it to Raedon or the king. Instead, he stood in the small circle of light cast by the flickering fire and waited in silence.

Toroth sank into the plush chair at the far side of his grand desk and raised an eyebrow at the pair of them, asking for their report without permitting them to sit. Dimitri opened his mouth, but Raedon beat him to it.

"I can't work with this *spy*," Raedon spluttered. Toroth's thunderous brows knitted together as he glared at Raedon, then Dimitri. "He tails along after us, appearing here and there without warning or courtesy. He sits and skulks and never seems to do anything. He disappears, and no word do I hear of what he has done to earn his place."

The king stood, his fists resting on the desk, and turned to Dimitri. "Is this true?"

"Not at all, Your Majesty." He smiled blandly at Raedon. "The dragon master does not understand the nature of my work. Why, if I had the same courtesy of him, I would have said he did nothing except shout orders all day and fly about on his dragon. Did you find what the king seeks?" he asked Raedon innocently—and savoured grim glee as Raedon squirmed.

"No, as you well know," he muttered. He looked at Toroth and straightened, the picture of defiance. "I won't work with him. His shadiness sullies the name and good reputation of the Winged Kingsguard."

"Won't?" Toroth whispered dangerously before he exploded. "You are *ordered* to work together. I don't give one *damn* whether you like it or not! If you dare defy me, I shall give your title to a more deserving rider."

Raedon subsided, but Dimitri had the spark of an idea. He dropped into a low bow. "Your Majesty?"

"*What?*" Toroth snapped. Dimitri knew one false word and they would both be out of favour.

"Forgive me." Dimitri's words were as smooth as smoke on the wind. "I believe the general may have stumbled upon a grand idea, though entirely for the wrong meaning. Perhaps we would be better off parting company."

When the king stood tall, glowering at him, Dimitri held up his hands in a placating gesture. "Apart, we can cover more ground. If we split up, we can cast the net wider, find what you seek twice as fast."

Dimitri leaned forward, putting every ounce of persuasion into his voice that he could. "Of course, my king, you know best of all. It is no trouble to me. I only wish to better serve you. I humbly submit to your judgment."

Toroth narrowed his eyes at him. Dimitri could see how much Toroth hated to agree with him, but it was not his first time playing this strategic game. It was almost like a game of *chatura*. Just with people, not pieces upon a board.

"Fine," Toroth relented. "Part ways. Search faster, and harder. It has been too many days." He sat once more, and his attention turned to the contents of his desk, dismissing them.

Raedon bowed and left. Dimitri followed suit. The general spoke not one more word to him as he peeled away down a corridor to his chambers. Dimitri stared after him before he turned the opposite way to his own quarters. It had been so many years, but the resemblance was still uncanny. Five years separated Dimitri and Aedon. If Dimitri had been a legitimate son, he considered he and Aedon would probably have been close friends. After all, their houses were allies, though Aedon's was held in much higher regard than his.

He huffed as he walked the dark, deserted corridors. They had grown up as far apart as could have been. Dimitri, the illegitimate shame, hidden away. Aedon, the golden son, afforded every privilege. Aedon was everything Dimitri had ever wanted—and everything he could never be. How different their lives had been. Dimitri shook his head. Their fortunes had reversed in a strange way. Now, Aedon was as infamous as he was famous, and Dimitri was the one with a place at court.

It seemed Aedon travelled with others as infamous as himself. Dimitri had used his time earlier that evening, arriving home well in advance of Raedon, to dig into the elf's companions. Brand, the exiled Aerian rebel. Erika, the nomad with unknown origins. Ragnar, the disinherited dwarf. Nowhere was there mention of another woman by the name of Harper. That pulled at Dimitri. He had to know more. To both sate his curiosity and find the Dragonheart.

More than that, he also had to find Saradon—still morbidly curious as to where the cursed one rested, what had happened to him—and the strange prophecies that surrounded him. Somewhere in it all, Dimitri was determined to find clues that would help him follow in Saradon's footsteps and break the wheel.

Dimitri halted with an epiphany. The halls were utterly silent around him, as if waiting in anticipation. He could use it to his advantage. First, he would use the quest for the Dragonheart to cover up his own search. Then he would use it to seek Saradon. All the while, he would keep a watchful eye on the elf and his misfit accomplices. A grin split his face, and he strode forward with a new spring in his step. It was lucky indeed that he had a swift way to travel, for there would be much ground to cover in order to accomplish everything he had hoped. Time was of the essence.

When he entered his own quarters, the upended vase of roses on the floor reminded him of his other duty. With a sigh and a wave of his hand, he made them, along with the mess on his fine rug, vanish. His first duty would be to the court. Of course, he would have to ensure his eyes and ears watched there, too. But there was one place they could not aid him.

"I see you called upon me, my princess." Dimitri bowed low to Rosella, who reclined before her fire, her body covered in a thin, silken nightgown. Her quarters were far more warm and welcoming than the king's. Every touch of comfort had been added. In truth, he despised the ghastly plumpness of all the cushions, the cloying softness of her furnishings, and the overbearing heat. It was just turning to autumn, for heaven's sake, and she hardly needed the hearth raging in every room. He said none of this, betraying nothing of his true feelings on his duty there.

When Rosella flicked her hand, the servants vanished in silence, setting down their trays of choice canapes and drinks on the way out. Rosella lifted her chin imperiously. "You have been absent." Her beauty paled when she was petty and angry, but he pretended not to notice.

Dimitri strode forward to kiss her on the cheek, but she pulled away, so he stepped back to a respectful distance. It was not an unfamiliar game. Rosella liked to do the abandoning, not the other way around. "I can only apologise, my princess. Your father sent me away on urgent business. Would that I could have seen you instead."

Her pout subsided just a little.

He shifted his weight, so her gaze angled toward a suggestive part of his body, and grinned wickedly. "Did you miss me?" he purred.

Her pout disappeared, opening into a mischievous smile,

and she tilted her body toward him, letting her gown slip from a shoulder. "Show me you're sorry, Dimitrius."

His body ached with tiredness and he wanted nothing less than to serve her, but that was the dangerous game he had to play. He showed no hint of it as he unfurled a dark smirk that promised her hours of pleasure.

The next morning, with the tension in his body released after his dalliance, Dimitri returned, even more tired, to the king's task. He longed to seek Saradon using the relic from Karietta's tomb, but it would have to wait. He glanced toward the item's hiding place, tempted to recover it.

Not yet. Soon, he promised himself.

It would be the easiest of his tasks, now he had the relic. Like called to like. The relic would guide him to Saradon's remains, wherever they were. If only he had even a part of the Dragonheart to do the same. Something more than the teasing tendril of memory of its power coursing through him.

The dead could wait. The living could not.

Dimitri did not delay. He slipped through the shadows to the valley where he had left them. The woods were empty, save for the steady pitter-patter of rain falling on the canopy above him. Mist and low clouds clung to the valley, and with mild irritation, Dimitri spelled himself against the cold and the wet. There would be no saving his fine boots from the mud. *A Dragonheart is worth muddy boots*, he reminded himself.

He moved like water through the air, cutting from one place to another as he followed the scent, the feel of the Dragonheart's unique power, deeper and deeper into the woods. Stronger it grew as he covered a day's worth of travel in minutes, finally finding them. Dimitri remained in the shadows, ever watchful and careful, lest he be detected. He did not need to alert Aedon and his companions that he watched them. First, he wanted to see them relaxed. Off guard. Magic thrummed next to him, an invisible net that threatened to wreak havoc should he cross those lines. Dimitri leaned close to the wards Aedon had set, then carefully stepped back with a curl of his lip.

Rudimentary. Aedon ought to have done better. Careless. They practically invited him to take it. Dimitri could have broken through the wards with a single thought, but that would have served no purpose. Not yet. It would give him the greatest pleasure when he could tear through them like a spider's web. Instead, Dimitri cast extra wards, ones Aedon would not detect, sinking them into the earth, the trees, the very air outside the paltry camp where Aedon and his companions toiled. It would not do for someone else to take advantage of the shoddy protections.

He could not care less for Aedon or his companions, not even the mysterious young woman, but Dimitri was determined to protect the stone. Now, no one outside the vicinity would be able to follow that telltale scent of magic... should they know what it was. Toroth might not have been the worst thing seeking magic like that. There was no doubt in Dimitri's mind that it was there, with them. The trail ended here. He shivered as the wind picked up and the fog descended farther, turning the already murky day into premature dark. He slid back into the shelter of the tree, regarding them slightly enviously as they all shuffled closer to the fire.

Through the wards, he could not hear what was said, but he watched, eagle-eyed, to discern the relationships between them. The nomad woman, terse and a lone spirit. The dwarf, warm. The Aerian, a protector of all. Dimitri did not want to think about the elf. *Cocky. Arrogant. Conceited.* His mind filled in the blanks as he watched Aedon lean toward Harper in an entirely overly familiar way. And this Harper...

She held a beautiful desolation in her grey eyes and proud, straight back that called to the familiar ache in his soul. It was obvious from the group's relaxed body language that they were in good company but her... she held herself slightly apart from them, and her smiles did not quite reach her eyes, as though she did not feel the same level of comfort. He had already surmised she was a newer companion, and his observation supported that. It opened more questions— to which he had no answers, and nothing he could glean from watching her.

The group was open, friendly, chatting and laughing amongst each other with easy camaraderie that Dimitri knew was born from years of companionship. They seemed at ease with the new addition to their group—except the nomad. She watched Harper with obvious wariness, glances thrown from the corner of her eye when no one else watched, and a body coiled in readiness. Dimitri could see that it was her nature, yet his gaze lingered on her.

What is the reason for such distrust?

Harper chuckled, then sent some quip back at Aedon that had the elf and dwarf howling with laughter. Even the big Aerian grinned. Dimitrius could not look away as that smile finally reached Harper's eyes, infusing them with an infectious light, one that he wanted to see more of. He cut off the thought, turning over the problem at hand instead once more. She spoke the Common Tongue with a strange twang. One he did not recognise. Yet she was of clear Pelenori descent, with elven blood coursing through her veins.

Their talk turned more serious—smiles fading and brows furrowing. He longed to sneak through Aedon's wards to hear the outlaws' words, but he did not have the time to unpick them without detection. Dimitri shifted from one foot to the other, pulling his black cloak tighter about him as he strengthened his protective magics against the worst of the elements. True darkness was falling, and the chill seeped into his bones. A blast of warmth banished it back to the forest.

Then the woman, Harper, pulled something from inside her cloak. It sparkled in the shattered firelight. Dimitri stilled. His heart stuttered for a moment before thundering into life once more. There it was, plain as day. The Dragonheart. The girl handled it with care, but without the reverence and respect it deserved, as if she had no idea of the power she held in her slim hands.

It was, without question, the Dragonheart he had attempted to take. And it went to *her*? Dimitri flexed a hand involuntarily, as if he could reach out and grasp it. *Not yet*, he told himself, but immediately questioned why. *Why wait? Why not crush them all and take it?* His hand sparked with magic, then subsided.

He did not know why he withdrew into the shadows when the magic called to him. It was like a physical tug, almost sending him tripping over his own feet. It took all his will to turn away from it. *You don't yet know what you're dealing with*, he rationalised to himself. The nomad, the Aerian, the dwarf, the elf—they were probably predictable. But who was the young woman, Harper, who travelled with them? She was an enigma, one he wanted to solve.

He could afford to wait a day, he decided, against his better judgment, watching how the young woman's grey eyes filled with warmth and laughter at one of Aedon's jokes.

There was obvious attraction in her body language towards him, the way she angled closer, the way her gaze lingered—Dimitri scoffed and kicked a stone. His mood soured as he looked at how easily, *naturally*, Aedon managed it. It was outrageously frustrating that even as a criminal, Aedon could still command hearts and minds.

Unable to watch him anymore, Dimitri slipped away, back to the city. The last thing upon his gaze before he faded into the shadows was the young woman and the stone illuminated in the fire, with the Dragonheart shattering iridescent light in her laughing, grey eyes.

31

HARPER

That night, Harper found herself restless, twisting and turning under the folds of her cloak until she was tangled within it and unable to find comfort, still her thoughts, or banish a certain set of violet eyes from her mind. Aedon's words had unsettled her, though she still refused to believe it would be as difficult as he suggested to approach the king for a way home. If she had a Dragonheart, and he prized them above all, *surely* that was leverage enough? There was no way other than to focus on that—to admit to anything else would be to fall into the hopeless void on either side of that knife edge.

The next morning, she rose early with the dawn mists around the dell, and went to bathe in the stream. The water was freezing, despite the time of year, but it was just the rough awakening she needed. As she hurriedly dried herself and scrambled to dress, the reeds stirred behind her. She spun around, and a frisson raced across her skin as she found herself face to face with the chest of a shirtless Aedon. Her cheeks heated and her eyes flicked to his muscled and tanned chest before she wrenched back to his gaze. His lazy smile widened.

"Sorry to disturb you. Morning." Aedon covered a yawn with his hand.

"Morning, Aedon. I was just finishing up. Stream's all yours." Her voice was carefully even, and her attention locked on his face, refusing to be drawn to his muscled torso again.

"Actually, I came for some quiet time, to contemplate. Would you care to join me?"

Harper's eyebrow rose. He did not seem the thoughtful type. "Sure." It would be a while before anyone else arose or Ragnar needed her help with breakfast. Was this his way of inviting her back into the fold? She had worried they would cut her adrift and she would be left lost in a strange land. Much as it pained her, she needed them.

Aedon grinned, though his eyes were still clouded with sleep, and jerked a thumb over a shoulder. "I think this spot would work best." He slipped on his shirt to her mingled dismay and relief. She followed him through the mist to a grassy hillock, carefully arranged her cloak on the dew-laden grass, and sat opposite him. She didn't fancy having a wet behind for the rest of the day.

Aedon took a deep breath and exhaled loudly, the air whooshing from his chest as he gazed around with a serene-ness Harper had not seen of him at any other time. "What?" he asked at her cocked head.

"You don't strike me as the type to sit and think."

He chuckled. "I'm not, but I do occasionally enjoy sitting and watching the world go by. Though the fog isn't so great for that."

Harper's lip curled. He was irritatingly infectious, curse him.

"I hope I didn't scare you with the tale last night, Harper. Or what was said afterward."

"You didn't scare me," she said softly. "But I do worry that I don't know what my place is here—or when I get back home." The mist had closed around them. They could barely see each other, let alone anything else. It made her feel even more lost.

Aedon sighed, his smile full of sympathy. "Don't dwell on it for now. Enjoy the present." He shuffled closer until both sat cross-legged, their knees bumping, and reached out, palms held toward her hands. "May I?"

She slipped hers into his, looking at him with questions bursting upon her tongue. As their skin connected, she inhaled sharply. Her hands tingled—part attraction and part something quite unfamiliar—and she fought back another rush of heat across her cheeks.

"You felt that, yes?" She nodded, not trusting herself to speak. He laced his fingers with hers, and his voice dropped, low and alluring. She leaned in. "That's magic. Right there. I said you would be able to feel it. Mine is strong. I've lived here all my life and I'm a pureblood elf. My blood is charged with it. Yours will take a little while to accumulate within you, but soon, you'll feel it. It'll be like a stream of water filling up a vessel. Close your eyes. Try to imagine it, feel it."

Harper did as he asked. Her breathing evened out—hitching for a second as he traced a circle with his thumb on the back of her hand and energy of an entirely different sort cascaded through her. Harper forced her attention inside herself for the source of this energy he spoke of. Deep within her it sat, lurking somewhere in her belly, but she didn't know if that was what magic felt like, or whether it was the buzz of attraction at their physical contact.

Her bare hands stiffened, even in Aedon's warm hold, and

the frigid damp seeped through her cloak. She felt ridiculous, truth be told, glad to hide behind closed eyes. She still didn't believe him. Not really. They sat there, motionless, until Aedon squeezed her hands. She opened her eyes to find him smiling at her with an open warmth.

"I know. It seems silly at first."

She winced. Could he read minds?

"You'll eventually understand what I speak of. Come. I'll wager the others will be rousing soon, and I'm starving. I want to wake Ragnar so he'll make me breakfast."

She laughed. "You can make it yourself, you know."

He grinned, shaking his head. "Why should I when I have the best cook this side of Keldheim tending my fire?"

Aedon helped her to her feet, then slipped his fingers from hers. Harper slowly pulled back her hands, acutely conscious of the sudden rush of cold the absence of his warm skin created. She was glad when he turned his attention away from her and strolled into the mists, back to camp.

Pull yourself together, she chided herself, pressing her cold fingers against her warm cheeks. There was no denying it. These elven males were attractive—ridiculously so—and utterly outside her reach. To even try would be folly. He didn't *feel* bad, however. Would she know for sure if he was? Perhaps she was insanely naïve to think that impressions could not be deceiving. Either way, she had started to develop feelings for the enigmatic thief. Where did that leave her morals?

"Harper?" As if on cue, he called for her through the mists.

Even the way he says my name, with that slight twang. Harper clenched her fists until her nails dug into the soft flesh of her palm. "Stop behaving like a lovesick girl," she snapped at herself. This wasn't like the tanner. She couldn't indulge.

There was far too much at stake for her, and she was already perilously out of her depth. "Coming," she called and hurried back to camp, wrapping her cloak around her as if she could banish such treacherous thoughts along with the cold.

"Ragnar said it's my turn to make the fire today," Aedon said, scrunching up his face and glaring in the direction of Ragnar's still resting lump close by, sticking out his tongue. "But it gives me an opportunity to show you how to use magic to make fire. Want to learn?"

"Yes!" Harper suddenly didn't feel cold anymore, but heated with excitement at the prospect.

Aedon smiled and directed her to build the fire as they always would. "There's really no shortcut for that," he mused. Once she was done, he nodded. "Okay. Now's the fun part. Hold your hands over the wood, like this."

He demonstrated, grasping her hands and holding them above the fire, as if she were warming her palms on invisible flames. As she did, he shifted, moving behind her and fitting his body flush to hers. She tensed, suppressing an inhalation of surprise and trying to banish the tingles that spread down her arms as his palms covered her hands.

"I'm going to share my magic with you. Don't be alarmed."

She shivered as his warm breath brushed the nape of her neck, making something swoop low and deep within her, but she could not hold in the gasp at what happened next. It was a feeling she would not later be able to describe. An energy rushed through her, cold and hot, tingling and smooth, sending every nerve ending into overdrive.

"That's magic, as it ought to feel." She heard the smile in his voice. Energy rushed through her, sparking from her fingertips and arcing toward the fire. It was both there and not there, an ethereal light that disappeared when she tried to focus on it. An instant later, the fire sprang to life before her. She scrambled back, pushing into Aedon's chest at the surprise of its intensity and the sudden onslaught of heat.

He caught them both from falling and laughed, steadying her with his warm hands on her arms. "How was that?"

"Magical," she breathed out. "How?"

He cocked his head. "You have to summon the magic, but when you know how, that's instinctive. I can teach you. You'll accumulate magic like a spring accumulates water. Eventually, it'll be happily bubbling away for you to draw on whenever you please."

"He's showing off," Brand quipped.

"Well, it's true. We're born of magic, and magic is born of us. But perhaps you might need to learn it the hard way." Aedon flashed her a grin. "Soon, it'll be as natural as breathing to you, Harper." He clapped his hands. "Right. Ragnar, how about breakfast now?" He grabbed a stick and poked the dwarf, who sprang from his bedding like Aedon had poked a sleeping bear—loud, displeased, and grizzly. Ragnar chased the elf around camp, shouting obscenities in a language she did not understand. Harper cackled as she ducked out of their way.

"Bloody elf!" Ragnar grumbled. "I was having a lovely dream. Warm hearth, *proper bed...*" He sighed.

"You can dream about it again tonight, Ragnar," Harper said, grinning. "But for now, breakfast. I spotted some berries. Want me to fetch them?"

Ragnar's face brightened at that. "Thanks, Miss Harper. You're a good help. Brew a tea when you return. I'll prepare the food."

Harper dashed off to collect the crimson berries and set to making a tea, whilst Erika and Brand rose, completed their morning training, and patrolled the area as the mists burned away to reveal a rolling, grassy plain before them.

Aedon was nowhere to be seen, but he soon returned with some larger fruits. He tossed them toward Ragnar, who caught them with surprisingly sharp reflexes, though his fingers struggled to close around the furry, bumpy surfaces. Aedon bowed theatrically. "By way of apology for waking you up, dear sir."

Ragnar grunted in reply and sent a stinging glare Aedon's way, still looking unimpressed.

"Your first lesson of the day," Aedon whispered to Harper as he passed her. "Never wake a sleeping dwarf, for they shall resent you 'til the end of time."

Harper stifled a smile. "Tea's ready, everyone."

"Good. I'm dying for a drink," Brand said, taking the pot. "Ladies first."

He offered it to Erika, who took it with a nod of thanks and brought it to her lips. She took a gulp, then immediately spat it out, showering them all in globules of spit and hot liquid.

"Idiot!" she snarled, whirling on Harper. "Why on earth would you make a tea of sun-damson berries?"

The camp stilled as they all turned to Harper. "What? I…"

"They're poisonous, you foolish girl! You could have killed us all!" Erika tossed the entire pot onto the fire, almost extinguishing it in a hissing plume of smoke, and dashed to the stream to rinse out her mouth.

"I didn't know," mumbled Harper. The berries and the plant looked just like ones she brewed in Caledan—perfectly safe to consume. "I'm sorry."

Ragnar patted her shoulder. "It's all right, Harper. Don't worry about it. I ought to have checked. You don't know the flora and fauna here. All's well that ends well—no one was hurt."

"Lucky that Brand's a gentleman," drawled Aedon. "If he'd have quaffed it all himself, he'd have paid the price."

Brand swatted at Aedon, who dodged out of the way. "I'd have known."

"As you were doubled over dying." Aedon stuck out his tongue. Brand returned the gesture with a ruder one of his own.

"See?" Ragnar said dryly. "No harm done."

"Erika's furious, though," Harper said in a small voice, her eyes downcast. It tasted bitter, the frustration she felt— towards Erika and towards herself. This place was still so foreign to her that she still felt as though she was drowning but for the support of Aedon and his friends. Feeling so dependent on others *stung*, and she resented it. Failing them —having them think her weak? Even worse.

"Hmm. She'll be fine. A little thing like an attempted poisoning won't—"

Harper glared at him, eyes full of hurt.

"I'm *joking*! She's survived far worse. Believe me."

"All the same, I think I'll leave the cooking to you." She was done. Done before words she couldn't take back spilled from her mouth. Harper clambered to her feet and retrieved the pot from where it had bounced, then went to a different part of the stream, far from Erika, to rinse it out and fetch clean water. That would have to do for breakfast.

32

DIMITRI

Curiosity grappled with caution as Dimitri returned to Tournai, unsure whether he ought to have crushed them all and taken the stone—and not at all willing to evaluate why he had hesitated. Why did she have it? The question taunted him, and that stayed his hand more than anything else. Why *her*? Her storm-filled silver eyes stared him down defiantly as he thought of her— and there was something in that fearless challenge that enticed him. There had to be a reason, and he needed to know it.

It would be easiest of all to eliminate her—eliminate them all—and be done with it. Yet something faltered at that cold thought too. He balked at doing it for his own ends. He hated doing it for the king's bidding, after all. Stooping so low as doing it for his own selfishness was a new line of depravity even he had not yet crossed.

He could not stop the tingle of excitement that added a spring to his step at the threads beginning to unite, however. He now knew where the Dragonheart was, though not the part it played. He had the relic. Now he would discover Saradon's true fate. The moment he returned to his chambers in the sprawling palace, he took the relic from its hiding place, a nook deep within the impregnable castle walls that no one else could find. He still heaved a sigh of relief that the ring was there, that it had not mysteriously vanished or, worse, been discovered.

The large, oval, multi-faceted gem sat between golden claws twining around it. He looked inside the band, through the back of the ruby, and saw Saradon's Mark, the riven circle, carved into the face of the gem with a perfection that only came from a master craftsman… or magic. He made to put it on his index finger, but stayed himself at the last second. Something about this ring felt different, and he had long been cautious of magical artefacts. It was innocuous, really. At a passing glance, it was a gem fit for a lord or lady, but nothing so garish as to draw undue attention. Was the little pulse of power he felt emanating from it his imagination? Dimitri squinted at it suspiciously, but it glittered in the bright lights with no hint of any dark purpose about it.

His fingers closed around the cold, smooth metal as his eyes slipped shut and he inhaled deeply—a focusing breath. His heart jittered at what he was about to do, but he ignored it, walling himself off from any emotions. He buried his mind into the ring in his palm, feeling it, understanding it, being it, until its essence and that of its previous owner filled his mind—for the ring had been in Karietta's possession since her death, but its true owner had been Saradon.

Just like the Dragonheart, the tiniest thread burrowed into the distance, quickly vanishing, so tenuous was it. The ring was warm in his hand and hummed with energy. Dimitri focused on that, seeking its likeness as he sank into the void to follow the thread back to its owner. He slipped from the world and flitted through the shadows, skimming over distances like a stone over water. There were brief flashes of the landscape as he touched down or slowed for a moment. Sunset over the mountains. The deep, silent shadows of a forest. Open plains. The welcoming golden glow of a fire surrounded by travellers, a brief flash of warmth in the cold. The further he travelled, the more the relic warmed in his palm until it almost burned him.

Then, with a start, he was there, and stumbled uncharacteristically into rough stone that grazed his palms. Crushing weight. Pulsing silence. Energy charged around him, so strong it set every hair on his body on end. Dimitri blinked rapidly, clearing his eyes after the sudden rush of dizziness. His senses fired on full alert, ready to repel any attack. None came, though he could feel the magic of this place. It was so strong, it forced itself down his throat, through his skin, pushing itself into him as though it would absorb him if it could.

Daring a small faelight, he found himself in a small cavern with no entrance or exit. Sensing around him, far beyond the reach of his arms, the weight of the mountain atop him was a looming keeper, its essence slow and sonorous. The hand-hewn walls contained all manner of markings in a script he had never seen before, made so finely he knew it was magic that had scoured the marks from the rock, not the hand of man and chisel. He realised they captured the magic that sealed everything in. That magic pulsed through the air and stone of the cave, like the beating of his own heart. Despite the mountain's cold stone all around, a heat burned him corrosively until the unpleasant prickle of sweat soaked his skin and the expensive, fine fabrics of his clothes.

He did not need to read the glyphs to understand the

magic. The wards sealed the space with the worst magics he had ever felt—death, destruction, curses. Realising he held his breath, he released it in a slow whoosh when he noticed how the wards swirled lazily through the stone and air. Even though they felt him, and he could taste the threat behind their acrid, metallic tang, they did not seek him.

For the first time in many years, he felt a magic older and far more powerful than he. It could crush him in less than an instant. He rolled the ring between his fingers, feeling it hum with small vibrations against his skin—and realised that was what had given him safe passage. It protected him, he marvelled, staring at the innocuous jewellery. The likeness in the magic of the cavern recognised something resonant in the ring.

Dimitri widened his faelight, shining it on the corner of a raised structure. He cast it farther out and up, until the whole cavern was illuminated before him, bouncing his warm, golden faelight back at him with some strange red corruption. Tingles ran down his spine. Before him stood a great, stone sarcophagus. More glyphs adorned it. Many he did not know, but some Aurarian elvish runes were smattered here and there. They embossed the stone in a rosy metal he did not recognise. He glanced closer at the Aurarian runes, noticing they were not as he expected. Somehow changed, marred, their meanings cursed and corrupted. A shiver of dread lingered down his spine. Yet like called to like.

The sarcophagus inexorably pulled him closer.

The stone reached the top of his thighs, and now, looking down upon the surface, he saw the carvings continued in columns and rows, swirling clockwise from the bottom right to the centre of the great slab of stone, where there was a strange hollow. Dimitri leaned forward—careful not to touch the stone. The raw power rolling from it singed his senses. Either something powerful lay here, or it had sealed the tomb.

A tingle of fear stroked his spine, but Dimitri had come this far. He would not be denied now. If only he could figure out how to enter it without triggering the wards that lazily swirled under the surface. The answer he sought could be within that stone—and used to unite a rebellion. He scoured the runes. There appeared to be a void of magic in the centre of the stone where the runes and the magic ended. The little dimple looked like an accident, or as if something was there and had fallen out. Dimitri frowned and bent closer, holding back his tunic so it did not touch the stone.

In the hole lay a raised symbol. With a rush of energy, Dimitri understood. He uncurled his fingers and stared at the ruby in his palm. It had become almost burning hot. He felt around the gem until he found the flaw in the frame, then popped it from the setting. The giant ruby glittered in the warped light of the cave. Slowly, he lowered it to the sarcophagus and slipped the ruby into the hollow. It fit perfectly, one piece of a jigsaw to another, upon the Mark of Saradon carved into the stone.

The stone shuddered under his fingers as the ruby sealed against it. With a hiss, the lid of the sarcophagus creaked. Dimitri leaped backwards as it slid away and dissolved into swirls of sparkling magic. The glittering particles of light faded. Another tingle, one of fear and wonder, ran down Dimitri's spine. He recognised the perfectly preserved face of the male within the tomb. Saradon.

They were still days away from the plagued village. Harper spent the long days of endless trudging mostly in silence, dawdling at the back of the group, even farther behind than Ragnar. Not even Aedon could chivvy away her glum spirit after almost accidentally poisoning Erika. "She's really not so bad once you get to know her, you know," he said as they pushed their way through grass so long, it was as if they swam in it.

She made a non-commital grunt in response.

"Honestly, Harper. Chin up."

"I hardly think Erika's opinion of me will change. The sooner I return to Caledan, the better." Frustration rose, bitter on her tongue.

Aedon stopped beside her, and she stopped with him. "Do you truly think that?" He looked almost hurt at the suggestion.

She scowled.

He shook his head. "Then you are a fool. Harper, this is your birthright. You were meant to be born here and live here. It's going to take a little catching up, but you ought not be defeated at the first hardship. Are you really so easily persuaded away from your path?"

Harper bristled. "No. I just—"

"Exactly. You just *nothing*. Life isn't meant to be easy. You're doing pretty well for only being here for mere days. I mean, you're not dead yet. That's actually a pretty huge accomplishment."

"Thanks to you."

"Well, yes." For once, Aedon didn't puff up with self-importance. "But still. You're alive. Besides, if you left…" He took a deep breath, "I'd miss you." His words halted her steps and she glared up at him, her face blooming with heat and her tongue stumbling to form any coherent word.

He gave her a wink and, whistling a jaunty tune, jogged ahead to catch Ragnar. It took a long moment for her to gather herself and follow him. Had he just said that? What did that mean? And… what did she want it to mean? It left her skin crawling, so unfamiliar was she with attention like that—but there was something pleasurable there too, a low heat in her stomach that had nothing to do with the flush of embarrassment on her cheeks.

Harper swallowed down the unfamiliar feelings. Aedon was right. She had never been one to give up easily. Why start now? Sure, she'd nearly poisoned a woman who seemed to hate her for no reason, but it had been an accident. Everyone made those. There'd been no harm done—and that was what mattered. She forced herself into motion. This was all becoming too uncomfortable.

When they stopped for a midday meal in the middle of the wide valley, she plucked up the courage to approach Erika. "Please can you teach me about poisonous berries?"

she asked in her most powerful voice, though it quaked a little with nerves.

Erika regarded her with a flat stare. "Ask Ragnar."

Harper had no reply, only the burn on her cheeks of embarrassment, and turned away to hide her scowl.

Ragnar threw a dark look at Erika. "Sure, Harper. *I'll* teach you, though Erika is better at it than I. Perhaps she can give some tips when she sees fit to get off her high bloody horse." He glared pointedly at her.

She ignored him.

Ragnar glowered. "Fetch some water, please, Harper."

They had followed running water fairly closely all day, and the stream remained nearby. Harper disappeared into the long grass, her eyes on the hazy hills in the distance. She almost fell into the stream, which was far closer than she had thought, and bent to fill the waterskin and pot.

"You don't have to be like that with her," she heard Ragnar say angrily.

Harper froze. *He's talking to Erika?*

"Like what?" Erika replied, her quiet voice muffled by the swaying, rustling grass. Harper strained her ears.

"You don't have to be such a damn harpy to her!"

"Don't speak to me like that."

"Like *you* speak to *her*? I won't have it, woman."

"Don't call me *woman*!" Erika's voice rose, shrill against the breeze.

"Calm it, you two," Brand said, his gravelly tones breaking the friction between them.

"You know, you *both* know, how damn hard it is to be an outcast," Ragnar pressed. "Erika, I thought you would relate to it more than anyone. How did you feel when you were shunned, cast away from everyone and everything you knew and loved? I bet that was like falling into another world, wasn't it?"

"You don't know *anything* about that," Erika spat at the dwarf, "and you have no right to speak of it!"

"I think I do, because I also know what it's like. It feels like your entire world has fallen away. Like everything and everyone has died. You're alone, and everything is a clean slate—it is a blessing and a curse." Ragnar's voice sounded desolate. Harper's heart ached for him.

"Somehow, you have to pick yourself up and carry on. When did you become so bitter and twisted, Erika? Harper hasn't done anything to you. *It isn't her fault.* Quit acting like she's the chip on your shoulder. You think she'll achieve anything if you're always putting her down? Telling her she's stupid? That she can't do it? We're a team… nay, a family, and right now, I couldn't be more ashamed of you, sister. You're acting exactly as you were portrayed. This is the behaviour you were cast out for. This is the person people feared you would become. Do not become her."

She did not answer. When Harper heard the rustling of grass coming closer, she bent low, hidden amongst the tangle of foliage, as Erika passed close by, leapt over the channel of water, and strode out of sight. Her heart hammered as Ragnar's words echoed in her mind.

What is he talking about? Harper clutched the pot between her hands and returned to camp, the tense atmosphere there dissipating with her arrival.

"Ah, thank you, Harper. Much appreciated. You've saved my old hands and knees."

She set the pot down and smiled, but it did not quite reach her eyes. "Oh," she said, struck by a sudden thought. "I might be able to help with your hands." She had noticed how he sometimes struggled to pick things up and fumbled when he held things.

"May I?" She gestured toward his hands.

With a quizzical glance, he offered one to her. Harper settled on the ground at his side and took his gnarled hand between her own, massaging it slowly from palm to fingertip. Ragnar groaned in bliss. She worked on one hand in silence before transferring her attention to the other. He sat back with a sigh when she was done, flexing his fingers and examining his hands.

"That was wonderful, Harper. Thank you. That's really eased my aches. Where did that come from?"

"My old—" She wasn't sure what Betta had been—part mother, mentor, caregiver, friend. "—friend suffered terribly with arthritis, and this used to help. She couldn't pick things up, her fingers were so overworked. In the winter, it got that bad she could barely use her hands."

"Well, I thank you." Ragnar's smile was genuine and warm, reaching right to the corners of his crinkled eyes. "That feels much better."

"Are you offering those to everyone?" A swoop rushed through her belly as Aedon seemed to appear from nowhere beside her, his voice low and suggestive, and the heat of his body close enough to radiate to her. The skin on the back of her neck prickled at his proximity. "Can't be giving the old dwarf an advantage over us at *chatura*, you know."

Crashing through the bracken spared her from answering. Erika returned. There was a long moment of awkward silence. Harper held her breath.

"Here," Erika said abruptly, thrusting a handful of berries toward her. "Red ones are occa berries. Edible. Nutritious. Green ones are poisonous. Don't eat them."

"Thank you." Harper caught the berries before they

tumbled to the ground, and Erika strode away again. Harper examined the berries for a long moment, noting their shapes, sizes, tones, and distinguishing features. They were nothing like what she foraged for in Caledan.

She offered the red ones to Ragnar for his tea, but he refused. "Have them as a snack. I think we'll drink up and move on. Slim pickings here if Aedon the Great Hunter hasn't found anything."

Aedon held up his hands apologetically.

"Jerky it is." Ragnar pulled some strips of dried meat from his pack and passed them around.

Harper ate it without complaint. It was rich, tangy, and extra salty, but too small to fill the gnawing hunger in her stomach. It was as if Aedon could read her thoughts, for he offered her some of his own.

"You don't have to do that."

He shrugged. "You need it more than I. Did they starve you in Caledan?"

Harper pulled her cloak around her self-consciously. "No. I mean… It's just a hard place to live. The king takes his tithe, then the lord takes more. There's not much to start with, and even less when they're through."

"That doesn't seem fair." Aedon shared a glance with Brand.

"That doesn't happen here?"

"The king is greedy, but not so much for peasant's food. He prizes dragons and magic."

"You said all dragons belong to the king. How is that?" Harper could not imagine the dragons from her stories being subjugated.

"By law, all dragons in Pelenor belong to the king, who can do with them as he pleases. Of course, all of them become members of the Winged Kingsguard, his personal winged army. He has no other use for dragons. Besides, I hear they're a bit more malleable if you can train them out of the egg. Otherwise, they're rather hard to tame."

"That doesn't seem fair, either."

"It's the law," Aedon said, as if it were that simple.

"You're quite right," Brand said, catching Harper's gaze and scowling. "Just because it's law doesn't make it right."

"Exactly my thought," Harper murmured.

"You'll find a lot of that here in Pelenor," Brand said, "though I'm guessing Caledan is no utopia, either."

"No," said Harper sadly. "There are plenty of people with power who abuse it, plenty of outdated or unfair laws, and just those who think they can take what they will." She meant the lecherous men in the inn, but as her gaze strayed to her companions, she realised they were quite possibly the same, though in a different manner. Something uncomfortable settled in her stomach at the thought.

"Such is the way of the world," Aedon said. "This is why we're here. To bring a little bit more fairness back." When he saw the flicker of skepticism on Harper's face, he nodded. "You'll see."

"How big do dragons grow?" she asked quickly, keen to cover her tracks. *Don't bite the hand that feeds you, Harper. Criminal or not.*

"Huge. The size of a house or more," Aedon said. "It is said that King Menoth's own dragon, some four hundred and thirty years ago, was as huge as a hill."

Brand snorted. "Poppycock."

"Were you there?" Aedon challenged him, puffing with indignance.

"No, and neither were you, young elf."

"Don't 'young elf' me. I'm older than you!"

"In years, but not maturity," Brand sniped, grinning as Aedon's cheeks reddened with annoyance.

"How old are you?" Harper asked curiously. She glanced between them. Brand looked older than Aedon by far. Maybe in his late thirties to Aedon's mid twenties. *How long is a year here?* she wondered. *Maybe they measure it differently.*

"Old enough for everything to ache when I wake up," Brand grumbled.

"Shouldn't spend so much time banging weapons about then," sniped Aedon. "I, my dear Harper, am one hundred and eighty-four summers young."

Harper gaped. "What? Are you serious?"

"Yes, quite. We live a lot longer than humans, you know."

We? "Wait. You mean… I will live that long, too?"

"Oh, undoubtedly."

"How long?" Harper whispered.

Aedon shrugged. "It depends on how strong your elven blood is. Perhaps we will find out one day, but it's not something to worry about now."

"Right." Reeling, Harper sat back. *Just when I think I can handle all this, another surprise comes my way.*

"We need to move on." Ragnar stood, brushing the dust from his trousers. "We still have a long way to go."

"Must I?" Aedon sighed. "What I'd give for a break."

"Less of the cheek," Ragnar said, bustling past him.

"I don't know what in Pelenor you're talking about," Aedon protested, the picture of unconvincing innocence.

"You're the biggest reprobate of us all," Brand called back, already out in front.

"Charming."

Harper jogged to Erika, who strode down the trail at her usual breakneck pace. "Thank you for the berries."

She shrugged. "No problem."

"Hey, Erika!" Aedon caught up. "Wait up. Ragnar's washing pots in the stream before we head out. You know, now Harper's here, she needs to know how to defend herself. Why don't you show her how to use a weapon whilst we wait?"

Erika gave him a stare that could have surely reduced him to cinders, as if she simply could not imagine anything worse.

"Please?" Aedon gave her his best smile.

Erika scoffed at him. "Fine." She pulled out one of the twin blades strapped to her back and thrust it at Harper. "Here."

Harper reached out, nearly dropping it as Erika let go too soon. She caught it clumsily, almost slicing herself in the process.

"Lesson one. Pommel. Grip. Guard. Blade. Point." Erika pointed to each part of the blade in turn.

Harper examined it. The handle was made of an ivory-coloured material she did not recognise. Not wood, metal, leather... *Bone?* she wondered. It was smooth from use, a grain ran vertically up the length of the grip, and strange characters were carved into the side. The pommel was a slightly widened knob on the end of the grip.

The crossguard was simple, made of steel-like metal, leading into a slim blade longer than a dagger but shorter than a sword. Rippling patterns covered the blade, almost like a frozen metal river, and the cutting edge was so sharp, Harper felt she would cut herself by looking at it. Already, the weight of it tugged her arm inexorably toward the ground. How did Erika wield *two* of them? Harper eyed Brand's huge, two-handed longsword strapped to his back. She probably couldn't even lift that.

"Lesson two," Erika continued. "Take care of your

weapons better than you take care of yourself. That way, they'll last longer and won't fail you. A badly maintained blade is as good as nothing."

Harper nodded. "How do I take—"

"Lesson three." Erika seemed determined to get through this as quickly as possible. "Don't get hit. Block your attacker whenever possible. Cut off their attack. Better yet, avoid it altogether. Footwork and balance are key to that. Lesson four. Hit your target."

Harper stifled a grim chuckle. "I should have seen that one coming."

Aedon grinned at her, but Erika's visage did not waver from grim indifference. "If you can't hit them, you won't be incapacitating them any time soon."

Harper squirmed under Erika's glare. Could she attack someone? The thought was deeply uncomfortable. "But—"

"But nothing. The middle of a battle is not the time to be shy, not the time for cowardice, not the time to develop concern for your enemy. If they're trying to kill you, they should be as good as dead in your book. I can already tell that's going to be a problem." She sent a shrivelling glare Harper's way. Harper had no reply to that. Indignation burned her throat closed.

"Lesson five. Always be ready. Threats can be all around you. You have to constantly know what is in front, behind, and to your sides. You have to be able to assess everyone, right down to the sweet old granny who doesn't look like she can lift a sword. Believe me, when you're not expecting it, she can stab you in the back just as good as anyone else. And—"

"All right. I think that's enough for now. You'll scare her off!" Aedon protested. He turned to Harper. "Not *all* grannies are evil cretins, I promise you. I wasn't anticipating quite that deluge, but, uh… Erika's tips are good. Think you can remember them?"

"Hmm." *Not a chance.* Erika was a terrible teacher—she clearly didn't want to share a scrap of true knowledge. Anger seethed in Harper that the woman thought so little of her. She'd done nothing to deserve that.

"Perfect. Perhaps you can show her some of that fancy footwork when we break for camp tonight, Erika."

"Hmph." Erika looked less than impressed as she held out her hand, raising an eyebrow at Harper. It took a long moment for Harper to realise she wanted her sword back. She passed it hurriedly to Erika, who spun the blade in her hand expertly and sheathed it on her back once more. Without another word, she jogged away and disappeared ahead to scout as Ragnar caught them up.

"That went well," Harper said bitterly.

"Oh, don't mind her." Aedon waved a hand. "That was actually pretty good. Most words I've heard her say all month. She must like you."

Harper snorted.

"All right. Perhaps that is pushing it, but believe me, that's friendly for Erika."

"I feel like she hates me, but I don't know why."

"Oh pish. She doesn't hate you. You can see she's the type who takes a while to warm to people. It's nothing personal. When she starts to teach you some proper techniques, I'm sure you'll be the best of buddies in no time."

Harper laughed. "I won't hold my breath for that."

"Probably wise. You can help me with the fire again tonight. See if we can stoke some of your magic whilst we're at it, hmm?"

The suggestiveness of his tone curled her toes. She tried to push away thoughts of his skin on hers and only focus on the excitement of the magic rushing through her. If she tried really hard, there was a tingle deep down in the pit of her stomach. It was small and weak, but still there. Maybe, just maybe, like Aedon had said, it was starting to well up. Or maybe it was just nerves. Any good feeling she had left ebbed.

"Sounds good," she said, her voice painstakingly level.

"Good. You ought to learn how I keep our camp safe every night, too."

"I thought that was Brand and Erika. You know, with all the swords and scariness."

"Oh, that's all for show. Magic is far better at protecting us." He extended a hand to help her over a fallen tree blocking the trail. Those green eyes of his were mesmerising, and she risked losing herself down a dangerously irrational road indulging any of these fickle feelings he elicited. Harper swallowed, and reached for his hand.

34

DIMITRI

Saradon looked as perfect as the day he had died, right down to the wave of still-raven hair upon his head that streamed across his shoulders. Not a hint of decay marred him. The question floated through Dimitri's mind—he was dead, wasn't he? Why else would he be in a grave? This was undoubtedly nothing else. A hidden shrine to a once great threat.

Dimitri ought to have left well alone. Sealed the place and left. Curiosity would not let him. Unconsciously holding his breath, Dimitri's eyes trickled across the still form before him. Saradon's eyes were shut—much to Dimitri's relief—his face stern and taut, even in death. Anger ran down every line upon it.

His clothes were not too dissimilar to Dimitri's own. The fine silken overjacket and matching pants, all embroidered in chasing patterns. Yet Dimitri could tell they were from a different time. The wider, flaring sleeves, loose-fitting bottoms, and shining knee-high boots on his muscled calves… It was dated compared to current court fashions.

A blade lay beside him. The match of the sword he wielded in the painting Dimitri had viewed in the royal galleries. The long, slim blade gleamed, and the ruby in the pommel was a larger sister to the signet ring. Saradon's Mark gleamed upon it, inset in rose gold. Saradon's fingers clenched around the grip, his hands covered in black gloves of a leather so fine, Dimitri had never seen its like. There was no hint of decomposition upon him. None that Dimitri could see or smell. Tentatively, to satisfy his own curiosity, he sent out a tendril of power toward Saradon's still form, seeking something more. A spark of life, or the absence of it.

A power greater than his own snapped closed its jaws around him.

It froze Dimitri where he stood, gripping his mind and body in an instant. Dimitri could not even breathe. The magic seizing him felt ancient, foreign. An impenetrable wall of black adamant smothered his senses. It crushed and constricted him, squeezing his life and power out of existence. Dimitri threw up his mental shields. Had the magic allowed him an ounce of movement, he would have shaken with the effort of it. He had never encountered such overwhelming power.

There was barely an instant to wonder if Saradon had other innate elven gifts no one had known of, besides the magic he had been denied, or whether he had bought, bartered, or stolen the power that now surrounded Dimitri. He knew he only had a moment to fight back before the power winked him out of existence. It was the first time he had ever encountered a power so much greater than he that there was no hope of defeating it once it fractured his barriers and cracked his mind.

Saradon would own him, control him, and destroy him. Dimitri was not sure which one was worse. He sent out every ounce of energy he had, pushing back against the black adamant around him. The assault halted. A momentary curiosity sized him up. Dimitri felt the power well up again, so he appealed once more, holding Saradon's Mark clear and firm in his mind. The attack halted again.

"*Who are you?*" a deep voice spoke in his mind.

The pressure drew back a little, allowing him the breath to answer. Dimitri gasped in the warm, stale air gratefully. "Dimitrius Vaeri Mortris of House Ellarian," he choked out.

Anger rippled through him. Not his own, but that of the being who spoke to him. "*I know of House Ellarian.*" Memories that belonged to someone else flickered through him. Cruel faces. Darkness. Hate. Fire. Pain.

"I am not them," Dimitri added hastily.

"*Who dares disturb the rest of Saradon Ettrias Thelnar of House Ravakian?*"

Excitement muddied by fear shot through Dimitri. Saradon was alive. Had somehow survived five hundred years of exile. How could it be? Dimitri was quick to answer, but not with his mouth. He pushed images of the kingdom at Saradon's consciousness. He showed him Toroth's greed and corruption, five hundred years of prejudice, bloodshed, and anger, and finally the burning of the false traitors in Saradon's name. Rage shuddered through Dimitri as Saradon's mood soured further.

"*My name has been used in vain?*" Saradon thundered.

"Yes, Lord. Five hundred years have passed and nothing has changed. Pelenor is as corrupt as ever it was."

"*Five hundred years?*" His surprise rippled through Dimitri, swiftly replaced by anger once more. "*Curse them all,*" Saradon spat. "*Why have you come?*"

Now was his chance. "I want to break the wheel. I—" He

fell into silence. He wondered what? Whether he could break the wheel himself? Whether somehow it would be possible to raise Saradon to do the selfsame thing, now that he had found him apparently in some stage of life or animation? *He could be so much more than the talisman I sought.*

"*You wondered if you could use me.*" Saradon's accusing voice cut through his thoughts.

"No!" Dimitri hastily replied. "I find you here—alive?" he asked tentatively. A silent affirmation replied. He cleared his throat. "Perhaps we can ally for a common cause."

"*I have power. Why would I need you?*"

The rumble of power threatened to sweep Dimitri away, but he felt how the magics twisted around him, more curious than angry. *He cannot raise himself,* Dimitri realised, somehow entirely certain of himself. "You cannot free yourself without assistance—without *me.*" Dimitri drew back, as if readying to leave, although, in the back of his mind, he was not entirely sure he could.

The foreign magics shrank back in surprise before tightening again. He felt Saradon scowl—though his body remained entirely immobile—and the magic trickled back again, prowling around him. Still a threat, but not an imminent one. "*It was not meant to be five hundred years. Merely a temporary stasis. It seems I was let down.*"

"There was a prophecy that you would rise again," Dimitri suggested cautiously. "Is it true?"

Saradon snorted, and a dark rumble of laughter echoed around the cavern. "*I will rise again. I care not for any prophecies made by the elves.*"

Dimitri privately agreed, though he did not say it. "How is it done?" he asked instead.

"*I would not trust that knowledge to anyone.*"

"Then let me prove myself to you. I shall be your eyes and ears in the kingdom—and beyond, as the royal spymaster—and when you rise, I shall gather those that I can to your banners. I have already planned the fall of Pelenor." Dimitri made it sound far more developed and grand than the wild idea it really was, but his resolve did not waver as he stood firm, knowing Saradon would be sensing him out.

"Why do you want this?" Saradon asked slowly. *"Are you simply as greedy as the rest of them?"* He sounded bored, but his voice held a bite of curiosity and still, that ever-present anger.

"No," Dimitri was hasty to placate him. "Like you, I am sick of being oppressed for that which is not my fault. I will show you, if you wish, so you will know I speak truthfully." It was a daring move that Dimitri was not entirely sure would succeed, but he had nothing to lose, and the greatest weapon in his potential arsenal to gain.

"Show me."

Dimitri lowered the shield to his mind, opening a tiny chink in the impregnable wall he had never yielded to anyone.

The summer sun tickled his skin through the chink in the shutters. Dimitri pressed his face against the cold metal bars, as if he could somehow sink through them, through the shutters, to outside, to where life, light, and joy reigned—for others, but never for him. A cloud scudded across the sky, cutting off the slim ray of light in an instant. Dimitri sank onto the bench, his back against the cold stone. Out there, it was warm, but here, in the bowels of the castle, the cold of the earth was almost as pervasive as the cold of the stone.

He shivered and drew his knees up to his chest, but he did not draw away from the rock. It soothed the lines of fire across his back where his father had whipped him mercilessly. An anger as hot as the pain seared through him at the thought of his brothers' smug faces. The bastards had taunted him, as ever, with their legitimacy, and when he had bitten back with a taste of magic far stronger than theirs, it was he who had borne the punishment. As if his life were not punishment enough—confined to the shadows, as though his father's shame was his fault.

He skipped from memory to memory, lingering as little as he could, for even now, they brought him nothing but pain and anger. His years of childhood confinement and punishment at the hands of a cruel father, step-mother, and step-brothers. His repeated snubs from the king. His dogged efforts to raise his standing, always hampered by the glass ceiling of the taint in his blood. His unanswered questions of who his mother was.

Finally, he let the last memory slip away. How he had gotten his revenge, at last, upon his brothers. They bothered him no longer. He had always felt he had not made them suffer enough. Saradon's anger fuelled his own, but he locked it away, pushing it back into that dark part of himself that he kept under the tightest confinement at all times.

"A Heart of Dragons. Find me one so I may yet live."

A thrill chased through Dimitri.

Saradon continued in a low growl. *"Find more, and I shall break the wheel."*

Dimitri bowed low. "I will make it so, Lord."

The magic aided him, pushing him away, as Dimitri slid into the veils of the world again. His heart hammered as he alighted in his own quarters. So normal, safe, and welcoming after the hot, raw power of the chamber. The Dragonheart was the key—and he had to take it now.

35

HARPER

That night, when they stopped in a narrow valley by a stream, sheltering under a rocky overhang, the weather closed in. Harper was glad for the added shelter as the temperature sank and the clouds piled high.

The humidity was unbearable as the first storms of autumn fought the summer into decline, and Harper made the most of the waterfall that plummeted off the overhang. Fully clothed, she walked into it, groaning with relief as the cool water engulfed her. It stripped away the dirt of the road and swept away the uncomfortable mugginess for just a few minutes. As she returned to camp dripping, she sank gratefully onto a rock, wriggling her toes as her aching feet pounded.

"Good idea." Brand stripped to his breeches and dived under the waterfall. Harper gawked at him. Every inch of him bulged with muscle and strength. But, scars riddled his skin, some old, and some decidedly less so. She had never seen someone so battle-worn before. He was a fearsome warrior for certain.

"A wash is indeed a good idea!" Aedon said brightly, making to follow Brand. Ragnar grabbed him by the scruff of his neck.

"Not so fast, laddie. I need some wood before this storm arrives. Go on. Off you go."

Aedon groaned. "Make Erika do it!" Nevertheless, he lowered his vest and turned away. "Harper, want to help? I can show you the camp enchantments at the same time."

"Yes!" She scrambled to her feet, now regretting her decision to soak her clothes, because shivers wracked her body.

"Hang on. Your lips are blue." He stood face to face with her, and held his hands out to her, running them down her sides but never touching her. As they moved, she felt his magic sweep through her, warm and tingling, and when he stepped back, she was dry. He threw her a wink and strode away. She swallowed, wrenching her gaze away from the fine sight of him retreating, and hurried to follow. They gathered pieces of wood, twigs, and suitable kindling in short order, then returned to the outskirts of camp. Aedon paused. "Dump your wood here. We'll set the wards and return for it."

Harper emptied her armful on top of his.

"Take my hand. You'll feel it then."

Harper laced her fingers through his, hating how much the simple feel of him brought her pleasure. How could it be that she was undone so easily? Was she that starved of attention? She shoved the thoughts aside and matched her stride to his, focusing on one step and then the next, as the surge of his magic stroked through her. Harper revelled in it flooding her body, radiating out from him in pulsing waves. Her senses changed, as though the outside world muffled, then sharpened, repeatedly peaking and diminishing until they had walked around the entire camp, hopped over the stream, and were back where they had started.

"What did you do?" she asked breathlessly, heady on the energy tingling throughout her as it faded.

"I made us safe. That will keep us unheard and unseen, secret until we leave tomorrow." He faced her—but had still not dropped her hand.

She felt the heat of his body. "Will I be able to do that?" she asked, as much to distract herself as to sate her curiosity.

"Yes. When your magic is strong enough, that will be an easy one for you." He smiled, and she noticed he did not look tired at all, despite the amount of energy that had cascaded through her. He lingered close to her, his gaze dipping to her mouth for a fleeting second before he retreated, slipping his fingers from hers after a light rub of his thumb upon her hand that was so small, she was not sure whether she had imagined it.

"Come. Tell me of your life," he said in a light voice. "What is it like to dwell in Caledan, the land of no magic?"

"Hmph. Hardly as interesting as your escapades."

"Oh, I suspect that isn't true." He grinned, his merry, twinkling eyes fixed upon her. She looked away, pushing down the flutter in her stomach.

"There's not much to tell." She recounted her life in recent years with Betta, but kept the years before that she never spoke of to anyone to herself. No one would want to hear of the young waif who survived on scraps of charity and waste, who came from goodness knows where and whose earliest memories were of the dull ache of hunger and the cold of no bed. She did not like to often think of it herself.

Aedon was silent for a moment once she finished. "Well, then, I suppose our company is much more pleasant and thrilling."

"It wouldn't take much," she muttered darkly. For a moment, she was back in the dingy, stinking inn with its undesirable patrons. He laughed at her scowl, and bent to retrieve some of the wood. She gathered the rest and returned to camp behind him.

"Did this arse make you carry all that? Let me help you with that," Brand said to Harper as she returned to camp, shooting a reproving glare at Aedon, who ignored him as he built the fire. Brand rose from where he had been playing *chatura* with Ragnar.

"I'm all right. I've got it." She dodged out of his way and dumped the wood on the rocky shelf by Ragnar. "Is that enough?"

"That'll do." He did not lift his eyes from the board for more than a second, absorbed in the game of strategy.

Aedon lit the fire with a thought and in moments, fuelled by magic, it burned merrily, just as the air cooled around them and the heavens opened. They huddled under the overhang out of the driving rain and glad for the fire, though there was no meat to go on it that night and they had to make do with more jerky and some sour fruit Ragnar had found that day.

Separated from all of them, Erika sat as immobile as a statue with her back to the rock. Harper could not help but wonder what had happened to make her such an inhospitable character.

The rain stopped before darkness fell, taking the chill with it. Harper watched the stream run by before them, lost in the babble. She startled as a shadow fell over her.

Erika stood before her, holding out one of her blades. "I'm cold and stiff. We can start your practise now."

Harper scrambled to her feet and took the blade. Her arm fell involuntarily, just as it had the last time, unused to the weight.

"Hold your blade upright," said Erika, irritation biting in her voice. "And watch your feet. Stand with them farther apart, one slightly behind the other. Your balance will be better."

She darted forward to slap Harper on her thigh with the flat of a blade.

"Ow!" said Harper. "I wasn't ready."

"Always be ready. And move your feet. Don't stand still."

She darted forward again. Harper dodged backwards, but not quickly enough, and she grimaced as her heel jarred against an errant tree root. Her feet felt like bricks, her legs wooden. Erika rapped her again. It smarted.

"Try and attack me. Maybe your attack is stronger than your defence."

She reddened. Erika thought her defence was bad enough, and it was clear she did not think her attack would be much stronger. Harper dashed forward, her arm sailing through the air, but travelling a different path than she intended with the weight of the blade. Erika easily knocked it aside. She turned and gave Aedon a look that said, "*really?*"

"We all have to start somewhere," Aedon murmured.

Erika huffed. "This is going to take a lot of work." She sighed and pinched the bridge of her nose between a forefinger and thumb. "Right. We'll go again. Perhaps this might help. Think of a fight much like a dance. You dance with your opponent back and forth, teasing them, pushing them, leading them on."

"I can't dance," mumbled Harper.

"Of course you can't," said Erika through gritted teeth.

Erika demonstrated manoeuvres with Brand, moving with exaggerated slowness. Each time, Harper had to copy them against Erika, movement perfect. Even that felt like too much. Every movement was so alien to her. Muscles she did not even know she had were forced into action and complained thrice as hard for it, until she trembled with tiredness. This was awful. Shame and disappointment burned in her chest, and her throat clogged with thickness that threatened to brew angry tears. The grand tales made this sound so glamorous. Reality was far from it. Swordplay was intolerable. It was hard, loud, and impossible. Harper's patience had worn out, and it seemed so had Erika's.

"I think we're done for today. If you remember half of that, well, you might not get killed immediately."

Great.

"One final thing. Stand just like that with your feet in… Yes, that position. Hold your blade out, as if you're facing off an attack. Stay there."

"Until when?"

"Until darkness has fallen and you can see the stars above you."

Harper gaped at her. "Why?"

Irritation flashed across Erika's face. "Discipline is critical."

Harper didn't drop her gaze.

"Because you need to grow your strength. You need to be able to hold your blade and wield it for long periods of time. You're already tired. You have no stamina, so you must build it." She slapped the underside of Harper's arm with the flat of her blade. "See? You're drooping already. Stand up straight." With a low growl, Erika turned and stalked to Brand. "I can't take this," she hissed.

Brand stared at her flatly.

"I don't deal with novices."

"Patience." His voice was low and soothing, but Erika scowled all the same. "I know this isn't easy for you. I'll take over from here."

"I can do it," Erika snapped.

A weary flare of irritation spiked in Harper. Erika hated her and didn't want to train—but would do it out of pride if she had to, rather than cede the responsibility to someone else? Harper didn't understand the nomad at all.

Brand huffed. "But it's better if you don't. I insist." His tone brooked no argument.

Harper's cheeks burned as she returned her gaze to the woods. *Did she mean for me to hear that?* Erika did not seem like a good teacher at all. Harper wondered if there was more to her than met the eye, because so far, she did not like Erika. *I am trying. What's her problem?*

Harper straightened and forced her complaining arm to rise again, though her muscles ached fiercely. As the sunlight faded and the moon rose, Erika stood there, watching her. She stayed silent, only moving to slap Harper's arm or tap her back to indicate she faltered once more. Harper dug deep until every part of her hurt, but she clung doggedly on until her stare could have burned a hole into the scenery. She would not give Erika the satisfaction of seeing her fail.

When Erika finally allowed her to relax, Harper's whole body trembled, but Erika offered no sympathy. Harper made no complaint, though her eyes pricked with tears, over-whelmed in her exhaustion by fears that assailed her merci-lessly, taunting her about how useless and out of place she was. Harper gave Erika her blade and stumbled back to collapse upon her cloak, ignoring Ragnar's offer of a seat at his game of *chatura* with Aedon as she fell fast asleep.

Harper woke early the next morning. Though exhausted, she could not return to sleep. Erika's scathing tones burned in her mind as she tossed and turned— and eventually gave up. She rose silently, glancing around camp. Brand was also awake, gazing into the woods.

"I'm going to wash," she whispered.

He held up his hand to stop her. She paused. He drew out a knife from within the folds of his cloak, though it looked more like a dagger to her, so huge was it.

"Never go anywhere unarmed, just in case. Be on guard."

She took it, her hand barely fitting around the wide grip that was formed for his big, broad hands. "Thanks."

The ground remained sodden and muddied from the previous night's storm, though the sun had risen, already creating a warmer, more pleasant, day. Harper looked at her feet, focusing on not slipping on the moss- and mud-covered rocks as she rounded the outcrop. She followed the stream far enough that she would not be seen or overheard from camp.

Clambering down to the stream, she unclipped her cloak, resting it and the dagger atop a high rock, stripped to her undergarments, and gave herself a brisk wash in the cool water using a chunk of moss. It felt refreshing to wipe the visible layer of grime from her skin that the fire's smoke had gifted the previous night.

"What I'd give for a hot wash," she murmured to herself, laughing dryly. Had she ever gone so long without a proper wash? Definitely not. No matter how poor she had been, water was free and wood plentiful. A hot bucket had been her treat after an unbearable shift or long hunt. It did not bear thinking about.

She clambered from the water and found a rock that caught the early morning sun. She perched upon it and closed her eyes, soaking in the light and warmth as it dried her skin. Before too long, she was almost dry, so she hastened to put on the billowing shirt, just in case anyone else should have awakened and followed her. She bent to pull on her breeches. As she tugged them over her hips, an arrow shattered on the stones beside her.

36

HARPER

arper spun around, almost falling on the uneven rocks. She glared up at the bluff, squinting into the sun. Two silhouettes leapt down with inhuman agility. She gasped when they left the sun's piercing corona. Elves. Both armed and dressed in slim-fitting dark clothes that camouflaged them amongst the foliage. Braids contained their long, mahogany hair and their golden eyes were narrow and hostile—yet they hung back with an edge of wariness whilst they took her in, as though they expected her to be trouble.

"Where is it?" the taller, female elf snarled. She stalked closer, a long, slim blade pointed directly toward Harper. Harper inched back, bumping into the rock where her cloak lay. With her hand behind her back, she fumbled for the knife. The elf's male companion, armed with a bow—which was drawn, an arrow nocked and pointed toward her heart— circled away from them both to cut her off from running.

"Where's what?" Harper asked, turning slightly to try and keep an eye on both of them at once. Every nerve in her was alight, and her body trembling on the edge of bolting, because there was no way she would be able to match them in combat.

"You know what," the male elf answered. "We've tracked you this far. We know you to be with the thief and his pack. Where is the *aleilah*?"

"I don't know what you're talking about," Harper said guardedly, but her heart thundered and her nerves shot with lightning. *Do they mean the Dragonheart?* "I'm an innocent traveller."

"Ha!" the female elf scoffed. "No one who runs with the Thief of Pelenor is innocent, but I shall give you a choice. Where is the elf, or the *aleilah*?" she said, leaping across the stream to land feet away from Harper.

Harper backed against the cliff, cursing silently that she had run out of options. There was nowhere to go. She rolled the knife around in her palm. It was utterly inadequate. "Look, I don't know what you're talking about. I was travelling with them. I take no part in their affairs."

"Was?" the male cocked his head.

His sister scowled. "She lies. You're still with them. Their trail does not leave this area. I know they're close—I can taste it. I will not be denied him now. I owe him thanks for the merry little chase he's led us on, and for the damage he caused our beloved Tir-na-Alathea."

With an icy rush, Harper realised who they were from the snippets Aedon had shared. *These are the elves who held the antidote. The ones Aedon stole from.*

"If you won't tell me voluntarily, I'll draw it from you!" The female elf thrust a clawed hand toward Harper. An invisible force ripped Brand's knife from her hands. It spun through the air and landed far from her reach with a clang upon the pebbles. Before she could react, the elf's attention returned to her, and pain shot through her like lightning.

Harper screamed, unable to hold it in. It was like nothing she had felt before. An unbearable burn that seared through her. A moment later, it passed. She slumped to the ground as all strength in her body left with it.

"Tell us where the thief is." The she-elf advanced.

Harper bared her teeth. If they thought she would tell them before, that was no way to persuade her. "Go to hell!" As the next wave of pain hit her, she tensed, screeching through gritted teeth as it wracked her body with great shudders, the power making her limbs involuntarily dance. It sent her crumbling to her knees.

"Tell me!" the she-elf screeched.

Her companion took over. Using invisible hands of magic, he lifted Harper from the ground and slammed her against the wall of rock. Its rough grit dug through the thin overshirt. All the air was knocked from her body and she gasped for breath. Her chest burned as she slid down. He loomed over her, casting his bow aside. One strong hand hauled her up by the neck with ease and shoved her against the rock, whilst the other pressed the gleaming, sharp point of an arrow into her throat.

"I suggest you tell my sister what she wishes to know," he said in a low, even voice. His eyes ensnared her. They were liquid amber, but cold and entirely devoid of emotion. "It will not go well for you if you resist."

Harper spat into his face. He quickly masked the flicker of anger, but she had seen it. Despite her pain, a smugness rose. "I can't tell you what I don't know," she said, enunciating every word with the small amount of breath she had.

"Enough! Get out of the way!" His sister bodily pushed him aside and stood before Harper, her blade raised.

Suddenly, her eyes widened. "Unh!" she grunted in surprise, looking down at the arrowhead protruding from her collarbone.

Her companion whirled around. As Harper slumped to the ground, fading in and out of consciousness, familiar silhouettes loomed on the other side of the stream. Relief flooded her.

A roar she barely recognised, far fiercer than any she had ever heard emanate from him, washed over her as Brand's huge form launched across the stream. He crashed into the she-elf, who went down screeching. Aedon, Ragnar, and Erika targeted her companion. Aedon shot a hail of arrows at the elf, who leapt out of the way. Not fast enough to avoid Erika— she barrelled into him and sent him crashing into the cliff face.

Ragnar rushed to Harper's aid. With surprising strength, he hauled her to her feet and dragged her away, supporting her body with his. Behind them, the screams of the she-elf receded as she dashed into the forest with rivulets of blood pouring from her whilst Erika gave furious chase. The male elf was lost in a clash of metal as he engaged with Brand, and she presumed Aedon. Ragnar rushed her back to camp, setting her down by the fire.

"Harper, can you hear me?" His voice faded in and out. "Harper?"

It hurt too much. Harper's eyes closed as she sighed, and everything faded into blackness.

37

HARPER

ool, wet fabric grazed across Harper's cheek. Then the other. Her forehead. She clung to it, ascending into the light where the pain met her. Harper groaned.

"Wake up, Harper." Aedon. She groaned again. Her lungs felt like they were on fire, and her chest burned as she tried to inhale. "Harper, you're safe." Aedon's reassuring voice swam to her in the depths. She forced her eyes open just a crack. Blue skies. Rocky overhang. Aedon hovering above her.

"I'm alive," she rasped, lifting a hand from the rough, cold rocks to rest on her stomach, though her body screamed at the effort it cost—after Erika's beasting the previous night, she hurt from head to toe, and every part of her felt weak. "What happened?"

Aedon's brows furrowed. "I was hoping you could help us on that count. It seems we are still being tracked. The elves of Tir-na-Alathea do not give up their secrets easily."

"Did you expect anything less?" Brand's voice held a bite of anger.

"No, I suppose not."

"We're sorry you paid the price for our venture, Harper," Brand said more gently. "What happened?"

She recounted everything in as few words as possible. Her throat was raw and her voice hoarse after the screaming. When she finished and fell into silence, the group shared troubled glances.

"We grew complacent," Erika said. "Neither distance nor time means anything to an elf. They will track us for as long as it takes."

"Then we need to do more to cover our tracks," Brand growled.

"Consider me on it," Aedon said. "I'll make sure there's no trace of us when we leave here. They shall not find us again so easily."

"They should not have found us so easily the first time," Ragnar said. His quiet disappointment bit into Aedon, who flinched.

"It's my fault. I was lax. It won't happen again. I'm sorry, Harper," he whispered. His fingers rested gently on hers for a moment, then withdrew.

Brand stirred. "Harper, we need to move on as soon as possible. Now they know we're in the area, it's not safe. Can you sit up?"

Harper winced and groaned as she tried. Her entire body felt broken. Hands supported her—Ragnar and, to her surprise, Erika—until she sat upright.

"I didn't even get a chance to fight. I let you down," she said to Erika. Now the nomad would despise her even more.

Erika blinked in surprise. "Are you kidding? That you

managed to fend off two elves of Tir-na-Alathea at all, let alone unarmed, is a miracle. You ought to be dead."

"You did well, Harper." Brand's monstrous hand patted her shoulder gently. He turned to Aedon. "You cover our trail —*properly*—and I'll fly patrol up ahead. Ragnar and Erika can travel with Harper."

They helped Harper stand, but she swayed on her feet. All strength and energy had been drained from her. She hated to admit it to herself, but she wasn't in any fit state to trek.

"We're going to struggle today, I fear," said Ragnar as he offered more of his support to Harper with a hand around her waist.

"Then I'll carry her with me. I think that's easiest for us all." Brand glanced around the group, but no objections came. He nodded. "It's settled. Harper, you'll be with me. Ragnar and Erika on the ground, and Aedon bringing up the rear. Who carries the cure today?"

"Harper should," said Ragnar. "She's earned it." Erika nodded, to Harper's surprise.

"Guard this with your life." Aedon slipped the small glass vial from inside his top, where it had been tucked close to his chest, and handed it to Harper. She took it reverently, admiring the small, crystal bottle with its stopper containing the precious liquid within. The lump in her throat now had nothing to do with the hoarseness of her voice. She clutched the vial close, its surface cool on her palm, before tucking it into the depths of her clothing. "I will."

"She—and it—will be safe with me," Brand said, and he held out a giant hand to Harper. She took it, grateful for his solid weight to hold her up, for her legs still shook and every part of her body hurt. "Right. We have no reason to delay. Let's go."

"Going anywhere nice?" a familiar voice drawled. One that sent Harper's heart into a frenzy.

Dimitrius stood far too close for comfort, in yet another immaculate suit as dark as night, his hands in his pockets and his smooth coiffed hair shining in the morning sun. Those violet eyes were only for her, and the world fell away as she met them with a stare. She raised her chin defiantly, forcing her screaming body to draw up tall and proud. She would not show him one ounce of weakness.

Brand swept Harper behind him as Erika drew her blade and Ragnar hefted his axe from his belt.

"You sent them?" Aedon launched an assault of magic. His barrage disappeared into nothingness. Dimitrius did not so much as twitch. Again and again, Aedon sent everything he had, until Harper's ears rang and black spots danced across her vision from the volume of magic that crackled and blasted across the space. But his assaults vanished each and every time.

Harper's stomach swooped. She had thought Aedon powerful, but Dimitrius was incomparably more so. Aedon's shoulders drooped, heaving with each ragged breath—yet their opponent did not even appear slightly winded. Still, his violet eyes stared them down—and a jolt of something intangible zinged through her as his gaze grazed hers for the barest second. She drew her own knife with a shaking hand, hopeless as it felt against his. Not to mention her own battered body could barely lift the knife, let alone wield it.

"Are you quite done?" Dimitrius narrowed his eyes at Aedon. "Or do I need to teach you a lesson?" Blue lightning bloomed in his hands.

DIMITRI

Aedon bared his teeth in a feral snarl. *Skulk back to your pack*, Dimitri thought, watching his retreat. "Now, who did I send?"

"You well know," spat Aedon.

"Ah, you mean the two I saw scurrying away with their tails between their legs?" Dimitri cocked his head. "What are two elves of Tir-na-Alathea doing here, chasing you? And why do you think *I* am involved?"

Aedon glared at him, but did not answer.

Dimitri shrugged. "Fine. Have your secrets," he said mockingly, even though his mind was alight with wonder and worry. Did they know of the Dragonheart? He could not afford for them to. Then he recalled a report from the forest about a recent theft of one of their secretive elixirs—and the pieces clicked together.

"I hope what you took from them was worth it." He smirked, but relief washed away the edge of nausea. There was no way for the elves of Tir-na-Alathea to know what he had accidentally sent into Aedon's hands—

but doubt still lurked. Could he afford to take that chance? He already knew the answer. It changed everything.

They glared at him in stony silence. He shrugged off their wariness, circling them like a predator. They shifted with him as he moved, their defences flowing like water, always keeping the strange girl in the centre of their eddies. He did not need his other senses to know she carried what he sought. He could feel it, temptingly close. And, their actions betrayed them.

"I know what you carry." His gaze flicked to Harper's, and he gave her a coy smile, showing one of his sharp canines. She returned it with a momentary widening of her eyes, quickly masked by a snarl.

He sent his magic to sense her. She felt strange. She was magical, that was certain, but hers was weak, suppressed deep within her. He cocked his head. She seemed foreign. Her scent was other, yet her blood was elven and sang to his own, calling him closer, drawing him in. They were kin, as all elves were. How could she be elfkind, yet not? He had never met anyone like her.

When none of them replied, Dimitri suppressed a sigh. Just as he did not wish to reveal his personal interest in the Dragonheart, they did not wish to reveal they had it. He continued to circle them, keeping them constantly on guard and shifting. "The king knows his Dragonheart is missing and he wants it back," he said casually, admiring the surroundings as though he strolled through the beautiful manicured gardens of the palace. Meanwhile, he noted with pleasure their shock and suspicion that he knew what they carried. Suspicion toward him, and perhaps toward Harper, as their emotions roiled over one another in quick succession.

"You can give it to me now, and I will leave you to your miserable existences, or I shall take it from you."

He felt Aedon's magic well up before he saw the elf's crackling palms. Aedon's companions raised their own weapons, and even the girl wielded a knife.

Dimitri laughed. "Are you going to carve me up like a roasted dinner?" he asked Harper sweetly, then leapt back as they attacked as one.

Aedon's fireballs scorched the earth where he had stood. Any trace of mirth dropped from Dimitri's face. *Now it is my turn.* He straightened his collar and glared at them. They froze, gasping as his vice-like grip of magic tightened around them, just as Saradon had done to him.

"I can crush you without a second thought. I suggest you not be so foolish next time." After a few moments, he released them. "There. See?" he added mockingly. "That's not so hard. I'm not a monster. I'll give you a little time to decide." *Whilst I eliminate the competition,* he thought to himself, wondering where the Tir-na-Alathean elves were. "I'll be back."

Dimitri faded into the void, watching with glee as their eyes widened at the sight of him vanishing into nothingness. Once he was gone, he raced away quicker than a flash of lightning, seeking a different trail—that of the Tir-na-Alathean elves.

He was almost certain they sought something different from Aedon and his outlaws, but Dimitri had to be certain. The last thing he needed was the wood elves stumbling onto his Dragonheart. They would take it into the living forest for their queen, never to be seen again. If that happened, his hopes—now more alight than ever—of crushing King Toroth, his father, and the entire blasted establishment of Pelenor would be dashed.

It was a complication he did not need, but whilst the stone lay hidden from Toroth, and other prying eyes, Dimitri would eliminate the only potential leak of information. It would be worth it to know he would be secure in the knowledge only he would have the stone's location.

He found the wood elves not far away, nursing their wounds. Dimitri sundered their cocoon of protective magic. They were on their feet at once, casting around for the source that had broken their barrier. As they espied him, their welling attack turned into a rush of defences. Good. They knew who he was.

"What would two wood elves of Tir-na-Alathea be doing so very far from home, on a miserable day such as this?" he asked, keeping his tone light. They would know he meant business. Anyone who knew of his reputation did. As he felt their defences rising, he flicked his finger, wiping them out. "There's no need for that. It's a pointless waste of energy."

Despite his words, their defences began rebuilding once again. Dimitri clenched his jaw. "Fine. You brought this on yourselves." He had not decided how to deal with them. That depended on what they knew. He took a deep breath and shattered open their minds, walking through centuries of memories without breaking a single bead of sweat. He did not need the previous centuries. They would make for interesting perusal on another day perhaps.

He saw their Queen's recent anger at the theft of some *aleilah* potion from her stockpile. Their own dogged attempts—all failures—to waylay the elf, Aedon, and his companions to recover it. Their latest skirmish. Dimitri raised an eyebrow at the bravery of Harper, despite her naïveté. She had no training, magical or otherwise. It was an unforgivable weakness for an elf, but he had already drawn the conclusion she was no normal elf. He stilled as he found the memories he needed most. Their knowledge of Aedon, their meeting with Harper, and their sudden realisation that she carried a magic more powerful than that which they sought.

They knew. His own blood sang with the first tinge of fear. He saw their desire for the Dragonheart's powerful magic. Their wishes to take it for themselves—for their Queen. Dimitri listened to their conversations through their memories.

"It could be useful to her," the male said.

"It is an object of great power. She will desire it whether it be useful or not," his sister remarked, then raised an eyebrow. "What of the girl?"

The male elf paced back and forth. "She feels... strange. Great power resides in her, yet she does not know how to use it. I suspect she does not even sense it."

"A curiosity."

"Yes, quite."

"The queen enjoys curiosities."

"You think we ought to take her and the aleilah, sister?"

"Precisely. She carries something of great power that the queen would no doubt covet, perhaps punishing us if we return without it. And the girl, well... She might be of use or interest to the queen. If not..." She let the sentence hang in the air.

Dimitri knew the girl would be disposed of, or become a toy at the leisure of the queen. It was not uncommon. The queen liked collecting pets.

The he-elf smiled. "We shall bide our time and strike them when she, and whatever she carries, is most vulnerable."

And indeed they had. The elves stilled as Dimitri relinquished his grasp upon their minds. They knew precisely what he had seen. "Well," he said, keeping his tone conversational as he shoved his hands deep into his pockets to save them from the chilled air. "We seem to have a problem, don't we? It's wrong to steal, you know."

"Not if it's from a thief," the he-elf growled.

"Not if it's the King of Pelenor's property, Ta'hiir of the Forest," Dimitri fired back.

The elf glared at him with defiance, but did not seek to attack. He knew it was futile. "Our queen does not recognise the authority of Toroth as above her own."

"Your queen can recognise whatever she likes—or not. I don't give a damn."

The she-elf took an intake of breath at the insult, puffing up before him. In a second, he had advanced upon the elf, looming over her. His hand encircled her throat and he squeezed before releasing the pressure—a warning. Not to toy with him. She bared her teeth at him—a testament to the enduring defiance of her people. If it hadn't annoyed him so much, he would have admired her pluck.

"I want the king's property back, and you shall not stand in my way. We can do this amicably or not. It's your choice." His words were cool, but Dimitri's mind raced. They were elves under the protection of the Queen of the Living Forest, the realm of Tir-na-Alathea. Not an enemy to Pelenor, and a powerful one to anger. He could not kill these elves. Not if he wished to avoid war. Like a game of *chatura*, this required one precise move—anything else would result in the downfall of his carefully arranged plans.

"The thief is fair game." Ta'hiir gripped the handle of his bow, his knuckles white. Dimitri could see how his fingers twitched, itching to nock an arrow to the string.

"I do not care about your *aleilah*, elf. But what the girl carries is mine, and I don't trust you." Dimitri narrowed his eyes. No matter how he looked at it, they were a threat. Without waiting for their response, he waded back into their minds, seizing them whole. El'hari and Ta'hiir shuddered, their eyes bulging as they stood frozen. "I will take all memory of Aedon's journey from you. You never found his trail. He escaped with no trace. You are to concede defeat, and give up in your hunt for the *aleilah*. You did not see the girl or feel what she carries. You know nothing of it. You will return to your queen and make such a convincing account of your failure that she will concede the hunt. You will bear your punishment."

Dimitri gave his instructions in a voice of steel, crushing carefully chosen memories with each word. Before he surrendered their minds and bodies back to them, he gave one last instruction as he slipped into nothingness. "I was never here. You did not see me. If you fail in this, I will end you both."

39

HARPER

With Harper in his arms, Brand took to the air. She squeaked and clung to him as he leaped into the sky, though she need not have worried. Brand's arms did not flex or waver for a second as his wings pumped powerfully, thrusting them up. She did not dare look down as the rolling land swept away.

"Won't they see us up here?" she asked, raising her voice slightly so he could hear her. *Or him.* Dimitrius's eyes still burned into her memory, though he was gone. Harper squinted against the wind rushing past them, making her eyes water, stealing the scent of Brand's leather and musk from her nose.

"No. We're to fly close to the ground, and Aedon sends us with extra protections to ensure we will not be spotted."

This was close to the ground? Harper gulped and chanced a peek down. Treetops sped past far below her feet. "I'm sorry I lost your knife."

"I found it. Don't worry." Brand paused for a moment.

"You don't need to be ashamed, you know." He glanced at her, then gazed ahead, impassive as always.

"I ought to be able to defend myself. Erika is right. I'm not good enough."

"You had one lesson, if that, before you were pitted against elves of Tir-Na-Alathea. That was an outcome nothing could have changed, Harper. It's all right to be the underdog."

It sounded as though he spoke from experience. "You can't possibly know what that's like. You're so..." Strong? Fierce? Invincible? Nothing seemed fit enough to describe how capable Brand seemed as a warrior.

"I wasn't always as I am now. I've had to learn to take care of myself. As hard as it might be to believe, fighting isn't everything. I was once the underdog, just like you. Sometimes there are other strengths just as important."

"Such as?"

"Like today, for example. You could have given us away. I'd wager a lot of folks would have under such duress. Yet you held strong. That takes a special kind of courage. Thank you for not revealing us. Things might not have ended so well had we been taken by surprise. I respect you for that."

Harper swallowed. He *what?* It seemed impossible that a strong warrior like Brand would have respect for someone like her, especially when she felt so weak and inconsequential. That made something warm and hot well up in her chest so far it caused her throat to block—and her eyes to sting.

"You have more strength than you realise," he said, as if he could read her mind. "Physical strength is not all that is important." He fell into silence. The wind whooshed past them to the powerful drum of his wings pumping through the air.

"But it is for you now?"

"Yes, in a way. My strength counts for a lot. It helps me in combat, but it also helps *prevent* combat. It's somewhat intimidating to face an opponent of my size." She heard the smile in his voice. "That has its advantages. I don't enjoy fighting needlessly. I never did."

"But you have to."

"Sometimes, yes." Brand fell into silence, the only sound the air rushing past them and the periodic beating of his wings. "I lived with my own kind once," he finally said. "I had every privilege given to me, though I did not realise or appreciate it then. I did not fight at all, you see. I had none of these scars." He laughed mirthlessly. "I thought all anger could be tamed with words—or money. I was wrong. There are many different battlegrounds, each for a different type of engagement."

"What happened?" Harper dared to ask.

Brand did not reply immediately, then sighed. "I fell in love with the wrong Aerian. You see, there are two classes of Aerian. The differences grow from there." Brand's voice grew bitter. "*My* kind is the privileged. We command the higher positions, the more economically fortunate situations. Every advantage in life is ours, deserved or not. Our cousins have to work much harder for their share, but never are they elevated to the same levels. Even as a privileged Aerian, who took it all for granted, I could see that it was unfair." He shook his head.

Something painful bloomed in Harper's chest at his words—and the feelings underlying them.

"Her name was Nyla." He said it with such softness, so uncharacteristic for the grizzled warrior, Harper was taken aback. She strained to hear him, because his voice was so quiet the wind snatched away his words as they flew. "She was the most beautiful Eyrie inside and out that I had ever seen. I did not care that she was 'lower' than I. It did not matter. Yet my family thought differently. They were appalled by my behaviour and disowned me." His voice hardened. "It was not suitable for an Aerian of my station—of Skyrie—to fraternise with an *Eyrie*." His voice hardened.

"I was determined to prove them all wrong, that Eyries were worth as much as Skyries. That my Nyla was worth as much as any Skyrie female. I tried to give the Eyries a voice so I could live happily with my Nyla, free from judgment, from unfairness. We revolted. It failed. Nyla was killed. I was imprisoned. I escaped—I can never return."

"I'm sorry," Harper murmured, aching with sadness for him.

"It's not yours to be sorry for, but I thank you. I learned how unfair life was, regardless of what was just or right. I was determined to never be weak again, to never fail those who mattered to me. It took me many years to understand what strength was. Not just strength in body, but mental strength, strength of character. I know what it is to be the underdog. Persevere; don't lose heart. Sword fighting, or other forms of combat, may not be your forte, but you have other skills. Take Erika's frustrations with a pinch of salt. She hates that some can't protect themselves. But I see the resilience within you—you are stronger than you believe. I hope one day you see it too. I hope one day you grow into your most powerful self, so you can leave the world a better place than you found it. I'm certain you will.

"You're better than you give yourself credit for, you know. Look how you helped Ragnar with his hands. Look how you protected us today. Look at me." He chuckled. "I haven't told anyone this story in years. Keep practicing your fighting—I'll help you—and whatever else you can learn. You can always find new ways to be strong. You never know how you might grow."

"What happened to Erika?"

"That's her story to tell. It would not be right of me to share it."

Harper nodded. "Thank you."

He gave a sharp nod, returning to his gruff, taciturn self, but Harper was honoured by his confidence. Despite the pain she was in, a warm glow filled her middle. Brand was right. She was good at other things— resilient and resourceful, fair and hard-working, and she could turn her hand to whatever she needed to survive. Whether she agreed with him on the value of combat, she was not entirely sure. It surely would have helped her that morning, but still, it soothed something raw and painful in her that felt small and weak for not being able to fight. She knew that was not a path she wanted to follow.

By the end of that day, they had covered an even greater distance than the days before, spurred on by the knowledge of their hunters. Brand watched Aedon like a hawk as he laid extra protective enchantments around their camp. For the first time, Aedon's eyes were shadowed and his shoulders sagged, as if the effort of covering their tracks had taken a great deal from him on top of their encounter with Dimitrius.

It was a quiet evening. No one wanted to break the silence, each straining to hear any trace of pursuit, as futile as they all knew that would be. The elves of Tir-na-Alathea were fleet of foot and as silent as the night. Of Dimitrius…

He was worse than any other denizens of the night. Even Ragnar was subdued and did not suggest any *chatura*.

It was to be their last evening before they reached the village that had started all this—the one that had driven Aedon and his friends to steal the *aleilah*. Gentle undulations in the earth had once more sprung up into hills, and Harper saw hazy blue mountains in the distance that slowly disappeared into the darkness as the sun sank. Their camp backed into an impregnable crag soaring above them, scant shelter provided by tall trees of great girth that somehow clung onto the stony terrain. It was hard to reach and almost inhospitable. Precisely why they had chosen it.

Harper kept her thoughts to herself, but she wished they had more shelter. The cooling winds already drove into them. They were all restless that night and woke tired with frayed nerves. Even the ever friendly Ragnar was silent as he and Harper prepared breakfast. The smell of woodsmoke and livestock lingered on the stray breeze as they descended to the forested valley with one more small pass to climb. It smelled foreign after days of nothing but pine forests and nature. Harper quickened her step, as did her companions, and checked again that the small vial was still within the pocket of her cloak.

"I'll take that now," Aedon said quietly, gesturing to it. She slipped it to him. "I hope this will be enough."

"How many people are affected?" she asked.

"A dozen or so, but they ought to only need a drop each. The antidote is powerful."

Harper eyed the small vessel. It didn't look potent. In fact, it looked like nothing more than water glistening in the ornate, tear-shaped vial.

"That'll really be enough?" She wrinkled her nose.

"The elves of Tir-na-Alathea are some of the best potion

masters in all of Pelenor, perhaps even Altarea. Nothing else has worked, and this sickness needs to be cured before it spreads further. Which reminds me. You need to protect yourself." He opened the vial and dripped one single drop onto Harper's waiting tongue, before stoppering the vial again.

The liquid was almost tasteless, only having the slightest hint of sweetness. "What about everyone else?"

"Already protected," Brand replied gruffly.

"Come on now. We're almost there, and they're relying on us. We've been away long enough," said Erika.

"That we have," murmured Ragnar.

Something pricked at her intuition long before they came upon the village. Their good cheer had dissipated with the growing altitude, then the freezing fog that met them as they journeyed over the pass. It marked the end of the long reach of the elves of Tir-na-Alathea's territory, Aedon had declared, though Harper was not entirely convinced they were safe yet. The feeling amongst the rest of the group was mutual.

Brand scouted before them, leading the way, as he eased his short sword out of the scabbard at his waist. Erika skulked behind, her twin blades guarding their rear. They were silent shadows, watching, every ounce of attention sent out into the forest, seeking. Even Ragnar was more watchful. Hardly the fighter his fabled people expected, his hand was upon the handle of his knife, ready to draw it should he need to.

"I don't like this." Brand's voice was low. "Something doesn't feel right."

"It's the only pass. We have little choice," Aedon replied.

"The elves will not be here, will they?" Ragnar's voice held an edge of trepidation.

"No," said Aedon, though there was every possibility as far as Harper reckoned. El'hari and Ta'hiir were fast and ruthless. It would not be hard to set up an ambush. Ragnar's hand fussed on the handle of his axe, tapping the wood with a nervousness that leeched through the air to Harper.

The valley narrowed ahead, and high, grey stone soared into the mist and out of sight above them. Beyond the cleft, the village lay in the shelter of the far side of the pass where the valley widened once more. Between the pines, stone walls sprouted from the earth and earthen roofs blended seamlessly into the environment. At such an altitude, there was neither material for thatching nor the weather for it. It was deadly silent. A warning stroked down her spine. Erika and Brand wordlessly drew closer.

Harper's neck tingled with premonition and wariness. "Where is everyone?" she whispered, unwilling to break the heavy silence. Not even birds sang. Even the rustle of the trees had stilled, as if the air knew something was amiss too.

"Weapons out," Brand's command was barely more than a growl. He drew his sword and lowered into a fighting stance, casting his gaze warily around them as he surveyed their surroundings.

Harper fingered Brand's knife and pulled it from her belt, holding it before her, though she felt more like a liability than an asset. Erika moved to the other side of the group to flank them. Aedon drew his long, slim blade with a whisper. Ragnar's hand moved from his knife to the haft of his axe. He hefted it from his belt to hold it, two-handed, in front of his torso, ready, waiting. Brand stalked to the front. "Move in."

40

AEDON

Aedon sent his awareness out into the forest. Nothing. The trees were a light of life against the black of the rocks surrounding them. And yet—there. A pulse. The faintest glow of life dotted around them. In the huts, he realised. Aedon's heart beat quicker and his hand tightened on his weapon, ready to meet the threat, before his grip slackened again.

"There are people here, but they are—" *Ill? Dying?* He did not know. "They need help." Aedon sheathed his weapon and rushed toward the dwellings.

"Wait." Brand's command rang through the cold air. He pointed toward the doors. They had been marked with a giant "X" across the weathered, greying wood. It had already darkened and dried. As Brand leaned closer and touched it carefully, little black flecks flaked off. "Plague."

Every door had been painted thusly. Aedon drew close, touching the markings. When it came off on his fingers, he thoughtfully rubbed it between his finger and thumb, holding it close to his nose and sniffing. "Ash and mud."

"It's the same here, Aedon. What does it mean?" Brand looked on edge as he circled, his back toward the group, casting all his attention outward for some sign of life.

"It means it is catching… and that we might be too late." His shoulders slumped for a moment, but only a moment. "We need to search the village from top to bottom. There may be survivors here."

"They're hiding," said Erika in a low voice. She pointed at a window. A shutter swayed, but there was no wind to move it.

Brand strode over and threw open the door, his weapon ready. He had to stoop in order to enter the small dwelling, then he backed out, such little room was there inside. "One female. Alive, but weak. And most definitely ill. Aedon, you need to see this."

Aedon rushed over. Harper followed. It was a dank hovel, with a bare earth floor, and a bed made of furs and rough, woven cloth. The pallet was lumpy. He realised with a start that not one, but three lay within the folds of the blankets.

It was dark, the only light entering through the doorway. Cold ash lay in the small hearth. A woman's small frame was barely noticeable under the pile of blankets covering her, and her children less so, curled into her sides. Her gaunt face loomed in the shadows as Aedon approached. Her eyelids fluttered weakly. Without touching her, he knew she burned up with fever. He felt it raging through his blood, his entire body wanting to recoil. The children's almost lifeless faces were pale ghosts in the dark as they stirred a little. Ragnar followed Aedon in. Taking his pack from his shoulders, he rummaged through it for medicinal supplies.

"They don't need those," Aedon said softly. "Open your mouths. I have the antidote."

They offered themselves to him like chicks in a nest

waiting to be fed, and he carefully gave each of them just one drop of the precious liquid. "Rest. You'll feel better tomorrow," he said before turning away. "Ragnar and Harper, fetch water. Erika, Brand, if it is as I fear, then the rest of the village is also like this, and those unaffected have fled." He did not voice aloud the thought that filled his stomach with lead. *And we do not have enough aleilah to treat them all.*

Harper and Ragnar collected water from the village well as everyone else swept the village until every abode had been checked. Harper, Ragnar, and Aedon worked long into the night, whilst Brand and Erika stood guard, watching either end of the village in the fog and eerie silence. Ragnar's skills were utterly tested as he worked until his eyes reddened with tiredness, Harper helped to make their patients comfortable, and Aedon used every fibre of magic he had until fatigue dragged his limbs down. Still, they could not turn the tide of the fever raging through the victims who were left.

That evening, the five huddled around a fire that was too small to truly warm them. All were stiff and numb with cold.

"There's only one cure I know," Aedon said to the others. He pulled the stoppered vial from his breast.

"There's not enough," Ragnar said dully.

"I know," Aedon replied. He rubbed his creased brow with a hand. "It's spread so quickly. We don't have enough to cure everyone, and there's nothing else we can do to help them. Damn. I should have stayed. I should have tried to get *more.*"

"Don't blame yourself," Brand said. "That you managed to procure any *aleilah* at all is a miracle. Anyone who receives it will be grateful."

"But we don't have enough," whispered Aedon. "How do we choose who receives it and who…" He trailed off, but he did not need to finish. They all knew what he did not dare say.

"Women and children first," Ragnar said. "As always. If there is any left, the men may partake."

"There is not even enough for that." Aedon looked into the small vial. Somehow, it seemed tinier and emptier than before, as though it carried the last dregs and nothing more.

"Then the young ones first," said Ragnar, hanging his head in sadness.

Erika stirred. "We can still make them comfortable."

"We need to tend to everyone." Aedon could not deny the reality of the situation—but he would not give up whilst there was still something to be done. "No doubt they are all in a state of severe weakness and will not eat or drink properly. Brand, help me distribute the water. Harper, can you and Ragnar look around, see if there is any food to be had in the houses? Erika, see what bounty the forest holds. Then we can decide who is most in need of the cure."

Ragnar clapped Aedon on the back. "Don't be hard on yourself, brother. It's not your fault."

Aedon grimaced. That was easier said than done. Every person he met gazed at him with such hope in their eyes— and he saw the moment it guttered out when they realised he had failed them. Every time, it was a punch to his gut. A personal failure. Not one death was acceptable. Not one. And there were already three fresh graves marked with cairns at the edge of the village since they had left. He could not bear to ask who they belonged to.

They had little time to dally. Whilst Aedon and Brand returned to the dwellings, Harper, Ragnar, and Erika set about collecting firewood and anything edible, distributing it amongst those who were ill and setting fires in hearths to warm the cold homes through.

The young woman Aedon had tended first woke before the others. "Thank you," she said weakly, her face drawn and her pallor grey. "It burns through my blood. I feel it even now, but by whatever grace you have given me, I sense it slipping away."

"What happened?" Aedon dared to ask. He held a beaker filled with cold, fresh mountain water close to her lips so she could take a sip.

"We do not know. When you came, only a few were sick, and it burned slowly through them—like you, we thought we had time when you and our healer could not mend them, for their condition worsened slowly, and so few were affected. When you had departed to find a cure, we thought we were safe, but it spread so swiftly and we could do nought to stop it. Old, young, fit, and healthy. It did not discriminate. Most fled to protect themselves. The rest of us..." She sagged. "When you did not return, we asked them to leave us behind."

Heaviness sat upon Aedon's chest as a fierce ache burned there. They had been gone *weeks*. All the while, these people had suffered. And some had died. He felt personally responsible. He should have been better. Faster. Returned sooner. "Where did they go?"

"Down the pass, into the next village."

"We will send them back to you."

Her eyes lit up with burning fear. "There's no risk to them?"

Aedon hesitated, uncertain. "No. You have no sickness in you any longer. Burn everything you can to purify the area. If there are any of magical blood here, set new wards against sickness upon your households. It should suffice to halt the spread for now. Confine those still sick to their homes. Only those who have weathered this illness should have contact with them to sustain their care."

Brand immediately flew to the village where the others had fled, soon coming back with word they would return with the coming dawn. Aedon bid their patient farewell.

"I owe you a life-debt, Aedon Lindhir Riel of House Felrian," she said formally, using his full title.

"I hope to never call upon it. Be well."

HARPER

That evening, Harper sat beside the campfire with the rest of them, just outside the village. Her body ached from a day of labour and activity, and she longed to cleanse the smell of smoke and sickness from her, but there was nothing to wash with. She rubbed a hand across the back of her neck, grimacing at how clogged with dirt and sweat it felt.

"You all right there, Aedon?" Brand's deep voice broke the silence. Harper watched her companions. Aedon was uncharacteristically quiet that night.

"No—how could I be? *Look* at what's happened here." He shook his head. "We were gone weeks."

"We couldn't have done it any faster," Brand replied. "You know that."

"I... there could have been a way. Somehow. We should have got horses. Something." He dragged a hand through his hair, and in the flickering firelight, shadows yawned under his eyes. The anguish in his voice was clear, and Harper softened, longing to comfort him, but she did not know how.

She did not see a thief or a criminal anymore. Now she saw someone who just wanted to help, who punished himself for failing.

"You know as well as I that that was not an option. Nowhere we passed had horses, for one," Brand replied.

Erika added firmly, "There's nothing we could have done. Don't beat yourself up—use your energy to help them now. That's all we can do."

"Hhmph." Aedon did not reply. He drew his knees up and rested his crossed arms upon them, and his chin on top, staring into the flames. He did not invite further conversation. Their persuasion would not help change his mind, Harper surmised. The guilt he wore was heavier than that.

"You did a good job today, Harper," Ragnar said as he offered her slightly stale bread from the village, pressed upon them by a grateful patient. A luxury.

"Thank you," Harper murmured, ducking her head and hiding behind a curtain of tangled hair. Praise was not something she knew how to receive. She'd just done her best helping Ragnar tend to the villagers, that was all. Anyone would have done the same in her position.

"She has a knack for putting people at ease." Brand took his share of the loaf, and gave her a tired smile.

"That she does," Ragnar replied. "Mighty glad was I for her help today."

Harper coloured. "I just did what felt right."

"The world needs more of that," Ragnar said around a mouthful of crumbs and smoked meat.

They ate as night fell around them, but the forest was still and silent. Brand broke the silence first. "I don't like it here. Too quiet."

"It's like the forest knows. The creatures give this place a wide berth," Erika said, glancing warily around her. Harper noticed how neither of them had settled down, each alert.

"It does," said Aedon softly. "The very magic of the plants and animals is tainted here. It makes me feel nauseous, this disease on the air."

"Is that what happened when Saradon cursed Pelenor?" Harper asked. The tale he had spun to her in a similarly dark night preyed on her mind when the sun set now. In her story book, such tales had seemed impossible to be true, but now? Now, she wasn't sure what was fact or fiction.

"Yes. The earth, the plants, the creatures were left untainted, but even so, such darkness resonates. Magic is as much a part of this land as the people are."

"What could cause it?" Erika asked. There was a bite of another unsaid question to her tone that Harper could not fathom.

Aedon gave Erika a long, slow look. "I do not believe it to be Saradon or dark magic, if that is your meaning. He's long dead, as you said. Nothing more than a tale to scare children at night. This is but a pale imitation of the blight he left upon the land, and no doubt natural in cause."

He shrugged and spread his arms wide. "We have no idea what brings this sickness, but we will do our best to contain it." He glanced at the tiny vial. Harper knew what he was thinking. That it could not be done with such a limited quantity of the cure.

"What can be done?" Ragnar asked, stroking his beard. The beads holding together his plaited braids clinked together gently.

"Can we not get more of the cure? Or even make more?" Harper asked, desperately wishing she had a solution.

Aedon shook his head sadly. "I'm afraid not. Perhaps the elves of Tir-na-Alathea have a way, but if they do, they have not shared it, and are not likely to. Everything comes at a price with them. If this has spread so fast already..." He trailed off.

She waited for him to continue.

"We can still help plenty," he said quietly.

"Perhaps not enough, though. What else can be done?" Ragnar turned back to his cooking, because he knew the answer. *Nothing.* Erika did not reply at all.

When Aedon stilled, the others turned to him.

"Are you all right?" Brand raised an eyebrow. It was unusual for Aedon to be quiet or motionless. Both meant he was entirely out of sorts.

"We need to make more—or rather, make this spread further," Aedon said.

"I beg your pardon?" Ragnar leaned forward.

Aedon shook the tiny vial at them. Erika hissed and dove to catch it, lest he drop it into the fire, but he snatched it back and clutched it to his chest. "I believe there's a way we can make more."

"I don't follow," said Erika. "I thought the whole point of taking this from the wood elves was because we *couldn't* make any?"

"How? How is it done?" Brand asked.

Supper was forgotten as their attention fixed upon Aedon. "No, you're correct. We couldn't make it—but we can make *more.* There's a difference, I promise. There are certain substances which can be used to make potions more potent, so you can use smaller doses or even dilute them. They're rare, of course, and pricey, but they exist. There's no reason it wouldn't work."

"Are you certain?" Brand pressed him.

The light faded from Ragnar's eyes. "If you're wrong and the potion is spoiled, they'll all die."

Aedon faltered, but only for a moment. "Course I'm sure. That's what we need to do."

"What can be used, and where do we find it?" Erika's dagger and whetstone sat forgotten in her lap.

"Wait," Ragnar said before he could reply. "Dragonhearts," he said slowly. "Yes?" He looked to Aedon.

"Precisely." Aedon's grin widened. Harper stilled. That lump nestled in her clothing dug into her. A Dragonheart?

"Hmm?" said Erika. Brand rustled his wings and cocked his head, but stayed silent, dark eyes evaluating Aedon.

Aedon gestured to Ragnar. "You know the lore then?"

Ragnar inclined his head. His voice took on a grave cadence as he recited an obscure passage. "The Heart of Dragons is a substance most potent. A crystalline structure, hued and jagged as the dragon it comes from, contains such magics as are yet misunderstood. The Heart of Dragons may affect potions or incantations in many different ways, most notably lending the strength of the dragon to the magics performed."

"Thank you, oh wise one," Aedon said, a hint of fond mockery in his tone. "Ragnar is quite right. Dragonhearts are incredibly potent. Part blood and flesh, but part magic and spell, too. The very essence of a dragon is captured. They're beautiful. They shine with iridescence and their own inner fire. Almost as if the dragon isn't truly gone." Aedon stared into the flames.

"Do you mean their *literal* heart?" interjected Brand, narrowing his eyes.

Aedon winced. "I do mean the literal heart. You won't be able to obtain one from a living dragon, of course." He swallowed. "But they can be harvested from a dead one."

Brand's face softened and he nodded to the elf, a sympathetic grimace on his face that Harper didn't understand.

Aedon smiled half-heartedly in return. "They're very rare. I'm sad to say the King of Pelenor stockpiles dragons, alive and dead."

Erika scoffed. "What man thinks he can own a dragon?"

"The king believes he can own *every* dragon, as you well know." Aedon pursed his lips. "So he also considers Dragonhearts to belong to him. He never allows them to have final rest, as befits them. They are *impossible* to get ahold of. Except," said Aedon delicately, "we have one right in our midst." As one, Aedon, Brand, Erika and Ragnar turned to Harper and affixed her under their scrutiny.

"You want my Dragonheart," said Harper, and now her hand did wind into her garments to touch the rough, hard surface of the Dragonheart.

"Yes," said Aedon quietly.

Harper's hand trembled, and she swallowed audibly. How did she feel about that? The Dragonheart was her pass to freedom—her only opportunity to return home to Caledan.

"There's just one problem."

Harper's attention snapped to Aedon, and her breath stalled.

Ragnar groaned. "You don't know how it's done."

"No." Aedon admitted, biting his lip. "Not a clue. That knowledge is beyond anything I learned in Tournai. The answers we seek, however, are there. I have no doubt. The royal archives are famed for their comprehensiveness. To understand how to use a Dragonheart to create more of this life-saving potion, that is where we must go."

Harper felt nauseous. Everything she had set her sights on—a trip to the royal court, where she could use the Dragonheart to leverage her return home—was in jeopardy, because now, her companions wanted, *needed*, that prize for their own ends. And it could not fulfil both.

There were four of them. One of her. They were highly trained—and magical. She was… she pushed that thought away, because the answer that floated to her was viciously unkind. *Useless*. Would they try to take it by force if she did not want to give it? Her hand grasped the Dragonheart so tightly under the folds of her cloak that pain bit into her palm. She couldn't breathe.

"Well, there's no chance of getting it overnight," said Brand, his voice calm, unaware of her spiralling thoughts. "What's to be done about this village? We must stop the sickness spreading amongst the people."

"Nothing that I know," said Aedon, dragging his hands through his already messy hair. "We don't have enough cure to make everyone immune. We're going to have to choose, or let the villagers choose, who to save immediately and who must wait for our return."

"I agree," said Brand. "If there's a chance of some kind of cure, even if it'll be nigh on impossible to get, we have to try. If we don't, there'll be a lot more in the same position. We promised these people we would help."

"Let it be done then," Aedon said with a heavy sigh. "At first light, we'll wake everyone and the decision shall be made, then we'll leave for the capital. We need the knowledge of the archives to have any hope of making this potion spread further."

Erika groaned. "I think dealing with the Tir-na-Alathean elves would be easier than this."

Aedon answered, his voice muffled as he placed his head in his hands. "What other choice do we have?"

"We're going to the royal city?" Harper asked, taking a shuddering breath.

Aedon looked up at her. "It looks like you got your wish after all. We're going to Tournai." He made no mention of the

Dragonheart, but Harper was certain the same thoughts were already running through their heads. Surely they had to have already conceived of taking it from her too?

A frisson flickered through Harper at the potential—she was closer, perhaps, than she had yet been at finding a way back to Caledan. Yet, the threat lingered. Her new companions needed her Dragonheart—for a purpose far more noble than her own. Guilt and worry tangled within her.

42

HARPER

The next morning, the hushed villagers assembled, and Aedon dealt them their predicament. Too many for a limited cure, and nothing to be done there and then about it. It left a sour feeling in Harper's stomach. Yet again, a tale of the poor suffering whilst the noble elite possessed all the wealth and resources to end it. Perhaps Pelenor was not as different to her home as she had hoped.

"You must choose, I'm afraid. I'm sorry it has come to this. We did our best, but alas, we did not realise this would spread so quickly. We'll leave at once to obtain more elixir, whether we have to beg, borrow, make, or steal it. I promise, we will return. We will not forsake you in your hour of need."

Their leader stepped forward. He stood tall and proud, but Harper saw the wobble in his step and the sweat beading upon his brow as he strained to hold himself up with the aid of a cane. The others looked to him. "If that is what it takes, so be it. We are grateful for your assistance. We know the risks you have placed yourselves in to even procure such a small amount for us. Others need it more than I. I shall wait until you return."

"It may be a while, Ralkan," warned Aedon.

"We place our faith in you," Ralkan said in an even voice. Even though he put on a brave face, Harper saw how his shoulders sagged. "You did not fail us once, and I'm sure you will not fail us now."

"Who shall take the cure?" Aedon asked, casting his gaze about those assembled.

Ralkan pointed at a child. "Him. Children first." The villagers nodded, muttering and pushing their young forward.

"Form a line," Aedon called. "One at a time."

They trudged forward, each offering their upturned faces to him as he carefully dripped one drop of the cure on each of their tongues. The women stepped forward next, youngest to oldest, until the vial was empty save for three, last drops. That which they could not afford to give, for it would be the only way to secure more.

"No more," Aedon said, slipping the vial inside his breast pocket once more. "I'm sorry." Half the women remained, and all the menfolk. But no one glared at him. With wondrous expressions and a light in their eyes, the villagers surrounded their young, who already seemed to have a little more spring in their step.

"I can feel it. Magic," Ralkan said hoarsely.

"It'll take a little while, but they will recover. Now, keep to yourselves. Do not stray from the village. Woe betide that this should spread," Aedon warned. "We'll return as soon as we may."

"Dragon's speed to you," Ralkan said.

"You're in a good mood today, aren't you?" Aedon grinned at Harper. He had lightened in spirits since they had left the village earlier, as though he had left his sorrow behind. Harper was glad to be away from the place too. It had been a draining experience to see such hopelessness. He had regained some of the spring in his step and twinkle in his eye. She knew he would be distracted by the thought of a new adventure, though she suspected mostly because of the illicit nature of it.

"I'm looking forward to seeing Tournai. Dragons, magic, and the king, and all." It was enough distraction from her sore, throbbing feet to wonder at what lay ahead. And easier to distract herself with what was to come, not what they had left.

Aedon shot her a sideways glance. "You might not see the king, you know. He's not the type to wander around the streets of Tournai. I don't know any king who does."

"Well, then, I'll go to him."

"And what? Receive his blessing and his help to return to Caledan?"

"Yes." She could see it now. Kneeling in a grand hall before a throne. The king would sit upon it, regally benevolent. His face shadowed. Perhaps he would have a beard. A kind smile, too, and a grace beyond anything she had seen. He would be exceptionally grateful for her gifted Dragonheart—and only too happy to return her to Caledan and send aid to the village. Nothing like the miserly and mean lord of her lands only seen from afar on feast days in the town. She frowned. Somehow, the image of the noble king blurred into the image of the Lord Denholme, greed and anger marring his stern visage.

"What then? You'll return to your old life?" Aedon interrupted her thoughts.

Harper stilled. She had only thought about returning—not what might come after.

"What is it?" Aedon pressed, his hand brushing her arm.

Not able to bear his touch, she surged away as though he had stung her. Guilt and longing warred within her—the Dragonheart was her way home. *Hers.* Whether it could save lives or not was irrelevant—she owed nothing to anyone. She'd always taken care of herself. No one save Betta had ever looked out for her. But, no matter how many times she told herself that, guilt seethed sourly inside her. "I don't want to go back to that life," she admitted. "I have to return, though. At least to Caledan. What else do I know? Betta needs me."

"What if you didn't have to return? What would you do?" He stood closer now. His hand dropped away.

Harper met his eyes. "I'd… travel, I suppose. Find a new home. Adventure. I'd find a way."

Aedon cocked an eyebrow at her. "Oh, really? What kind of adventure?"

Emboldened, she continued. "Ever since I was a little girl, I've loved reading about and hearing tales of dragons, knights, and epic quests. I dreamed about being like the heroes in the stories. Wouldn't it be amazing?"

"Hmm." He gestured around. "Is this adventure not grand enough for you?"

Harper laughed. "I suppose this is an adventure of sorts. I've always imagined becoming a dragon-rider or something grand, like the old tales of *Ulric and the Dragon.*"

"Hmm. I haven't heard of that one. I imagine that's not

impossible," Aedon said, though she could see his suppressed smile.

"Really?" she burst out, unable to help herself. *I wonder if I could trade my Dragonheart for a place with the king's dragon-riders*, she thought, all ideas of returning to her dreary life in Caledan lost for a moment.

"You *do* realise it's not that simple, right?" His lip curled and her heart sank. He was toying with her. That stung.

"How so?"

"He means that you can't just stroll up to the capital city —or the king, for that matter—and decide to be a dragon-rider," Brand said from behind them, making her turn to look at him. "It's more complex than that."

"Go on."

"Well, for starters, to become one of the Winged Kings-guard, you must have trained with the Royal Kingsguard for many years, starting your apprenticeship young. It's not unheard of for someone to be taken on at your age, but it's certainly unusual." Brand quickened his pace to draw level with her and Aedon. "Then there's the matter of being accepted for the training. You already have to be proficient in a number of physical and magical combats and arts, as well as rounded in your education."

"I can read and write," Harper replied. *Just about. Thanks to Betta.*

"Hmm. I don't know what education is like in Caledan, but for starters, I'm going to wager you haven't studied philosophy, magic, or the healing arts. Nor can you speak, read, and write Pelenori, and that is what matters here."

Harper gave him a blank look.

"Then there's the small matter of your *breed*." Brand scrunched up his face. "It's as crude as the Aerians. If you have the wrong type of blood, well, they simply won't look at you twice. You can't be a mere mortal, that's for sure."

"So I'm out," Erika said from behind them with a snort of derision.

"You cannot be another kind of race, either. So that rules myself out," said Brand.

"And me," said Ragnar. "Not that I want to ride dragons anyway."

"Nor can you be a half-breed any less pure than a half-elf. They like to keep the magic pure and strong. Half-elves or stronger are the most able-bodied for combat, and their magic runs strongest to bond with their dragons."

"I don't know about that," said Harper. "But that means there's a small chance, right? I mean, if I *am* half-elf, and they *do* take applicants my age, perhaps I can learn all those other things."

"Sure," agreed Brand affably. "Never say never. Few things are truly impossible. But Aedon is right. It isn't as easy as strolling up to the king's gates and saying 'pretty please'."

Harper sighed.

"Why are you so hung up on it?" Erika asked.

"I've dreamed of adventure all my life." What Harper did not dare admit to was that those dreams had been all that she had to keep her going on the darkest of nights. The promise of better times and the power to change her own fate. "Perhaps it's not the same here where such adventures are common for you. Besides, I want to know more about the Dragonheart, how it came to me. I don't know where else to get answers."

Erika snorted again. "If that's the case, you have a pretty messed up idea of what's important. Riding dragons and pratting around like you're better than everyone else? Pah!" She strode ahead.

Harper glared at Erika indignantly, but no one spoke to excuse her. "You all agree with her?"

"'Fraid so," said Brand.

Aedon nodded. "It's an easy choice for us. Look at what we're doing. We're on a mission to save lives. We'll make a real difference in the world."

"But so will the Winged Kingsguard, right? They must do such noble deeds far and wide!" Their scrutiny—and self assurance that she was in the wrong—made the back of her neck burn. She angled defensively, eyes darting between them.

Brand chuckled.

Harper narrowed her eyes at him. "What?"

Aedon cast his friend a glance. "I think what Brand's thinking is that it's not so clear-cut. When you're on the orders of the king, you do what you're told—not what you want to or what you think is right. You may even have to complete tasks you believe are abhorrently wrong because they're your king-given orders. Would you really be happy to do that?"

"That depends, I suppose. What's the king like?"

Aedon shrugged. "A king."

Harper waited for him to elaborate, but Brand spoke up. "Rulers often believe they're doing the right thing, whether for themselves or for their kingdom. Seldom are those things aligned. A king may often act outside the best interests of his people. A king is but one person, and people are fallible, especially when not held to account."

"That's treason," Ragnar said cheerfully.

"Your point? Join in if you feel like you're missing out," Brand retorted.

"Gladly. Kings are asses," Ragnar said loudly with relish. "Have you ever really thought it fair that gold gets spent on those grand tournaments and parades when folks out in the country are starving on a bad harvest? There's no way anyone can justify that. And being a member of the Winged Kingsguard will mean you have to stand by and watch that happen, even actively take part in it."

He continued, "Notice how the king is not rushing to cure this sickness? Why bother? He might not have heard of it, just to give him a fair chance, but if he has, what's one village to him? Hardly worth the effort, to be sure. Now, if it were his *own* household, I'm sure things would be different. Why, the Winged Kingsguard themselves would be sent the length and breadth of the kingdom to find a cure and retrieve it by any means necessary. Any price would have been paid to the elves of Tir-na-Alathea for it," Ragnar scoffed, then muttered unintelligibly to himself.

Harper turned back to Aedon and Brand.

"That pretty much covers it," said Aedon with a shrug. "It's hard to join, but if you get in, don't necessarily think you'll be off gallivanting on grand and noble quests. More likely, you'll sit, growing old and fat, until the king sends you out on some selfish behest."

"You're just bitter," Harper said, sticking her chin up and surprising even herself with her audacity. "Can't be helped that some folks have privilege and others don't. Believe me, I know the hard truth of it, but it doesn't mean those with privilege are all bad. It doesn't mean the king is bad, or that the Winged Kingsguard are all old, fat, lazy, and have no morals. I want to be a dragon-rider, or a warrior—*somebody* better than the nobody I've been all my life. Plus, I won't be like that. It's not in my nature. So at least there'll be one good one."

"Suit yourself," said Aedon, more coldly than she had

expected. He and Brand strode ahead in silence, leaving Harper to walk on her own.

"You really want to go to the King?" Aedon asked her that night as they sat around a small fire.

Harper tensed. "I do."

Erika huffed and shook her head. "Foolish," she muttered. Harper pretended she hadn't heard. Ragnar pursed his lips in silent disapproval, and Brand didn't move a muscle. Harper massaged her aching wrists. Before their evening meal—skewers of some unidentified, tangy meat—she had sparred with Brand and practiced her footwork.

"You want to do that over helping us?" Aedon pressed.

"I'm no help," Harper insisted, shrugging. "I'm an extra pair of hands and another mouth to feed. I'd be more of a hindrance than anything. I'm no good at fighting, or magic, or anything you Pelenori value, so is it really such a problem if I don't stay with you?"

When they all shared a look, Harper scowled, frustrated by the unspoken words running between them that she was not privy to.

Aedon looked at her, his expression inscrutable, until she squirmed and dropped her gaze. "I thought we had made ourselves clear, Harper, but perhaps not. Look, I think it's a really bad idea. We all do."

He reached out to grasp her hand, squeezing it, his worried gaze searching hers. Harper swallowed. She tugged away, determined not to be distracted. "But how will I return home? If it truly is the only place I can find answers and a way to return home—or a better life for myself—where else can I go? Why should I *not* go?"

"Sure, we said that," Aedon replied, slowly nodding, "but remember, we've also warned you that you will be thought of as a thief first. You don't know the punishment, do you? Trust me, it's not a quick death."

"But I'm innocent. I'll do whatever it takes to prove that, then they'll have to listen to me and send me ho—"

"They don't *have* to listen to anything you say, and they won't," Aedon snapped. "Before you can say 'Dragonheart', you'll be in irons." Aedon huffed, glancing around at the others for support. "Come on. Help me out here. She's so… *stubborn!*"

"I know someone else like that." Brand sniggered quietly, glancing at Erika.

"I'm not stupid, though," Erika said bluntly. She glared at him in return, then at Harper, her eyes full of disdain.

Harper scowled at Erika, but before she could retort, angry words jumbling thick and hot on her tongue, Ragnar spoke. "We welcomed you into our group," he said quietly. The disappointment in his voice cut to her core, quenching the anger that had arisen at Erika's coldness.

"We shared our food, our hearth, and all else we had with you—even our quest. We are grateful you assisted us in the village, but so much more is at stake. We need every pair of hands we can get, and yours have far more value than you think, even to us *Pelenori people.*"

Aedon bared his teeth at her. Harper flinched and cast her gaze aside.

"It's a betrayal," said Erika. "Now you know what's at stake, you ought to stay and help us. Do you know what an asset you would be to us with a Dragonheart?"

"Erika," Aedon said sharply, but she continued.

"It's selfish to walk away, to throw yourself on the mercy of a king who will kill you for treason and take your Dragonheart in a heartbeat. You will never see your home again if you follow that path. Only death."

"*Erika*," Aedon cut her off, then turned back to Harper. "You know we run on the wrong side of the law. I hope you've realised we're not the criminals you thought at first and that we have a critical task at hand. We need your help. We'd be honoured for you to continue with us. You might not yet have magic or be proficient at fighting, but you have other skills that are equally as valuable. Please, stay with us." She opened her mouth, but he raised his hand. "At least consider it."

Harper nodded. The group fell into an uncomfortable silence. Harper did not want to laze around the fire a moment longer. She rose and strode from camp.

"Don't stray far," Brand called after her.

She raised a hand in acknowledgment and kept walking.

What was worse? Erika's disdain? Brand's unfathomable silence? Ragnar's disappointment? Aedon's frustration? Harper did not know. And what should she do? She did not know that either. The alternative—pleading with the king to send her back to Caledan or to train her as a warrior—seemed equally ridiculous when she truly thought about it. Her heart sank.

43
AEDON

Aedon paced back and forth around the fire. Wanting to follow Harper—and not, at the same time. His blood ran hot with frustration and he saw no way out of this that ended well.

"What's to be done with her?" Brand asked gruffly, folding his muscled arms over his chest.

"We ought to take the stone and be done with her and this damned charade," said Erika with no shadow of hesitation.

"You know that's not the right thing to do," said Ragnar, giving her a baleful glare.

"Hasn't stopped us before," she snapped.

"We take from those who deserve it, or can afford it, to help those in more need. Harper does not fit that. Never have we taken from anyone who could not afford it."

Erika scoffed at him.

"He's right," Aedon said, running a hand through his tousled hair. "We cannot take it."

"Not even if she leaves?" Erika sprang to her feet, pointing after Harper. "That girl could walk away with the only way to cure those villagers—who knows how many more are infected by now—and you'd be happy to let that happen? Are you insane?"

"Erika," Aedon snapped. "For once, it's not so black and white."

"You're right. This is all kinds of shades of grey. You like her, don't you?" Erika fired at Aedon, eyes narrowing.

"That's not it," he replied steadily.

"Then what is it? You seem awfully familiar with her."

"I do what I must to protect us."

Erika scoffed. "This has strayed beyond you using your charm to keep her close, elf. Why are you so protective of *her*? She's a stranger. She means nothing to us and is standing in our way. Life would be a lot bloody easier without her right now."

Aedon winced. "Admittedly so. But I stand by what I say. We do not take from those who can ill-afford it."

"Since when have you been so vaguely charitable?"

"Erika," Brand's voice rang with warning.

"No, I don't care. We all know his past. Well, boo. We all have terrible shadows behind us. I'm not going to mince my words to spare his feelings about a girl who means *nothing* to us."

Aedon swallowed. "You're right, Erika. We all have darkness behind us, but that's all the more reason to move forward into the light. It doesn't sit well with me to take the stone from Harper. But more than that, I sense something in her. I'm not sure what. At first, I thought she could be dangerous or malevolent, but it's clear she's neither. In fact, she doesn't have the first clue about the potential she contains, nor whatever connection she has to the Mark of Saradon."

"What is it?" Ragnar asked.

"I still don't know." Aedon frowned. "Whoever she is, aside from the Dragonheart, she needs our protection. She couldn't survive here alone. At least with her close, so is the stone. Whatever her fate, her origins, her purpose, she runs with us—for now."

"Harper is a good person," said Ragnar, his glare daring Erika to argue with him. "We'll make it right." His attention turned to Aedon once more. "In the morning, once all this has blown over, we'll come clean with her and ask for her help—for the stone."

"She won't say yes," Erika said flatly. "She thinks the Dragonheart is her only way back."

"If that's the case, we'll find a way to help her," Ragnar said firmly.

Erika let out a disbelieving bark of laughter. "Good luck with that."

That night, Aedon remained too unsettled to rest. He watched Harper's still form, peaceful, her torso rising gently with each soft breath, and wondered if she slept, or whether, like him, writhing thoughts kept her awake too.

Were they doing the right thing, giving her a choice, rather than taking the Dragonheart by force? She was so determined to single-mindedly follow her desire to petition the king for a way back home to the life she so hated. He could not make sense of it. If push came to shove, they needed that Dragonheart—and he knew that he would take it by any means necessary. Despite his nefarious reputation, that rankled.

44

HARPER

Harper had returned long after dark, guided back by the slowly dying fire. Her heart hammered in her chest, afraid of what she would find, but she need not have worried. The camp slumbered. With the silent grace of a practised hunter, she slipped into her bedding with hardly a rustle, turned over, and eventually drifted off to sleep, her mind a whirring jumble of thoughts that took an age to settle.

A *crunch* of twigs snapping tore her from sleep. Harper's eyes flickered open, widening at the shadow looming over her. She shrieked and threw the cloak back, a knife already in her hand and swiping out at the shadow. The rest of the camp roused at the noise as Erika stumbled backwards to avoid the slicing blade, swearing. She lunged and grasped Harper's wrist, squeezing until Harper dropped the knife. Harper howled in pain and clutched her arm as Erika released her.

Erika flung the knife away, which landed in the fire just as Ragnar threw on a fresh log to light up the situation. As Erika dodged the sparks, firelight illuminated her.

"What are you doing?" Harper growled, springing to her feet. Her heart thundered. Neither made a move.

"What's all the commotion?" Brand's gaze flicked between them as he sat up.

"I have no idea. I woke to find *her* standing over me," said Harper. "What were you doing? Wait." Her gaze narrowed. "How dare you!" She strode forward and reached out to snatch the Dragonheart from Erika's grasp. Erika stepped back, holding it out of reach.

"Give it to me, you thief!" Harper's shaking hands balled into fists.

Aedon stepped between them. "Calm down. What's happening, Erika? Why do you have that?"

Erika raised her chin—and Harper's fury sharpened at her defiance. "I took it."

Aedon sagged, and muttered a curse under his breath. "Why?"

"Because she has it and we need it. I'm done playing games."

Harper bared her teeth, but before she could speak, Brand intervened. "Give it here." Glaring, Erika handed it to him. Brand held it out to Harper, who snatched it to her chest and backed away, scowling at Erika. "We decided that is not the way forward," Brand said flatly.

Every vein in Harper's body burned with the hurt of their betrayal. "I want to know right now what's happening. Don't think I don't see all your secret little glances and hear you muttering away. I'm not stupid." She felt it, though, for letting down her guard at all with any of them, and the hot, heavy weight of it crushed her chest and clogged her throat.

Aedon sighed. "Let's sit."

Harper scoffed. Not a chance. She and Erika remained standing at opposite sides of the crumbling embers. Tension sung through Harper as she eyed her meagre pile of belongings. She could carry it all, snatch it up in a moment if she needed to flee on foot. There was absolutely no chance she was going to sit quietly whilst Aedon and his silver tongue wheedled their way out of this. She was done being the doe-eyed, foolish girl.

Aedon ran a hand through his hair. "Harper, I'm sorry. We ought to have been more honest with you, but you must understand. You were a stranger with a wild tale who stumbled out of thin air in our hour of need. And you have what we need to make a real difference. We had no choice—but it wasn't supposed to happen like this."

"How was it supposed to happen, Aedon?" she said, hating how thick her voice was, hating the desperate edge of pain on every word. Because as much as she hated him in that moment, she hated herself more, for falling for any of it, for believing she had ever had a place amongst them, for being grateful that they had taken her in. All along, they had known the value of the treasure she held—they would have taken it one way or another, and this was just a reason to do it that made them feel better about themselves. They were criminals. It was all an act. And she was done.

He quailed under her attention, his eyes darting to meet hers and then dropping swiftly away, burned by the ferocity in her. Oh, how he squirmed—and how good it felt to make him do so. She had been so stupid. A hot lump blocked her from swallowing.

He cleared his throat. "As you know, we're on a quest to cure the sickness of a village for whom no cure could be found. We journeyed to the living forest of Tir-na-Alathea to find a potion the wood elves were famed for making, *aleilah*. It is rare, and precious, but it can cure most anything. The price was beyond a king's ransom and the elves would not barter with us, so we took it. You must understand. We never take from those who cannot afford it. The wood elves can always make more *aleilah*. They alone hold the recipe."

"I understand your motives, though I still think stealing is wrong," Harper said. "Why are you telling me what I already know? There's no way for you to spin this horse shit in your favour, Aedon."

"There's just not enough of it." He tore at his hair, and she steeled herself against his distress. He was a con artist, and she would not be fooled. "There are a few substances that can be used to make greater quantities of things like medicine without diluting them. The Dragonheart is one such substance. They are more precious than kingdoms, so rare are they, and the king keeps all that he can find locked away in his vaults.

"You can imagine our surprise, and our wonder, when you arrived in our midst at precisely the moment we needed a Dragonheart most, it seems. Yet you carry the Mark of Saradon upon your wrist, you speak the Common Tongue with an accent none of us recognise, and you—forgive me—were the strangest woman we had ever laid eyes on. Who were you? How were we to know you were as innocent as you portrayed yourself to be?"

Harper rankled, straightening with indignation. "Don't you *dare* turn this around on me."

Aedon held his hands up. "We know you now, of course. We know you to be who you say you are. But you cannot blame us for having just as much suspicion of you as you had of us."

"So what?" Harper asked, her voice quiet, yet cutting

through the night and crackle of the fire. She balled her hands into fists, because she wanted to shake him. "What were you going to do? Take us all to the capital and steal the stone from me?"

"Of course not!" Aedon said. "To be truthful, we didn't know what we were going to do. Only that we hoped we could figure something out before we arrived. We had decided to make one last plea to you tomorrow and beg for your help, even though we know you have your heart set on the Dragonheart being your way home."

Harper scoffed. "Of course you were going to tell me tomorrow. How *convenient*." She dashed her sleeve across her eyes to catch the tears prickling there. She would not let them see her feelings. "All along, all of *this*—" she gestured at them all, "—this semblance of cameraderie, was nonsense, wasn't it? You've been playing me for a fool, using me for your own ends, and I was stupid enough to fall for it! I should never have listened to any of you. You're a bunch of criminals!"

"It's not like that. We promise you," Aedon protested.

Ragnar leaned forward. "Please believe him, Harper. It's true. I swear it."

Harper turned to him, the one she had deemed most trustworthy. Ragnar's shoulders slumped, mortification etched on his face at the judgement he found waiting for him in every rage-hardened line upon her face and the unshed tears glistening. She shook her head. "How can I believe it? It's so clear now. You were going to take it from me one way or another, weren't you?"

"Yes," said Erika.

The group spun toward her, snarling. "That's not helpful, Erika," Brand growled.

"Well, we were, by hook or crook, going to get that stone, weren't we?"

"Not like that!" said Aedon, his voice a desperate, hoarse shout. "Not everything has to be so black and white." He turned to Harper. "Harper, we would not steal it from you. We would only use it if you permitted us. There is always another way. We would have found one."

Harper shook her head. Every time he said her name, with that twang of his lilting voice, it drove the knife deeper into her heart. "Empty words. Lies. I'm leaving. Don't follow me."

She felt hollow as she scooped up her belongings and stormed off into the night, having no idea where she went or how far. Her steps carried her from camp as fury and shame fuelled her onward. Once out of the circle of light and away from their presence, she allowed her hot, angry tears to spill forth.

"You stupid, *stupid* girl," she cursed herself. "You knew they were thieves, yet you trusted them because they were *kind* to you. A full belly doesn't make a friend. Damn it all!"

She had been better fed than in years past, but now she wished she had refused it all. Every mouthful of food, every kind word, every smile… It had been a way for them to get her to lower her guard a little further. When she could walk no farther, stumbling over the peat-filled hollows and heather, she sank onto a rock on the side of the hill as the purple of dawn bled into the sky on the horizon. She watched as dawn illuminated the sweeping moors.

With sinking dread, Harper realized she had no idea where she was. Nor did she have any food or resources to help her survive, not even her knife, which had sailed into the fire. Harper cursed internally—she would not crawl back to them. She could not. Wrapping her cloak around her, she stood and trudged to the top of the hill, a spark of relief lighting in her belly. Far in the distance, a city rose against the mountains. Tournai.

Behind her lay the woodlands they had camped in, and before her lay miles of undulating moors and valleys hidden from view. The river swept through a vast plain beyond, a ribbon of silver against the green. There was nothing for it but to begin walking. Her stomach growled lightly to remind her it was, in fact, breakfast time. She could not help but think wistfully of Ragnar making eggs, meat, and whatever else they could forage or hunt, finished off with a fragrant, warming tea made from local plants. She took deep shuddering breaths to ride through the surge of emotion, picked a direction, and strode on.

45

HARPER

It was not long before they caught up with her. She faintly heard her name shouted on the wind long before she saw them, but no matter how fast she strode, she could not distance herself. That resignation drove into her like a stake to the heart with every step. Eventually, just beyond a ridge, and out of the cold breeze, Harper stopped and turned, waiting, her breath coming hard and her shoulders bowed with exhaustion. She straightened nonetheless, waiting for them to appear. When they did, she stared them down without a word.

"What can I say to make this right?" Aedon asked. Ragnar huffed beside him, slightly out of breath. Brand held back, and Erika lurked behind them all, a brooding, unfriendly presence that Harper ignored.

"Nothing," Harper said coldly, though her heart ached. Ragnar and Brand seemed regretful. "Nothing you say will make me trust you again." Unconsciously, her hand clung to the inside of her cloak where the stone lay, as if seeking to reassure herself it was still there.

Aedon shook his head. "Where will you go?" he asked, gesturing to the wide vista around them.

"I'm going to Tournai to return the Dragonheart to the king in exchange for passage home." Her voice betrayed none of her swirling doubts. She was still unsure what she would ask of the king, but Aedon did not need to know it.

"He won't send you home, Harper. He'll kill you."

"What do you know? You're liars and thieves. You'll say anything to get what you want." Harper edged backwards. Her pulse ratcheted up for another reason now. They outnumbered her. Her eyes darted between them, watching for any sudden movements—ready to turn and flee if they tried to take it from her by force.

"I suppose we deserve that. We'd have to find another way." Aedon glanced up hopefully. With one look at her stony gaze, his shoulders slumped.

"So be it. We won't be travelling with you anymore then. We have our own mission to fulfill. We need to find some knowledge in the royal archives to help those villagers and they do not have time for us to waste here with *you*," said Erika. She moved off.

Harper bit down on an entirely inadequate retort. The others remained where they were. Brand pursed his lips together. "Fair winds to you. Mayhap our paths will cross again."

A part of Harper wanted to thank him for her training. The previous morning, they had sparred again. He had shown her how to block attacks and find gaps in her opponent's attack. For the first time, as clumsy as she remained, something had seemed to click. She held her tongue, her throat blocked and her eyes stinging, and held her own head high, her mouth pressed into a thin line. Brand bowed his head at her silence and ambled after Erika.

She stood in silence with Aedon and Ragnar.

"I'll miss having you around the campfire, Harper," said Ragnar with a sad smile. "Goodbye, and good luck—I mean that."

That one felt like a punch in the gut. Harper exhaled shakily through her nose, blinking away the sting in her eyes. Resisting the urge to break.

Aedon lingered. "Please don't go," he murmured. His gaze burned with an intensity Harper did not understand.

She shifted, softening, before steeling herself anew. "My mind's made up."

Aedon reached for her, but she stepped beyond his span. He let his hand drop. "Very well." Aedon sighed, his shoulders slumped. He turned to watch the others, already a distance away, but did not move. "I can't stay with you, but I don't want to leave. You've barely seen how dangerous this land is, and I don't want to see any harm come to you." He pushed a hand through his hair. He did when distressed. Even the realisation that she had cared enough to notice that *hurt*.

"I can manage," she said stubbornly, even though she was quite sure she couldn't. Without even a knife, she could not hunt to sustain herself.

"Look, Harper, this is your last chance. Please, don't go to Tornai," he implored. "This will end in folly you cannot even begin to imagine. Plus, we need you. Just as much as your Dragonheart."

"I have to go," Harper said. *To Tournai, then home. Caledan feels like an ever-fading dream already. Betta needs me.* This had all been nothing more than a ridiculous and desperate dream. "This is what's best for me. Your mission was never mine. I'm grateful for your help," she allowed herself to concede, "but I can't stay. Erika was right. I have a different path to follow."

Aedon sighed heavily. The breeze sighed with him, grazing through the trees and grass, brushing Harper's hair from her face.

"If your mind is made up, I cannot dally any longer," he said dully. He reached inside the folds of his cloak and unbuckled his dagger. "Here. I want you to have this."

Harper took it, holding it gently in her hands. "I can't take this," she whispered. The ornate scabbard was a shadow of the beautiful blade within. She had already admired it. Silver filigree on red leather that matched the grip and guard inside. A small pommel of intricately wrought steel, and a leaf-shaped blade the likes of which she had never seen.

"You need it more than I do," Aedon said, stepping back and raising his hands when she held it out. "The handle of your knife was damaged and the blade nicked. I'm sorry. I hope this will serve you as well as it's served me. Take care not to lose it. One day I might ask for it back." His smile was half-hearted, but hopeful.

"I'm sure our paths won't cross again, Aedon." Harper fingered the dagger, feeling wholly out of her depth and ill-equipped to use it as it deserved.

"I hope they do, but promise me one thing."

"What's that?"

"On your honour, swear that if you ever become a member of the Winged Kingsguard or something so grand, you won't arrest me." A flicker of his usual light-hearted humour broke through the creases of worry etched on his face.

Harper could not help but crack a small smile. A part of her hated that he could worm through her defences so easily. "I'll consider it."

"Well, I suppose this is goodbye." Aedon lingered. It was clear he still wished for her to change her mind.

"I suppose it is. Thank you, Aedon, for everything." Despite how this ended, she was grateful to them. They had saved her life. She didn't want to think about what would have happened had she not run into him that day. "Goodbye."

Aedon nodded and swallowed, before turning on his heel and marching away. After a few paces, he broke into a run to catch up with his distant companions, and did not look back. Harper watched them crest the hill and disappear. Despite their short companionship, she had grown to care for them. She hated herself for it, but to see them receding into the distance, knowing their paths were unlikely to cross again, made her ache more than she wanted to admit to, even in spite of the hurt that had been caused. And in the end, had they not proved themselves? No matter how desperately they needed that stone, they had not taken it by force when they could have done. That counted for something. It eroded the hot anger she felt towards them—leaving only her own surging pool of guilt at her selfishness.

She followed the valley until the land flattened out, trying to outrun that feeling. The great city of Tournai stood proud on the horizon, stretching up into the mountains like a crown amongst the foothills. As she hiked toward it, Harper tried to be distracted by the promise of what awaited—but there was no way to outrun the turmoil churning inside. She would live or die by the decision she had just made.

46

DIMITRI

The order was a physical compulsion, a tug of magic deep within Dimitri. The king summoned at his will and Dimitri was bound to follow. He could have cursed Toroth in that moment. Having dealt with the wood elves, he now had to secure the Dragonheart. The last thing he wanted was to return to Toroth's side to falsify yet another report that he had not located it—and endure Toroth's inevitable wrath.

It took all his efforts to conceal the truth from his thoughts, but Dimitri took heart that the charade would soon be over. He listened to Raedon's reports, too, feeling a noticeable tinge of relief that the Winged Kingsguard weren't any closer to finding the location of the stone, but in fact drifting further away. He allowed himself a moment's smug satisfaction, hidden from both Raedon and the king.

"Is that all?" The king's furrowed brows suggested that it had better not be.

"Your Majesty, every member of the Winged Kingsguard searches from dawn until dusk for your stone."

"Bah," spat Toroth, pacing back and forth before the hearth so angrily, Dimitri swore he would wear a hole in the stone. "What of *your* efforts?" he fired at Dimitri.

He straightened, caught off guard by the sudden switch in the king's attention. "I am afraid my results are the same as the general's. It must have travelled far afield indeed."

They bowed their heads in contrition as the king erupted at them. Curses were shouted, objects hurled, items of priceless value smashed, before the king's anger abated and he dismissed them. Dimitri held his tongue, averted his eyes, and dipped his head for it all, despite the rebellious streak of anger that spiked in him. Every moment further pushed him towards that inevitable path. This was why the wheel needed breaking. Why Toroth had to be supplanted.

Knowing there was no time to waste, the moment Toroth dismissed them, Dimitri rushed to Saradon's chamber in the heart of the mountain. He had to make his reports and retrieve the Dragonheart. Now Aedon and his companions knew he sought it, he had no doubt they would do everything in their power to thwart him.

Saradon's crushing presence greeted him in the warm, stale air of the cavern. Dimitri bowed to the sarcophagus before opening his mind to the strange, not entirely welcome presence of Saradon, who brooded and lurked upon the fringes of his consciousness.

"I have located the Dragonheart, Lord," Dimitri said without preamble. "I was unable to obtain it due to a complication, but it is safe for now. As soon as I leave here, I shall retrieve it."

"*A complication?*" Saradon's tone was curt, with a bite of

impatience. Dimitri could understand that. Five hundred years was a long time to wait.

"Yes." Dimitri shared a flood of mental images with Saradon's consciousness, showing the encounter with the wood elves that drew him away from his pursuit of the stone.

"You should have crushed them," Saradon said flatly.

"They may yet be allies—and I do not want them for enemies."

"The wood elves ne'er were amicable toward my ilk. They were too high and mighty to associate with the likes of me."

Dimitri pursed his lips. "I understand that only too well. They were none too keen to cooperate with me, either."

"Yet your anger is not directed at them."

Dimitri started. He had not realised it still curled within him, like the embers of a fire that would not die. Before he could respond, Saradon had already stepped into his mind, living through his encounter with the king. He felt Saradon's disdain for Toroth before he voiced it.

"What a detestable creature. The bloodline has not changed, I see. I shall enjoy casting him down."

"And I will be glad to see it done by my hand also," Dimitri said grimly. "The court is a cesspit of greed and selfishness. None more so than Toroth. The kingdom suffers at his hands, and I would see it end."

"Not just Toroth, though?"

Dimitri realised that his thoughts had strayed to his father. "No," he admitted. "I still have scores to settle with my father and brothers." He had never really settled them to his satisfaction. With the court broken, he could seek retribution there too.

"And you shall see it done." The cave faded away as Dimitri imagined it, not for the first time. Saradon's voice caught

him in the midst of his fantasy. *"It will be a turning point for Pelenor. One that ought to have occurred five hundred years ago. I shall not be denied again."*

Dimitri found himself in unfamiliar visions. He flew as if on dragonback, but utterly weightless and without wind, over a lush, green vista. Blue skies reigned from east to west, across verdant valleys and rolling forests, and rivers of silver threaded through the land. They soared over hamlets and towns filled with healthy, laughing peoples. A pale city rose before him. Tournai, cleaner and more pure than ever Dimitri had known it. There was a sweetness in the air. A clean, fresh, natural fragrance that contrasted starkly with the stench of the city streets Dimitri knew.

"Pelenor will be restored to prosperity, peace, and health once more. No longer will the land and its peoples be exploited for all they have."

Saradon's anger brought thunderous clouds to the vision. The skies darkened, and suddenly, they were inside Tournai, at the very square where Dimitri had watched Toroth burn the false traitors. The pyres remained, but the figures upon them were very different. They blurred, shifting, but Dimitri saw snatches of faces he knew in them. The king, his father, his brothers, the court.

"I will see it done that Toroth and his kin of blood and spirit are punished for all they have done. The cruelty and greed of the court will be put to death. A fairer Pelenor will be born, and I will see that it does not fall into such depths again," Saradon growled. *"You will be well rewarded for your assistance, in whatever way you choose."*

Dimitri knew what Saradon meant. He could enjoy his fair share of riches if he chose, but he was more alike to Saradon than he had first realised. Righteous revenge was more important than gold to both of them.

"How do we make it so?" Dimitri asked, envisioning the green and prosperous land once more, daring to wonder what a fair court would look like.

"All I need is to break from the shackles of my self-imposed prison," said Saradon, sighing. *"I have power I never could have dreamed of, but it is wasted, trapped here."*

"Forgive me, Lord, but how did you come by it? All the tales tell of your struggles with magic and your use of arcane methods," Dimitri dared to ask, phrasing it as delicately as he could.

Saradon's mood flickered, but no anger rolled over Dimitri. *"It is enough to know that is not true,"* he said in a tone that brooked no further questions, but Dimitri was not satisfied. It did not answer what he had asked, and he knew Saradon had sidestepped his true question. Nonetheless, he nodded, even as his thoughts strayed once more. The portrait of Saradon, dark and evil. There, he was the darkness engulfing the light, yet the Saradon Dimitri found himself with seemed to hold himself as the opposite, a pinprick of light fighting against a growing dark. *History is told by the victors*, Dimitri reminded himself.

"Arcane powers may be misjudged," Saradon said, as if he could read his most private thoughts. Dimitri hoped he could not. *"Besides, magic is neither evil nor good. It is a tool. Magic is whatever and however it is chosen to be wielded. All magic can be used to do good, as ours shall."*

And evil, thought Dimitri, recalling the charred bodies of the false traitors. "What would you have me do?"

"Retrieve the stone without delay and bring it to me. Once I have the relic and the stone, I shall rise once more."

47

HARPER

When she stopped that night in sight of the huge city crowned with twinkling lights, Harper's confidence faded. Her sharp-edged senses spiked as she settled in a hollow in the shadow of an old, gnarled tree, exposed and vulnerable amongst the sweeping plain that undulated and rose to Tornai.

Harper settled upon the dry grass there, realising that without Aedon's help or any tools, she probably could not light a fire. She also had no food. As if a reminder, her stomach rumbled in sullen rebellion. When had she last eaten a proper meal, one that made her feel as though her sides would burst? Not since a few days prior when Ragnar had cooked a small boar with tubers and wild herbs, making gravy from the juices... Harper's stomach growled even louder at the thought. She groaned in annoyance that she had found nothing to sustain herself, for the moors seemed entirely barren after the bounty of the woods.

Had it been this cold of an evening in the forest, or was

she only noticing it because she was out in the open where there was no shelter from the breeze? Harper hugged her arms around herself and rubbed her upper arms. A strange cry split the air, making her jump. Her head whipped toward the source of the sound. She remained motionless for several seconds, her entire body tense. She glanced around, but saw nothing against the darkening sky.

Harper adjusted herself, trying to stave off numbness and a sore back from where she leaned against the tree trunk, which dug into her body uncomfortably. The dagger nudged her side. With a slightly shaky hand, she drew it from the sheath and placed it at her side, then wrapped her cloak around herself.

For what good it does, at least I'm ready. With a sigh that sounded as loud as a shout to her fraught senses, she realised she really had no idea what it took to protect herself from whatever lay out there. Just as she had begun to feel confident with some of Brand's training, it was over all too suddenly, and she was painfully aware how little she knew of it all.

There would be no chance of sleep. Haunted by the scurrying of nighttime creatures through the grass and across the earth around her, their cries, which were far too loud and close for comfort, only heightened her nerves. A hunter she may have been, but it had been many years since she had to sleep under the stars with no protection or company.

The creatures stayed away, for which she was thankful, but her frayed nerves would not allow her to rest. Long into the night, Harper kept her silent vigil, feeling as though she slowly turned into a cold, lonely, stone sentinel.

Harper must have eventually slept, for the next morning, she awoke with a start, cold, stiff, and covered in dew, just like the world around her. Blades of grass glittered, crowned with jewels of water. They adorned her hands with cold kisses as she pushed from the ground to stand, stretching her limbs and wishing she could banish her aches and fill her empty stomach. It gnawed at her relentlessly now. She sighed. There was no point in waiting. There was clearly going to be no breakfast that day.

Tournai was close, the road in the valley already full of morning trade and travel. She gawked at the gigantic city, just like how she had imagined Denholme that first time before seeing the grimy and pale reality of the citadel of her county. It rose from the plains, nestling into the steep cliffs of the mountains. A great palace, with hundreds of windows which caught the morning sunlight and crowned with crenelations, topped the walled city.

As she drew closer, she squinted at the wall. It was taller than she had imagined, pierced by windows and even balconies at the highest levels, as if there were perhaps dwellings within it. Watchtowers rose even farther, spaced by crenelations matching the castle's, as if the wall and the towers were a crown surrounding the city. She could see little inside the walls, only what rose above her, which was a tangle of buildings and roofs.

Now that she could see Tournai before her, the current of nerves and excitement in her belly churned together. Harper bounced on the balls of her feet as she increased her pace, her aching, stiff joints and empty belly forgotten. Aedon, his companions, and their mission were discarded for the moment, pushed to the back of her mind as it filled with grand thoughts of dragons, kings, and adventure. She was almost there. It was every bit as grand as she had imagined. A grin split her face. Soon, she would be inside exploring, and with any luck, able to see dragons and the Winged Kingsguard up close.

Harper's gaze slowly rose, drinking in every detail and straining to see more, despite being a distance away. Far above the palace, she saw more construction in the same white stone, great openings in the side of the mountain itself. Her heart constricted when she saw great, winged shapes, far too large to be birds, wheeling in the sky above it. Were they dragons?

She joined the throng of people flooding toward the city, marveling at the variety of beings she saw. Humans of all skin colours. Elves, some on foot and others on horseback. Men, women, and children of all ages surrounded her. Carts drawn by draught horses or donkeys carrying all kinds of loads bumped, rolled, and groaned around her, some covered and some open. The smell of their wares mingled with that of the crowd—sweat, smoke, and dirt, the faint fragrance of perfume and soap threading throughout. The clamouring of voices overwhelmed her. Shouting, chattering, and calling all around her, layered with a cacophony of clopping of animals, and the creak and racket of carts.

The rising sun was warm, and Harper soon started sweating under her cloak. The heat did not help the smell, either. The faint whiff of excrement from all the animals rose too, so Harper breathed through her mouth, carefully stepping over the steaming piles of manure so as not to trail her cloak in them.

Harper gawked, unable to stop staring. As they drew closer to the city and the imposing white walls, she had to crane her neck more and more to look at them. This close, she could no longer see over them. They towered over the rush of people climbing the incline from the wide valley. She could clearly see the windows and balconies now. Drying clothes hung from the highest, the coloured garments flying in the breeze. Flags whipped back and forth high above them, too far away for her to see the crest. Occasional faces, which were just pale blobs from such a distance, peered over battlements or flashed past windows.

The crowd bunched together as people waited to pass through the gate, arms holding papers or tokens in the air. From the middle of the pack, Harper shuffled along with the rest of them. Soldiers lined the way, scanning those papers with every passing sweep of their attention. Their gleaming armour shone in the sun, blinding her momentarily as she moved. It felt overwhelming. The crowd pressed closer, and with every step, people bumped against her body, feet kicked her legs. Harper could do nothing but grit her teeth and edge forward. She glanced up at the gates looming over her. The crowd passed through in a constant stream.

Anxiety tempered the rush. Where was she supposed to go? The city looked huge. Where was she to start? Who should she seek? Should she try to go to the palace first? Surely that was where the king would be, and he was the one who would give her the means to go home. The moment of misgiving niggled at her. She had been so concerned about getting to Tournai, she had not once stopped to think about what she ought to do when she finally reached the royal city.

"Oy!" The shout cut through her thoughts. She turned her head. She was about to pass under the gate, which was only a few people and one cart wide. Its shadow engulfed them all. Ahead, mounted guards scanned the crowd. One stood tall in the stirrups as he called again, a word she did not understand, and pointed toward her.

She looked around, but the rest of the crowd had their heads down. As they all passed through the gate, they showed papers or tokens to the various guards, who nodded them through, before they peeled away into the maze of streets on their own business. She had nothing, she realised with a cold rush. Did she need a token of some kind to enter?

Me? she mouthed, pointing to herself. The guard met her gaze and nodded, beckoning. She forged through the crowd. Perfect. She would ask him—this was fine. Quicker, even, she reassured herself. As she approached, he dismounted, his scowl deepening.

"Where are your papers?" he asked in accented Common Tongue, placing a hand upon the pommel of his sword as he strode forward.

"Papers?" Harper replied, scrunching her face in confusion. She stumbled as a group of men passed, knocking into her. They hurried away as the guard stepped toward them with menace. He then called to her in another tongue she did not understand. At her look of confusion, he switched back to the Common Tongue.

"Do not move. What is your name and purpose?"

Harper froze. The man looked even more wary now, as though he expected her to pull forth some giant and fearsome weapon from beneath her cloak. "I... My name's Harper. I need to see the king," she said desperately, all rational thoughts leaving in her panic. The crowd surged around her once more, pushing her closer to the guard, his sword, and his comrades, whose dark looks fell on her one by one, and overwhelm threatened. For the first time, a surge of true fear, laced with crushing doubt, shot through her as she realised how ridiculous and far-fetched her naïve idea was. She ought to have practised this—what she would say, and how.

His feet inched forward, and her pulse shot up as her body flooded with white-hot fear. This was going wrong. She felt her chance slipping away. "I'm coming to see the king. I have something for him," she said desperately. On an impulse, she brandished the Dragonheart before her.

At her movement, he pulled his sword free and raised it to strike, but he halted at the sight of the small stone she held. His comrades surrounded her, their own hands lowering to their weapons.

"That is a Dragonheart," he said darkly, eyes narrowed. "Where did you take it from?"

"I didn't take it. I found it." In the din of the crowd, no one heard her. Panic rose from the pit of her stomach.

"It belongs to the king, by law of Pelenor. Lay it upon the ground and step back."

But Harper clutched it tighter, sure it was her only way out of the mess she had willingly and inadvertently walked into. "I didn't steal it. I swear. I *must* see the king!"

"The king does not bandy with thieves," the man snarled. He looked at one of his men. "Does it match the description?"

He nodded. "Aye, Captain. Looks like the one that was stolen from the vaults."

"I haven't done anything wrong," she said. She gripped the folds of her cloak as if it could somehow steady her, because it felt like a rug had been pulled out from under her. But he stepped forward, pushing Harper back. This close, with his plumed helm and broad, muscled shoulders, he loomed as tall and wide as the wall.

"Please! I must speak with the king! I will not let that out of my sight until I speak to the king!" Her voice rose in volume and pitch as panic set in. She knew nothing she said would change their minds. She had made a terrible mistake.

She tried to back away, but they had surrounded her, so she was met with a wall of silent, cloaked, muscled men, each readying to draw his weapon.

"You will make no demands of us," he snapped. "Our king will like to deal with you personally, thief. Seize her!"

48
DIMITRI

A nerve twitched in Dimitri's temple as he stood, rigid as iron, before the court. It ought to have been an unremarkable night. The usual banquet after the day's work, the relaxed hall filled with the tinkle of cutlery and glasses, as well as the muted laughter of lords and ladies. In reality, they were silent, circled like carrion crow around him—their prey. The bright lights stung his eyes and making him feel especially naked before them, despite his sweeping, dark robes. Before him, Rosella's laughing eyes teased him, but with none of the mirth and lust they usually held. She taunted him today, publicly humiliated him, took glee in his suffering.

"Are you not going to kneel before your princess?" she said with mock astonishment at his supposed insubordination.

Never. With a blank expression that masked raging emotions within, Dimitri bowed instead, the motion smooth and automatic.

"Good," she purred. The crowd tittered.

Hell to you all, Dimitri cursed them silently.

"I find myself insulted by your lack of respect to me. Princesses ought not to have to ask for such things." She ceased circling him, but at his lack of reply, his measured stare into the distance, resumed it again with a a twitch of annoyance to her lips. She wanted him to bite.

"I think you should beg for my forgiveness." She stopped before him, her hips level with his head, and extended a jewelled, slender hand toward him.

Dimitri clenched his jaw. "I beg your forgiveness, Your Royal Highness. No male would ever insult such beauty and wit as yours." He was tired and irritable from his constant travelling and lack of sleep, and it took all he had not to shake with weariness and keep the snap from his voice.

"You have such a way with words. You may rise."

He did, and remained silent, his stare blank as he filtered the loathing from it.

"Come, ladies," Rosella called to her retinue, the flock of sparkling, noble elf-maidens who followed her wherever she went for any favour she would give them. To Dimitri, they were a cacophony of shrill, gossiping, backstabbing sparrows he preferred to keep at arm's length.

Sensing their fun would go no further that night, courtiers began to turn away, and conversation rose around him. The stiffness in Dimitri's shoulders eased a little at his humiliation being over—for now. As Rosella swept past him, the caress of her favourite perfume was a heady scent teasing his nose. "You will visit me tonight," she whispered to him alone, her voice covered by the noise around them.

I'll be damned if I do, little harpy. "I regret, I am too busy, Princess."

She stopped in surprise, but by the time she turned

around, her mouth a perfect "o", he was already halfway to the door.

He punched the cushions on his lounger with a growl of unbridled anger. He had finally had enough. As glorious a prize as Rosella was to parade before his father, and better yet, insult the king with—adopted daughter or not, she was still Toroth's daughter and it irked him to no end that Dimitri dallied with her—it was worth it no longer.

I'm done with her, I'm done with Toroth, and I'm done with this entire festering court. No more duplicity. It's time to play my hand. His body ached from head to toe. It screamed at him to rest, to sink into the sumptuous, soft bed just one room away, but anger coursed through him, banishing the weariness.

Minutes later, he stood in Saradon's chamber once more. Saradon's watchful, wordless presence observed him, waiting for him to speak.

"I'm done with Toroth—with them all," Dimitri said shortly, sending a mental barrage of images to Saradon, who absorbed them thoughtfully. "There is no more time for delays, but I want *assurances*. I will raise you, but only if you make me your right-hand advisor. I will deliver everything we have discussed. I will not be a spectator in this. I want to orchestrate it. I want to crush them myself. If you agree, I will make it so. If you do not, I walk away and find my own way for revenge."

"*You dare to speak against me?*" Saradon's customary flickering anger lapped at the edges of the cavern, ready to spring. He laughed at Dimitri's resolute silence, his set jaw. "*No matter. I know it is born from anger, not insult. Our ends are aligned, Dimitrius Vaeri Mortris of House Ellarian. You have my word it will be so. I promise once. I promise twice. I promise thrice."*

Dimitri felt the warm, tingling magic wrap around him, clutch sharply for a moment, and then fade into nothing as their agreement bound to the magic of the world around them. "I'm going to reclaim the stone."

Dimitri executed a short bow and fled into the world once more, hungrily seeking the area of his last dalliance with Aedon and his companions. When he arrived, he found the remnants of their camp empty, as he had expected, since they moved on every day. He followed their essence, drawing closer, until he stood on the moors before the great plains of Tournai.

They practically sat on the king's doorstep, yet Toroth knew nothing of it. Dimitri could have laughed at the irony. But his amusement was soon tainted by fear. They were so close to being discovered. He knew he had been right to choose now. There was no more time. He drew himself toward their small fire, a tiny pinprick of warmth against the cold landscape, until he stood just outside their barriers.

With a cold rush that swept through him, he realised Harper was nowhere to be found. When he sought back along the trail he had followed, he discovered her essence was gone. Panic drenched him. He shattered the wards around Aedon's camp only to discover the worst. Hidden behind their wards, there was no trace of the Dragonheart, either.

"Where is she? Where is it?" he thundered, striding into the firelight. Aedon had already blanched at the crushing of his wards, visibly reeling with the power of it. His companions jumped to their feet at the intrusion. Weapons appeared in their hands, and magic bloomed around Aedon. They formed a barrier against Dimitri, their backs to the fire.

"Back off!" Aedon snarled, raising a hand full of crackling, magical energy.

"Where is Harper? Where is the Dragonheart?" Dimitri enunciated every syllable, his voice dangerously even, though he shook with fear and anger.

Ragnar spat at him. Dimitri thrust a clawed hand at the dwarf. Ragnar sailed into the air, landing on the ground with a crunch. He moaned and was silent. Erika slowly backed up to tend to him, her blade raised, not daring to turn her back on Dimitri. Brand and Aedon, filled with defiance, tightened the gap between them.

"If you won't tell me willingly, I'll drag it out of one of you." Dimitri swept his hand in front of him. The two males collapsed to the ground, their legs plucked out from beneath them.

"Over my dead body," growled Brand.

Dimitri unleashed an avalanche of pain. Aedon paled, his fingers clenching into balled fists. Brand grunted, eyes shut against the agony. Ragnar lay still, and Erika shook as she dropped to all fours, still huddled over him protectively.

Again and again Dimitri blasted them with his magic, until all four lay on the ground, twitching, their veins running with white-hot fire. With a jerk of his hand, he ceased the magic. It ebbed away, along with some of his frustration. He knew they would not tell him anything. He did not know whether it was more out of loyalty to Harper or spite for him, but it did not matter.

"I will find her," he promised them with a growl, and vanished.

49

AEDON

It was a long, dark, restless night as the four aching warriors huddled around their fire, built as high as resources and energy would allow, refusing to rest in case Dimitri should return. Even Brand drooped with weariness by the time the sun rose, its pale light blinding to their swollen, heavy eyes. Every limb was stiff, the pale flickers of the fire failing to permeate the freeze of night.

In silence, they broke fast that morning on unsatisfying, cold rations. Every muscle hurt as though Aedon had run for days with a heavy pack, and his fingers shook. Rage bubbled through him at the spymaster's cruelty—but fear laced the edges. What would he do to Harper when he found her? Now, Aedon was certain she went to her doom.

Aedon had renewed the wards thrice, but even so, they had not dared speak for fear Dimitri would be listening. Brand scouted the area, ambling back uncharacteristically slowly. "If he is here, I can find no trace of him."

"We have to find her," Ragnar said. His eyes were as dull

as his voice as he stared listlessly into the flames. "She is in danger from that *monster*."

Brand shook his head. "If we're not too late."

Aedon glanced at Erika, who remained silent on the matter. "I fear you're right, Ragnar. As much as she swore she was capable of independence, Dimitrius is too great a match for her." He shook his head. "Even if she's not walking into a trap, she goes to her doom. It would be unforgivable if we let her."

The group sat in silence for a long moment.

"There's a slim to none chance that we will procure any more Dragonheart, powdered or whole," Brand said carefully. "I think we all realise that. We have no Dragonheart and no knowledge of how best to use one. Going to Tournai may be our own doomed mission."

Aedon gritted his teeth. "We made a promise, and I will not renege on it. Lives are at stake. We might find another way to fulfil our oath and save her at the same time. She'll be branded a thief and imprisoned—or worse."

Brand held up his hands in submission, though he knew Aedon had taken his point on.

"Besides which, Harper is in trouble. I know she is not what some of you would consider one of us, but even so, I feel a duty to help her. Do you not agree? The quest for the stone might be futile, but at the very least, we could save one more innocent life from Toroth. Is that not worthwhile?"

"You know where I stand," Ragnar said. "I'm ready to go when you are."

Brand dipped his head. "You are right. It's foolish, beyond madness, but you are right. I could not live with that on my conscience."

Aedon turned his attention to Erika, who sat there as taciturn and imperturbable as always. He fidgeted as he waited for her answer, disturbed by a sudden sense of urgency that they had to leave *now*, find Harper before it was too late.

"It's idiotic to risk ourselves for a stranger," she said shortly.

"You were a stranger when I risked my life for you." Brand stared at her until she dipped her gaze.

"Dimitrius hunts her," Aedon said. "*Dimitrius*, the spymaster of King Toroth himself, *personally* hunts her. If that is no clue to the danger she finds herself in, I do not know what is. She is clever and fit, especially now she's eaten better than I suspect she has in her entire life, but she is no fighter. She does not understand politics, at least of Pelenor. Leaving her is worse than leaving you to the wolves—which we could have done to make our lives easier, and did not," he added pointedly.

Erika stirred. "Fine. I do wonder what he wants with the stone, and she is not safe in his path." It was as close to an acknowledgment, and agreement, that they would receive.

"We are settled then?" Aedon looked at them in turn. "We are going to venture into the jaws of the dragon itself, into Toroth's very court, to save Harper—and the Dragonheart, if we can—from the clutches of that bastard Dimitrius." He dashed to his feet, bouncing upon his toes. His entire body sang of the urgency that pulled him towards Tournai. "Come on!" he chided them impatiently.

Ragnar struggled to his feet, with Erika's help, as Brand scuffed dirt over the last of the fire to douse it. "We have a girl, a stone, and a village to save." *And a spymaster to foil*, he added to himself, wondering darkly what Dimitrius's intentions were.

50

HARPER

"No!" shrieked Harper, but before the word was out of her mouth, soldiers wrenched the Dragon-heart from her. A vice-like grip seized her arms and shoved her to the ground. Her torso and face smashed into the stone, winding her for a few precious seconds whilst they restrained her with ease.

She wriggled, trying to buck off the man who held her down, but her strength was no match for his weight. Soon, another man took one arm, pinning it to the ground. Others stamped on her legs until she was entirely crushed to the stone, unmoving, and then tied with bonds that dug into her skin.

A man's loud voice boomed across the square, but she understood none of the words. Gasps and mutters followed, then turned to shouting and curses in a variety of tongues. Objects started to pelt her, and more than one foot was aimed her way. The guards let it happen, watching her with cold disdain for a moment.

Harper struggled, fully bound, to hunch into a ball to

protect herself. As a hand grabbed a fistful of her hair and yanked her head up, she screeched, but was quickly muffled by a dirty rag shoved between her teeth. Harper gagged on it as they hoisted her up by her arms moments later and dragged her away. She cried out in pain as her unsupported legs scraped against the sharp edges of stone stairs. She tried to shout through the rag, but all that emerged was an unintelligible yelp.

A hood—a sack of some sort that stank of old, mouldy potatoes, and worse—was jammed over her head, clogging her nose. She retched into the gag. Her eyes streamed with every jarring impact on the ground, and the strain on her elbows and shoulders felt as though they would be pulled from their sockets with every rushed step.

The world was reduced to sounds as they rushed her through the city. She could smell nothing but the foul sack, taste nothing but the fouler rag, and see nothing but darkness inside the rough-woven fabric. Darkness that lightened and deepened as they dragged her through patches of shadow and sun.

Her feet and legs scratched over stone flags and then small, bumpy cobbles. Aside from that, there were no clues as to her surroundings. The sound of the city rumbling around her was no comfort, either. The maelstrom of voices and sounds was overwhelming, and she could distinguish nothing to give her any point of reference, save for up and down.

She tried to still her juddering sobs, for they only made the breathlessness worse. Tears streamed down her face. Eventually, she felt cool darkness envelop her and heard a door slam shut behind her. Several more banged open and closed in quick succession before and behind. Her feet stumbled over thresholds as she crossed them blindly.

The bag was suddenly ripped from her head and the gag torn from her mouth. She retched with relief and sucked in a huge gulp of air. It was cold and filled with the fetid stench of excrement and rot, but she did not care. She blinked, but need not have. It was dark. Small lamps threw flickering shadows and paltry light over the rough, dark stone. There were no windows.

Harper tried to control the rising feeling of claustrophobia. She twisted her head, to see the way they had come, to determine if there was a scrap of daylight somewhere, but she gleaned no clues. A moment later, they hauled her forward again, opened a door, and tossed her into a pitch-black cell.

The door boomed shut behind her. When she heard a thump from the other side, she knew it had been barred. She scrabbled for it, pushing against the unyielding wood, to no avail. Trapped.

Time was immeasurable. Harper had no idea how long she sat on the frigid, hard floor. Not even her stomach or energy could mark the passage of time. She was already starving and exhausted. Her face pounded from the impact upon the ground earlier, and there was a crusted trail of dried blood from her nose. She gently picked it off, carefully touching her tender face. One hip throbbed, sore and angry, where she had been hit. She did not need to see it to know a gigantic bruise had already started blooming.

Harper's only companion was the dark. The smallest amount of faint light slipped under the door. That one solid, thin line connected her to the outside world, but it was small comfort for it offered no illumination on her situation. In here, the smell was even worse. Even before she explored its cramped confines, it was not hard to determine she was in some kind of prison cell.

Moving agonisingly slowly, in no small part because of her complaining body, she crawled around the space. It was narrower than she was tall and not much longer. Straw, or perhaps rushes, covered the stone-flagged floor. The shafts were wafer thin and trampled. Some crumbled as she picked them up.

There was no mattress, bed, or blanket that she could find as she felt around, her fingers sinking into the corners of the floor. They trailed through dirt, grime, and slime until she was certain she would be a creature of dirt, grime, and slime herself. She raised a hand to her face to sniff it—immediately regretting the action—and fumbled for the hem of her cloak to wipe her fingers clean. There was a bucket in the corner, which had an even worse smell. Harper recoiled from it.

After a period of sitting in the dark, huddled against a wall and wrapped in her cloak, which offered no resistance against the cold around her, she stiffly rose and stumbled to the door, leaning against the hard wood. At least it was slightly warmer than the stone, for what that was worth. Yet no matter how she searched for any crack or weakness, pushed it, or slotted her fingers into the edges to try and pull it—there was no handle on the inside of the door, perhaps for good reason—she could not get even a whisper of give in the stout wood. Her palms caressed the worn boards as she rested her forehead against it with a sigh. Through it, she could hear faint sounds. It was low and deep, the drone of men talking.

Think. There has to be a weakness somewhere. An idea struck her. She scraped some of the paltry, slightly soggy straw into a pile and reached down into the middle of herself, feeling for that slight tingle, the deep well where she knew the magic was. Knowing what it felt like to have Aedon's strong magic coursing through her, she knew exactly what to look for. Somewhere deep inside, there it was, the tiniest little nugget, slightly bigger than it had been before. She clung to it. Perhaps she did not have to sit in the cold or the dark after all.

The magic slipped away. She grasped it tighter, focusing on the tiny trickle. The faintest warmth heated the very tips of her fingers, but no more. Eventually, she shook with the mental strain and her hands fell to her sides. She slumped against the wall with a huff of resignation. Aedon had made it look so easy. It appeared it wouldn't be that way for her, at least not yet.

Harper gritted her teeth in silent frustration. There was no way out that she could tell. Her weapon—Aedon's beautiful knife—was gone. And she had no means, magical or otherwise, to facilitate her escape. She would have to wait for whatever was coming, and that was the most terrifying thought of all. It made her stomach flip and body shake with nerves. Slowly, she pulled her cloak about her, retreated to the far corner of the cell, and slumped onto the floor with her knees drawn to her chest.

Fitful sleep was the best she managed. Harper's eyelids drooped, exhausted, then jerked open again with every small noise from outside. Every sound put her on high alert. Were they coming to fetch her? Where would they take her? What would they do? Would she—*could* she—escape?

Then the sounds faded again and she huddled deeper into her cloak, wishing for the comforting presence and warmth of Aedon and his companions. The growing torrent of anxiety also taunted her about him. Every nerve was frayed, and her thoughts were a runaway horse of worry. He had pleaded with her, but she had not believed his nature ran true. Perhaps, just perhaps, she had been wrong about him… about them all.

She looked about her, from one dark corner to another, glad she could not see anything. If only they could see her now. They were right. Erika most of all. Harper was glad she would never have to admit it to Erika's face. Then again, her thoughts trailing in loops and circles, she returned to worrying about her own hide. Concern over what her own fate would be stifled her breath in her chest. Not for the first time, she berated herself for making the wrong choice. She'd probably never get the chance to admit anything to Erika's face. She should never have come.

There was nothing to do but wait on her fate now. Perhaps someone would come to rescue her. Harper laughed mirthlessly at the thought. Who would come for her? Who even could? Certainly not Aedon and his companions. They had made their feelings abundantly clear. She could not blame them. She had walked into exactly the folly they had predicted, and now she was in a strange world, about to be charged with a crime that seemed punishable by death or "worse", whatever that meant. None of her own kin or friends would come. They did not exist. She fleetingly pondered how long she had been gone since the hours and days had blurred together. She stopped that thought before it went any further, wondering what everyone would think had happened when she seemingly vanished without a trace.

She did not know whether she hated herself or the situation she found herself in more. She had been foolish to believe she would be taken for her word. This wasn't

Caledan, but there wasn't justice in either realm. That was blatantly clear. No "innocent until proven guilty". This place was unjust, unfair, and she didn't belong. It was as far from her vision of being a noble knight or intrepid adventurer, or being sent home by a gracious and understanding king, as she had hoped.

"You're so stupid, Harper," she growled at herself. "Should have stayed with Aedon. At least they accepted me, as useless as I was." They would have used her Dragonheart, but that was better than it returning to the king's vaults to gather dust. She scowled and punched the floor, as if she could punch her regret, frustration, and fear. It did nothing other than earn her a new pain.

No one came for her in what seemed like an age. Harper did not bother moving from her corner, huddled up in her cloak, shivering from head to toe. The light and warmth of the turn of summer to autumn seemed like a distant memory already. What had once seemed like a thick cloak, stifling in the heat, now felt like nothing more than her old, thin, tattered cloak, and offered her no shelter, comfort, or protection.

When the door clunked open, Harper startled. The dim light outside was blinding after so long in the dark. After a moment of surprise, she scrambled forward. A dark form dropped a wooden bowl in the room and set a wooden beaker down, spilling most of the contents of both in the process. Before she could reach the door, it slammed shut again.

Harper cried out. The muffled thump of the bar slipping into place rattled the door. Then receding footsteps. Then silence.

She felt around the floor for the bowl and cup. Water. It smelled suspiciously unclean, but she downed it in one gulp all the same. The gruel in the bowl was weak and tasted barely edible. The hunk of bread was so stale that she could have mistaken it for a stone. She ate it all anyway, grateful for something to fill her stomach.

Once finished, she retreated back to her corner. Her stomach still rumbled unhappily. A few mouthfuls of paltry food and tainted water did nothing to still its mutiny. She hung her head. Her forehead pounded mercilessly, as though she had spent the night before downing too much ale. Unfortunately, Harper knew she would not be able to shake it off so easily. She could not help but wish that this was nothing more than a bad dream. The assault on her senses told her it was very real indeed.

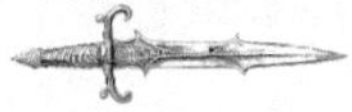

The next time they came, she had no idea how long it had been, but she was ready. There was only one name that might curry her some kind of favour, or chance, as much as she hated to use it. It had repeatedly taunted her, but would it help or damn her? She had no idea. She hoped it would not land her in a worse predicament.

When the door slipped open to allow a meal in, she shouted past the burn in her throat. "Dimitrius Vaeri Mortris! I demand to speak with Dimitrius Vaeri Mortris of House Ellarian!"

The dish paused in midair, before the hand holding it dropped it. The door shut a second later, but with a quieter slam than before. Harper's heart pounded. What had she done? This could make things even worse—but she had nothing else to gamble.

51

DIMITRI

imitri longed to run, but he forced himself to take measured, unhurried steps, schooling his features into boredom with a hint of indignance at being disturbed for such paltry matters. Under the surface, he was a torrent of crashing storms. Was it her? How had she come to be in Tournai? Who knew?

"My apologies, Lord Ellarian," stammered the guard again. "She asked for you by name, and we weren't sure whether she was one of your associates."

Dimitri waved a hand in dismissal. The man resumed scurrying ahead, taking fearful looks back at the spymaster, who stood a head taller and was a good deal more imposing than the human guard. The rank air inside the dungeons did nothing to help his nerves. He stifled a retch at the foul stench of damp and decay, gritting his teeth against the insipid freezing chill of the place. A flick of magic warmed him and banished the scent, and sent a faelight blooming above him in the constricting corridor.

The guard led him to a cell at the end of a passage, heaving open the door with a grunt. Dimitrius sent his faelight in first. He stilled as their eyes locked, and his heart stopped for a beat before thundering back to life. It was her. Harper. The bottom dropped from his stomach.

Steel-grey eyes met his. In a moment, she changed from wide eyes to sharp anger. "You! Tell them to let me go at once!"

Dimitri raised an eyebrow. He had not been expecting that. *Feisty,* he thought with a flash of amusement. This was precisely why his thoughts had lingered over her rather more than he cared to admit was professional.

The guard's mouth dropped open. He barged into the cell, an arm raised to strike her.

"Stop!" Dimitri barked. "There's no need for that. Where is the item she carried? I need it at once."

"M'pologies, Lord. It's already been sent to the king."

A flash of fear spread through Dimitri, but he crushed it swiftly. *I hope not.* He pressed his lips together in a thin line, biting back his anger. "Of course. Release her at once then."

"M'pologies, Lord. The king's orders."

"You know my position." Dimitri advanced. "Release her to my custody. I shall deal with the king. She's one of mine."

The man shrank away from the brunt of his full attention. Harper had the good sense to stay quiet, her attention flicking between them with confusion. *She has no idea what she's gotten herself into. Why is she here?* The questions could wait. First he had to get her out of there, away from the king and his scrutiny, which Dimitri feared would eventually fall upon himself.

"I—I can't, m'lord. King's orders. I can give you her property, that's all."

"Fine," he said after a pause. He knew she would have little on her worth anything to him, but it never hurt to collect such things for whatever useful means he could find. Harper glared up at him, though she remained huddled in the corner, covered in filth. She knew she was no match for him. He stared at her coldly in return, before spinning around and striding away. Part of his anger was directed at her, at how stupid she had been to walk right into the king's hands. But most of it was just anger at himself. Fury that he had dallied too long.

The anger masked his fear, too. He could not let the Dragonheart fall into the king's hands. He would never get another chance. In the wake of the thefts, the king had doubled the security upon his vaults. Besides which, if there was some way to link him to the theft, he was done for. Dimitri could not dwell on that. It was a dark path to walk down.

It provoked his desire for self-preservation and success more than ever. His thoughts jumped back to Harper, sitting in the cell. To his surprise, he felt a wisp of pity for her. He could still see her grey eyes staring him down. For a nobody, she had a compelling presence, a challenge in her gaze he rarely received from anyone given his fearsome reputation.

He stifled a dry laugh. She had no idea who she dealt with, free from such prejudices, yet she still disliked him. He supposed he had never given her any reason to feel other-wise. But even though he had demonstrated just how powerful he was, she did not seem to fear him. She was an interesting one.

"H-Here, m'lord."

The guard thrust an armful at him containing a dagger, a small bracelet, and a pair of boots. He eyed the dagger. One of elven make. He had noticed the same one hanging at

Aedon's waist. *What a charming gift,* he thought disdainfully. *Or did she steal it from him?*

His entire being stilled when the charm on the woven leather bracelet caught the paltry light of the dirty lamps. Saradon's Mark. With barely a hitch, his gaze passed to the clasp on the boots. He examined them for a second, appearing as nonchalant as he could, though his heart thundered in his chest. He cleared his throat, and the guard's attention flicked to his face. "Has anyone else looked through these?"

"No, m'lord."

With the guard's attention on his face, Dimitri slipped the bracelet up his sleeve and thrust the rest of the things back at the man. "Then I leave them with you in case the king should desire them too."

"M-M'lord?" the guard stuttered, holding the things and staring after him. Dimitri was already halfway out, striding toward the door and the faint hint of a fresh breeze, the silver bead burning cold upon the inside of his wrist.

The bracelet taunted him, revealing no secrets, as Dimitri reclined on his sumptuous couch. He fidgeted, unable to find comfort, turning the item over and over in his hands and examining every minute detail of the silver charm.

"Where did she get you from?" he breathed out with a shake of his head. Mysteries upon mysteries. He tried to piece together all he knew of her. The memory of her brazen silver eyes taunted him. What secrets was she hiding?

Harper, an uncommon name in Pelenor, who spoke the Common Tongue with a twang he was unfamiliar with. Definitely foreign. She was a companion of Aedon and his ragtag band—but that gave him little. They were all outcasts. Yet she seemed young, naïve, and inexperienced in comparison to them. Was she a new associate? Something did not quite fit. Then there was the matter of the mark upon her bracelet.

Dimitri growled, and his fingers drummed upon his leg as he rested. *Did I send the Dragonheart to her somehow? Why her?* Even with the bracelet, it was a tenuous connection at best. An answer eluded him. He huffed in annoyance. Still, her steel-grey gaze taunted him. She was temptation and distraction incarnate, and he could not afford to deviate now.

If he was sensible and callous, he would end her. She was nothing more than a loose end that could incriminate him. He had no confidence she would last through torture without revealing whatever she knew. Though he was certain she did not know the importance of what she carried, she could certainly incriminate him enough for the king to question why he had taken so long to recover the Dragonheart when he had plainly known where it was.

She could destroy him. His entire body seemed permanently flooded with nerves since his discovery that she had arrived in Tournai, but the more he dwelled upon it, the more he realised just how much trouble it could land him in. At the very least, the king would have grounds to charge him with treason for his disobedience. Without the Dragonheart and the means to raise Saradon, Dimitri's plans were dead in the water.

I should kill her at once and be done with it. Even if that would make him as bad as the king. Something sour and heavy settled in his stomach at the thought. He fingered the charm again. She carried Saradon's Mark. There was more to this than he could see—somehow, she mattered in this mess.

And he had no idea how. Dimitri closed his eyes and let out a silent scream of frustration.

He had to salvage this. The stone could not remain in King Toroth's hands—and he could not allow her to condemn him to death. *Think!* he urged himself. At any moment, the Kingsguard could be at his door and Toroth's blade at his neck.

52

HARPER

The small light from the corridor momentarily blinded Harper after her stint in total darkness and she shrank into the corner as its glare swept across the cell. Her pulse ratcheted up, thundering through her ears as shadows crowded the doorway. As her eyes accustomed, Harper couldn't separate the churn of fear and relief at the sight of Dimitrius's face looming before her.

Her body remained flooded with terror, but she refused to show it to him. Folding her arms around her to stop them from shaking from fear and cold, she glared at him, her gaze unwavering. His brow rose in momentary surprise before an unexpected mirth glittered through his eyes, tugging something swift and foreign within her. He turned back to the guard and they conversed in a tongue she did not understand.

Dimitrius seemed unhappy with whatever the guard said, for with a final icy glare that sent a thrill of fear to the pit of her stomach, he left with a swish of his cloak that sent a sharp, sweet scent with an aftertaste of musk rolling across her before the door slammed shut, leaving her in darkness.

It was not long before they came for her again, but to both her dismay and relief, Dimitrius was not with them—one miniscule piece of familiarity in a sea of the unknown. Two guards, their faces obscured by helms and beards, hauled her to her feet. Their breath and sweat was almost as bad as the cell. She struggled as they dragged her down the corridor and into another room that was big enough to accommodate them all. It was dimly lit and cold—even colder still when they tore her cloak away.

Harper felt naked without it. Terror flamed anew as she caught sight of metal instruments hanging from one of the walls and a chair with straps affixed to it in the centre of the room. No matter how much she struggled, it was barely any effort at all for them to drag her to it and strap her in. Tighter and tighter they bound the straps until spikes on the chair's arms pierced the flesh of her arms. Struggling only made it worse, so she forced herself to remain as still as possible. It was impossible. Fear, and exhaustion had her body shuddering wildly, and with every movement, pain lanced through her.

A dark cloaked male entered, his face obscured behind a black mask and only the glint of his hard eyes visible. As he raised his hands, pain seared through her entire body. She cried out as the agony burned white hot, worse even than when the wood elves had attacked her. Her struggles caused the metal spikes upon the chair to dig deeper into her flesh, adding to her pain.

Harper's eyes rolled into her head as unconsciousness threatened to take her, and she gladly reached for the darkness. Suddenly, the pain ceased. She rebounded back to waking with a rush of dull, fresh pain, but not as excruciating. Hot wetness soaked her feet. With a flush of humiliation, she realised she had wet herself.

"How did you steal the Heart of Dragons?" the black-cloaked figure asked.

"I didn't," she gasped, struggling to still herself once more to prevent the spikes from aggravating her wounds. Pain crashed over her once more and she sank into unconsciousness.

A bucket of ice-cold water drenched her. She woke, gasping in air and water, having no idea how long she had been unconscious. Pain wracked her as she spluttered and the spikes bit harder into her skin.

"Do you see where we are?" her torturer remarked in a gravelly voice that betrayed no compassion. He gestured with a giant hand around them. "I have many means, physical and magical, to make you suffer. You can end it sooner. How did you steal the Heart of Dragons?"

"I swear, I did not steal it."

"How did you steal it?" he growled, sending claws into her gut.

"I found it in the woods. I didn't take it," she forced out past her blinding fear.

"Which woods?" he yelled into her face.

She flinched away from the spear of his pale eyes. "In Caledan, far from here."

His eyes narrowed. "Such filthy lies!" He struck her across the face with a backhanded blow that sent her reeling and dimmed her vision momentarily. When he raised his hands, a different kind of pain assaulted her. A pressing all across her body that compounded the pounding of her head and the heavy weakness of her limbs crushed and distorted her.

"Stop," a cold voice commanded with quiet authority. "Touch one more hair on her head and I will obliterate you from the face of this land." A familiar voice. One she should have dreaded even more than her current captor. Dimitrius. And yet, he had stepped in to stop this—to come to her defence. Harper did not understand—but she could not be more glad for a reprieve, no matter how temporary. Harper did not think she had any more fear to give, and yet it electrified her fraught nerves anew.

Through tears and the throbbing of one side of her face, she watched the cloaked figure rise, puffed with indignance, before he melted into a bow. "My lord." The two words were edged through gritted teeth.

"I shall take over from here. Out. Now."

"I am here on the king's orders, Lo—"

"Now. Or would you like me to inform the king of your disobedience? Whose orders do you think have me in this foul pit? She is one of mine—this charade should never have gone so far. Begone before I have you in the chair."

"At once, my lord," the man murmured, gave a deep bow, and left.

The moment the door shut, Dimitrius rushed over and knelt before her, his gaze searching her face with a surprisingly caring intensity. "Are you all right?"

Harper trembled. What fresh tactic was this? She had nothing else to give, strapped to a chair, bleeding, in a pool of her own… She swallowed. It hurt. Everything hurt.

"Of course you're not," he murmured, running his gaze down her. As his attention lingered on the pool at her feet, her cheeks burned. She hoped he could not smell the urine mixed in with so much water. Her teeth chattered as a wave of cold rushed through her once more, and she could not hold in the yelp of pain as the shivering jarred the spikes in her arm.

Dimitrius swore when he noticed her injuries and worked to release her. His hands were surprisingly gentle, his fingers warm on her cold, clammy skin. In seconds, he had the restraints open and ran his palms down her arms. Harper expected pain as he raised her arms from the chair, but a soothing tingle ran down her limbs. She turned them this way and that. With a strange itching sensation, she watched, her mouth hanging open, as the torn flesh knitted itself back together without leaving even a scar. In a rippling wave, warmth spread through her, banishing both cold, pain, and a good measure of exhaustion from every inch of her body. Harper stared at Dimitrius, mute.

"Better?" he asked levelly, with no hint of the coldness she had felt at their last encounter—or the threat of violence he had just made.

"Yes. Thank you," she whispered.

"What have you told them?"

Them? Not us? "Nothing. I mean, I found the stone. I didn't steal it from the king. Please believe me." She shifted in the chair, desperate to escape, but her legs were still tied to it.

"I believe you," he said quietly, much to her surprise. His voice was low, his words gentle, and that violet stare penetrated to the centre of her soul. He was a lifeline that she did not want to cling onto—but he was her only way out. His hands lowered to her leg restraints, then halted, his fingers brushing against her ankles. "Did you mention anything of me?"

She paused, brows furrowed. "No. Why?"

"Good." He untied her. "Can you stand?"

I'm not sure, she thought, but she would not admit it. She started to push herself up on shaky legs, but Dimitrius held up a hand.

"Not yet. I need you to follow my lead. Can you do that? I promise, I will see you out of here alive."

She stilled at his words and met his gaze. *So I won't leave here alive if I don't?* Harper swallowed, nodding. "I can do that. You promise?"

"I promise once. I promise twice. I promise thrice."

Warmth flared across Harper's skin. A tingle of unease curled in her belly at the recognition of magic in his words.

A weary smile of relief formed on his face. "Do as I say, and I shall make our escape quick."

Harper nodded, consumed by a strange blend of fear and confusion that left her nauseous. For once, she was glad of an empty stomach.

"Follow me."

53

HARPER

Harper stumbled after Dimitrius. Relief leapt in her, but she dared not believe she was free. Dimitrius had his own agenda. She just did not know what it was, and she did not know whether to be more scared of that or the torture she had just escaped.

Dimitrius opened the door and strode out. Harper followed. The guard's instant advance made her stomach lurch. Their unfamiliar language flew off his tongue with the same strange lilt Aedon spoke with. She shoved him from her thoughts. It was too painful to think of her mistake now when she was so vulnerable, and when Aedon and his friends' misgivings had proved so right. The discussion became heated between the guards, the cloaked elf, and Dimitrius, but with a final threat that was clear from his tone even across tongues, the others retreated and left the way clear.

He strode with purpose as Harper staggered after, bolstered by whatever magics he had cast upon her but still exhausted and only kept on her feet by terror and desperation. He took her through a labyrinth of tunnels until she was even more disorientated. Finally, he slowed and stopped, and she too halted with relief. At an involuntary wobble, Dimitrius's hand closed around her upper arm to steady her. Warm. Solid. She was too exhausted to hate herself for finding comfort in the contact. Her eyes fluttered shut and she took in a deep, shaking breath. When she opened them, the world was still spinning and her legs threatened to buckle.

"Close your eyes."

She looked up at him, a question in her expression.

He smiled—grim, but sincere. "Trust me. Close your eyes."

Trust him? She was not sure whether she could—and definitely certain she shouldn't—but there was little other option. Harper closed her eyes. His hand on her arm was the only steadying touch as a strange tugging sensation pulled her this way and that. Light flared and warmth surrounded her. The scent of lemon and his musk. Silence blanketed. She opened her eyes and gasped. She was somewhere entirely different—and for a second, that had felt so familiar to how the Dragonheart had taken her.

It was more luxury than Harper had ever seen. She drank it in, mouth open. Sumptuous rugs and furs covered almost every inch of polished wood or stone floors. Drapes made of fabrics finer than those she wore framed tall windows that reached up to high, ornate ceilings. It was dark outside. She fleetingly wondered what time it was and how many days had passed in the cell. Fine furnishings filled the large space —plush sofas, book cases, side tables, framed paintings, dark cabinets—and metal chandeliers and lamps burned with none of the soot and stench of the tavern's tallow candles, but a floral scent that left her refreshed and dizzy with its sweetness. Harper started as Dimitrius's hand left her arm.

"You are safe for now. These are my quarters. We will not be disturbed here. I shall make sure of it. Would you care to wash?" He gestured to a separate room, behind an ajar and intricately carved redwood door.

She did not answer as she huddled into her cloak, feeling suddenly aware of how painfully out of place she was… and just how filthy.

Dimitrius's lips twitched, trying to hide a smile. "I offer you a chance to regain some of your dignity. Please, take me up on the offer. You could use a wash."

Harper's ears burned and indignant retorts burned on her tongue so fast she could not utter more than an unintelligible noise of frustration in retort. It would be nice to wash, but she bridled at his insult. She considered refusing just to spite him.

"If you want to punish me, feel free not to bathe," he said airily—he had seen the flash of stubbornness pass across her face, then. "But the offer is there." He waved at the open door. It was too tempting, and she had no clarity of thought left to evaluate her position.

"Thank you," she mumbled and picked her way across the fine woven rugs to the room. Inside was a wide, deep bowl big enough to sit in. She glanced at it, cocking her head. "Is there a bucket of water anywhere? I-I don't mind if it's cold." She had washed with far worse.

Dimitrius scoffed. "Nonsense." He strode in and turned a metal protrusion above the basin. To Harper's surprise, water gushed out, billowing steam. Another turn of another metal knob, and cold water flooded out. Both streams swirled together in the huge space.

He laughed at her evident surprise. "So you do not have running water in your corner of Caledan?"

She shook her head. Something hot and seething spiked at the way he provoked her shame so easily. He uncorked a large bottle and poured in a stream of liquid that erupted into bubbles when it hit the churning water. It filled the air with the delicious scent of... him, she realised. Horror swept away the more pressing fear that had remained a permanent undercurrent for so long. Dimitrius gestured to the water, and once more that inscrutable dark gaze met hers, and she could glean nothing from it.

"Enjoy." His tone was genuine, not a joke at her expense, but she eyed him suspiciously nonetheless. After a moment, she forced her hackles down. He was powerful and an ally for now. She needed to find out what he wanted—and where the stone had gone. It was all the leverage she had.

Soon, the basin was almost full of warm water. Dimitrius had fetched her a linen sheet to dry herself, a soft scrub to wash with, and a set of fresh clothes to change into—though she noted they were men's and would not fit her.

"I'll leave you to your bath," he said and backed away. She watched him still, her brows furrowed. "There's a lock on the door. I won't come in. Believe me, I'm not interested," he said flatly. She did not answer. "If you're worried I'm going to harm you, I would have done it already. Bathe, then we can eat—and talk. We have much to discuss."

Unease curled in her belly at that promise. She had no idea what his agenda was—but he was dangerous. Did she really want to be naked in a bath on the other side of what seemed a flimsy door when compared to what she had seen of his power?

"Hurry up. I'm famished." He turned and left, closing the door behind him.

She swallowed. She would take the chance. Harper scurried to bolt the door, though it felt like a meaningless protection. The mechanism was frail in the face of his power. Yet, she reasoned he was right. If he had meant to hurt her, he would have done it already. Her gut—and her nose—made the decision for her.

It was hard not to gag as she peeled the wet, stinking clothes from her body and piled them upon the stone floor, wishing she could burn them. For the first time, she had enough light to examine herself. It was an appalling sight, and not one she enjoyed. Between the bruises and the dirt, there was barely a clear inch of skin.

She hurried to the bath and sank into it, moaning with relief at the warmth that flooded over her. After a minute, she fetched the scrub and attacked herself with it, scrubbing furiously until every inch of her skin was red, wincing with every stroke. Soon, the clear water was brown, but her skin was gloriously *clean*. To her dismay, a variety of bruises, most of which she could not recall receiving, mottled her legs, arms and torso.

She rubbed the soap over her skin, emitting a moan of comfort at how good it felt to be clean, and the delicious scent it exuded. She stilled at a realisation. The soap smelled like *him*—some kind of sweet, sharp fruit she had not encountered before—and now she would too. She put down the soap at once. That thought was all too uncomfortable. To associate such sensory pleasure with *him*. She had hated him only hours before. Harper frowned. Did she still hate him? She had no reason not to, but he had saved her from torture, or worse. If she had learned nothing else from her time with Aedon and his companions, she had learned that not all was as it seemed and first impressions often did not stand.

It was all too much. She stood in a rush. Water sluiced

down her, a river running between her breasts and down her belly from the wet hair plastered to her shoulders. She wrung it out and clambered from the bath, snagging the towel. She had to suppress another moan as the soft fabric enveloped her. This was luxury. Pure luxury. She would enjoy it for the moments she could. Taking an extra few moments to dry herself, she breathed deeply, enjoying the feel of the soft fabric on her bare skin, before donning the clothes.

Harper could not help laughing. They were far too large—comically so. The shoulders sat too broad, causing the sleeves to cover her hands, and the trousers both too wide for her slim waist and too long for her legs. They sagged at her hips instead and trailed at her feet. She rolled up the sleeves and trousers with a sigh, and turned to the digusting pile of dirty garments at her feet. She dumped them into the bath and scrubbed them as best she could, wringing them out. They were not pristine by any measure, but they were better. She would take that.

"Hello?" she called through the bathroom door.

"Hmm?" came the muffled reply from the other side, some distance beyond the door.

Harper's stomach churned. Had he been listening? Had she actually *moaned* with bliss at any point? Her cheeks burned again, damn it. "I don't know how to make the water go away."

Harper heard his fingers snap, and gasped as the filthy water vanished. She swallowed. Both an amazing feat and a reminder of the power and danger Dimitrius bore. He had been kind to her—she was washed and about to be fed—but that did not mean she ought to trust him, she reminded herself. She had learned that lesson the hard way, with Aedon and his companions. The knife in her gut twisted as she thought how they had betrayed her, and, in a way, she them. She steeled her resolve, raised her chin, and unbolted the door.

Dimitrius reclined on a couch before the fire, one arm slung over the side, one leg crossed over the other, and a book in hand, his brow lightly furrowed as he read. The picture of relaxed ease. His jacket was gone, slung over a nearby armrest, and under it he wore a shirt of pale smoke with the top buttons undone. Her gaze fell to his open neckline. It revealed the deep curve of his neck as it joined his shoulders and hinted at the muscle on his chest. Dark tattoos crept up the side of his neck, now revealed by the open fabric. Harper snapped her attention back to his face as he chuckled at her.

"Well, don't you look a charm. Come. I waited for you." She followed him through carved wooden doors to a table big enough for six. He pulled out a chair and gestured to it. She sat, acutely aware of his presence so close behind her, and allowed him to tuck her in. He sat opposite, so close her feet could reach him if she stretched her legs.

Between them lay a veritable feast, and her tongue hurt as she salivated for it. She stared. Cold, cooked meats, cheeses, green leaves, breads, and other assorted foods she had never seen before were piled high on fine crockery. So *much*. So *fresh*. She'd never seen anything like it, such an abundance of food, and so fine. Was she permitted to eat? She fisted her hands together under the table. Waiting for him to make the first move.

"You can eat it, you know," said Dimitrius, leaning over the table to scoop food onto his plate. "It won't poison you."

Harper chose a few things, but he tutted. "For goodness sake, you're going to starve. Eat more, please." He gestured at the plates, then pushed back his chair and stood, striding around to lean over her shoulder. This close, her breath caught. The air moved against her cheek, her neck, her hands, as he leaned over her plate and piled it high from the serving dishes. "There. Better. I will not have you starving."

And then he was gone, slipping back into his chair and tucking into his food as though nothing had happened. As though he had not repeatedly attacked her companions. As though he had not just rescued her from a hellhole. As though they were casual dining acquaintances enjoying a meal together.

Harper had no idea what to make of it—or of him. She picked up a fork, holding it awkwardly. The metal implement gleamed. Metal was saved for weapons, not eating implements, in Caledan—the best she had used was a wooden spoon and her hunting knife. She used the fork to stab a mouthful of ham and cheeses and filled her mouth. Who knew when she would get another meal?

She was clean, and now she could feed—she decided to make the most of it whilst she could. It would make her stronger for whatever came next. She savoured every bite, trying not to think about that. It was the finest food of her life. Spiced cheeses, breads made with honey and herbs, cured and smoked meats cut wafer thin. Her tongue burst with the intense flavours of each fresh mouthful. Was this what it was like to be rich? She turned away from the bitterness of that thought—it was too much to face alongside everything else. She could not restrain herself. After so long without, Harper ate and ate and ate until she could eat no more, then sat back in her chair with a groan.

"Enjoyable?"

"The nicest meal I've ever had." The words slipped out before she could stop them, but Harper forced any hint of a smile from her face. He was still an enemy. She remained a prisoner. She would not fall for the charm of a free meal or a safe bed again. His own smile faded with her dourness.

"To business then," he said with a brittle tone that made shivers crawl up her spine and alighted the fear curled in her stomach once more. "If you do exactly as I say, Harper, you might make it out alive."

54
RAGNAR

Ragnar sat in the corner of the dingy inn. He puffed on his pipe, nursing his flagon of ale. He had purposefully slumped in the seat, eyes unfocused and dazed, as though he were already filled with drink, but his mind followed every conversation within reach. That afternoon, he had gone from inn to inn, soaking up the gossip that ran rampant and unchecked away from the ears of the city guard.

It was just his luck to be the most inconspicuous of them all. Brand, the giant Aerian, would stick out, as would Erika with her unusual attire. Then there was Aedon and his well-known reputation. To the humans and elves of Tournai, one dwarf was much like another. Ragnar played to it as much as he could with a generic cloak and none of his usual beard embellishments or hints to his identity.

Wrapped in that dark cloak, as anonymous as the rest of the patrons, he listened for any mention of Harper. He did not hear her name, but the theft of a secret, most magical treasure and the ensuing capture of the thief could be no coincidence. *It's got to be her*, he thought, his heart sinking the more he heard. They were too late.

It was almost impossible to walk as though he were drunk, bumbling and stumbling from the city to return to the others. He longed to run, but it would be too suspicious, so he endured the laughs and jeers of the guards as they taunted him and slammed the gate shut so quickly behind him it stung his backside. He ambled into the dark countryside away from the city. Only when he was away from the lights of the towering walls did he break into a jog, savouring deep breaths of the pure air. Time was of the essence. It did not take long to find them tucked up in a vacant shepherd's hut, and even less to relay the day's events.

"We're too late," Aedon said, adding to Ragnar's own trepidation.

"Aye," he replied, slumping down beside the paltry fire.

"She is probably in captivity as we speak."

Erika pursed her lips. "She will be suffering the worst treatment, especially if they have seen the mark on her bracelet."

"And whose fault is that?" Aedon snapped. "You're the reason this blew up, that she is where she is. If you hadn't been so high and damnably mighty, she wouldn't be in such danger."

Erika did not return his scowl, frowning at the ground. Ragnar knew she believed Aedon was right, though she would not admit it.

Brand ruffled his wings, making the shadows dance across the half-fallen walls. "We are all to blame. We all could have managed this better."

Aedon ruffled his hair. "We have to rescue her somehow. I can't bear to think what they must be doing to her, how much she's suffering at their hands." He shook his head and shuddered. "I know it seems futile, but it's our fault she's in there. Damn the stone, but we cannot abandon her. She needs us even more now."

"Of course," said Ragnar. "But where can we find her? How? Will she have even made it to the castle? Tournai is so big, it will be like searching for a needle in a haystack."

Aedon rubbed his chin, deep in thought. He slowly turned to Ragnar. "*Please* tell me you did not throw away her knife."

Ragnar raised an eyebrow. "It's in my pack. Why?" He couldn't bear to, truth be told, even though it was most certainly not worth salvaging. He rummaged for it and held it out to Aedon. The handle was burnt and cracked, and the blade dulled.

Aedon's face split into a huge grin, and he clapped Ragnar on the shoulder, surprising him. "Divining. We can find her with it. Like calls to like. It will lead us right to her."

"How certain are you?" asked Brand.

"There's only one way to find out." Aedon took the knife from him and held it out across both palms.

55

HARPER

Harper felt her eyes drifting shut as another wave of exhaustion threatened to take her. She blinked furiously and straightened in her chair, determined not to be vulnerable in Dimitrius's presence. He felt like a predator—and she, the prey. Dimitrius smirked as though he knew exactly what she thought of him.

His attention turned to the bottle of wine between them, and he made a small sound of disapproval. "I rather prefer the red to finish. One moment." He slipped from the chair and took the bottle to a side-table where a rack held many other bottles. He perused them at leisure, tapping a bottle here, pulling one out there.

Harper's eyes darted to her place setting. There were five different types of knives. Holding her breath, she slipped the middle knife from the table—the one with a serrated edge and a sharp point—and tucked it up her sleeve, wedging it in with another fold of the loose fabric. The cold metal implement burned against her arm. She did not move, did not react, as he returned with another dark bottle, and poured out a measure for them both.

Dimitrius raised his glass to her. She watched him guardedly. What was this? What was she supposed to do? He wasn't holding it out to her, just holding it in the middle of the table. His expression faltered. "Cheers," he said, and took a sip of his wine. "You can drink it, you know. It's not poisoned. You don't have to wait on ceremony."

Harper picked up the crystal flute between her forefingers and thumb like him. It felt so delicate that it would shatter if she clenched her fist around it. The ruby wine looked uncomfortably like blood, and she wanted to recoil from drinking it—but he watched her. She would not baulk. The small sip coated her tongue in rich, tangy liquid that was not at all unpleasant. "Oh!" She hid the exclamation poorly under a clearing of her throat and put the glass roughly down on the table. To her relief, he did not remark upon it.

"Come. Let's enjoy the evening air." Dimitrius stood and took both of their wine glasses in hand. He looked back at her and cocked an eyebrow expectantly. She shoved back the chair and followed him through a set of tall, carved, wooden doors out onto a stone balcony.

Harper shivered—the night had dropped cold with the promise of autumn's coming, and after a warm bath and a hot meal, she had grown contented and sleepy. It was just what she needed to banish that and reclaim her alertness. She followed him warily, scanning their surroundings—and all the while the knife hung hidden in her sleeve, a heavy cool weight against her skin.

Dimitrius set down both glasses on the edge of the balcony of ornate stone and leaned against it, looking down at the city below. In the darkness, it was warm and welcoming with pricks of light shining from every window in a carpet of light that blanketed down to the edge of the city. Beyond the walls, the land lay, a strip of inky black under the open heavens, where paltry clouds chased across a backdrop of stars. The balcony was empty and dark, the door behind them throwing out warmth and light. Harper drifted closer to the edge, glancing down on the pretence of admiring the view.

"Who are you, Harper?" he asked her, swirling the wine around in his fluted glass.

"What do you mean?" she asked guardedly, her attention snapping to him. So close in the dark, Dimitrius was a looming shadow over her, his dark eyes glinting in the sparse light. She fought back a shudder.

"Exactly that. Who are you? Where do you come from? You're not from Pelenor."

She winced. Was it that obvious? "I'm not," she allowed herself to say, crossing her arms. The knife dug into her uncomfortably. "I'm from Caledan." She looked up at him to see if he knew of it. His expression remained unreadable.

His reply was level. "Caledan is far away. What brings you to this land?"

Harper swallowed. Even now, she did not know how far away she had travelled, nor did she dare ask, for it seemed to be impossibly distant. "I don't know," she whispered. She told him of the night she had found the Dragonheart, lost amongst the blizzard-covered forest, and how it had seemingly transported her to Pelenor. Words tumbled out, one after another, and she could not explain why she told him, of all people. It did not feel like revealing anything of value—she was already at his mercy—but if he could give her *answers* then she might not be clawing in the dark. She clung to that faint hope. To her surprise, he did not question her, though his eyebrows drifted farther up his forehead as he listened.

"When the villagers chased me, I ran as fast as I could. I didn't know where, but I needed to get away from them. That's when I bumped, quite literally, into Aedon." Harper grinned at that—then pinched her lips together, wiping the mirth from her face. She might have told him some of her story, but she would say nothing of Aedon and his friends. It was not lost on Dimitrius.

"You aren't so surly when you smile, you know. You almost look pleasant," he offered in an offhand voice. He took a long sip of his wine, holding her in his magnetic gaze.

What a ridiculous statement to make. He lounged there, undoubtedly the most handsome male she had laid eyes on and garnished in finery worth more than her life's earnings. In contrast, she was what? A dirty peasant from a foreign land? She could have scoffed at him if she wasn't still so apprehensive of the threat he posed. Harper glowered at him, but he only laughed her away.

"When was this? How long have you been here?"

"You believe me?" An unfamiliar relief hesitantly surfaced.

"Of course."

"Why?" The relief bloomed, along with curiosity.

"Because it's not as impossible as it sounds, and you seem like a terrible liar to me. I would be able to tell."

She raised an eyebrow. He certainly had a high opinion of himself. "Hmph." When his silence and undivided attention demanded an answer, she continued. "I've lost track. I suppose it's been a few weeks."

He nodded. "That makes sense. That's when the stone vanished."

"From the king's vaults?" She searched his expression, but it remained frustratingly unreadable.

"Correct."

"But if you believe me, then the king will, too, right? If the stone brought me here, there must be a way home."

"I'm afraid it's not that simple, Harper." Dimitrius's face closed as he set down his glass upon the stone once more. "I hope for you to never meet the king. He is not a kind elf."

Harper nodded slowly, but a part of her still refused to believe that all hope was lost. "Then why do you serve him?" she asked, though she already knew the answer. Why did anyone serve the unworthy? She was guilty of it herself, working to sustain the greed of Lord Denholme, like the rest of her countryfolk.

Dimitrius let out a cold bark of laughter. "Why are you poor? Because there is little other choice."

The back of Harper's neck pricked at that. "But you hope for better?" Like she did.

He looked her over, coolly, as if evaluating her worth. "Yes." She sensed he would say little more. She was pushing —and she could feel him closing up.

"Aren't you little better?" she dared. "You're the king's spymaster, are you not?"

Dimitrius's face darkened. "Have you not realised yet that not all is as it seems? Or are you so naïve that you do not realise people may be far more than they present to the world?"

She subsided, but it did not stop her from wondering who he was and what dark things he did for the king. It sobered her to be reminded of his danger—and the danger she was in, if she displeased him. She did not know him. He had fed her, allowed her to wash. It did not mean he had a shred of decency. And he was most certainly using her for whatever information she had to offer. When he realized she was worth nothing—what then? Harper did not want to think too hard on that.

"Another reason to return to Caledan. I know nothing of this court and its ways." *Nor do I want to.*

"Of course, but the king will not be your means to get home. I suppose you have loved ones waiting for you to return? They shall be worried for your absence."

"No," Harper mumbled. "Nothing like that. There's someone I look after. She made sure I survived, so now I'm returning the favour. I think she might be the only person in the world who needs me." *The only person who cares if I'm dead in a gutter or not.*

What was she wanting to return to? She stared at the stars until they blurred before her. She had no family, no prospects. Just a tiny hut, a worn book, and a forever depleting pile of coin that would be long gone when she returned. It was too much to contemplate. Her drive since arriving in Pelenor had been to return to Caledan, but what was that worth if there was nothing to truly return to? Where did she belong if not there?

"Don't look so wan. That's not such a bad thing. Family is overrated," Dimitrius said darkly.

"I wouldn't know."

He raised an eyebrow. "You don't know your family?"

"No. I'm an orphan. Do you have family?" It was impossible to imagine him with a wife and children—to imagine him capable of kindness and love.

"Unfortunately."

Harper waited expectantly.

"I prefer not to associate with them whenever possible." He shrugged, but she could tell it was a casual movement meant to hide an old pain, because he had a small crinkle in the centre of his brow that seemed out of place with his usually smooth expression. "So, what do you know of the Heart of Dragons, Harper of Caledan?"

She allowed herself to follow the change of topic. "Hardly anything. It's a powerful thing, said to be the actual heart of a real dragon, but dragons haven't been seen in Caledan for centuries, so it's a myth, right?"

Dimitrius tipped his head to one side. "Not exactly. It is true. The Heart of Dragons is literally that. I daresay they are rarer in Caledan than they are here, where the king hoards dragons—both dead and alive."

His disdain was clear, oozing from his tongue. Harper filed that away. She needed to know whatever little tidbits she could of him, if it would make a difference for her own survival. He hated the king, yet he served him. Interesting.

"Their magic is legendary. Not that anyone would know, given the king's penchant for collecting them."

"And what about you?" Harper asked. She felt cold to the core now. They were here to talk business, but she still did not have a way out of any of this mess.

"What about me?" His brow lifted, and the corner of his mouth tugged into a smile at the change of tack.

"What do you want with me?" Harper straightened, but she was no match for his height. He towered above her as he took a slow, deliberate step forward.

"You are in a great deal of danger—and it is best for both of us if that disappears. If *you* disappear, perhaps."

The threat lingering in his voice had her moving. If she was lucky, she could leap the balustrade and climb down on the ivy that curled around the building. Harper slipped the knife from her sleeve and swept her arm up to his throat.

56
HARPER

Dimitrius moved faster than Harper could perceive in a blur of shadow and grabbed her wrist, the knife suspended between them at his throat. "My goodness. You are a murderous little thing, aren't you? First you try to shoot me, now you try to cut my throat with my own silverware? That's poor thanks for saving, bathing, and feeding you, little huntress. Or perhaps I should call you a wolf? Your bite is sharp and wicked, and it seems I shall not tame you today."

"Let go!" She wrenched away, but his grip was iron as he drew her closer until they were almost chest to chest, so close that she could see the curl of those shadowy tattoos creeping up his collarbone. His smile was deadly as he looked down upon her with revenge promised in his heavy gaze. Lightning sang through every nerve and muscle in her, and she had never felt so alive as in the danger of that moment.

"To do what, precisely, hmm? Shall I help you?" He drew her arm closer and cocked his head. Then bared his neck to her and to that blade, drawing it closer until it nicked his skin. "Is this what you want? Please, be my guest. Put me out of my misery in this foul place—but be prepared to deal with the consequences."

Harper stopped breathing. Her wrist throbbed in his grasp. He grazed his throat across the very edge of the blade—to no effect—and laughed as he twisted her arm. She dropped the knife with a cry of pain, and a moment later, the blade was in his grasp between long, elegant fingers. It clinked as he set it down next to his wine glass on the stone.

"What were you hoping to achieve?" he scoffed. "Oh, don't bother answering. I suppose I cannot blame you for trying to escape—but do not mistake my courtesy for kindness, or my generosity for weakness, Harper. You are here because it serves my purpose. For now."

Dimitri took her chin between his forefinger and thumb and tipped it up, forcing her to meet his eyes. This close, his stare paralysed her, the threat of the power brimming within enough to make her heart stutter. "Do not try that again," he warned. "You will do as I say, or we will both die. Know that I am as invested in keeping you alive as I am myself, for at this moment, they are one and the same."

At last, he let her go and Harper staggered back into the stone railing, crashing into it with a painful impact. She breathed heavily, unable to shake the dread that curled through her, nor the exhilaration of the moment. Her eyes darted over the railing. If she jumped now, would she make it?

"The answer is no, Harper," Dimitrius said softly, watching her. He tipped his glass and drained the last mouthful. "If you try, you will fail, and we will both die. I cannot allow that to happen."

She swallowed, and his attention flicked to the bob of her throat.

"I mean you no harm. Truly," he offered. "I commend your pluck, that you would choose to take me on, despite the vast impossibility of your success. Turn that foolish bravery to your real chance of survival." He watched her—but she could not respond, frozen against the stone, her chest heaving. "If you do as I say, I will ensure you leave here alive. I promise once. I promise twice. I promise thrice. Do we have an agreement, Harper?"

His magic caressed her, charging the feelings raging within her. Her legs shook, and she was glad for the stone to hold her up. Before her, he simply stood. The pure, raw power of him balanced in that moment, waiting for her choice. Those dark eyes were impassive once more, no feeling betrayed in his masked expression. She could glean no emotion from the preternatural stillness of that predatory body of his that oozed the promise of darkness.

Her agreement was the best hope for her survival in that moment. That was all she had to do. All this was. One step after another. And at each one, she simply had to choose the path to surviving. To freedom. "Yes," she breathed. And his magic coiled around her like the jaws of a wolf promising a beautiful death.

"Good," he crooned.

That was not the word she would have chosen. But she was not dead—and so she had won this step in this very real game of *chatura* she now found herself playing. Exhaustion dragged through her, and she sagged against the stone.

At once, his hand was at her arm, steadying her. Her stomach swooped with the threat of his proximity as his citrus and musk scent washed over her. She pushed him away and stood, swaying slightly. They had an agreement—

yet it did not mean she trusted him. She had let her guard slip over dinner, lulled by warmth, unthreatening conversation, more food than she had ever been allowed to eat, and a seemingly generous host, but she had since shown her hand. There was no way that his kindness was genuine and without motive. Or that he would trust her in the slightest after the stunt she had just pulled.

"You must be beyond exhausted. Come, rest." Fear bloomed in her belly as her thoughts turned to sleeping arrangements. Would he expect payment for his hospitality? He knew she had no money and nothing else to offer, which meant… She knew what men wanted from women—the men at the inn, at least. She *wouldn't*. She would fight him tooth and nail if he forced her.

"*Come*," he repeated at her reluctance. "I have a spare bedchamber that you are welcome to use. No one else knows you are here, so you are safe tonight. I promise you."

She blinked. That wasn't what she had expected from this dangerous male. *Am I safe from you?* She did not dare to ask. No doubt the bedchamber had a latch on the door that would be equally as ineffective as the bathing room's at keeping him at bay.

Dimitrius tsked. "Sleep in there, sleep on the floor out here. I care not. For your own safety, however, you may not leave my quarters, may I make that expressly clear. I can return you to the dungeons, if you find that a preferable option." He smirked at her visible shudder, and those violet eyes drank her in. "I thought not. Come."

She followed him in and he led her a short ways down a dimly lit panelled hallway. "This chamber is yours for the night. I shall not bother you, have no worry of that. Good night."

"Wait," she called, then swallowed, worried at her boldness.

Dimitrius turned and fixed her in an impassive stare, an eyebrow raised.

"There…" Harper took a deep breath. "I had a bracelet with me. A leather thing, old and worn, with a silver bead on it. It's nothing much. It has no worth to any but I. I don't suppose you have it?"

Dimitri narrowed his eyes. "Why do you want it?"

"It's the only thing I have left of home."

"Where did you come by it?"

"I've had it for as long as I can remember. Please, it really is worth nothing to anyone else. I don't even think it's real silver. May I have it back?"

"I shall see if I can find it. Perhaps." He inclined his head and slipped down a corridor to what she presumed were his own quarters.

She walked to the bedchamber and opened the door. Harper swallowed, looking around. She doubted even Lord Denholme had chambers so fine. With a backwards glance at the empty living quarters, she slipped inside and shut the door behind her, before leaning against the cool wood and letting out a lengthy exhale. None of this seemed real anymore.

It was almost dark but for a few lamps dotted about, all of which contained small, bobbing faelights that cast the room in a faint, warm glow. Harper edged into the centre of the room and spun on the spot, taking in every detail of the wood panelled room as her toes scrunched in the furs beneath her feet. She looked down. It must have been a huge beast to almost cover the parquet floor, but its fur was as soft as a rabbit pelt.

Slowly, she approached the bed—a giant four-poster that

shamed her rough, wooden pallet—and ran her fingers along silken oversheets, thick undercovers, plump pillows and cushions. It was hard to put a price on such luxury. Certainly more than she could have earned in ten lifetimes of eking out an existence in Caledan. It put a lump in her throat.

The room was hers. Again, her gaze flicked to the door. The image of Dimitrius between the sheets before her flashed through her mind. He terrified and attracted her in equal measure, and she was not entirely sure what to feel about that. She crushed the thought.

Trust... Do I trust him? she wondered. Not in her lifetime. Yet it was no prison, at least not the same one she had been in earlier that day, nor did she seem to be in mortal danger from Dimitrius. Another yawn threatened. She swayed with tiredness, but remained standing. *What's better? To knowingly sleep in the home of my enemy, or to collapse from exhaustion?*

57

DIMITRI

He couldn't sleep, though her light snores showed she had no such qualms. Exhaustion had finally taken Harper. Dimitri leaned against the doorframe, his eyes narrowed, watching the gentle rise and fall of the covers on Harper's prone form. Despite their conversation, he still could not fathom how she came to be there, from Caledan to Pelenor, and the strange series of events, not the least of which was the Dragonheart's bizarre destination.

Had he not seen the Mark of Saradon that she carried so preciously at the expense of any other treasure or talisman—and the only thing she had asked for to be returned to her—he would have said it could be nothing of his making. But with the mark of the infamous half-elf, and the elven blood running through her veins that marked her as different from all others in the non-magical realm of Caledan, there had to be an element of destiny within it all.

Why did it come to you? he silently asked her still form. Did it have something to do with Saradon? Perhaps because he had somehow recovered the relic when his magic had failed, the stone had found some form of Saradon's likeness somewhere else. Did it have something to do with her tattered bracelet and the Mark of Saradon upon it? What did that mean far away in Caledan? It all seemed entirely impossible, yet there he was, grasping at the smallest explanation.

An enigma.

Was it his own miscalculation, or fate? He did not believe in chance. No, it was by some design that she of all individuals had found the Dragonheart, that she of all people had come to be there. The mystery of her consumed him. What an individual she was. He uttered a quiet laugh and shook his head. His spirit leaped at the challenge in her. He could do little else but wonder at her.

The first time he had seen her, he might have forgiven her misdemeanour to draw a bow with an arrow nocked in his very face. He had been so amused then by the defiance in her silver eyes. She might have not known his identity, but she had recognised him for the danger he was and she had not backed down. But now? Now, she knew precisely who he was, had seen—had *tasted*—his power, and still, it had not brought her, practically a mortal, to her knees begging for mercy.

No. She hadn't done that at all. She had stolen a knife from his very own table and put it to his throat. He had never met anyone quite like her—and she thrilled him. No doubt it would be beyond tricky to navigate what was to come next, especially if he needed to finish with the Dragonheart in hand, but he had no doubt whatsoever that she was going to make it deliciously interesting. He started at a small tapping on the outside. With a last look at Harper, he silently closed her door and answered the tapping. One of his operatives at the door to his suites.

"Yes?"

"Rook reporting, sir. Word has made it back to the king that you have the prisoner he detained for the theft of a Dragonheart. You're about to be summoned."

He nodded, and Rook melted into the shadows. Dimitrius barred the door again, locking it and putting up his wards, then charged back to Harper's room, pulling a bell cord on the way.

"Harper, wake up," he called in a low, urgent voice. She stirred. After a second of grogginess, she jumped from the bed, whipped something gleaming from under her pillow and brandished… a candlestick holder at him. Amusement and something deeper bloomed. She was untameable.

"What are you doing in here?" she demanded, her eyes narrowed, every muscle in her body tensed. He noted that she still remained fully clothed.

He decided not to remark on the makeshift weapon, which she had somehow filched from the dining room without him knowing. "It *is* my abode." He raised a brow, but continued without waiting for a venomous response. "I apologise, but there's no time. I thought we had until morning, but alas, I was mistaken. The Kingsguard is on its way. They come for both of us." He knew there remained only one card in his arsenal. To take her to the king as his own tool.

"You called, m'lord?" A maid appeared, and Harper jumped at her presence. Her blank eyes slid over Harper without lingering before settling upon Dimitri.

"Emyria, I need you to obtain a squire's outfit for this young lady at once. Nothing too fancy or too shabby."

Emyria sized up Harper with a critical eye, before bobbing her head and scurrying away.

Dimitri turned back to Harper. "I need you to listen and follow my instructions to the very letter. Do you understand me? For goodness sake. Put down that trinket. You know that's no defence."

"What's happening? What do you want?"

Dimitri sighed. "What I *want* is a different matter. What I *need* right now is to make sure the pair of us survives the night. The king's men are coming. If you want to avoid an excrutiatingly painful death, I need you to act exactly as I tell you. I assume you would like to remain alive and well?" He raised an eyebrow.

Dumbfounded, she nodded.

"Fantastic. Get ready to meet the king…"

58
HARPER

Harper gawked at him, still groggy from sleep and a full stomach. *The king.* But nerves assailed her. She had been arrested, charged with theft, and tortured in this king's name. And now, Dimitrius wanted her to… what?

As if he could read her thoughts, Dimitrius ceased pacing. "I realise it sounds ludicrous, but this is the only way I see that we can succeed."

Her chance was slipping away—how could she bargain for her freedom and passage to Caledan if she went along with this? But, if she did not… Aedon had warned her it would be a painful death. Now, she believed him. Perhaps the only win was leaving there alive.

She wrinkled her nose. "So I have to pretend that I work for you, and I found the Dragonheart for the king?"

"Exactly. It won't be hard." He looked at her, and with a rush of fear and something she could not name, his voice sounded in her head. *"Do not fear. I will be with you the whole time. Anything you do not know the answer to, I can help. Any moment you doubt, take a deep breath and my answer shall be there on your tongue."*

That snatched her breath away, to have him inside her own head—far too intimately close for comfort. Harper swallowed and glanced down at herself, suddenly self-conscious. The squire's clothing fit decently and was finer than anything she had ever worn before. The pants were made of a charcoal cloth that hugged her legs and tucked neatly into new, stiff, brown leather boots that were only slightly too big for her. A charcoal tunic bearing the royal symbol—a tree, mountain, and stars—dropped to her mid-thighs, the fitted sleeves covering the length of her arms and threatening to spill over her hands.

Emyria had done her level best to tame Harper's flyaway hair into a neat braid that sat squarely between her shoulder blades, but no matter how much she had tried, Harper felt like she did not belong, and that she was well out of her depth.

The guards waited outside, loitering like crows. Dimitrius had dismissed them, so he could present himself in a more befitting manner to the king. It had bought them time, but no more than scant minutes to dress as best as they could.

"You look fine. Fitting to be in my employ," Dimitrius said with a smirk, which Harper answered with a glowering scowl.

As she followed him out the door and into the company of the king's personal guard, she thought she caught the faintest tremble of Dimitrius's hands as they smoothed down his impeccably tailored tunic. That scared her more than anything else. If he feared the king, what chance did she have?

Seated in full regalia upon the throne at the far end of the vast hall, King Toroth could have been a statue. Harper shivered, and not just due to the frigid cold. A far contrast to the surprising warmth of Dimitrius's chambers.

Toroth's face was carved in stone, and the stern, uncompromising harshness in his expression made her even more anxious. Trailing Dimitrius, she forced herself to take one step after another and bowed as he did before the king, halting a respectful distance away.

The king's booming voice echoed around the empty hall and up into the lofty heights where no light pierced the shadows of the vaulted ceiling. Silent, unmoving guards, who could very well have been empty suits of armour for all she knew, were just as imposing as their master. Harper's gaze nervously flicked around them all. Unconsciously, she shrank toward Dimitrius, the only semblance of an ally she had.

Toroth spoke in Pelenori, but Harper heard the cutting disdain in his tone and saw Dimitrius's tall posture wilt slightly at the king's words. She mentally rehearsed what Dimitrius had instructed her to say.

"What say you, girl?" the king's voice in Common Tongue cut through her focus and she startled, covering it with a deep bow to the king and remaining there, her eyes upon the floor, as Dimitrius had told her to. "What account can you give of this? Am I to believe what he says?"

"Your Majesty," Harper said, trying to keep the tremor from her voice. "I am not worthy to address you."

Toroth clenched his jaw. "And yet I order it of you."

Harper bowed lower. "I was instructed by Lord Ellarian

to infiltrate the company of Aedon, formerly of House Felrian, on grounds that he was suspected to have had involvement in the theft of an item of your esteemed property."

"*Good,*" Dimitrius's soothing voice murmured into her mind. "*Keep going.*"

"I found that to be true, but not possessing the magical or physical strength to take it by force, I had to ingratiate myself with them until such time as their trust in me allowed me to take the stone from them."

Toroth's eyes narrowed. "You do realise, girl, I have an entire army at my disposal. Why did you not report it to me at once?" He looked at Dimitrius. "Raedon and his Wings have been working *pointlessly* on this. You ought to have informed me at once, so I could have tasked them with more important matters."

"Forgive me, sire. Aedon has ever been a slippery target, as you well know, and I did not want to give him any reason to spook."

"So you *did* know. Are you certain it was not your ego that came between you and your task?" Toroth growled.

"Absolutely not, sire. We gained valuable information into the workings of Aedon, his associates, and their machinations."

Toroth snorted. "And you invite this peasant into your very chambers? Do you *dally* with all your spy scum?"

Harper stiffened at the insinuation, but Dimitri remained confident. He flicked his gaze at her and gave her a sideways smile that sent a shiver down her back and stirred something uncomfortable within her. "I do whatever it takes to obtain the information you desire, sire. I would never compromise Pelenor. My chambers are private—no prying ears of your enemies there."

Toroth bristled. "I have no enemies in my own kingdom. What is this *valuable* information you obtained?"

"Aedon and his outlaws currently flee the wood elves of Tir-na-Alathea."

Toroth's attention sharpened at that. "Those jumped-up feys? Ha!" he barked. "I welcome them to him—to each other. I am still not satisfied that you did not procure it sooner."

Harper felt the rumble of his anger reverberating through her, but it was directed at Dimitrius, who faced it unflinchingly. She dared a glance at him, but his shadowed face was impassive. Toroth rose from his throne. Around them, the clang of armour sounded. The guards, readying themselves to jump to their king's command.

"You think yourself better than us all, don't you, little bastard?" he said in a dangerously quiet, even voice. The spark in his eyes invited Dimitrius to rise to the challenge, even relished it, but he did not.

Toroth's eyes flicked to hers. Harper immediately dropped her gaze to the floor, holding herself with rigid determination, even though she trembled at his approaching power, the pressure of which she felt in her very bones like an ache of dull pain.

"Not at all, sire," Dimitrius replied in an even voice. "*Bow,*" he said into Harper's mind. They sank low before the king. "I live to serve your wishes, sire. This mission was of the utmost importance, and I did not wish to leave it to chan—"

"Silence!" snapped the king, then added more in Pelenori that Harper did not understand. She felt Dimitrius stiffen beside her—both of them still locked in a bow—and saw his jaw clench and the flash of his gritted teeth. Dimitrius replied to the king, who prowled around the pair of them. Harper's heart thundered, until all she could hear was the blood rushing through her own ears and all she could feel was the swooping sickness and trembling of her aching limbs.

At last, the king stopped. "Get out, bastard, and take your alley scum with you."

Harper struggled to hold in a sudden surge of tears as they left the room. How different he had been than the noble monarch she had pictured. It was not so. Toroth was hard-hearted and rotten to the core. He would not send her home if she asked, and she could not begin to unravel what that meant for her prospects.

It was clear that she did not belong there. The court was a strange machination to her with its own set of rules and goals she could not fathom. For the first time, she felt as insignificant as one snowflake amidst a blizzard.

59

DIMITRI

imitri cursed in Pelenori. "He did that on purpose. Held audience with us in the formal throne room to intimidate me." He scowled, and his balled fists shook by his side as he strode the halls so quickly that Harper had to jog to keep up. When they had escaped the reach of the king, Dimitrius halted. He searched her face, and he could tell it startled her. "Are you all right?"

"Y–Yes."

That was a blatant lie, he reckoned. Dimitrius swallowed. "Good." It was a reminder to them both that he ought not be kind to her. Anything he showed kindness to was destroyed. He could not risk her, above all others, for she could destroy him too.

"Are you?" she asked haltingly.

Dimitrius closed his eyes and turned away, hating the feeling that slunk through his chest at her care. No one ever asked him that. She did not belong in this damned court. *Fool of a woman. Guard yourself better.* "I'm fine," he said with a hint of a snap that he immediately regretted. Her face closed, but not before he saw the hurt that flashed across it.

Once in the safety of his own chambers, he relaxed. Harper stood awkwardly by the door. He gestured to the sumptuous armchairs before the hearth. "Sit. I apologise. The court is an intimidating place to you, I imagine."

Harper nodded.

"It's not easy to be here and not understand any of it. I'll grant you that. You did well. I understand what it is like to stand before him for the first time."

"You understand how I feel?" Doubt laced her voice.

"Well, of a sort. I imagine Toroth made his feelings toward me clear, no matter what tongue he spoke in." Dimitrius scowled. He still felt that uncomfortable swoop in the pit of his belly. The shame never left. He glanced to the shuttered windows, but no light yet slipped through the edges.

"Come. To bed with us both." He ran a hand across his face, wishing he could erase the creeping tiredness that had plagued him for weeks. "I fear the ordeal is not yet over, and we had best be fresh when next the king sends for us."

Harper padded obediently to her room, but Dimitri made no move, staring into the flickering flames that danced across the logs, hungry for their fuel, like he was hungry for change. Any other lord would have been indignant with rage at such treatment—whether from the king or not—but Dimitri had no anger left in that moment. It was not the words that concerned him.

There would be no way to obtain the Dragonheart. Not now it was in the king's possession. He closed his eyes, as if he could banish the thought of failure and hopelessness, but of course, that bore no fruit. He could not deny it to himself.

Dimitri cursed. It was the only way to save himself and erase the madness from the kingdom. A part of him was still in the throne room at another time and place, flinching as the king's spittle landed upon his face, enduring Toroth's tirade with a stony face.

Times do not change, no matter how much they need to. I must find a way.

But no matter how much he thought, he could not find one. He was in over his head, too closely associated with the stone, and through Harper, there was the possibility of somebody finding out he took it in the first place, if anyone dared to dive into her mind, steal the truth of their encounters, and calculate from there. He had no doubt Toroth would, given the reason to, for they were all bound to serve him. Dimitri only wondered how soon he, and Harper, would be summoned once more. Only the king's trust in his own authority protected the both of them thus far.

Get rid of her, his mind goaded him. *She is the weak link.*

He shook his head, as if he could deny his own mind. *I cannot kill her.*

You've done it before...

I will not kill her. It is not my nature.

There had to be another way. Maybe he could return her to the company of Aedon, or perhaps even her homeland, where the king would never find her. But even as the thoughts bloomed, they slipped away. They were desperation. Nothing more.

Over breakfast the next morning, Dimitri pried for more information. Judging from the shadows under her eyes,

Harper looked to have slept as little as he after their audience with the king.

"What made you stay with Aedon and his merry band of criminals?" he enquired in a light voice. "We never did finish our chat yesterday about your adventures."

Harper glared at him, full of suspicion.

Dimitri laughed. He could not help it. This young woman was a curiosity—no one else would have dared to treat him with such defiance. It surprised him, but he enjoyed the novelty. More than that, he liked her, he realised, and that was a very unfamiliar feeling. "Do not worry. I don't expect you to share any valuable secrets."

After a moment's hesitation, Harper chewing on her lip, she spoke. "Well, they were kind to me, for a start, and I didn't have anywhere else to turn. What else could I do?"

"You seemed clear that you wanted to see Toroth, to petition him to return you to your homelands. Did they escort you here?" A part of him still hoped they lingered. Their capture would be a sweet present to the king to curry his favour and perhaps buy himself more time.

Harper winced. "Not exactly. We had a disagreement. Their goals and mine did not align, shall we say."

"Oh?" Dimitri raised an eyebrow, but did not say more. Neither did Harper. He suppressed a smile. *Oh, she's determined not to incriminate them. How does Aedon do it?* he wondered with a flicker of resentment for the easy grace with which the disgraced elf always managed to charm everyone. It was no wonder he had eluded capture for so long.

"Come now. If that's the case, they cannot be as friendly as you seem to think. You've seen what they abandoned you to."

"They didn't abandon me," Harper said stubbornly.

"Oh?" Dimitri spread his hands wide. "Forgive me. I don't see them coming to save you."

Harper's shoulders crumpled at that. Dimitri regretted being so callous, but he capitalised upon it anyway. "Where are they journeying to?"

"I don't know. But they're not as bad as they seem."

"Hmm."

"They're trying to help some villagers cure a sickness that seems to be spreading, almost like a plague."

Dimitri stiffened and leaned forward. "A what? Where? When?" He gripped the table, his knuckles white.

"I—I don't know. I don't know Pelenor."

With a giant whoosh of breath, Dimitri sat back in his chair and tapped his fingers upon the table. "You're sure it was a plague-like sickness?"

"That's what they said, and what we saw. Why?"

"Because the king knows nothing of it. Or, if he does, he's said nothing, which I would not put past him," Dimitri growled. "Either way, this is grave news." He sighed. "Come. Eat your breakfast. I fear today will be a long day."

Harper ate obediently, though it did not take much persuading. He had not failed to notice how thin she was, as if she had never had a full belly. Dimitri pursed his lips and dropped his gaze to his own plate.

It was the same wherever he went. No matter whose kingdom, abject poverty and inconceivable wealth existed side by side. He fleetingly wondered if the rulers in her homeland were as cruel as the king. If he could somehow send her back, what kind of life would she be returning to? She had said precious little about it, but that spoke volumes in itself.

It was another reason not to pursue sending her home by whatever means he could. It was an excuse he could focus on, rather than think about why he really wanted to keep her under his watch. At her heated request, he had returned the charm bracelet to her, but with a heavy sense of foreboding and a warning to her to always keep it hidden.

It has to be connected, his mind taunted him. *The stone, the charm, the girl, Saradon...*

The request to join the king's presence arrived sooner than he liked, just as they finished eating.

"Come," Dimitri said, grim-faced. "The king requests your presence 'to reward you for your services'."

"Isn't that a good thing?" Harper asked, her eyes wide. "Perhaps he could return me to Caledan."

"I would not raise your hopes. Harper, you saw his true spirit last night. Do you think he will be so benevolent?"

She did not answer.

"Do not ask it of him," he warned.

At Dimitri's request, Emyria fussed over Harper, making sure every inch of her was impeccably presented in the squire's clothing. As a last thought, he stopped her before they left.

"Wait. I have something for you. A peace offering, if you will." She frowned, but watched as Emyria handed a wrapped object to him. He held it out to Harper. "Here."

She unwrapped it to discover a familiar dagger. The one Aedon had given her. Her hands closed tightly around it. She met his gaze, radiating confusion, her fire quenched by the surprise of his action. Her words, when they came, were gentle enough to surprise him too. "Thank you."

He nodded stiffly.

"Why?"

"Because today will not be easy. Consider it a talisman of courage. One condition though?"

She hesitated, a question in her eyes.

"Don't use it on me, will you?" He could not help but grin.

Her answering smile was glorious, like the coming of the sun, and it sharpened to steel as her vicious fire returned. "I can't promise."

60

AEDON

Aedon's heart thundered with the thrill of evasion as he vaulted from Brand's back. The shadow of the giant wings over him vanished as the Aerian soared away, Erika still within his arms for her own mission. Aedon landed upon the battlements with a soft thud, cushioning the impact with his knees. He pressed himself down to the ground and into the shadows and stilled, surveying his surroundings. Tournai at night. The city never slumbered. It thrummed with life, though a different tune to its daytime cacophony.

Seeing a fleeting gap between the patrolling guards, Aedon flowed from shadow to shadow. With a running leap, he vaulted from the wall onto the roof of a nearby building. Before he could be spotted, he slid down the rough thatch, stopping just before the edge—and the perilous drop to the cobbled street below.

Checking his handholds before he committed, he swung from the roof onto a shuttered window sill below, and from there—after confirming he had escaped notice so far—used his momentum to grasp a hanging sign closer to the ground, swung once, and jumped, alighting on the ground with a wet slap.

Aedon groaned. "Of course I've landed in a pile of—"

"Oy! What're you doing here? There's a curfew in this quarter, lad. Stop!"

There was no time to shake the excrement from his boots. Aedon launched into a sprint as two watchers gave chase. Down streets and up alleys he ran, but they knew the city far better than he and he could not shake them from his trail.

When he heard the two of them separate, he swore under his breath. It was a predictable move. They were going to cut him off. He turned a corner, slipped into a shadowed doorway, and made himself one with the night, at the same time sending a shadowy phantom of himself up the street. The watcher thundered past him, each loud step matching the drum of Aedon's heart. As soon as he passed, Aedon peeked from the shadows. The man was already halfway up the street after Aedon's spectre. Aedon grinned, slipped from his concealment, and ran the other way.

It was easier to lose himself in the inner city where the curfew was much later. The taverns were full, the brothels were fuller, and the streets thrummed with throngs of people still going about their business. Markets hawked their last wares of the day. Traders came and went. Aedon slipped between them all, his cloak wrapped around his body, his head shadowed by the generous hood. Though he was nowhere near safe, he relaxed slightly. This was where he belonged, on the edge of the thrill, where he felt most alive. He wound up to the higher city, leaving the bright lights behind as he ascended into the quieter, affluent quarters of Tournai. Now his smile faded, his gaze roving this way and that, and his senses rolled out as far as he could send them. Once more, he skulked from shadow to shadow, following the dagger's pull from underneath his cloak. *This way. This way*, it called to him. *Faster. She's here.*

Far above him, the castle walls rose, but for a well practiced climber, they were easy to scale. Aedon liked to think he could get anywhere a mountain goat could—and then some. Even so, the trip was perilous and fraught with danger, for if anyone happened to look upon the walls, he would be exposed. With the calculated mind of an experienced thief, he used the shadows of trees and houses to conceal his climb before forcing his screaming, straining joints and muscles to haul him over the lip and into the gardens on the other side.

Aedon leapt into the dark, safe arms of the tree branches before stilling to survey his surroundings. It had been decades since he had last come to this part of the palace—as an honoured guest, no less. He pushed the thought from his mind and gritted his teeth as he slipped down the tree trunk to stalk through the once familiar terraces of the royal gardens. It was a part of the royal quarters that was seldom guarded. Who could scale such a wall? In the king's arrogance was his weakness. Aedon still despised Toroth just as much as always, though he had once been the king's most favourite and trusted pet.

Through the palace he crept, avoiding wards and guards with ease, following the growing pull of the dagger—then he saw her. It took a beat longer than normal to register Harper's presence, because he did not recognise her. He ducked into the shadows and pressed against the wall as she—they— passed. Questions and doubts assailed him. Harper looked like a guest, as if she belonged there, wearing the very king's livery herself. She was clean, her hair braided, and her eyes bright. Yet the bruises blooming across her face were not lost upon him. The sight stirred anger in his belly.

And Dimitrius... She walked beside him as an equal, seemingly without fear. Aedon chanced a glance and watched their retreating backs with disbelief. She walked freely, without restraints—magical or otherwise. Her back was ramrod straight, and his miniscule glimpse of her face had shown a serious visage.

Suspicion uncurled in his stomach. Had he been mistaken? Had she duped them after all? Did she know Dimitrius? It had not seemed to be the case when they had met Dimitrius in the woods. Aedon watched as he placed a gentle hand upon the small of her back and guided her around a corner. She did not shirk away, but smiled at him. It was tight-lipped and serious, but a smile nonetheless.

They are far more familiar now than ought to be the case.

Aedon's feet moved of their own accord, sneaking after Harper and Dimitrius, pulled by curiosity and a burning need to understand what was happening. They halted outside the king's audience chamber. Aedon, shrouded in wards, dared not approach or follow them farther. For the first time, he saw Harper look up at Dimitrius with worry. He answered with a smile of reassurance and a light touch on her arm, before the guards opened the door and the two entered. At the physical contact, cold pooled in Aedon and his skin prickled. Aedon normally considered himself an excellent judge of character and an almost infallible detector of lies. Harper had seemed entirely honest when she had been with them. But she lived another life here. Did Harper need liberating at all, as they had thought? Which Harper was the 'real' one? The doors boomed shut behind them, leaving Aedon with only his raging thoughts and dumbfounded disbelief. None of it made any sense. He dared not ask himself the greater question. *Was I taken for a fool?*

61

HARPER

A talisman of courage, Harper thought, squeezing the reassuring weight of the dagger. She swallowed. She might need to be stronger than she hoped. It pained her to think of her companions, wherever they were. *Former companions*, she reminded herself. With a deep breath, Harper tried to fill herself with Brand's immovable strength, Ragnar's steady faith, and Erika's unflinching boldness. Last of all, she turned to Aedon's optimism. *I can get through this,* she told herself, repeating the mantra until it gilded her with the pretence of truth.

"Are you ready?" Dimitrius asked.

She opened her eyes with a start. "Yes." And she half believed it. One more step. One at a time. If she could win each one, then she could proceed—and there was hope. She belted the dagger around her hips, where it proudly bounced off the fine fabrics as she strode beside Dimitrius with more outward courage than she felt. If nothing else, the dagger would be a scrap of the familiar in a world where she knew nothing.

The king was nowhere to be found in the great hall. His throne stood there, empty and cold, with only an elf standing at its foot. At the lack of the king's presence, Harper's growing anxiety cooled a little. Even so, she had no idea what to expect.

The man turned as they entered. "Lord Ellarian, the king requests her presence in his personal study."

Dimitrius frowned. "And myself?"

"Your presence is not required, Lord."

Dimitrius paused. "Very well." He turned and nodded to Harper, his expression inscrutable, but she was certain she saw a flicker of fear, swiftly covered, that did not aid her own confidence. "*I will be with you in spirit,*" he spoke into her mind. "*Do not fear. You are not yet beyond my protection.*"

His protection. It sent a thrill of something she could not identify through her. She supposed fear, that she needed it, and relief, that she had some lifeline. She had no choice but to follow the king's man, with Dimitrius left waiting in the shadows of the great hall, staring after her.

The king's study was surprisingly small and cold. The minute fire in the grate did nothing to warm Harper's limbs and the chill that slowly crept through her.

"Your Majesty." Harper bowed as low as she could.

"Sit." His voice was abrupt, and as cold as his surroundings.

She took a seat obediently, sinking onto the hard, wooden chair but not daring to recline against the back. Her gaze flicked from the king to the floor, uncertain where she ought to look. She settled on the floor, picking a small spot between the stone slabs to meticulously examine.

Toroth remained standing, prowling around the space like a wolf waiting to pounce. Harper felt like a rabbit, frozen and trapped in his baleful glare. "You are not from Pelenor, are you? You do not speak Pelenori, and your Common Tongue holds a strange accent."

"No, sire." At his silence, and his expectant glare, she continued. "I am from Caledan."

"That is very far away. How did you come to be in Pelenor? Surely your failure to learn our tongue hinders you."

"The way an orphan does, sire," she replied, as Dimitrius had told her, for they had fleshed out a back story in anticipation of any questions. "I have travelled to many places, most of which I do not know the names, until I arrived here and Lord Ellarian took me into his employ. I have worked for him since."

His eyes narrowed. "Why you?"

"I—I don't know, sire. I only know that he spotted me and I fit the task he wished me to complete—"

"Which was?"

"To follow a man, unseen, and report back."

"What sort of tasks do you complete for him?"

"Following people, reporting, sending messages and retrieving them, infiltration…"

"Infiltration of?" Toroth asked sharply, circling closer.

Harper sat up straighter. "I blend in wherever Lord Ellarian requires me. In this case, a thief and his outlaws." It was easier not to call Aedon by name, to be as cold as the king. If she thought of them too much, she was sure she would crumple and all would be lost.

"Tell me everything. I want to know precisely how you charmed the criminals that have eluded me for so long."

Harper wet her lips nervously and forced her shaking

hands to lay flat upon her knees, though she longed to fuss with them. Her clammy palms fused to the fabric.

"*Keep going, Harper,*" Dimitrius's voice floated into her mind, and she saw his disembodied smile. "*You're doing brilliantly.*" At his words, the tension building in her shoulders relaxed just a little.

"Yes, sire. Lord Ellarian tasked me with recovering an item of great value that was suspected to be with them. I followed them for days, to be sure that they did indeed have the item—*your* item. I used one of my stories to gain their trust. I pretended I was far from home, lost, and without means to provide for myself. They took me in—"

"So easily?" Toroth interrupted sharply.

"No, sire. Some were deeply suspicious, but I ingratiated myself with the weakest of their members, those most susceptible to my story." It made her heart hurt to speak of them so. As though it had all been a lie. Despite everything, they had taken her in, and she would not have survived without them. "It did take a couple of weeks to fully gain their trust, travelling with them, listening to their conversations, giving them small favours and reason to include me in their business. I did not get far, but far enough."

"Then you took it?"

"Not quite, sire. Lord Ellarian was most insistent that I could not afford to fail. It was of utmost importance I not act too soon for fear of spooking them and losing your treasure forever. Besides which, I have neither magic nor strength to overcome the elf and his companions, some of whom are fearsome warriors."

The king scoffed at that.

"When they fell soft on me, charmed by my vulnerability, I wormed my way into taking the night watch. After a few nights, I took the stone from under their noses and brought it to Lord Ellarian at once—or tried to, but the city guard intercepted me."

The king laughed, a cold, mirthless bark. "I would not have thought it possible a scrawny thing like you could retrieve a treasure not even my entire Winged Kingsguard could find, yet here you are. Well, let it never be said that I do not reward those who are loyal to me. I have a gift for you, girl." Toroth nodded to a servant, who walked up with a bundle in his arms.

Harper stood to receive it, awkwardly juggling the item in her arms.

"Open it."

Harper unfolded the soft, grey fabric to reveal a thick cloak of a quality wool and weave, lined with delicate fur that would keep out any winter chill. The finely crafted silver clasp was a sigil matching her tunic—a mountain over trees and under stars.

"It is beautiful, sire," she said in a hushed voice, not sure what else to say.

"I thank you for your boundless generosity. I am unworthy," Dimitri whispered into her mind. She repeated the words to Toroth, who seemed satisfied at her humility.

"Do you know what the crest you wear means, girl?"

"No, sire."

"You ought to know what you wear," he said, frowning. "I shall have words with Lord Ellarian, who obviously does not educate his people properly."

Harper winced, but Dimitrius's voice was cool. *"Don't worry. I've been in worse trouble. I'll be fine."*

Sorry, she thought, hoping he would hear it.

He pointed to the crest. "This is Pelenor, throughout time, and I. We are the mountain—strong and unyielding, born of the earth and reaching for the sky. We are the tree—

life and vitality ever thriving. We are the stars—everlasting in our magnificence and power, always enduring." Toroth stood tall, filled with his own esteem.

Harper dithered. *Am I supposed to say something?*

"*Stoke his ego,*" Dimitrius replied with a sigh—to her relief. "*Tell him how strong and powerful he is and always shall be, or some such useless sentiment.*"

"You are all of those things indeed, sire," she said dutifully to the king. "I am honoured to have an audience with you."

"Yes, you are. Perhaps we shall speak again." She did not like how his eyes, his cold, dark eyes, fixed upon her with a hunger that had not been satisfied, but he turned away after a second, leaving her containing a sigh of relief. "You are dismissed. I have more important business to attend to."

It was clear from the way his gaze had lingered that he did not wish to finish with her then, but she was glad for the interruption of his next business. She bowed and was escorted out. When she returned to the great hall, Dimitri met her with a tight-lipped smile of relief.

"Come," he said coldly, then turned without another word. The hall had started filling with others—lords, ladies, and every manner of servant. Harper stared after him for a moment, wondering what she had done to earn his coldness, before hurriedly dodging through the throng before she lost him amongst the bobbing heads. She chased his long strides all the way back to his quarters, down cold galleries and passages, which would have had her lost in a heartbeat, until she espied the familiar door with relief.

Dimitrius closed it behind them and leaned against it, his eyes closed. Harper waited. He finally sighed and opened his eyes, looking at Harper with tired relief. "You did very well, Harper. Just as I planned. The king is placated, though I sense he is not done yet. We shall deal with him as it arises."

She watched him. He was so hard to fathom, his mood as slippery as water.

He raised an eyebrow at her blank stare. "I apologise for being so cold, but you must understand. Out there, I have a façade to present, a reputation to uphold."

"But you're sweet and kind behind closed doors?" she added with a bite of sarcasm.

In a flash, he was upon her, backing her to the wall. His hands crashed to the stone at either side of her head as he leaned in close, his eyes flashing and his mouth twisted in a snarl. "Do you not realise how hard I'm working to keep us both alive right now? You would already be *ashes* without my intervention. We balance on a precipice, Harper. Do you want to die?"

With Dimitrius suddenly so close, Harper felt a swoop of surprise, fear, and something unfamiliar—exhilaration—overtake her as his sweet, citrus scent surrounded them both. Her fingers bunched in her cloak with the shock of his advance and the sensory assault of his nearness. That tart, alluring scent wrapped around her as his gaze captured hers and refused to let go. He breathed so heavily that every warm breath ghosted over her skin, and this close, his violet gaze consumed her.

"You have no idea of the danger we are both in, Harper… from all sides. We do not leave the palace because we are not permitted. *I* am not permitted." His nostrils flared. She could not look away.

"If even the slightest whiff of any of this escaped, we would be worse than dead. So I will act however I damn well need to in order to make sure I survive, as I always have. You're welcome to your freedom once this is done, but for now, we have an act to play. So be done with playing the innocent, naïve girl and start running with me. Stop being so open. I can read you like a book. You might not know this court, but I do. Learn how to play; otherwise, we will die."

He stormed away, leaving her pressed against the wall and blinking after him. Harper had stopped breathing. Dizziness passed over her. She gulped in a deep breath before letting it whoosh out.

This place is full of secrets, lies, and games—with people's lives. How do I survive it?

62

HARPER

They ate dinner in silence. Harper picked at the fine foods, but the succulent meats melting on her tongue and the berries bursting with juices were hard to enjoy. Not when they came with such a steep price. Part of it awoke a yearning within her to live this life, to be able to enjoy such food every day. Was it not everything she had dreamed of in Caledan? She was safe, warm, dry, and fed. It was hard to wish for more. She had never been so clean or worn such fine clothes made of materials so cosy and soft they felt like kisses raining upon her skin. She had not felt the bite of the autumn chill since arriving.

At the same time, she had never been in so much danger. The more she partook of this other life—the food, the strange politics, the confinement of the luxurious palace— the more she longed to escape back into the woods. It was a harder life, but a simpler one. One where she knew the trees, the animals, and her own land. One where survival was earned with earnest toil. One where she did not feel as out of place as a fish up a tree. She felt a nobody—and meant to remain that way. She wasn't meant for these schemes and this place, where everyone had a hidden agenda, and where words were veils of lies that she struggled to unpick. It was impossible not to think of Aedon and his companions, out beyond the tall walls and stone of Tournai, living the life she had imagined, adventuring without restraint.

Life was so much simpler. I miss them. She swallowed past the lump in her throat. She had been so foolish. The irony was not lost on her. The criminal seemed more trustworthy than the king. Though she could still not figure out Dimitrius's agenda. He had seemed despicable since the moment they had met and yet he protected her now, when she could see no obvious reason for him to do so. It left her uneasy. That, and the overpowering effect he had upon her with the proximity forced between them.

"Are you all right?" His voice broke through her reverie and she jumped, clattering cutlery on the table and knocking a knife to the floor.

Harper bent to retrieve it with burning cheeks. "Fine. Just thinking."

"Coin for your thoughts?"

"Oh, nothing." At his expectant silence, she continued, "I wish I had never come here."

Dimitrius regarded her solemnly. "Truly?"

"Yes. It's a hopeless case, returning home. They warned me. I should have listened. I thought I would find a benevolent king, but instead, I—"

"I would not finish that thought aloud," Dimitrius said lightly. "Ears everywhere, even here sometimes. I know what you mean. I did not think it would be this way, either."

"It?"

He gestured around. "The court." He sighed, and his next words spoke into her mind. *"I thought this would be a place of fair rule, a pinacle of our society, but instead, I found it to be the deepest cesspit of sin imaginable."*

Harper frowned at him. He seemed so at odds with the detestable, predatory, dark male she had first encountered. Were the hidden depths he was allowing her to see now a calculated choice? Some kind of deception? "You're the king's spymaster. Surely you are amongst the worst of them all?"

His face clouded and eyes darkened. "I've done what I needed to survive."

"What have you done?" she dared to ask, her breath stalling, though based on her encounters with the king and the hospitality of his dungeon, she truly did not wish to know the depths of his depravities.

"Things you cannot even imagine. I will not speak of them, least of all to you. Do not think that because we dine together and I clothe you, that I am your ally, Harper of Caledan." Dimitrius stood stiffly and scowled at her. "Good night." He tossed his napkin onto his unfinished plate of food and strode from the table, down the corridor and out of hearing, until she heard a door slam in the distance.

Harper stared after him for a long moment before abandoning her own plate and slipping into her room. Just when she thought she had something figured out, away it slipped again, like smoke between her fingers.

Harper wore her new cloak to the next audience with Toroth, this time in the royal gardens that she had walked through the other night with Dimitrius. They were stunningly beautiful in the daylight. If Harper had been at leisure to view them, she might have admired the precisely shaped bushes and the delicate way flowers intertwined for a heady mix of scents and fierce colour. Perhaps she would have even noticed the artificial warmth, heated by the magic of the king to keep summer for just a while longer. Harper saw none of it. Toroth stood so close beside her, she could have reached out and touched him. Of course, she did not dare, and stood like one of the garden's statues, buzzing with nerves, waiting to hear what he would ask of her. This meeting had not been anticipated, and it confirmed Harper's worst fears—that for some reason, the king did not find her beneath his attention.

Dimitrius had not been invited, but he lurked not too far away, listening. For that, she was grateful. Despite his outburst the night before, he seemed determined to see them both out of this predicament, though Harper had the feeling she did not know the half of it.

"What do you know of Lord Ellarian, girl?"

Harper stiffened at Toroth's words, her heart thundering into life. It was not what she had expected, nor what she and Dimitrius had practiced. "Not much, sire," she said after taking a steadying breath she hoped he did not notice. As seemed to be his way, he glared at her until she continued. "He is a lord, and I am nobody," she said, hoping he would find that acceptable. It was true, after all.

The king did not need to know how he snapped at her when she brushed a nerve, or how he had been kind to her when she was scared, or how he insisted that she eat well at every meal. The king did not need to know how it made her feel when Dimitrius offered her safe quarters, or when he slammed her against a wall filled with wrath, or rushed to steady her when she was so tired she could no longer stand.

She supposed Dimitrius was much kinder than he had first appeared, but the nature of the court made her wonder whether it, too, was just an act, and whether the truth of his character lay in the darkest of his conduct with her. Everything there seemed to be a lie—and Dimitrius had said it himself, he was not her ally.

"That is all?" Toroth raised an eyebrow, oblivious to the torrent of thoughts and emotions washing through her.

"Yes, sire."

He stared at her with an intent focus that made her squirm. "And would you say Lord Ellarian is trustworthy?"

"I have no grounds on which to speak of him, Your Majesty. He has never borne me ill, if that is what you mean, and everything he asks of me is for your employ."

Toroth narrowed his eyes. Harper could see his interest was fading. *Good. I'm useless. Dismiss me!* Self-consciously, she tucked an errant strand of hair behind her ears, which promptly flopped loose again.

Toroth's eyes followed her wrist as the loose sleeve fell back, and his attention locked upon the shine of metal there. "Where does a girl like you afford a bracelet like that?"

A rush of terror flooded Harper's body. She tucked her arm under the cloak as subtly as she dared, though her heart hammered. "It's an old trinket, sire. It's nothing. Just a scrap of leather and a bead."

"You did not steal it, girl? Lord Ellarian would certainly disapprove of a thief in his employ. Let me see it."

"It is unworthy of your great attention," she squeaked and shrank away, clutching at the folds of her cloak in panic.

"I command it."

"Your Majesty." Dimitrius seemed to appear from nowhere. Relief rushed through Harper. "I beg your forgiveness. May I have a word with the girl? I have some urgent business for her to attend."

"Of course," said Toroth, but as Harper turned away with a wordless glance of appreciation at Dimitrius, Toroth snatched her wrist. She squealed and wriggled in his iron grasp, but he tightened his grip until her arm screamed with the pain. Inexorably, he pulled her closer and lifted her by her arm to examine the worn leather strap and tarnished silver bead.

"Hmmph," he said, pursing his lips. "This is nothing."

"I am unworthy of your notice," said Harper, biting down on her lip to stop herself crying out in pain as he held her arm up, straining her shoulder.

Toroth started to lower her arm when his eyes grazed over the metal, catching on the crudely stamped mark upon the bead. In an instant, he threw Harper away, as if burned by her touch. She landed in a jumbled heap upon the ground.

"Saradon-cursed traitor," Toroth growled and prowled toward her, magic erupting at his fingers.

Dazed and winded, Harper could do naught but watch him approach. With a jagged jab of his splayed fingers toward her, pain assaulted her, until Dimitrius stepped between them.

"Sire," he started.

"Did you know she possessed that—that *filth?*" Toroth rounded on Dimitrius, shaking with anger. Spittle flew from his mouth with every word.

"Filth, sire?"

"Th–That *treason!*" The king could barely utter words in his wrath.

"It's on your business, sire. She's with me." Relief stuttered in Harper as he stepped squarely in front of her, shielding her with the bulk of his body.

"Explain *now*, before I have you both executed."

"*What's going to happen?*" Harper asked Dimitrius desperately.

"*I do not know,*" he replied, a bite of worry in his own voice.

A cold fear spread through her stomach.

63

DIMITRI

Rage lined every cold edge in Toroth's face, his dark eyes, his thunderous brows. "Must I damn you for being incompetent or a traitor?"

Dimitri knew Toroth longed to punish him. Regardless of Harper's fate, he had to save himself first. He sketched a bow to the king. "Sire, I apologise for my duplicity. I did keep something from you."

Toroth ceased his pacing and fixed Dimitri in a piercing glare.

"The symbol means little—nothing even—to the girl. I asked her to wear it." Toroth had utterly stilled. Inwardly, Dimitri smiled to himself. *He worries I am a traitor. Ha. How little he knows.* "There are murmurings in the south. Ones I wish to keep a close eye on, for they portend possible rebellion. I was readying the girl to go to them."

"What rebellion?" Toroth said sharply. "Who?"

Dimitri inclined his head. "Forgive me, but it is just murmurings that have only reached my ears in snatches and shreds. That is what I wish to determine, and the girl will find the truth for me."

"Why does she carry Saradon's Mark?" Toroth advanced, full of menace.

"To aid me. I suspect they are sympathisers to his cause. I need her to gain their trust—be one of them—in order to break into their circle. If my suspicions prove true, I shall draw them out. We are just now working on her story and details of the task at hand. It will be dangerous for her, but she is well up to the task, given her success with recovering the Dragonheart."

Toroth paced back and forth, mulling over Dimitri's words. "And you are sure—beyond certainty—that she is loyal and no sympathizer of Saradon herself?"

"Yes. She is a foreigner. Our history means nothing to her." *For goodness sake, you paranoid, batty old dragon, let it be.*

"I would like to be certain. Mayhap I will have my own men question her on this."

Fear spiked in Dimitri. "That will be unecessary, sire," he said smoothly. "If anything, I would beseech you to grant her immediate release so I may task her at once on this mission of utmost importance."

It was precisely the wrong thing to say. "Do you think you know better than I, bastard?"

"No, sire." Dimitri bowed low to conceal his rage before he fought it under control.

"Because you do *not*," said Toroth, as if he had entirely ignored Dimitri's reply. He launched into a tirade of his ultimate authority and Dimitri's worthlessness, but Dimitri had heard it a thousand times before. He schooled his face into blankness and ignored the king, wondering how on earth he could secure Harper's freedom—if only to save implicating himself. A spark of an idea hit him. Perhaps he had missed something entirely obvious. As long as Harper was free of Tournai, she could not implicate him in anything, and he had one way to ensure she would be far from there and never return. His safety hinged on her... *Who else could I ask to rescue her but the grand escapee himself?*

Dimitri hid a smile as he realised just how he might reach all his goals in one fell swoop. The Dragonheart would be his once more. Harper would be safe and so far away she could not implicate him. And Toroth would soon see just how much he ought to fear the name of Saradon. When the pair of them were eventually released, once Toroth's rage had burned low, and the spymaster's assurances had sunk in, Dimitri spirited them away to his quarters at once.

When they arrived, she was shaking. "It's going to be all right, I promise." Dimitri didn't know why he was compelled to utter such foolish words to her, but the sight of her in such a state distressed him. He flexed his hands at his side, holding them ramrod straight to avoid reaching out to comfort her.

"I need to attend some business, but I will return for you as soon as I may," Dimitri said. "I have work to do if I am to see us through this safely. Have courage, and patience."

"How long am I to remain here?" she asked, a gleam of desperation in her eyes. But he had no answer.

"I will come soon," he promised again, though he did not know how on earth he would save himself, let alone her. With more regret than he thought he'd feel for a nobody like her, he left without another word, closing the door behind him.

I pity her, he realised. A part of him felt bound to protect her, despite the danger she posed to him. She was a victim of injustice, like him and so many others. And yet, despite a hard life, she had not given up her spark of defiance and hope for better, for more. She was precisely the kind of person the changes he would bring would ultimately protect, one way or another.

Dimitri's nerves ran on a permanent high as of late, thrumming through him with a corrosive energy that wore him down little by little. He did not welcome it. Whatever happened, he was at risk.

64

AEDON

Aedon watched Dimitrius cross the gardens alone. He frowned. Where was Harper? The knife now suggested she was far beyond his reach, which concerned him. He noticed Dimitrius's quick stride and the worry on his face. A curl of unease slithered to life in his belly. He prayed Harper was well. Despite his confusion and suspicion at seeing them together amicably, he still had a small kernel within him that worried something was amiss.

He followed Dimitrius to beyond where he could comfortably follow—the heart of the palace. His heart sank. *I hope she's not in there.* But the knife tugged him forward. He knew the answer he did not want to admit to.

After a short time, Dimitrius returned, looking more worried than before. As he entered an emptier part of the palace, he stopped. Aedon halted in the shadows behind him.

"I know you are there, elf." Dimitrius's voice rang through the vacant hall.

Aedon stilled.

"Reveal yourself. I have a proposition for you."

Nothing.

"If you wish to save Harper, you ought not ignore me."

Aedon could not resist. He melted out of the shadows and approached Dimitrius, halting a healthy distance away and eying him with suspicion.

"She *is* in there, isn't she?" Aedon spat. "What have you done to her? If you have harmed her, I swear—"

"Do not swear what you cannot deliver," Dimitrius snarled. "For once, you need to listen, Aedon, because there is no time. She is almost beyond my help for now. There is but one chance, and it is infinitesimally small. She is in danger from the king. I can protect her no longer, but I can give you a window of opportunity. You must get her out, or she will be made to suffer most horribly. It is not a death I would wish for."

Aedon bristled at that, but he stilled. It had been a century since Dimitrius had been able to bear calling him by name.

"There is far more at stake than you know, Aedon. Unless she escapes, Harper will be caught in the middle, and I cannot help her any more than I already have. Forget the Dragonheart. I don't know what you wanted it for, but it is in the vaults once more, under wards that require a power greater than you to break. If you save her, you can do a great deal more good than ever you shall know."

"Why do you speak in riddles?" Aedon shot at him with a scowl.

"Because I need not explain myself to you, thief. Time's up. I can dally no more. Make your choice, and make it well. If you act, act before the night is spent. She depends on you."

Dimitrius strode away before Aedon could respond. It would be easy to gain entry. He had done it before. *Go on. Do it,* a small part of him urged. But though he flexed forward, ready to bend to that will, the rest of him held back. It could easily be a trap. He would not put it past Dimitrius, or the king, who had longed to end him for decades.

Is it a trap?

Most definitely, he answered himself.

Harper was within the palace, but to know her state, he would have to look upon her face himself. It was not a decision he could make alone, for it would endanger them all.

"It's definitely a trap," said Erika flatly.

"I agree," said Brand.

"It probably is," Ragnar added glumly, his shoulders slumped in defeat.

"But she's definitely in there," Aedon reminded them. "And if she's in there, she certainly isn't being treated well. It probably *is* a trap, but that doesn't mean we can't outwit them."

"Even Dimitrius?"

Aedon looked at Erika. "Especially Dimitrius. I have extra reason to best him."

"This isn't a game, you know," she replied flatly, glaring at him.

"I know that," he snapped. "But this is what we do best. Manage the impossible, then slip away."

"You're forgetting something very important. She might be a traitor. You told us how she was with Dimitrius, how amicable they were, how she seemed ingratiated with his kind." Erika's suspicion was neverending, Aedon knew.

"I know. I cannot explain it. Perhaps she is doing whatever she needs to survive. Wouldn't we all do the same?"

"Why is he trying to save her, though?" asked Ragnar. "I

like to believe the best of people, but none of it makes any sense."

"It doesn't," Aedon said with a huff of annoyance. "But she is our friend. And she is, at this moment, in the dungeons of King Toroth, where she does not belong. Moreover, he has her Dragonheart, and many others, tantalisingly close. Isn't it tempting? We can rescue Harper and obtain a Dragonheart. Perhaps an unlimited supply!"

"You really think you can get us past the wards?" Brand was the voice of reason—as always.

"I am no ordinary elf."

The Aerian dipped his head in acknowledgment. "Even so, you are not as powerful as once you were."

Aedon's face was a mask of stone, but he knew they realised the turmoil of hurt roiling beneath the exterior. "I can do it."

"Let's take a vote," suggested Brand. "Who votes for rescuing Harper, despite the fact it's probably an obvious trap?"

Aedon and Ragnar raised their hands.

"And who votes against?"

Brand and Erika raised theirs.

"Two versus two. We appear to have reached an impasse."

"We don't have time for impasses," Aedon said, utterly exasperated. "If you won't come with me, I'll go after her myself. Trap or not, I have to try, for we owe her that. And, whilst I'm there, there's got to be a way to obtain a Dragonheart."

"Don't be so bloody foolish!" growled Brand.

"Well, what else can we do?" he snapped. "Time is running out. This is our chance. What say you?"

65

HARPER

ommotion outside woke her, but this sounded different. Harried. Panicked. In the end that evening, she had fallen asleep slumped in a chair in the drawing room nearest to the entrance to Dimitri's suites. Waiting for him, because she could not bear to know nothing for a moment longer than necessary about what was happening—and about the danger they were in.

The sounds were outside, in the main hallways of the palace. Harper's ears pricked and she tensed, holding her breath as she strained to hear more. Their voices were muffled, echoing down the passage. The noise grew louder, closer. Most of it was in Pelenori, and her inability to translate only worsened the prickling dread clawing up her spine.

Now they were outside the door. She scrambled to it, pressing her face to the floor and trying with all her might to see under it, but the gap was too thin. The light flickered, winking in and out as bodies blocked the faint light. The tramp of booted feet shook the floor, rattling her head.

Harper jumped to her feet, clutching the dagger at her

belt. Could they get in? Dimitrius had promised the door was secure—impenetrable—but she wasn't about to place all her faith in his promises. The door looked like a door, and the noise on the other side of it sounded like more than enough to batter it down. They were coming for her. This was it. The inescapable thought gripped her, hard, and it did not let go. She gasped for breath.

But no one battered on the door. They continued on and the rabble faded into the distance, muffled once more. And her chest unclenched, the panic dissipating with their passage. *What was all that?* she wondered, rising from the floor and retreating back to the chair, to curl up in its plush depths. All too soon, there was nothing but silence and darkness again, but it took a long while until Harper drifted off to sleep once more.

Something woke Harper with a start. She listened, frowning. *Scratching?*

There was incessant scratching on the wood of the suite's front door, as irritating as a fly buzzing around her head. She shuffled, gritting her teeth.

There it was again.

Scratch, scratch, scratch.

What is that? Harper forced her frozen body into action. Holding her breath, she crept closer to the door, trying not to make even the slightest sound.

Scratch, scratch, scratch.

Mice? Rats? Maybe she did not want to find out what it was after all, but curiosity pulled her nonetheless. It was more interesting than sitting in the cold and the dark with all her senses blinded.

"Hello?" she whispered. "Is someone there?"

The scratching paused, then started again.

"Hello?" she said a little louder, in the smallest voice she could—in case it was something dark and terrible. Did she need to call for one of Dimitri's servants? Fear clutched her chest, and her breath would not come. She was there alone, unarmed, without magic, against whatever was on the other side of that door—and she had just given away her presence to it so obviously. Her supple imagination fed her all sorts of detailed and terrifying possibilities. The scratching stopped again. Harper wanted to vomit. She clamped down on the churning in her stomach, and the impending light-headedness.

"Hello?" said a quiet voice from the other side of the door.

"Who's there?" she asked, a flood of relief threatening to overwhelm her. *A person?* The voice sounded strange through the door. Man, woman, or something else, she could not tell. The voice was far too quiet, as if they were also being cautious.

"Harper?" the voice whispered.

Wait, I know that voice. She tugged on the handle—locked. Scrambling to undo the bolts, Harper's fingers fumbled. She opened the door. Harper angled her head so she could see the face in the almost-dark.

"Aedon!" She threw herself at him as he rushed for her. Their bodies collided. He gripped her in a great hug that she returned, relief flooding her body.

"Oh, thank Pelenor I found you," he said, his voice muffled in the crook of her neck.

Harper struggled out of his grasp and stepped back. "It's really you? I'm not dreaming? How did you get here? How did you find me? And why? I didn't think I'd see you again." The questions rolled through her mind and off her tongue.

Aedon held up a hand. "We don't have much time, but suffice it to say," he said, drawing himself up tall and sweeping into an elaborate bow, "I am Aedon, the legendary Thief of Pelenor, and I have come to steal *you*." He gave her a crooked smile. "I thought you might like a change of scenery."

Harper did not know whether to laugh or cry, so she did both.

"I'll take that as a 'yes, please'. Come on. Let's get you out of here." When he turned toward the door, she grabbed his cuff.

"Wait. Why? How?"

Aedon didn't turn back, but some of the swagger dropped from his posture. "We realised we couldn't leave you to fend for yourself—not when we knew what you were walking into. It was too dangerous, and you were blinded to it. I hoped I wouldn't be so late, but the others took a little more persuading. By the time I arrived, the entire city was abuzz with rumours of the Dragonheart thief's capture and impending trial. I suppose I'm here to make sure you won't be attending. Unless you wish to?" He turned and cocked his head.

Aedon had no idea what had transpired between Dimitrius, the king, and her since her capture, it seemed. Events had unfurled so swiftly even she reeled from it. Something she could not name stirred in her stomach. Aedon was here to rescue her. But she was already safe— wasn't she? Dimitrius had promised her that and despite everything that had happened between them, she realised that in those quarters, and especially with him, she did feel safe. Harper swallowed. Safety was an illusion here.

"No thanks," she said, her voice hollow. She had the opportunity to leave. That was exactly what she wanted, wasn't it? She was a prisoner here—to the king, to Dimitrius, did it even matter? Her freedom was the goal. And now she had a chance to take it. So why did it feel empty and a tinge bittersweet to face the open door before her?

"Didn't think so. So what else was there for me to do but come and get you myself?" Aedon asked, his usual grin and twinkling, mischievous eyes appearing once again, oblivious to her discomfort. "This place wasn't a match for me."

Harper hugged him again as gratitude and relief bubbled over that someone cared so much for her to put themself in danger on her account. He squeezed her back and laughed, lacing his fingers through hers and tugging her with him.

"Come on."

Harper followed Aedon, overwhelmed by a strange stirring rekindled by his presence that she recognized. Somehow, it felt like she was going home. Yes, she decided. It was definitely right to leave. She owed Dimitrius nothing. He had his own agenda, and she didn't want to find out where that left her when he had no further use for her.

66

HARPER

Harper had no time to savour the moment. Aedon chivvied and tugged her along the dark corridor.

"What about the guards?" she hissed at him.

Their footsteps were far too loud, deafening to her after her enforced silence.

"Already taken care of," he said airily.

"Huh?"

He did not answer as she struggled to keep up on feet that felt like blocks of ice. Sure enough, the corridors were deserted, the noise of the guards always seeming at a distance, though too close for her comfort. She had no idea what he'd done or how he'd done it. It seemed too easy, too neat.

He soon pulled her into early morning sunshine. She slammed her eyes shut against the brightness of dawn, then slowly opened them again, looking around. There was not a soldier to be seen—or anyone, in fact. He slid his arm around her waist when her knees buckled, supporting her as it overwhelmed her for a moment—to feel light upon her face, wind upon her skin, and the hubbub of the city waking around her.

"Are you all right?"

She nodded. Words failed her, because she wasn't at all.

"Let's go," he said gently.

"We have to find the Dragonheart!" she blurted, refusing to be tugged away.

"I know. Don't worry! All part of the plan," he said, tugging her hand again. "We need to go. Timing is critical. The rest of them are waiting."

She set off at a jog beside him, hardly able to believe the others might have come with him after how they had parted company. "And we're going to get the stone? I don't know where they took it." She glanced around. The city was huge. Where would they even begin?

"Already in hand." Aedon was serene, as if he did this every day. Then again, she realised, this wasn't his first time. He led her through the streets and alleyways, always keeping to the minor routes, which twisted and turned through the heart of the city and were overshadowed by tall buildings. In a small, deserted square, the gang awaited.

Harper's mouth fell open. Even Erika had come.

"Got her!" Aedon said cheerfully.

"About time," Brand muttered. He pushed himself off the wall where he stood with his arms folded. "Let's get going. Plan's afoot."

Ragnar beamed. "It's good to see you, Harper."

"Why did you come?" she asked in a small voice. "I didn't think I'd see any of you again, after—"

Brand said, "Yes, well, Mr. Poetic over there wouldn't stop waxing lyrical about how you never ought to turn your back on someone in need, even when they were being completely and utterly daft—"

Harper winced.

"—So, just to shut him up, we decided to come along and help you out."

"I missed my cooking partner, too, if I am being truthful," Ragnar added.

"And the hand massages," Aedon whispered with a wink as he strolled past. Harper chuckled.

"Thank you," she said, loud enough for them all to hear.

"Time for that later," Brand replied gruffly. "We have a Dragonheart to steal back, and our own escape to master, before we're done here."

Erika bent to grab a pile of cloth from the ground. Harper cocked her head, wondering what it was. As Erika passed them around, she saw they were red cloaks. She took one automatically, but glanced at Aedon, a question in her eyes.

"Kingsguard uniform," he explained. "Help us blend in. Make sure you put it on right so it drapes over your clothes. That way, no one can see you're not wearing a uniform underneath. Did you get the helms, too?" he asked Erika.

She kicked the sack next to her, which rattled.

"Same again then. One apiece."

Harper slipped her red cloak and helm on over the squire's uniform and the king's gifted cloak. The helm forced her head into her shoulders uncomfortably. Its long nose-piece pressed down on the tip of her nose and reduced her field of vision to two vertical strips.

Harper turned her head this way and that to see her companions. They were indistinguishable from real guards, except Brand, who could fit neither head into helm nor wings into cloak. The only other who remained without either cloak or helm was Ragnar, who made no move to don either, to Harper's confusion.

"Right, where is it?" Brand asked.

"In the dragon hold," Aedon replied. "The king holds his Dragonhearts with the dragon eggs."

Brand frowned. "That could work to our advantage."

"Definitely. However, the fewer dragons we meet, the better. They'll be our enemy as much as the Kingsguard if they believe one of their own is in danger."

"Shall we?" said Ragnar, his wicked grin taking Harper by surprise. She did not expect such mischief from him. Aedon met it with one of his own.

"After you, my friend."

Ragnar nodded to them all, then hurried down another twisting alley.

"Where's he going?" asked Harper.

Aedon turned his mischievous smile to her. "Why, he's going to the Kingsguard to tell them the legendary Thief of Pelenor is at large in the city, of course!"

Icy panic flooded Harper. "Wh-What?"

HARPER

Aedon burst out laughing. "Not where we are! Ragnar likes playing *chatura* in real life, too, as you'll find out. He gets tired of wooden pieces on a board. Real people are much more interesting and unpredictable. It's a rather useful skill that's gotten us out of quite a few tight spaces. He just needs a little head start on us."

Harper shook her head in bafflement. *Reserved and kind Ragnar has a mischievous streak?* She would never have guessed. Perhaps he had been running around with Aedon for too long, though she left that thought unvoiced.

"Take this," Erika said. She gave Harper a slim sword with a scabbard and belt. "It's similar to my twin blades, so you'll be more used to the weight. You'll probably need it. Remember what Brand taught you."

"Thank you." Harper eyed Erika warily.

Erika huffed and turned away. "If all else fails, stay behind the rest of us and don't stab us. It's time. Ragnar will be in place by now."

Harper suppressed a wince. Hopefully she wouldn't be

that bad. A flicker of nerves ran through her at the thought of having to use a blade—and not in a training situation. Her first hope was that it would not come to that. She released a shuddering breath and followed Erika, Brand, and Aedon into the alley.

Ragnar joined them just before the buildings opened out into a grand square. Erika raised up her closed fist to her chest at the sight of him. He replied in kind, along with a smug grin.

"Done?" she asked, her brusque tone revealing her tension.

"As easy as taking sugared fruits from a wyvern," Ragnar said with a toothy grin. "They all legged it off to some poor, unsuspecting district that I suspect will shortly be in the midst of a total lockdown."

"Good. Let's go." She tossed him a cloak and helm, which he swiftly donned.

They all jogged toward the grand doors that led to the dragon hold. The stone doors were huge rectangles, three men high and two men wide, under a thick lintel set directly into the cliff soaring above them. To Harper's surprise, they pushed open on oiled hinges without a sound.

From there, the gang proceeded silently with no weapons drawn, so as not to draw attention to themselves. Harper felt naked without something to protect her, so she stuck close to Ragnar, behind Aedon, as they forged into the heart of the mountain.

She barely had a chance to glance around, and little vision to do so through the restrictive helmet, but it was as if she had stepped into an underground town of sorts. The ceiling, which was formed from natural crags in the rock, soared above them, stalactites hanging from the roof. Lights hovered above their heads. They were dim, but better than the pitch black of darkness.

The floor was the only smooth part, stretching through the heart of the stone ahead of them. To either side were doorways, both grand and small, and even windows, giving the illusion they were on some kind of underground street. Each wooden door was closed, barred, and bore a sign that Harper did not understand.

As they walked, it grew hotter until she regretted the oppressive cloak and helmet. Sweat trickled down the bridge of her nose and nape of her neck unpleasantly. There were Kingsguard here, all cloaked, some helmeted, who greeted them in the Pelenor tongue as they marched past. Harper remained silent as her companions cheerfully replied in kind. Her heart rose into her throat every time they sighted another red cloak, and she heard nothing over the rushing of her blood in her ears, but it seemed they raised no suspicion, not even Brand with his great wings. Then they reached another set of doors even larger than the last—and the guards who stood before it. Brand and Erika stepped forward without hesitation and knocked them out cold. Aedon stepped up behind them and passed his hands over their prone forms.

"A sleeping charm," he explained. "One that will modify their memories so they have no recollection of us when they wake."

"No time for chitchat. Move," Erika said. She and Brand opened one of the doors and they slipped through.

Harper gasped. It was as if they stepped into the heart of a great crater that stretched from the very top to the very bottom of the mountain. Faint daylight flooded in from the top, and yawning shadows tumbled from the massive caves peppering the inside of the mountain. Yet it was not that which had caught her eye. Above her head soared… *Dragons.* Big ones, little ones, blue ones, red ones. They called to each other with roars that echoed around the cave, and as they landed in the caves, the cracking of rock was akin to the snapping of whips. One blew a great stream of fire across the inside of the mountain, and a wave of heat rolled down upon them. Harper squeaked as it blasted her face.

"Keep steady," Aedon murmured. "Nearly there. This is the worst part."

"Won't they come after us?" she whispered back.

"That's why we have the cloaks. In them, we're friend, not foe. They think we're Kingsguard, and long may it stay that way." He gave her a reassuring smile and encouraged her forward. She struggled not to break into a run, feeling far too conspicuous wandering through a thunder of dragons. Each roar reverberated right to her core.

Please don't eat us. Please don't eat us. Please don't eat us.

"This way," Brand said in a low voice, walking into a wide hallway that plunged steeply down on the other side of the crater. "The egg vaults are down here."

There were more guards, too, standing before a thick, iron portcullis that barred the way. Again, Brand and Erika did not hesitate, and Aedon and Ragnar dove into the frey. Harper raised her sword and backed away, trying not to get in the way, certain she'd be a liability. Erika looked back at her with scorn that made Harper cringe. They raised the portcullis and hurried through.

A familiar feather-light touch caressed Harper as they crossed the threshold. She knew the Dragonheart was there. Instinctively, she recognised the imprint of it, the feel of it.

"It's here," she said as they rushed along the tunnel. "I can feel it."

They entered a large cellar with vaulted ceilings. Shelves

upon shelves were laid out in rows, bearing the most unlikely treasures—dragon eggs of every size, colour, and texture. Even Erika stopped for a moment of wonder.

"This way. Quickly." Aedon led them. "It'll be in one of the secure vaults. I'm holding back the wards with every ounce of our combined strength, but I can't protect us for long." Harper saw his jaw clenched, as though he were under some great strain, and a bead of sweat began to form upon his brow.

They followed him through the gloom. In every direction, the egg store was pitch black. Harper followed Aedon closely, keen to stay within the sphere of magical light he had cast to illuminate the way, small and inconsequential though it seemed.

"We're getting closer," Harper said. "I can feel something familiar. It's the stone. I know it sounds crazy, but—"

"Not crazy at all," said Aedon, changing course. "What you're sensing is the magical resonance of the stone. It's familiar to you after so much time together."

There was neither chance—nor breath—to question him as she followed him at a run. They came upon a wooden door, locked with a metal cylindrical mechanism of many revolving discs, the likes of which she had not seen before.

"A safe," remarked Aedon. "How predictable!"

"A safe?" Harper asked.

"The gigantic strongbox of rich folks," Aedon explained, wrinkling his nose.

"How do we open it?" Harper ran her fingers over the dials.

"Allow me, my dear." Aedon gestured for her to stand to one side and took her place before the door, raising his arms and wriggling his fingers, as though preparing. He whispered to the door, stroking the dials in a particular order. The dials rotated on their own until the door groaned and opened slowly. Aedon tsked. "Too easy. They always make it too easy." But, bravado aside, his mouth fell open at what lay inside. Piles of Dragonhearts of all colours, shapes, and sizes.

"There are so many," Harper whispered.

"Enough to cure a nation, if it came to it," Aedon said, his voice equally hushed. "It's too tempting. Think of the good we could do with all this! Grab as many as you can."

"Wait… What? We came for just one—mine!" Harper said. "We can't steal any!"

Aedon scoffed at her. "These could help us curtail what threatens to be a plague, and they're good for many more things beside. Start grabbing."

Harper refused, following the tug inside her to the small stone that was hers and hers alone. She grasped it and stepped from the vault. The rest soon tumbled out, their pockets, bags, and anything else that could be used as a vessel stuffed with as many Dragonhearts as they could carry.

"Quick," said Aedon through gritted teeth. "The wards are crushing me. I cannot hold them back much longer. We must leave."

They followed him out at a run. They heard a shout up ahead. Torchlights bloomed.

"Weapons out, team, and stick together," Aedon said calmly. Harper's heart lurched as more adrenaline flooded her system.

The Kingsguard melted out of the darkness in a cacophony of noise, light, and blood-red cloaks, until the group was surrounded from all directions.

68

HARPER

Aedon forged ahead, flanked by Brand and Erika, who cut down anyone in their way. Harper stumbled and fell, smashing her already battered body on the stones, but the rush inside her had her up and running a second later. She chanced a glance behind her. How could they be behind *and* ahead of her? Several red cloaks flapped in the gloom, spurring her on.

The portcullis ahead lowered by the second. Aedon and Erika sprinted through. Brand dove, barely making it out. He landed hard on the far side before scrambling to his feet. They fanned out to meet the wall of red cloaks awaiting them at the far side. Time stretched. Her legs felt like lead. Every step took her further away, not closer—and she wasn't going to make it.

"No!" screamed Harper, but it was too late. The portcullis slammed shut, cutting Ragnar off with her.

Aedon turned, and paled.

"Harper!" he shouted, slamming his hands against the impenetrable metal and looking at them helplessly. He only had a moment before he was forced to turn and meet blades with one of the Kingsguard on his side of the barrier.

Harper and Ragnar backed into a corner between the portcullis and the rough walls as the Kingsguard fanned out around them. Ragnar raised his axe before him. Harper swallowed. Fear fuelled her now, but as she looked at her companions, snarling desperately as they fought, almost like caged animals that knew they were already defeated, a surge of anger rose. This was not how it was supposed to end, but end they would unless she did something.

"We can do this." Brand's reassuring voice boomed over them all, as if to allay her fears.

"I say the same to you, Harper," Aedon called amidst the sound of clashing blades. "Fighting, just like you've practised—"

"But better," Erika chimed in. Harper could hear the smile behind her gritted teeth at the joy of the fight. Somehow, it sparked defiance in Harper too, a flicker of light against the crushing darkness of fear. If she thought about it, she would lose all nerve, so she didn't think. She threw herself forward, Ragnar at her side, as the soldiers descended on them.

Ragnar tore at their cloaks, nimbly running between and around them and tangling them in the folds. Somehow, her feet found the right positions, and she realised that Brand's training, limited as it was, made sense. She was still clumsy, and her short, light blade could not match the strength, reach, and power of the soldiers before her, but somehow, she dodged one soldier's attack and sliced his hand. Ragnar grabbed the man's hand in his vice-like grip and pulled him to the floor so Harper could smash the man's helm with the pommel of her sword. He went limp—out cold.

"You should have killed him," Ragnar growled.

"I can't!" It wasn't in her nature—but she could at least incapacitate them. That didn't cross her moral line.

There was no time to argue, for the next of the guards charged. Harper and Ragnar took him out together. Harper slashed at his cloak, then grabbed it as it flew past her, yanking hard so the man stumbled off balance. Ragnar leapt onto his back and dragged his dagger across the man's throat. He gurgled and fell as Ragnar leapt off him and advanced on the remaining guards with his axe raised, who surrounded them warily.

Harper backed up to the portcullis, a scream tearing out of her unbidden at the horror of it. An arm shot through the gate, grabbing her by the neck and pulling her back hard. Her air supply cut off instantly and she choked on nothing. A second arm grasped her around the waist, trapping her sword arm at her side.

Harper struggled, but the tightening grip was like a vice around her slender neck, and she could not move an inch. Stars danced in her vision as he slowly strangled her, the world around her beginning to fade.

Ragnar turned and froze. The anguish in his eyes was clear, and it cut her to the core. Harper knew they had lost. It was over. They would both die.

69

DIMITRI

Dimitri stood and watched. His only hope had been if Aedon rescued the young woman and took the temptation to chase the Dragonheart, too. It was easier not to think of Harper by name. He had succeeded in planting the seed with the thief, it seemed. It was not beyond Aedon's nature. Anything so daring would light the fire in him, if for no other reason than the sheer bravado and thrill of it. Harper would be gone—that felt like a bitter and hollow victory—and he had successfully goaded Aedon into doing his dirty work for him.

Dimitri could not care less if they left with one Dragonheart, a hundred, or none. As long as he also obtained one under cover of their theft. Then there would be nothing stopping him from raising Saradon and breaking the wheel once and for all. Unbeknownst to Aedon, he had also held back the wards, lending his strength to the elf. As much as he would have liked to see Aedon devoured by the protective magic, Dimitri's success depended on theirs. It was nothing else. Just self-preservation. He refused to admit to himself that he did not want Harper to be collateral damage. That thought was too dangerous.

In the chaos, it was easy to slip between the folds of the world remaining hidden. He flitted between them, tripping a guard here, blinding one there, just for the fun of it. He paused by Aedon and the tall Aerian. Their cloak pockets and bags hanging from their waists were stuffed to the brim with Dragonhearts. He found the biggest and spirited it to the in-between place with him. It was risky. He ought to have left, but he stayed, lingering just a while to watch the fight.

The dragon magic roared through Aedon, bathing all in fire, burning up wards, as well as air. Interesting. The dragon's bond of strength had not entirely forsaken the elf. Dimitri had no idea that could be the case when a rider's dragon died. It was a new reason to be wary of Aedon.

His attention sheared from Aedon as he saw Harper falter —saw a scar-faced soldier wrench her against the bars of the portcullis. Before any conscious thought materialised, his magic had already surrounded the man, choking the breath from him just as scar-face tried to strangle her. Dimitrius wrought savage pleasure in the crushing hold his power had upon the man's throat.

Around them, Dimitri felt the wards crumbling under the weight of magical assault and dragonfire. He was not yet free, and if he lingered, even for a moment too long—for her —all would be lost. She was no helpless maiden. The memory of her sweeping that blade to his own throat, a vicious fire in her gaze, was enough to make him grin. No. The huntress did not need his help. She could save herself. With that thought, Dimitri vanished.

70

HARPER

Harper focused on Ragnar. His presence was her anchor, all that kept her from falling apart and being dashed in the wind. She was going to give them hell. If she was going to die, if they both were, there was no reason not to go down fighting. Her fingers scrabbled inside her cloak, desperately seeking the dagger.

With a roar, Ragnar faced the Kingsguard, who rushed toward him. Harper plunged the dagger into the arm around her throat. All of the screaming and cursing around them were drowned out by a blaze of light and heat as flames erupted from Aedon, bathing the Kingsguard before him. The hands around Harper vanished. She collapsed to the floor and slumped against the portcullis, gasping for breath, utterly spent.

Aedon's fire grew. Slowly turning her head, she could see how he glowed from the inside out. *He's beautiful... and deadly*, Harper thought. Each breath hurt, as though her throat had been squeezed permanently shut and would not open, and the heat in the air around her burnt her mouth.

Stars still danced before her eyes, and her fingers were limp around the handle of the dagger.

I need to get up, she thought, but it was impossible, and Aedon was so captivating to watch. It was almost as if he was moving in slow motion. He turned, and an arcing jet of white-yellow-orange-red fire gushed from him. The cloaks of the Kingsguard caught fire. The red of the fabric deepened the colours of the flames. The plumes of their helmets flamed, too, like columns of flickering light shooting for the rocky ceiling.

Men ripped their cloaks and helms off, desperately trying to stamp out the fire, but as Aedon continued, they ran. Inferno after inferno he sent at them, advancing a step at a time, until they fled into the dark vaults. The portcullis rumbled to life at Harper's back. As it rose, she tumbled backwards, crashing upon the floor. Aedon rushed to her side, Ragnar and the others arriving soon after.

"Harper, can you hear me?"

She could not tell who the voice belonged to. She found the strength to raise a hand that did not feel like hers. Another grasped it, almost too hot to touch.

"Harper!" Aedon's piercing voice cut through her daze. He knelt beside her and helped her into a sitting position. She slumped against his chest. "Thank goodness you're alive." She heard them speak around her as though from a great distance. Her lips parted and closed, but no sound emerged.

"What in the blazes was that?" Brand spluttered.

"Er, can we discuss this another time?" asked Aedon. Brand narrowed his eyes and placed his hands on his hips. "Fine. Long story short, I repurposed the power of the wards into fire magic. It's not a big deal."

"Right," Brand mumbled, dumbfounded. "Not a big deal."

"We need to get her out of here," Ragnar said, biting his lip as he felt Harper's forehead.

"A moment, please. I need to give her strength to move."

Aedon dragged his bloodied hand across her cheek and cocooned her under his other arm. He murmured words she couldn't understand that slipped in and out of her ears as easily as wind through hair. Harper felt the tingle of magic rush through her. Slowly, the fog in her mind retreated, then her pain, until she felt well enough to sit up on her own.

"Better?" Aedon asked. She nodded, but he did not remove his support until she was on her feet and he was certain she could walk unaided.

"Let's go," snapped Erika. "The entire hold will have heard that din."

"We need another way out," Ragnar said with a pointed glance at Aedon.

"Remember, we're not the Dragonheart," said Aedon. "We're the decoy. The king won't be able to resist trying to pin me down now. Brand, take Harper and go. A tall, high place… You know what to do. We'll see you on the other side. Erika, Ragnar, come with me. We can't use the front door, so we might as well try the back."

"*Try?*" asked Ragnar.

"We've been in worse predicaments," said Aedon with a smile.

Ragnar spluttered.

"*Come on!*" Erika scowled and set off.

Harper looked at Aedon, completely baffled. "We have to split up?"

"Trust me," said Aedon. For once, there was no hint of mischief. He was uncharacteristically serious. "We'll see you soon."

"Harper, this way."

For a short time, they ran together through the hall. The clamour ahead set Harper's nerves on edge once more. At a crossroads, the group split in two without a word. Harper followed Brand into the darkness. The Aerian forged ahead along a perfectly flat corridor, which was lit by tiny lamps that offered little help.

"Stairs," was his only warning before they ran into the rising spiral. Harper pushed as hard as she could, struggling to keep up. Brand's giant wings, which barely fit in the narrow confines, rustled and scraped along the thick stone. He pulled farther ahead. Her lungs burned. Her legs screamed.

A different kind of light emerged. Suddenly, there were slitted windows in the walls that punctuated the stairwell at every level. The stone here was over an arm's length thick. As she raced past each opening, she glanced out. They were so high. Where were they going?

Soon, Brand came to a door. It offered little resistance against his bulk as he ran into it. He contorted his body to slip his wings through. Once he had made sure the coast was clear, he reached a hand in to tug her out faster.

Harper gasped. It was the pinnacle of Tournai. A watch tower. A walled ledge surrounded them. Brand peered over the edge. Harper followed suit. Her stomach flipped. They were so high up, she could not even comprehend the height. The road to the city was nothing more than a tiny ribbon trailing through the valley.

From where she stood, the wall around the city looked like parchment, the buildings a sprawling collection of crumbs. The wind tugged and tore at her, teasing that it would pull her off and fling her to her death below.

"Where do we go?" She turned in a circle, seeing nowhere

else to go, except down the staircase from which they had emerged.

Brand pointed out… toward nothing.

Harper raised an eyebrow. A suspicious inkling began to unfurl in her stomach, and she very much hoped it was wrong. *Oh no.*

"We're going to fly. Low and fast."

"Slight problem," she said, her tone light, though she felt like screaming. "I can't fly."

"I can," Brand replied. He smirked a little at her discomfort.

"But you can't carry me," she said desperately. *Not this high. Not this far. Not again.* "There must be another way."

"Nope."

"They'll see us!" The sun was high, and the sky bright. There was no way for them to escape undetected—and she did not want to be there when Toroth unleashed his dragons to hunt the skies.

"We really don't have a choice, Harper. Sooner or later, they're going to find us up here. If we're not gone…" He left the rest to her imagination.

"All right. If you're sure," she replied, swallowing her nerves. She nodded. "Let's get this over with."

Brand opened his arms wide for her to come to him.

"Please don't drop me," she whispered as she leaned into his chest.

His laugh rumbled through him as his arms closed around her, firm and strong. He lifted her with ease and turned to hop onto the parapet. Harper squeezed her eyes shut, clamped down on the rising nausea that threatened to overwhelm her, and clutched onto Brand's clothing. It was still not enough.

The door slammed open behind them, crashing into the stone wall. Brand wheeled around.

"You!" he snarled and crouched into a defensive position. One armed, he shifted Harper behind himself and drew his blade with his free hand.

Dimitrius stood before them, his hands up and magic balling at his fists in the face of the giant angry Aerian. Then he spied Harper. Their eyes locked. And the spymaster's magic guttered out. Silence hung between them.

"If you're going to attack, do it now before I make the first move, elf," Brand snarled, but Dimitrius's eyes did not leave Harper.

71

HARPER

"Do you have the stone?" Dimitrius asked. He was unreadable, as inscrutable as ever, but those violet eyes of his burned with an intensity she wished she understood. Was he furious at her for taking a chance to escape?

"Yes," she replied, raising her chin defiantly.

To her surprise, his shoulders slumped, that proud, tall stance of him folding ever so slightly. "Good. Go do some good with that."

Harper frowned. "You aren't going to fight us? Take it?" Because that was the truth of it. She had seen him at work. If he wanted that stone back, it was as good as his.

"No," he murmured.

She stepped around Brand. He placed a warning hand on her arm, but she shook it off and strode to Dimitrius. "What do you want? I don't understand."

For the first time since she had met him, he seemed lost for words. Something hidden flickered through his eyes, and for a moment, when his lips parted, she thought she would get an honest answer. However, his impassive mask slid on once more, and the heat left his gaze. "What I want is none of your concern, Harper."

His tone was so cold it sent a bolt of hurt through her. It stung—but it helped too. She straightened too and stepped back. She had been right to leave. She did owe him nothing. This was business and absolutely no feelings involved. She had served whatever purpose he needed, and he? She steeled herself. He had helped her survive. She needed him for nothing else. Wanted him for nothing else.

"Leave now," Dimitrius said, much to Harper's surprise, "and do not return. They're coming, and I cannot be seen letting you escape."

The mask slipped once more, and his eyes burned into hers with such an intensity, she was lost for words for a second. "I don't under—"

He stepped forwards, into her space, and his hand found her shoulder. Large, warm, and solid, his grip anchored her in place. "You need to *leave*. I don't know how you connect to any of this—to the Dragonheart, to Saradon, to *me*, but you are a danger to everything I have built, and if you stay, you are as good as dead if Toroth finds you. Sharp teeth or not, he will destroy you, little huntress."

And I do not want that, his violent gaze screamed at her. Or did she imagine it? Because at last, he broke the intoxicating eye contact between them, and his attention snapped over her head, to the hulking warrior behind her.

"Go! They are coming. Take her!" Dimitrius snarled at Brand, who needed no other encouragement. Dimitri stepped back as Brand wound an arm around her waist and tugged her towards him. Harper let him, turning only to step onto the parapet. She took a shuddering breath as the Aerian clutched her tightly against the rock hard plane of his chest

—some small reassurance in the face of the death-defying freefall she was about to face.

She locked eyes with Dimitrius as he stood, fists clenched, by that door. Watching her. Making no move to stop them. Brand leapt backwards, wrenching her with him. He plunged them into the abyss, severing the moment. Harper knew she had left her stomach behind with Dimitrius as they dropped like a stone, picking up speed. Her scream was lost to the wind, her questions too. *He let us go. Why did he let us go?*

Harper opened an eye just a crack. The grey-blue of the mountain rushed past them, making her stomach churn. Brand's wings cocooned around them, then snapped wide open. It felt like they had hit the ground, such was the force in his movement, but they quickly changed direction, wheeling out over the city. He hugged the edge of the mountain, his feathers almost brushing the stone.

Harper caught sight of the city rushing by and clung to Brand with a terrified squeak. She had never been good with heights, but this was too far. Brand's arms felt secure, yet they were so high, and he shook with every gust of wind that buffeted them, constantly adjusting course. He knew what he was doing, but to her, it felt like the very air itself might knock them from the sky.

Brand dove again. Harper's stomach left her once more as they dropped even lower, racing across the roofs that had been a patchwork quilt far below them minutes before. Now they were a shadow faster than the wind, crossing before anyone could see them.

"Why are we flying so low?" Harper dared to ask. "We'll be seen!"

"Not down here. People look to the sky, see a shadow, and know it is an Aerian. They will not see us now. We pass too low to the ground. The dragons will not think to look down, either. They also look to the skies." She hoped he was right. "No more talking. The dragons of the Winged Kings-guard have keen senses. My wings are quiet, but our mouths are not."

He banked again and flapped once, his mighty wings raising him just enough to get over the top of the wall, then they were out of Tournai and following the curve of the mountain out of sight from the city.

Harper shut her eyes and concentrated on not being sick.

Eventually, Brand slowed. The lights of Tournai were nowhere to be seen as he landed in a thick forest in the foothills.

"Where are we?" Harper asked as he set her down. For a few seconds, she stumbled as her cold, numb legs adjusted. She stretched and breathed a huge sigh of relief to have both her feet on solid ground again.

"North of Tournai. Why did he let us go, Harper?" The suspicion in his voice was clear.

"I don't know. I don't understand anything he does," Harper said with an edge of hysteria. "I don't understand who to trust anymore!"

Brand's impassive expression softened. "The important thing is you're free—and alive. Let's go. We can figure it out later."

The trees were tall, dark sentinels silently standing on the steep hills. Harper turned, holding her breath. Only the faintest trace of wildlife was audible on the breeze.

"It's quiet here," she murmured.

"Rather too quiet. Let's go. We have a rendezvous point to make, and we cannot be delayed."

"Can't we fly there?" she asked as she scurried after him.

She wasn't overly keen on going back to the skies, but it would have been faster.

"No. We don't want to be seen. The trees will give us better cover. Come now. The less talking, the better."

They jogged through the forest until it was pitch black, then slowly picked their way through until they emerged from the edge of the trees where the moonlight lit their way better. It had been hours since they had parted company with Aedon, Ragnar, and Erika. Harper's anxiety gnawed at her. Were they okay? There was no way to know.

When bulky, misshapen figures appeared between the trees, Harper slowed, her heart leaping into her mouth. She could take no more that day. Every part of her *hurt*, and she was so exhausted she felt as though she could drop with every step.

"Wait." Brand's command halted her. "Possible hostiles. Blade out. On your guard."

Breathing raggedly, Harper did as he asked, a desperate sob building in her throat. If the king's men had found them, they were as good as dead.

72

HARPER

When the three figures drew close enough to see, relief flooded Harper, a rush so vast her legs nearly buckled. Aedon, Erika, and Ragnar approached, each on horseback.

"Well met," Brand said, as though they had stumbled on each other by chance on a relaxing summer stroll.

"Another job well done." Aedon grinned. "Are you two all right?"

Harper grinned shakily. She hurt all over, and her nerves felt like they were frazzled beyond repair, but the bubble of relief consumed her. "Never better," she bluffed. "How did you know that staircase was there? And your escape route? And where did you get horses?"

"Lucky hunch, bold guess, and I'm tired of walking." Aedon shrugged.

Erika snorted. "Lucky hunch, my left arse cheek. It's not the first time we've raided that henhouse, if you catch my drift. We always research all the entry and exit routes. You never know when you might need one."

"Come now. We need to be far from here by dawn, then we can rest," Brand chivvied them along. Ragnar yawned, but nodded.

They trekked through the night, with Harper on Aedon's horse whilst he led them on foot with Brand. Harper was so weary, her eyes shut of their own accord, threatening to send her to sleep in the saddle. When they finally halted, she sank to the ground with a sigh of relief and promptly went to sleep.

The sun was high when she woke. Near the fire, Aedon sat chatting with Erika, who tended to her weapons. Ragnar was their silent companion, busy carving a twig with his knife. Brand flitted through the trees on the fringes of camp, no doubt keeping watch. Something warm bloomed in her to be with them again—and to be free, with the canopy of leaves and the sky above her.

For a long moment she simply laid there—still reeling from all that had passed. They now had the Kingsguard of Tournai *and* the elves of Tir-na-Alathea chasing them. Perhaps Dimitrius too, whatever his agenda entailed, because she did not entirely trust she was free of it. Harper shivered at the memory of him staring her down as they had parted for the last time.

Would any of them ever give up? Of the king and the wood elves, she doubted it. She did not yet know what to make of Dimitrius. She fleetingly wondered how many other enemies Aedon and his friends had made over the years before a pang of hunger wiped such thoughts from her mind. Harper sat up and stretched with a groan.

"Good morning," said Aedon with a grin, though judging from the position of the sun, it was clearly afternoon.

"Hmm," she said through a yawn.

"I think you owe us another story." Aedon glanced from her to the rest of them. "A rescue for a story. That seems to be a tradition we're making. Tell us what in Pelenor happened—and how the spymaster is embroiled in all of this." His tone grew more cold at the end, and Harper knew Brand had told him exactly how their escape had succeeded.

"Only if you tell me how you escaped Tournai," she said, her own tone guarded.

Unable to resist, Aedon puffed out his chest. "Naturally. I'm happy to recount our escapades!"

Erika rolled her eyes.

"And we talk about what happened," Harper added pointedly.

Aedon's smile slipped. He swallowed. His hands fussed with the twig in his hands. "Yes. About that. We're sorry, Harper. We shouldn't have gone about it like that."

Harper stared him down until he squirmed and dropped his gaze.

Erika straightened. "I'm sorry too. I should not have tried to take the stone from you." She swallowed and scowled. Harper waited. "It was my fault that things went so badly. And I am deeply sorry for that. For how you must have suffered. You did not deserve that." Her eagle-eyed glare met Harper's.

"Thank you," said Harper, giving her a sharp nod. The nomad's apology meant more to her than anything else—because she knew that the woman meant every word of it, and that her loyalty and favour were hard-won and well-earned.

"What happened?" Aedon asked. His voice was subdued—

laced with guilt, she realised, and the hardness within her softened to that. She told them what had happened since they had parted, not sparing a detail of her treatment in the dungeons, nor her inexplicable encounters with Dimitrius or her audiences with the king. They listened to her in silence.

Aedon blew out a breath once she was finished. "The spymaster's still plotting away, I see. Goodness knows on what. You were just a pawn to him in whatever scheme he has, Harper."

She nodded, though she was not entirely convinced. Some of the moments with the spymaster had felt so genuine, and that had taken root inside her somewhere. It hurt to cut that down, but she had to. She had survived in a court of lies and shadows. The spymaster had been using her and nothing more. She was back where she felt like she was finally starting to belong.

Yet still, she could not banish those violet eyes of his and the way they burned with so much unspoken feeling, making her long to understand his story. Harper cleared her throat. "Well, we agreed a tale for a tale. What's your story?"

Aedon told her of their gallant escape. After sneaking out of the dragon hold using hidden ways Aedon knew and with fresh sets of Kingsguard cloaks and helmets, they had 'borrowed' three horses and rode from the city.

"You make it sound easy," Ragnar murmured in disbelief.

"That's hardly as daring as our escape," Brand said.

"Perhaps not, but it required just as much guts." Aedon grinned crookedly.

Brand scoffed.

"Where to now?" Harper asked.

Now that she finally had a moment to think, with her life not in imminent danger, it struck her that she was once more without a way home. The city of Tournai, the king and his magic, were closed to her.

"To continue our quest," said Aedon. "Now we have a way to cure the sickness and eradicate it."

Harper's attention snapped to him. "Really?"

"Erika?" He looked at the quiet woman.

Erika stirred. "We had our own task to complete before we could think of rescuing you. I'm sure you understand. There is a particularly ancient text in the citadel archives that references an everlasting potion. If you can find this Dragonheart and have the method to use it correctly, you can make an infinite supply from the smallest drop."

She pulled out a tightly rolled scroll that looked hundreds of years old. "Now we can spread the cure as far as it is needed, for we have the perfect way to make enough to heal anyone and everyone afflicted."

"How is it done?" Harper whispered in awe.

"As luck would have it, a forgotten piece of magic that, when combined with the stone, has staggering potential," Aedon replied.

"That's incredible." Her thoughts strayed to the desperate villagers—this would be life-saving for them.

Aedon dipped his head to her. "The choice is yours, Harper. We would be mighty grateful for your assistance. I'm afraid our Dragonhearts were lost in the escape."

Erika shot him a glance.

Aedon returned it, shrugging. "Lost, used—what does it matter? Semantics. I had no choice if we were to escape alive."

Harper glanced between them, wondering quite what had happened in the vaults. That fire had been completely out of control.

"We're alive, but we only have your Dragonheart now, Harper," Aedon said. "May we use it? The choice is yours."

Harper did not know what to say. Her plans had changed by necessity, she realised. The Dragonheart was no longer her means to return to Caledan. Now, the Dragonheart had a greater potential use. The magic of how it had moved her was so unknown it could not be replicated. The king would most certainly not trade it for passage home. And, her time with the spymaster and his promise of freedom had never extended so far. He sprang into her mind—the slump of his proud shoulders, and his parting words. *Go do some good with that."*

She realised that she might have started to relinquish that idea after all—to return home. What kind of home was it? She had wanted to leave so badly, and she had nothing to want to return to. Only Betta. The thought of the old woman stirred familiar guilt, but if Harper was so far away it was nigh on impossible to return anyway, at what point did she have to accept that the notion of returning was nothing more than that—a thought that kept her trapped in an old life she did not want anyway. Betta would have to survive without her, because there was no other way about it—and Harper could not be responsible for that. The old woman was fiercely independent. She had survived before Harper and she would survive after.

This? This was an opportunity for Harper to find the courage to step up and embrace the opportunity she had always dreamed of. Everything she wanted to achieve lay on the other side of the fear standing in her way. Would she allow it to defeat her after what she had faced? Being dropped into a new and unfamiliar land, hunted by wood elves, withstanding the cruelty of a malicious king, surviving a court of sorcery and secrets—surviving the spymaster—

and more. Whilst she had scrubbed tankards, served patrons, and avoided their lecherous attention... this was exactly what she had dreamed of. Wasn't it?

Brand strode back into camp, distracting her. "No scouts that I can see. Perhaps we outran them, or maybe your charms have worked better than the last time we fled, Aedon."

Aedon winced. He would not live down that the elves of Tir-na-Alathea had tracked them so easily for quite some time, Harper surmised. She stifled a small smile.

"We're safe for today?" Ragnar asked.

"For today, and it's worth us lying low and resting. We have a tough journey ahead, even with the horses to speed our return. On the morrow, we must leave with the dawn."

Aedon turned to her, his face filled with expectant hope.

There were so many other questions she had—about Aedon's fearsome display of magic, about Dimitrius. So many about Dimitrius. Yet one was most pressing upon her mind.

Another journey, thought Harper, *but am I to join them on it?*

73

HARPER

Aedon swung his cloak around his shoulders and fastened the clasp around his neck. Behind him, Brand, Ragnar, and Erika waited, eager to put distance between themselves and the king, and to return to the village with the cure.

He turned to Harper, who was ready and waiting, too. She had never before appreciated how beautiful freedom was. Every blade of grass seemed greener, the rustle of the trees a sweeter lullaby, the kiss of the sun on her face more sensuous. The morning sun bathed them in light, and the clear skies were filled with the promise of better things.

"So," he said, his tone deliberately light, but Harper could see the worry that lurked within. "Do we have one more to journey with us on our quest?"

Harper scanned their faces. Anxiety lurked in the pit of her stomach. Each bore the same grim, yet carefully blank expression and stood with bated breath, waiting for her answer. This was it. Her resolve settled, the instinct within her humming with contentment at her choice.

"I wouldn't want to be anywhere else," she said. "If you'll have me, that is." She hesitated. They had parted on such poor terms, and even though they had come to rescue her, she still felt some kind of rift there, a bitterness on her part born of the hurt of their betrayal. That would take time to heal.

"You're one of us now," Brand said. Ragnar nodded in agreement, and even Erika jerked her head in what seemed to be support.

Harper's smile widened. "Thank you."

"Let's go," said Aedon, turning away. "Not another second to waste. People are counting on us for this cure." They mounted their three horses, and Aedon offered a hand to pull Harper up onto his mount.

She reached into her cloak, and instead of giving him her hand, placed the weight of the Dragonheart in his palm. He stared at her, the wordless question in his eyes. "Take it. It's needed."

"You're sure?" he breathed, as though he did not dare voice it too loudly in case she changed her mind.

"I'm certain." Dimitrius's words rang in her mind. "Let's do some good with it." And only then, when he had tucked it most carefully into the satchel on the side of the horse and murmured his astounded thanks, did she reach out her hand to allow him to haul her up into the saddle.

For the first time, she felt as though she lived the life she had sought. This *was* the adventure she had dreamed of—the chance to make something better of and for herself. And she did not have to do it alone. Here, she had a new family of sorts, a found one that somehow worked for all the odd individuals it brought together. Returning to them felt like slipping on a glove. They were as at ease with her as she was with them. Somehow, she fit in, in her own strange way, as though there was still room for her to find her feet—but they had her back. After all she had already endured with them, she felt as though she had earned her place there now.

"Come on, Harper. We haven't got all day." Aedon grinned and pulled her up behind him. Harper settled behind him and wound an arm around his stomach, as her own lurched with the rush of what was to come next.

For the first time in a long while, Harper felt *alive*. In that moment, she did not care when or if she returned to Caledan, and she certainly did not want to return to Tournai to see the king or the spymaster again. For now, she had a new home on the road, a new adventure whispering promises of novelty into her blood, and she could not wait to see what happened next. On to use the Dragonheart for good —and whatever lay beyond.

74

DIMITRI

When he was certain Harper and her companions had escaped, as sure as he could be that she would be safe, Dimitri left, as well, slipping through the world and racing to Saradon's tomb with the Dragonheart. Faster than his thoughts he travelled, running from any notion of *her*, because a part of him was not finished with Harper of Caledan yet—though for their mutual safety, he knew he needed to be.

The Dragonheart, he told himself. He had what he needed —and that was what mattered. Nothing else. This was the lock that fit the key in the puzzle he so desperately needed to unlock. To *unleash*.

It had only been too easy to take it from Aedon's unknowing hands. Dimitri allowed himself a smirk. How Aedon would despise accidentally helping his worst enemy. It was the perfect cover. The thief would be blamed once more for the loss. Dimitri would escape with no suspicion upon his head.

He marvelled at the well of power within it, greater than

even his own. His blood sang with anticipation. In the cave, Dimitri took a moment to adjust to the strange sense of crushing power that always left him reeling and dizzy. He sent out a greeting to Saradon, who responded with a magical touch of his own and the rumbling sense of his presence awakening. Silent, Dimitri offered the stone to the sarcophagus.

He felt Saradon's interest instantly snap to the white-hot star of power in his hands. It was so powerful, it threatened to shred his own energy and absorb him. He fought to keep his own magic from it, lest it devour him. It was exactly what Saradon wanted, for Dimitri felt his approval and excitement radiating through the space. His own life-beat was light and fast compared to Saradon's—a slumbering, ponderous, pulsing vitality that lay deep in the stone, under the swirls of glowing glyphs.

"Place it on the sarcophagus," Saradon commanded.

Dimitri obeyed and stepped back. In the living world, the Dragonheart seemed innocuous, a rock upon a pile of stone. But when Dimitri sank into the magical river of energy and bathed in its heady delight, the stone brightened to a star—undimmed, pure, and powerful.

At its touch, the scripts upon the sarcophagus wriggled and shifted before Dimitri's eyes, sinking into the vortex of swirling energy. They fell into it with glowing splashes, and the energy expanded and brightened with each rune that dropped into it. Saradon's voice rose around Dimitri, a monotone drone in a language he did not understand, but one charged with the buzz of magic that lifted every hair on Dimitri's skin, prickles crawling across him.

What is he doing? Something about the magic felt dark, wrong, as if the energy was tainted. Dimitri recognised the dark magic Saradon invoked—something far older and more dangerous than either of them—and the skin prickled at the back of his neck, an uncomfortable sensation crawling across his skin. A part of him questioned whether he was doing the right thing, but he silenced it. There was no room for doubt. Not any more.

Dimitri backed away as the energy constricted and sank into the sarcophagus, which melted into golden sparks until it was entirely gone. They swirled into a mass, and the outline of an elf-shaped form materialised. It rose on the stone base to stand before him. Slowly, the swirling golden marks coalesced into the form of a male, one Dimitri recognised only too easily as the glowing magic sank into his skin.

Violet eyes pierced Dimitri's as Saradon beheld him, then his stern visage broke into a grim smile. Slowly, Saradon slipped his eyes shut and deeply breathed the stale air of the cave as if it were the sweetest fresh breeze. He flexed his lithe, strong arms, clenching and unclenching his ring-adorned fingers, causing the fabric of his bell-shaped sleeves to bunch around his forearms. He ran his hands through loose, black hair that fell to his shoulders in waves, as perfect as the day he had been laid to rest, and fingered his neat, closely cropped beard. Saradon's gaze dropped to examine his form with wonder and a buzz of anticipation that was palpable to Dimitri before he grinned a triumphant, wolfish smile.

"It feels most wonderful to breathe again," Saradon said, inhaling a deep breath once more.

The tang of raw power still burned Dimitri, searing his skin. He watched carefully, wondering if Saradon had been as mentally preserved as he had been physically.

"You have my unending gratitude, Lord Ellarian," Saradon said, turning his attention to Dimitri once more.

He bowed. "What next, Lord Ravakian?"

"Revenge," Saradon said, savouring each syllable of the word. "Revenge on the royal line of Pelenor, and their abhorrent sins. Then the restoration of order and fairness to Pelenor, and as far afield as can be touched by my hands."

Dimitri smiled, a tight-lipped one of approval, as anticipation curled in his stomach. It would not be long before he would not return to Tournai as Dimitrius Vaeri Mortris, the king's spymaster, snapping at heels to find small favour. Soon, he would return as the right hand of Saradon and a new order.

He had started a mission for his deepest yearning. Now he stood a chance of overturning Pelenor's ruling class as Saradon's chief advisor. For once, he would be at the helm.

It was time to show his hand.

It was time to break the wheel.

It was time to build a new world.

THE END

THANK YOU FOR READING

This saga is for those holding tender but resilient hopes of a greater meaning in life, who believe that we have the power to make the world a kinder place. You have everything you need within you to make those dreams come true—for yourself, for those you love, for the world. Gather your courage, stand with those who lift you up— and go. Blaze from a spark to a star. Let your energy and light fill you up and ripple outwards. Overcome any darkness in your way. Make your impact. Bathe the world with your incredible light and fulfil your unique purpose on this good earth.

Want more?

Thank you so much for reading *Heart of Shadows*! If you want more before you read book two, join the Heart of Shadows readalong experience exclusive to my Romantasy Fellowship. Follow *Heart of Shadows* from the author's perspective—

discover behind the scenes, gorgeous artwork, and more in this email series direct to your inbox so you can read at your own pace. Best of all, this is completely free and you can revisit it as many times as you wish.

Join here: www.megcowley.com/heartofshadowsbonus

Stay in touch!

If you want to reach out to me, I love hearing from readers. You can find me in the following places:

Follow me on Amazon, Bookbub, or sign up to my Romantasy Fellowship newsletter to be notified of new books/releases/sales/news/etc.

Say hi on Facebook, Instagram, or TikTok (@megcowleyauthor)—I love hearing from you and seeing gorgeous pictures/videos of books out in the wild!

Join my communities on Facebook for social chit chat and Ream for early access and additional story content that isn't available anywhere else.

Find out more about my books and links to all the above on my website www.megcowley.com

Please leave a review

Thank you so much for reading *Heart of Shadows*! If you enjoyed it, please leave a rating/review on your retailer/book site of choice. Positive reviews really help my books find new readers to love them.

What's next...

I hope that you'll love the rest of the series. The stage is ready and the scene is set, and Harper, Aedon, Dimitri and the rest of the characters are ready to sweep you off your feet for the rest of the saga. Get ready for delicious tension and slow burn steam, the mother of all morally grey dilemmas for Harper, and some world shattering revelations in book two, *Court of Treachery*.

Happy reading!

Meg

BOOKS BY MEG COWLEY

World of Altarea stories:

EMPIRE OF BLOOD AND MALICE SERIES

Heart of Shadows

Court of Treachery

Heir of Darkness

Promise of Ruin

A slowburn, steamy, dark, epic quartet with enemies to lovers, forbidden romance, a courageous and vulnerable heroine, found family, high stakes, and a morally grey hero.

TALES OF TIR NA ALATHEA: DARKNESS OF THE LIVING FOREST SERIES

Flight of Sorcery and Shadow

Ascent of Darkness and Ruin

Purge of Flame and Song

A dark and immersive romantic fantasy of unlikely allies facing and overcoming darkness within and without together. Sequel series to Empire of Blood and Malice series.

MARRIED BY STARFALL

A fade-to-black standalone beauty and the beast inspired romantasy

ABOUT THE AUTHOR

Meg Cowley is a *USA Today* bestselling fantasy author from England, where she lives with her husband, son, darling golden retriever, two sweet cats, and her many book characters.

Meg writes slow burn steamy epic fantasy romances with courageous and vulnerable heroines, protective and brooding males, and lovable and welcoming found family in stories that will steal your heart long after the last page.

Meg's favourite past times are reading, hiking, and cooking. She can usually be found curled up with a cup of tea and a riveting fantasy romance book, cooking up a fantasy-book worthy feast, or out walking the wild, windswept moors of Yorkshire dreaming up her next story.

Visit www.megcowley.com to find out more, discover Meg's books, find exclusive reader bonus content, and join her Romantasy Fellowship newsletter.